# PRAISE FOR LARS IYER

## NIETZSCHE AND

"*Nietzsche and the Burbs* is an anthem for young misfits and a hilarious, triumphant book about friendship." —MICHAEL SCHAUB, NPR

"This is a near-perfect evocation of childhood's elegiac end." —MICHAEL M. GRYNBAUM, *NEW YORK TIMES*

"What a fun book this is! Delight is such a rare commodity nowadays and it is terrific to see it has not been hunted to extinction." —DANIEL HANDLER, AUTHOR OF *BOTTLE GROVE*

"Punk rock and philosophy coincide in the latest novel from Lars Iyer . . . Do you like smart observations about class and coming of age? How about some metal in the mix? Well then—welcome to the world of *Nietzsche and the Burbs*." —VOL. 1 BROOKLYN

"A rock-music caper loaded with adolescent yearning . . . pithy dialogue . . . evocatively rendered . . ." —HOUMAN BAREKAT, *SUNDAY TIMES* (LONDON)

"Readers . . . will delight in its wit. A model of originality. Clever, indeed." —*BOOKLIST*

"Lyrical and often moving . . . an affectionate satire on intellectual life." —ANDREW IRWIN, *TIMES LITERARY SUPPLEMENT*

## WITTGENSTEIN JR

LONGLISTED FOR THE FOLIO PRIZE

ONE OF THE TELEGRAPH'S BEST BOOKS OF 2014

"[Iyer] is a deeply elegiac satirist . . . He manages to both send up intellectual life and movingly lament its erosion." —*NEW YORK TIMES*

"One of the funniest books of the year, this philosophical bildung shows that intellectuality can be poignant, especially when its couched within a campus novel." —*FLAVORWIRE*, 50 BEST INDEPENDENT FICTION AND POETRY BOOKS OF 2014

"Iyer's lyrical novel unfolds like a prose poem, in fragments and scenes, compressed images and emotion, with rhythm and repetition that pull the reader through the novel . . . It is at turns a novel about England, the university, youth, madness, philosophy, love, which, when summed up, becomes a coming-of-age novel." —*HAMLET HUB*

"It isn't really a novel, or not only a novel. It's more interesting than that . . . Iyer has compiled an idiosyncratic–and surprisingly tender–paean to love and learning."

—TIMES LITERARY SUPPLEMENT

"Iyer already has a reputation for combining brainy dialogue with madcap action, but the triumph of his latest (and best) novel is that the cartoon turns out to have real substance."

—PUBLISHERS WEEKLY, STARRED REVIEW

"A droll love story . . . Existential angst is rarely this entertaining." —KIRKUS REVIEWS

## EXODUS

"The final volume in Iyer's gloomily brilliant trilogy about a toxic friendship between unfortunate philosophy dons, boozing and bitching in the great tradition of Beckett's double acts." —THE GUARDIAN

"The humor cuts broad and deep." —LA REVIEW OF BOOKS

## DOGMA

"Uproarious." —NEW YORK TIMES BOOK REVIEW

"*Dogma* by Lars Iyer is the kind of book that we are always told never gets published anymore: uncompromisingly intellectual, passing strange and absurdly funny. If Lars Iyer hadn't already written *Spurious*, it would be possible to call his second novel a unique event. As it is, it's just more of the same, only better. Iyer's weird talent continues to grow, and the misadventures of his miserable characters are starting to seem like the brightest things in modern British fiction."

—THE GUARDIAN (CHOSEN AS ONE OF 2012'S BEST BOOKS OF THE YEAR)

## SPURIOUS

"A tiny marvel of comically repetitive gloomery . . . [A] wonderfully monstrous creation." —STEVEN POOLE, THE GUARDIAN

"Who should buy this book? Intellectuals who face intellectual troubles in their own lives. There's a lot of biting satire about the shortcomings and general foolishness of the so-called life of the mind. This is graduate student wit, which is fearsomely funny." —WASHINGTON POST

# MY WEIL

## ALSO BY LARS IYER

### FICTION

*Nietzsche and the Burbs*

*Wittgenstein Jr*

*Spurious*

*Dogma*

*Exodus*

### NONFICTION

*Blanchot's Communism:*
*Art, Philosophy, and the Political*

*Blanchot's Vigilance:*
*Literature, Phenomenology, and the Ethical*

# MY WEIL

A NOVEL

## LARS IYER

⬆ MELVILLE HOUSE
BROOKLYN · LONDON

**MY WEIL**

First published in 2023 by Melville House Publishing
Copyright © Lars Iyer, 2022
All rights reserved
First Melville House Printing: July 2023

Melville House Publishing
46 John Street
Brooklyn, NY 11201
and
Melville House UK
Suite 2000
16/18 Woodford Road
London E7 0HA

mhpbooks.com
@melvillehouse

ISBN: 978-1-68589-060-5
ISBN: 978-1-68589-061-2 (eBook)

Library of Congress Control Number: 2023935681

Designed by Sofia Demopolos

Printed in the United States of America
10 9 8 7 6 5 4 3 2 1

A catalog record for this book is available from the Library of Congress

Pray, Lord.
We are near.
—PAUL CELAN

# C H A P T E R  1

1

**MONDAY NIGHT.**

The postgraduate social.

Room-temperature prosecco.

Ismail, to the most interesting-looking new arrival: Do you believe in God? Please say yes. We could do with a little faith around here.

I believe that I believe, she says.

That's good enough for us, Ismail says.

So you're really called Simone Weil? I say. Like the philosopher?

Simone, nodding.

She starved herself to death, right? Valentine asks.

She died as a martyr, Simone says. During the war.

She sounds like a nutcase, Gita says.

Are you a nutcase, too? Marcie asks.

Simone, smiling.

How come you're called Simone Weil? I ask.

Come on, Johnny, Ismail says. Like, duh.

I changed my name, Simone says.

Sure—this is *Manchester*, Valentine says. Fuck the CIS-stem. This is where you come to be reborn.

Are you actually *studying* Simone Weil, too? Ismail asks.

I want to . . . develop some of her ideas, Simone says.

Well, you're on trend—Christianity's coming in again, Marcie says. It's all the rage.

I thought *God is dead* in Disaster Studies, I say. I mean, I thought that was kind of a given.

Is that true, Simone? Is God dead? Ismail asks. Or is he just *playing dead*?

The God of the philosophers is dead, Simone says.

Isn't the real trial believing in God *after* he's dead? Valentine says.

No—the real trial's believing in God after *you're* dead, Marcie says.

Surveying the scene.

Disaster Studies PhD students mixed up with Sociology PhD students mixed up with Literature PhD students . . .

And *Business Studies* PhD students! Look at them! All cheerful! A mockery of the PhD student. The very *opposite* of the PhD student . . .

Where's their doom? Where's their crushedness? Their diseases of the soul? There doesn't seem to be anything *wrong* with them.

Discussion. What do *Business Studies pretend PhD students* even research? Kleptocracy? Corporate raiding? Debt leveraging? Overgrowth? Financial engineering? The pillaging of the system before the final collapse?

Do they even understand what doing a PhD means? *The final academic frontier.* There is no higher qualification! No course of study that's so open! So risky! Where you're carried away from everything known, everything certain! In a movement of *infinite philosophical eros* . . .

A PhD is a *passion of studious solitude*. A trial of the soul! A dark night of the intellect!

So why are the *Business Studies supposed PhD students* here? Why have they returned to the uni?

Because they sense what's coming in the world out there. They know this is just the looting phase . . . the before-the-collapse phase . . . the end-of-empire phase . . . the game-will-be-up-pretty-soon phase. Like in *Titanic*, when the ship goes perpendicular . . .

A *Business Studies fake PhD student*, actually coming our way . . .

Brace yourselves, Valentine says.

Why don't we try to turn him? Marcie says. He's cute.

You do it, Marcie—I'm out, Valentine says.

Marcie, pouring wine for Business Studies Guy . . . *Smiling* at Business Studies Guy . . .


Professor Sentinel, addressing us all. Bidding us welcome. Professor Bollocks, telling us we have an exciting year ahead of us. Our new method class lectures, compulsory for all PhD students . . . (Doesn't he understand that there's only an *anarchy of method* in profound study?) The inaugural Disaster Studies conference . . . (Doesn't he see that the disaster means the *impossibility of conferences*? The impossibility of networking!)


## 2

### ESCAPE TO THE STREET.

Police helicopters overhead.

So loud! Gita says. So blinding!

People are being murdered all around us, we tell Simone. Gang vendettas. Drug deals gone wrong. Manchester's a death trap! Manchester's the pit! Manchester's one of the circles of Hell!

3

But shouldn't they just let the world go down? we wonder. Let Manchester destroy itself? They can't keep it on life support forever . . .

Looking up at the towers. The new *mancunian skyline* . . .

There's something *true* about the Manchester streets, we tell Simone. Things are laid bare here. Things are revealed. Things those wankers in the towers will never see . . .

The Man's going vertical, we tell Simone. The Man's bought the sky. He's going to sit out the catastrophe in a luxury eyrie with a patio and a pool and a private helipad . . .

The towers are named after famous mancunian albums, we inform Simone. *Unknown Pleasures . . . Technique . . .*

They haven't called one *Bummed* yet, Marcie says.

*Power, Corruption and Lies*—that's what they should be called, I say. Meanwhile, we're down here with the rabble. With the homeless. The screamers.

It's the new Manchester, Valentine says. Tramps on the ground, elites in the sky.

Ismail, filming the heavens.

And there's the moon, too, shining down on everything, I say.

Johnny hates the moon, Valentine says.

It's the way it just hangs there in the sky, I say. Flaunting itself, all dead. I mean, the moon's just death, right? It's just white ashen death in the sky . . . And it's a *full* moon, too. A full moon brings out the madness in everybody. Mancunians don't need to be any more mad. They don't need the encouragement . . .

Johnny's been mugged forty-seven times by mad mancunians, Marcie explains. It's a local record.

You bring it on yourself, Johnny, Valentine says. It's your children's-home-orphan thing. People either want to shelter you or stab you.

Whereas Val would actually *like* to be mugged, Marcie says.

4

Gita, falling behind, on her phone.

Bet it's Russell, Ismail says. That's Gita's Russell-face.

Gita's queer in theory, but straight in life, Marcie says. She's bidding goodbye to heterosexuality by fucking her supervisor.

A *long* goodbye, Valentine says. A long, clichéd, abject goodbye . . .

Marcie, arm around Business Studies Guy.

Den mom, on the other hand, will fuck anyone and anything, Valentine says.

Ruin Bar.

Raw-wood tables. Exposed-brick wallpaper. Edison bulbs, hanging bare. Visible pipes.

Industrial chic, with a ruination twist, borrowed from the bars of Budapest. Décor, *ruined* (as-if ruined). Comfort, *ruined* (pretend ruined). Health-and-safety, *ruined* (supposedly ruined). And the canal, dark and silent outside.

*Picklebacks* all round. A Tennessee classic. The sweetness of bourbon . . . The tang of pickle . . .

Simone, declining a pickleback. Simone, sipping a mineral water.

Is there ever a good reason not to drink? Valentine asks. Is there ever a good reason not to start drinking right away? Is there ever a good reason not to drink yourself to death?

Drunken philosophy—that's our specialism, Marcie says. We follow the drunken path, that does not run in a straight line. That wavers, wanders. Goes its own way.

If we're not helpless with drink, what then? Valentine says. If we're not staggering from drink, who are we? Our purpose, or reason for being: drinking, now and forever. As refusal of our new teetalo-totalitarian world. As naysaying to the *soft Prohibition*. To the Man's anti-drinking nudges.

They want to outlaw drunkenness—of course! Marcie says. They

5

want to condemn drinking—obviously! In the name of public health, which means public *death*. They've declared war on us—on our kind. On drinkers.

They hate us—they hate drunken joy, Valentine says. But we're not haters, not in the end. We hate this world—this form of the world. But we love what we could be, right? We love Potentiality. We love what's Possible. We love Utopia.

So a toast to us, and our drunkenness! Marcie says. To living against the world, refusing the world, refusing to succumb to the world. Resisting this holding cell. This open prison.

We're looking to light the touch paper, Valentine says. Looking to launch. Looking to find thoughts that we could not have thought otherwise. So that our drunken nights will not have been in vain! So we'll understand them as a quest! As a search that can only be undertaken through drinking! That *needs* drinking! That begins with drinking, and perhaps ends with it, too!

It's time for some *pickleback reasoning*, people, Marcie says. It's Time to follow pickleback logic to the end of the night . . .

What we're working on.

Ismail: Performance philosophy. Showing that films can think.

And he actually gets to make films, too, Valentine says.

Yeah, but it's the stuff they show in art galleries, not on TV, Marcie says.

Pure artwank, in other words, Valentine says. In the international elitist artwank style.

Our job is to keep Ismail down, Marcie says. These *artists* . . . !

He's lucky to have us, Valentine says.

My turn. Ontological evil, I say. The evil that's actually in things.

The madness of evil, or the evil of madness—right, Johnny? Valentine says.

6

Yeah, I say.

Johnny's quiet but you'll have to watch him, Marcie says. One of these days he's going to *EXPLODE* . . .

Valentine's turn. The religious avant-garde, he says. Religious anarchism and the anarchism of religion. With special reference to the Acéphale group, led by Georges Bataille.

They were kind of like *Dead Poets Society* back in the '30s—but with human sacrifice, Marcie says.

Valentine's actually hoping to *conduct* a human sacrifice, Marcie says. So watch out.

Marcie's turn. My genius is in my life, she says. My dissertation . . . pah! Who cares?

Oh, come on . . . , Ismail says.

Lumpenproletariat revolt as ultra-politics if you must know, Marcie says. The figure of the knave, across world history. I'm reclaiming the idea of the *lumpen*, which means the very opposite of heavy and grey . . .

And now Gita. I'm sick of my PhD and I don't want to talk about it, she says.

Something about late heterosexuality, isn't it? Marcie says. About *queer communism* . . . *Very* radical.

Gita's a refugee from Victoria, the real university of the city, Valentine says. She began a PhD there. Dropped out for some obscure reason . . .

Well, you could hardly study queer communism at Victoria . . . , Gita says.


Pointing out our fellow Disaster Studies PhD students.

There's Weep, Severina and Merryn . . . Gothic types, never usually seen before midnight. A collective entity. One soul in two bodies.

Like rock climbers of life. If one falls, the other saves her. Their dissertation's about demonic invocation or something. About weird entities within the electromagnetic spectrum. Although it's disguised as a PhD on esoteric motifs in Deleuze . . .

The blond guy's the Dane—their friend slash lover. Studying over here for tax reasons or something . . . What is he writing on? Hygge or whatever . . . Abba or whatever . . .

There's Vortek. He corresponds with the Unabomber . . . or says he does. An *antitech radical*. Or an *ecoterrorist* maybe. *Very* left-wing . . . or very right-wing . . . one or the other.

Vortek will go on a rampage at some point, we agree. A real campus massacre. It'll probably be part of his PhD—the practical component . . .

Would the rampaging Vortek spare us, if he saw us cowering in a lecture hall? we wonder.

There's Originary Ron, Nostradamus, Romane Totale VI and the rest. There's Plastic Bertrand and Milquetoast. There's Rattus Rattus and Fox Piss.

There's Bitcoin. Son of a billionaire. Pretending to be one of us. He'll bore you to death about cryptos if you let him . . .

And there's Hector the apostate, who you'd never normally catch in the pub. There's Hector, all but carrying a briefcase, all but gone over to Business Studies. Hector, scholar of political grace, political conversion, who was once an integral part of our *League of Extraordinary PhD Students*, but has gone over to the enemy . .

The treasures of All Saints. Deplorables! Reprobates! From places you've never heard of, and of whom nothing is expected. Here to *study*, in inverted commas. Having lucked their way into three-year scholarships. How did that happen? Must have been positive discrimination for idiots. For people with *profound personality problems*. Must be some weird All Saints self-harm . . . A way for the uni to *deliberately defile itself* . . .

It shouldn't be allowed! *We* shouldn't be allowed! We're in bad taste. We're a bad joke. But here we are anyway, squandering our funding on Ruin Bar picklebacks every night ...

In the smokers' yard.

Do you despise atheists, Simone? Ismail asks.

There are illusions of belief that need to be . . . burnt away, Simone says.

And that's the role of atheism? Ismail asks.

I think faith has to pass through atheism as through a purifying flame, Simone says.

*God .. atheism* ... I don't know what these words even mean, I say.

Every meaning we give the word, *God*, is idolatry, Simone says. As for atheism ... I think it's possible to speak of *negative faith*.

Like, faith in negative stuff? Valentine asks. In universal doom and all that? That's our thing. We're experts on universal doom ...

Life on Earth is nothing but absurdity ... , I say.

All we know is lack, loss, powerlessness and evil ... , Marcie says.

*We're just broken and confused animals, scratching at the surface of the Earth* ... , I quote.

Ignore them, Simone, Gita says, rising to leave. They love pretending to hate the world. Saying they want to *let the world go*. Like they're some apocalyptic cell from the year 100.

I'd actually like to be in an apocalyptic cell in the year 100, Valentine says. Those guys really believed in things. Like, the destruction of the present course of the world. The wiping out of the Satanic powers. The termination of all pain and sorrow. The coming of the fucking kingdom of the God ...

Ismail, unscrewing the lens cap from his camera. Raising the viewer to his eye.

Put it away, Ismail, Marcie says. Fucking artist! Parasite! Fuck!

Let him film, Valentine says. He's trying to capture the beauty of drunkenness!

He's being a parasite, like all artists, Marcie says. He's stealing our souls. He's living off our discussion. Our ardency! Do you approve of being filmed, Simone?

Simone, smiling.

Very diplomatic, Marcie says. Can't you see you're disturbing our guest, Ismail? You can't film the revolution, brother! The revolution's live!

What revolution? I ask.

The *lumpen* revolution, Marcie says. The rising up of the social scum.

Is that us? I ask.

Technically, no, Marcie says. Technically, a PhD student can't be really lumpen. Studying in an institution working for bullshit credentials, hoping to put the word *doctor* before your name: It's anti-lumpen, right? But we're *spiritually* lumpen, with the possible exception of Gita. And Ismail. And I have my doubts about you, Johnny.

On your so-called logic, doing a PhD on the lumpenproletariat is the ultimate betrayal, Gita says.

Doing a PhD on queer communism when you're neither queer nor a communist is even worse, Ismail says.

Children! Children! Valentine says. Let's not bicker! Peace and love! Let's remember our common enemies! Fuck the Man, right?

More toasts. *FUCK THE MAN!*

Fuck Professor Bollocks! Marcie says.

*FUCK PROFESSOR BOLLOCKS!*

Fuck fatality! Valentine says. Fuck cosmic corruption! Fuck degenerate times!

*YEAH, FUCK THOSE THINGS!*

It's growing dark, Valentine says. The philosophers of the end, of the very end, are starting to appear. Us, maybe.

You wish! Ismail says.

We're holy drinkers—remember that, Valentine says. We're *hooleee* drinkers! We're antinomian! We're bearers of the alien fire! We're so atheist, so unbelieving, that we're purifying flames! Right, Simone? Purifying revolutionary semi-alcoholic flames!

Marcie, putting an arm around Business Studies Guy: Bet you never talk like this in *Business Studies*. Bet it's not all ecstatic nihilism, the lumpenproletariat and the void of God in Business Studies . . .

Simone, rising to leave.

Don't go! Valentine says. Don't leave us! God . . .

Marcie, calling after her: We're wretched! We're wretchedly drunk!

Valentine, calling after her: We need saving from ourselves! Save us, Simone!

Simone and I, walking to the bus stop.

We're crazy, right? I say. You don't need to say anything. I think we've spent too long in each other's company. I think we're sending each other mad.

Silence.

I'm afraid, I say.

What are you afraid of? Simone asks.

Of just about everything in Manchester, I say. Of the darkness. Of the night. Where they're planning their moves.

Who? Simone asks. Who's out there?

The evil ones, I say. The mad ones. The people of the void . . . They scream sometimes. Scream loud enough to wake up the dead—all the dead. Loud enough to give them a voice—a screaming voice. So that they can all scream up to the sky.

The disaster's crying out—screaming, I say. And laughing as it screams. Laughing at itself. At having to be . . . I shouldn't say these things, these mad things. Do I seem mad to you? I ask. I seem mad to myself, sometimes . . .

I think you've known terrible things, Simone says.

How do you know? I ask.

Your face, Simone says.

Do you hear the screams, too? I ask.

Simone, nodding

What do we do? I ask. How can we stop them?

*My solitude held in its grasp the grief of others until my death*: that's what Simone Weil's gravestone reads, Simone says.

Is that why you took her name? I ask.

I wanted to live deliberately, Simone says. I wanted to dedicate myself to something.

To God? I ask.

To others, Simone says. To God, if that is a name for others.

And that's what you're writing about: others? I ask.

I'm writing about the significance of the Cross, Simone says.

The Cross? I say. The crucifixion? No one cares about that. God's dead, right?

Not caring is part of the Cross—of the burden of the Cross. It's part of the scorn and derision and failure of the crucifixion, Simone says. It's only now that the crucifixion has become a reality. I think it's only appearing now—today—in its fullness.

In the time of disaster? I ask.

Yes, Simone says.

But if you believe in God, how can there be a disaster? I ask.

God's fallen silent, Simone says.

He didn't say anything at the crucifixion, did he? I say. When Jesus called up to him?

But his silence has a new depth today, Simone says. Because God is totally rejected from our thinking, our willing, our . . . projects. As if God had no importance. No . . . interest or significance . . . There's never been such an abandonment as now.

Wow, I say.

It's only now that Jesus is being put to death in the fullest and most radical sense, Simone says.

Because he's been abandoned . . . , I say. But we're abandoned, too. Is that why we hear screams? Because they're crying out and there's no one to hear . . .

Silence.

Look at the moon, Simone, I say. The Earth's dead daughter, shining to mock us. To remind us of the indifference of it all. That there's no one *bending over our cradle*. No one *singing us lullabies*. That no one knows or cares about our lives . . .

I don't think that's true, Simone says.

I wish it wasn't true, I say. Then: I'm glad you don't think it's true.

God will help us, Simone says. God will use us to engage with evil and disaster and brokenness and hopelessness.

But I thought . . . I thought we've been abandoned, I say.

God shows himself through us, Simone says. Through what we do.

How? What do we have to do? I ask.

Help others, Simone says.

And who will help *us*? I ask.

Simone, stopping to talk to a homeless man. Giving money to the homeless man.

The homeless man, thanking Simone. The homeless man, lifting up his tiny dog for Simone to pet.

I want to know, Simone—who will help *us*? I ask.

We help ourselves by helping, Simone says.

You forget yourself by helping, I say. Maybe that's all we want: to forget ourselves.

Perhaps forgetting ourselves is not such a bad thing, Simone says.

At the bus stop. The 143, pulling up.

Do you want me to come with you? I ask. Manchester's full of crazies.

I want you to pray for me, Simone says. As I will pray for you.

I don't know how to pray, I say.

Cry out and say, *Father, find me, I am your child*, Simone says. Cry out and . . . you will be welcomed home. You will be found by the father who made you.

Is that really true? I ask.


# 3

**TUESDAY MORNING.**

Al's café—always the same, always different, Valentine says.

Always the same, always the same, I say.

Ismail, in a speculative mood: This is my theory. Everyone's young in the morning and everyone's old at night. You live a whole lifetime in a day. You get born, then grow old. Right now, this is the *youth* of the day. Full of optimism. A break from yesterday's defeats . . . We're like children again.

Doesn't that mean we never learn? I say. That we just repeat the same thing over and over?

Exactly, Ismail says. But it means we're full of new hope, too—

Stupid hope, Marcie says.

But hope nonetheless, Ismail says. Every morning's still new. Young. A fresh take on the world.

So Al's café's new because it's morning? Valentine says. What about Al's plastic chairs—are they new, too? Are our macchiatos new? They *taste* the fucking same. Like day-old fucking piss.

You think that because it's nearly noon, Ismail says. We're almost out of morning. After noon comes adulthood: committing to things, getting on with things . . . being disappointed in things . . .

. . . Writing shit things in our rooms . . . , Valentine says.

*Trying* to write shit things in our rooms, you mean, I say. Prevaricating, mostly.

And procrastinating . . . Don't forget procrastinating, Valentine says.

And *masturbating*, Marcie says. The PhD student's essentially a masturbator.

. . . And then there's night, Ismail says. Full of regret. About things not done, roads not followed. At night, we search for consolation. Because of all the things we didn't do with the day. That's why we need to drink at night.

That's why I'm *still* drunk from last night, I say.

What about those of us who never actually went to bed? Marcie says. What does that do to your lifetime-in-a-day, Ismail? Business Studies Guy is *quite* the boy, I can tell you . . .

Jesus, Marcie, I say. We don't want to know.

I told him I'd fuck the Business Studies out of him, Marcie says. And I meant it . . .


## 4

BEECH ROAD VINTAGE. All upmarket. All boutique airs.

I'm sick of you guys just busting in here, Gita says.

We've come to spread the joy, Gita, Valentine says. It's a beautiful Manchester day. Rain pissing down.

Handing Gita her takeaway macchiato.

Oh great—now I'm going to get all buzzy, Gita says.

Handing Gita her takeaway muffin.

And *fat*, Gita says.

What's up, Gita? Marcie says. You can tell *us*. Bad night with Russell?

I don't want to talk about Russell, Gita says. I don't want to talk about anything.

Good thing this isn't just a social call, then, isn't it? Marcie says. We're on a mission—to inspire you, goad you on. You need to get back to work, Gita.

I *am* working, Gita says.

On your dissertation, fool, Marcie says.

Forget that. I'm doing *real* work. In the *real* world, Gita says.

When was the last time you had a customer? Marcie asks.

It's not all about customers, you know, Gita says. There's stuff to mend. Stuff that needs ironing . . . Anyway, I like it here, out in public. I'm not like you hideaway weirdos . . . And if you must know, I haven't touched my dissertation in a month. Not written *anything*. It's a total liberation.

What does lover boy have to say about that? Marcie asks. Must be getting worried.

He says it's okay, Gita says. It's okay not to write.

He's being soft with you, Marcie says. Pure guilt.

I don't know . . . Maybe I'm just not suited to PhD life, Gita says. I feel so lost . . .

All PhD students feel lost, I say. It's the PhD blues.

You guys are doing okay, Gita says.

We've got lower expectations, Marcie says.

We haven't the benefit of a *classical education* like you, Valentine says. We're not *well-rounded individuals*. We haven't got the *intellectual virtues*.

We can't even write lucid sentences, for fuck's sake, Marcie says. We hardly have our ABCs. Look at Johnny! He can barely speak!

You're taking the piss, Gita says.

Your problem is you've got too many options, Marcie says. You're a PhD tourist. A posh girl, interrupted. This isn't your real life.

Why are you always such bastards? Gita says.

That's a good question, Marcie says.

That's *quite* a question, Valentine says.

This is how the non-posh show affection, Marcie says. It's actual working-class behaviour. Cruelty makes us feel alive, Gita! Conversation isn't real unless it *draws blood*!

Oh please—I know what's *really* going on, Gita says. I'm dispensable now there's a new girl in town.

Is that *scepticism* we hear, Gita? Valentine asks.

The way you guys were buzzing round her last night . . . , Gita says. It was weird. *She's* weird. With her nun's shoes. Her nun's sense of style . . .

The real Simone Weil wasn't exactly a thermonuclear sex kitten, Valentine says.

Simone's recreating herself, Valentine says. That's what Manchester allows for, isn't it: reinventing yourself . . . being born again . . . joining queer bohemia . . . Not that you'd know anything about *that*, Gita.

Reinvention's cool, Gita says. Transitioning into some nutty nun-shoe-wearing ultra-Christian . . . no way . . .

Valentine, pulling a Happy Mondays teeshirt from the rails: fifty quid! Jesus!

It's got authentic sweat stains, Gita says. Bez could have worn that.

Who can afford it? Valentine asks.

Gita, shrugging: Beech-Roaders . . .

Don't see too many of them in here, I'd say, Marcie says.

The scene's tough now, Gita says. All the shops do so-called *vintage* . . . *I HEART HOOKY* badges . . . that kinda thing.

Don't you get tired of all this old stuff? I ask.

The proper element of messianic practice is the past: that's what Walter Benjamin wrote, Gita says.

Benjamin's incomprehensible, Valentine says.

We have to open the past to the needs of the present, Gita says. We have to search for the missed chances—unfulfilled promises.

What salvation is there in an Inspiral Carpets cow teeshirt? Marcie says.

*Ceremony*, Joy Division's version, on the shop speakers.

No wonder you're miserable listening to this stuff all day, Marcie says.

*Such* a beautiful song, I say. So tender. So heartfelt.

So *forlorn*, Valentine says.

Why were they so *sad*? I say. They were only about twenty . . .

Mancunian sadness, Ismail says. Barney Sumner said he didn't see a tree till he was sixteen. Manchester was still a bombsite. The buildings were black with soot . . .

But it's not just sad—it's tender, Gita says. So melodic. And listen to that bass. It's really searching for something. A kind of *connection* . . .

Marcie, grabbing Gita's phone. Yeah . . . *melancholic* connection . . . You've been reading far too much Benjamin, Gita . . .

Marcie's song.

Skanking guitar. Four-four beat. Hi-hats. Congas . . . *Wrote for Luck*. Happy Mondays. The Oakenfold mix.

Marcie, doing her googly-eyed Bez impression. Shaking imaginary maracas. Mancunian street funk, guys! Lumpen Funkadelic! . . . Come on—better Shaun and Bez out for a *grand majestic wander* than Ian Curtis hanging from the ceiling.

There's a whole way of life in this music, Marcie says. Scally gangs, heading into the Haçienda from the squats . . . Unemployeds, not up till three or four in the day . . . Smoking a few pipes . . . Necking a few brews . . . Microdots at the ready . . .

You can hear it all in this music, Marcie says. Stoned scallies, crossing the day like a desert caravan. Minor drug dealers. Petty thieves. Common-or-garden *lumpen*. Just drifting through squat-land into town . . .

Those guys had a real scene, Valentine says.

It's probably still out there somewhere, I say. Where the middle-classes fear to tread.

Forget it—there's no dole culture anymore, Valentine says. Even the squats got knocked down. *Lumpen freedom* disappeared when they demolished old Hulme . . .

I don't believe you, Marcie says. They're definitely out there somewhere. Doing their own thing. Dealing drugs. Nicking stuff. Having a laugh. Staying one step ahead of the Man . . .

So there's a *lumpen cavalry*, and they're going to save the world? Valentine says.

They've already saved the world, Marcie says. Just not for us.


## 5

AFTERNOON. Fallowfield.

Using Gita's car to move Simone.

A student glut. Why must there be so many? Aren't they appalled at themselves? How can they actually *stand* themselves? How can they go on?

Student concentration, at its greatest. Undergraduates, at their densest. Too many of them, all at once, and in all directions.

And all of them exactly alike. All of them, mirrored constantly. A horrible multiplication. Hundreds and thousands of undergraduates, crowding the horizon.

Youth! Middle-class youth! Come for the *student experience*! Come to party *with their own kind*! Flocking! Shoaling! Cramming themselves into the smallest possible space!

The tower block . . . The halls of residence . . . Rows of Victorian terraces taken over by students . . . Street after street of them. A rash of *To Let* signs. And crappy dormers. And concreted front gardens.

How can the city let itself be used like this? How can this be allowed, year after year?

It's the Fallowfield plague . . . And it's wiped out the original inhabitants. It's *colonisation*! It's *hegemony*!

Imagining the outbreak of some student disease. Some student autoimmune sickness. The student condition, somehow attacking itself. An intolerance of students to themselves . . . To their own state of being . . . Auto-allergy, manifested in para-suicides—in semi-suicidal acts . . .

No chance! They all look as healthy as anything...

That Simone was here, even briefly. That Simone was here, in amongst them all...

## 6

**MOVING SIMONE TO ISMAIL'S (TO MICHAEL'S).**

Where's the great man? Marcie asks.

I dunno—church or something, Ismail says. He did want to be here to welcome you, Simone.

It's okay, Simone says. I feel welcome.

Who even goes to church these days? Valentine says.

Michael's the cantor, Ismail says. He has to be there half of Sunday. The Orthodox have these really long ceremonies.

Is he, like, *really Christian*, then? Marcie asks.

He believes in reincarnation, Ismail says. Which is odd. And he's a bit polytheist—the house is full of Hindu statues. And he says Jesus was an anarchist...

This place is so big, I say. You could get lost here. Just wander from room to room forever...

It just *reeks* of boomer privilege, Marcie says.

Michael's owned it for decades, Ismail says. Members of Buzzcocks used to live here—some of them, anyway. Michael's famous, actually—he keeps cropping up in people's memoirs. He met the Sex Pistols when they first played Manchester. And he was at school with Tony Wilson...

He's *old*, Valentine says.

Nearly eighty, Ismail says.

Who lives here now—just you and Michael? I ask.

People pass through... A couple of people just moved out, Ismail says.

He must have serious money, Valentine says.

He was basically the head of the humanities, Ismail says. Retired aged forty-nine.

That generartion, Marcie says. It was all so *easy* for them.

What does he do all day? I ask.

Have very lengthy discussions with all kinds of people on every subject under the sun, Ismail says. Living room symposia, he calls them. Get visited by monks—loads of them. They're collaborating on some encyclopaedia of the Eastern church. He still teaches a bit— Indian philosophy, at the temple. And writes queer fantasy novels, which never get published.

. . . And his fridge is always full of saag aloo, Marcie says, eating from a bowl. Which is a great thing.

Sure, he likes to cook, Ismail says. He hosts great dinners . . .

And all for free for you tenants . . . , Valentine says. Fuck . . .

We do make a contribution, Ismail says.

Free, basically, Marcie says. Which is how it should be. We all deserve a *boomer subsidy*.

He likes company, Ismail says. He likes having young people around.

I'll bet he does, Valentine says. *Cute* young people . . .

Simone's room, at the top of the house.

Dumping her boxes. Her iron teapot. Her outsized pepper mill. (Simone's stuff . . . The stuff she's saved. That she's willing to carry through life. Is the secret to Simone amongst these things?) Volumes and volumes of books. Books in French! In *FRENCH*! She must have had a proper education. My God, there are even books in Latin! In *Greek*! And it can't be . . . It's quite impossible . . . scholarly editions of books in Sanskrit . . .

You can look out over the rooftops, Ismail says. And you can decorate if you like. Paint the walls . . .

I like it as it is, Simone says.

There's wonderful light when the sun's out, Ismail says. Which it never is.

Just don't say yes when he asks to film you in it, Marcie says. Don't let him get all arthouse on you, whatever you do.

21

It's so peaceful, I say. Like no one's lived here for years . . .

A lot of people pass through Michael's, Ismail says. They've worn the room smooth . . .

I like that, I say. I like the impersonality. You could be no one here. Just fade into the air . . .


# 7

**WEDNESDAY MORNING.**

At the bus stop with alkies.

Why do they have to hang out here? Why do they have to make bus-waiting so intimidating?

They're just being who they are, Marcie says. Unashamedly. There's a glory in that. Squandering their lives . . .

What if alkies are the clue to it all? Valentine says. The only ones really awake. What if they grasp the truth of everything?

The truth of, like, pissing yourself. The truth of swearing at passersby, Gita says.

They know things, I'm certain of that, Valentine says. They know because they're drunk.

No: they know and *then* they drink, Marcie says. Because it's a terrible knowledge.

They don't seem that unhappy about it, I say. That one's dancing.

At least they don't just lie in bed all day, Valentine says. They have an *interest*.

Uh . . . They're *alcoholics*, Gita says. They've come out for their first drink of the morning . . .

But they've done it *together*, Valentine says. They're drinking *together*. They're companions in defeat.

It's an *honourable* defeat, Marcie says. Better to destroy yourself in your own way than be destroyed by the Man, right? Better self-murder than being murdered by the Man.

## 8

**THE BUS TO UNI.**

Ismail, filming.

We're pathetic, Marcie says. We don't even have to be in today—and we're going in anyway. Why?

Maybe something will be happening, I say.

Maybe it won't, Marcie says.

It's a change of scene, Marcie, Valentine says. Keeps the deadness off.

*Multiplies* the deadness, more like, Marcie says. *God*, this route is so fucking *slow*! Have they deliberately *prolonged* it? Is it supposed to drive us mad?

Yeah . . . It's a big conspiracy, I say. A big *bus* conspiracy.

So many *stops*! Marcie says.

People have to get on and off, I say.

There are too many people! Marcie says.

This is *public* transport, Marcie—the clue's in the word, I say.

You've actually gone purple from misanthropy, den mom, Valentine says.

There are people *eating* on this bus! Marcie says. It should not be allowed! I can *hear* them! And it's so *crammed* . . . Everyone's breathing each other's air . . .

You're very particular for a former Scouse street urchin, Valentine says.

Why do we even have to *travel* to uni!? Marcie says. Why isn't teleportation a thing? We should have police outriders clearing the road ahead of us . . . *Don't they know who we are?!*

Who are we, Marcie? I ask.

People who deserve better, Marcie says. Fuck, Ismail!—put your fucking camera *away*! The revolution really can't be televised. You're such a leech . . . I'm lamenting here. Baring my soul. And you're . . . What *are* you doing?

Preserving things, Ismail says.

What are you actually filming? Valentine asks.

Everyday stuff, Ismail says. Ordinary life . . .

Why? Valentine asks.

To remember all the days that didn't catch fire, Ismail says. The days without drama . . .

Jesus, there are plenty of *those*, Marcie says. We're fucking sick of those . . .

I want to make an *ordinary epic*, Ismail says. The story of nothing in particular.

That's all we need: an apologist for dullness, Marcie says. Why do you have to film *everything*, Ismail?

The everyday's vast, Ismail says. No one can control it—not even the Man. You can't *direct* the everyday . . . It barely exists . . . And yet it *insists*. It's *there* nonetheless . . .

*What's* there? Marcie says. Drizzle? Road works? Traffic jams? The same route we've travelled fifty thousand times? The same fucking passengers crunching their fucking crisps?

We're so immersed in the everyday that it's hidden, Ismail says. We see through it rather than see it. We move through the everyday constantly—it's the medium of life. But we don't know it and we don't know we don't know . . .

I know it, believe me, Marcie says. The everyday is where life goes to die.

Things are happening all the time, Ismail says. They're trembling at the edges of our awareness.

You've got a pretty low threshold for *things happening*, Valentine says.

Things do actually happen on the bus, I say. Violent things. I saw a holdup once. These guys threatening to acid-spray the driver if he didn't hand over the cash . . .

And . . . ? Valentine asks.

They just scooped up some change and ran off, I say. Driver

couldn't drive afterwards—too shaken. We had to wait for another bus to pick us up.

Just another day in Manchester, eh? Marcie says.


## 9

### ALL SAINTS' HUMANITIES BUILDING, EIGHTH FLOOR.

Looking down from the atrium.

Corridors, thick with undergraduates.

Discussion.

Aren't they appalled by their sheer number? By the *fact* of their number?

This is mass higher education. To be followed by mass office pseudo-jobs. Mass fake employment.

Look at them: the finest fruit of institutional processing. From nursery to school to breakfast clubs to after-school clubs to soft-play centres to activity camps . . .

The *effort* it's taken to produce them! The resources! The *time*! Years and years! And all they've got to show for it is obedience . . . victimhood . . . dependency . . . And the deep-seated conviction that *there is no alternative* . . .

Student-drones, preparing for the world of non-work. Student dullards, being processed for a society of *busy nullity*.

Then what about us? What are we here for? Why were we given scholarships?

Because our processing was not complete. They've brought us back to finish us off . . .


## 10

### ALL SAINTS LIBRARY.

All space. An ocean of floor tiles. Vast windows.

All Saints Library: half café, half foyer. Forget the actual books. It doesn't need actual books. They aren't necessary to its sense of itself, actual books.

Open space, instead . . . A glut of space, instead . . .

And listen to it hum, All Saints Library. The library even *hums*. That's the sound of efficiency, that humming. Of busy computers. Of hard-at-work servo-mechanisms, keeping the air circulating. Switching the lights off and on. And the sound of chatter, over the hum . . .

Walking Business Studies Guy through the stacks.

*Phenomenology of Spirit*, Business Studies Guy! *Concluding Unscientific Postscript to the Philosophical Fragments*! *History and Class Consciousness*! *The Legitimacy of the Modern Age*! *Matter and Mind*! *The Visible and the Invisible*!

Have *we* read all these books, Business Studies Guy? Not really. But we've been in their presence, Business Studies Guy. We've been close to them. We've kept them on our bookshelves. We've laid them beside us on our bedside tables. And we've read *about* them—some of them. We've skimmed the introductory guides . . .

We've *imbibed* these books, Business Studies Guy. And now, so must he . . .

## 11

### BADMINTON IN THE SPORTS HALL.

Showing Business Studies Guy the badminton ropes.

The humanities PhD student needs an outlet, we explain. The humanities PhD student isn't entirely cerebral.

Badminton's the humanities PhD student's sport—all weathers, all seasons, sheltered from the ceaseless mancunian rain.

Oh, we know badminton's farcical, Business Studies Guy. We

know it's farce itself. But perhaps that's the only place where we can succeed: in farce.

We're even *good* at badminton (farcically good? actually good?)! Well, *Marcie's* good at badminton. Marcie's a badminton champion. Marcie and Hector all but won the Manchester Postgraduate Badminton Cup last year . . . They all but lifted the trophy . . .

Hector was Marcie's last protégé, Business Studies Guy. You should know in whose footsteps you tread. You should know the dangers—the *spiritual* dangers—that lie before you.

You have a gift for badminton, Business Studies Guy—anyone can see that. You're a natural. You could take this all the way to the final—we can see that already. But we said the same thing about Hector. We thought Hector was our great chance . . .


**12**

**EVENING.**

Student work-in-progress exhibition.

This better not be all artwank, Marcie says. And then—Oh God! It's all artwank. *ARTWANK!* Art for wankers!

Keep your voice down, Ismail says.

Looking around the gallery. All this *art*. The great *art glut* . . . The great *art mountain* . . .

All these *student artists*. Fledgling *postgraduate artists*. Who thought for a moment that they needed encouraging? Who thought for one second that they should be *brought on*? Does anyone want more art? Haven't we all had enough art?

*Gallery art*—not *of* anyone; not *from* anywhere. Nothing necessary about it. Nothing that *had to be*.

Examining the artworks.

Crap. Crap. Crap. Crap. Now yours, Ismail . . .

Marcie, reading Ismail's plaque. *SMILE*. In capitals. *A video piece.*
*Focusing on a single gesture . . . Loosening a moment from a chronologi-*
*cal sequence . . . from anything that proceeds or succeeds. A moment that*
*won't pass—won't settle . . . That just hovers . . .*

On the screen: a smile, in black and white. Broadening, very slowly.
In flickering light.

A smile without a face, Marcie says. Your precious everyday, everywhere all around—and this is what you film?

What's anyone got to smile about, anyway? Valentine says. Life's
going to shit.

It's not really a *happy* smile, though, is it? I say. It's ambiguous. Like
the *Mona Lisa* . . .

Yeah—I didn't want to show anything definite, Ismail says.

Perish the thought! Marcie says. Typical fucking *artist* . . .

What's the smile smiling at? I ask. What's happening off-screen?

Smile-boy's getting a blowjob, I reckon, Valentine says. That's
what's going on.

You think it's a man's smile? Gita says. I think it's a woman's.

Then smile-girl's getting fucked, Valentine says. But it's an ambiguous arthouse fuck. She isn't sure whether she likes it or not.

No—it's just *art* smiling, Marcie says. Smiling at itself. Totally
self-involved. Nothing to do with the world . . .

Light fading on-screen. The smile again. Widening. Only it's all
darker this time. Like the film stock has deteriorated.

*Smile II: This Time It's Drearier*, I say.

Reading more of the plaque. *Exploring permutation . . . Isolating*
*a single incomplete gesture and iterating it with variations, with tiny*
*differences in lighting and projection speed . . . Unfolding through its*
*own fragmentation, never finally happening . . .*

Kill me now, Marcie says. This is what's left of art—abducting living moments and taking them to art-land. Whittled down to this
smug floating fucking *smile*.

## 13

RUIN BAR, AFTER.

Marcie, looking decisive. There's only one thing for it, Ismail: We have to collectivise your project. Like in the Soviet Union, when they took over the farms from class-enemy of the proletariat. Only we'll be seizing art from the class-enemy of the lumpenproletariat: that's you, Ismail, by the way.

Don't I get a say? Ismail asks.

No you do *not*, Marcie says. The enemy of the lumpenproletariat should keep quiet unless addressed. Isn't that right, comrades?

Give him a chance to defend himself, I say.

He's had his chance! Valentine says. He's bored us to death with his chance!

If anything, we should have a *show trial*, Marcie says. Ismail should be made to publically repent for his *artism*. For his reactionary solemnity. For his individualism. For his *petit bourgeois attitudes*. Slow cinema, indeed!

What kind of film would the lumpenproletariat make? That's the question, Valentine says. Do we have to go all socialist realist or whatever? Make Stalinist art about the glorious workers?

The lumpen are not Stalinist, comrade Val, Marcie says. They're not into *socialist realism* or any of that. They're not bothered with agitprop. Or Billy Bragg. Or folk songs. They're against anything *forced*. *Pious*. They're for whatever arises directly from the *lumpensprung*. Whatever releases *lumpen energies*.

Just think of it: a film full of *lumpen laughter*: of those who want no stake in our rotten world, Marcie says. Who can't take the world seriously . . . Who have no care about the morrow . . . Who don't worry about earning a living . . . Who are too busy with *lumpen life*—with chaos and japes and *life itself* . . .

The lumpen could never make art, Valentine says. They couldn't get it together to make films.

They made *music*, comrade Val, Marcie says. Just think of the miracle of the Mondays.

The lumpenproletariat is actually a negative category in Marx, as you should know, Marcie, Gita says. It's just a name for pickpockets and idlers.

Exactly, comrade Gita! Marcie says. Our kind of people! Scallywags! Idlers! PhD students who have no intention of finishing! We're your *lumpen conscience*, Ismail. Forget this arthouse wank. We're here to save you from pretension.

Maybe we should go populist, Valentine says. Make something the people might actually give a fuck about.

A musical! I say.

A *lumpen musical*..., Valentine says. (Singing:) *Maybe it's because I'm a lumpenprole that I love Man-ches-ter*...

Vortek could sing, I say. He's got a *great* voice. Deep. Like Lee Marvin doing *Wand'rin' Star.*

We could make porn, Valentine says. The people want porn, surely.

I'm boooored of porn, Marcie says.

We could make *classy* porn, I say. With a European edge.

I think we should revive the screen romance, Gita says. Flirtation...bashful looks...coyness...That kind of thing.

We should make a *genre* movie, I say. That's where all the energy is now. All those zombie films . . . superheroes . . . Things people actually *watch*.

I think we should revive kung-fu cinema, Marcie says. Do a version of *Drunken Master.* Did you ever see that? It's fantastic...Some drunk guy everyone had written off turns out to be the greatest kung-fu fighter of all . . . Except we'd call it *Drunken Thinker.* He'd seem as stupid as we are. And perpetually drunk. And then he'd be revealed as really profound. He'd come out with the most brilliant ideas.

We could make *Drunken Scouse Bitch*, starring you, Valentine says.

We could make *Rochdale Hyperslut*, starring you, Marcie says.

Of course we lack a) kung-fu skills, b) any ability to make kung-fu films, c) actors who have kung-fu skills, Ismail says.

*Intensity*—that's what we want, Valentine says. Sensations, transmitted to *bodies*. We should make something *shocking*. Something to challenge every middle-class account of the world.

What would that be? I ask.

Something hardcore, Valentine says. A snuff film, maybe . . .

And you'd star in it, right? I say. *Such* a suicide queen . . .

No—our snuff film would snuff out all film! Valentine says. We'd *sacrifice* film. No—we'd sacrifice all of art. Make art sacred again. Like that Vietnamese monk who poured petrol over himself and set himself alight in the '60s. He didn't cry out . . . He didn't move a muscle . . . He made himself totally sacred!

That guy had, like, a noble cause, Gita says. He was protesting against the Vietnam War.

We'd be protesting against art! Valentine says.

No one cares about art, Gita says. Art doesn't matter.

Any attempt to destroy art just becomes more art, Marcie says. The history of the avant-garde shows nothing else. Art-death feeds the art-monster. Art *lives* on its own suicide.

You could film us talking about film, Gita says. It could be kinda *Brechtian*.

Too meta, Valentine says. I hate meta.

You know what we should do: make the film *after* the last film, Marcie says.

What's that mean? Ismail asks.

Things happen twice, first as tragedy, then as farce, right? Marcie says. We can't kill art, that's the tragedy. We can't destroy film. But we can reveal it as a farce.

Everything we touch becomes a farce, I say.

Exactly, comrade Johnny, Marcie says. *EXACTLY!* We can't start anything new, we know that. We can't make new art. So our mission is to despoil the art that's been . . . Repeat it—*farcically*. We can only laugh at art and laugh at ourselves laughing . . .

All that's left is farce: that's what the lumpen understand, Marcie says. We *affirm* farce. But we also want to push farce beyond itself. There's a superior farce that is part of the greater play. A *delivering* farce—that laughs at the entirety of the world and laughs at itself laughing.

I think Ismail should be allowed to speak, I say.

Tell us, comrade Ismail: Do you understand your role now? Marcie asks.

You guys know nothing—*nothing*—about making films, Ismail says.

But we have instincts, comrade Ismail, Valentine says.

And we have your best interests at heart, Marcie says. We're helping because we love you, comrade Ismail.

Why are you so fixated on art anyway? Ismail asks. Why can't you just leave art alone?

That is a very good question, comrade Valentine, Marcie says.

A question that deserves an answer, comrade den—comrade Marcie, Valentine says.

Because art is where all the bourgeois hopes and dreams have gone since religion collapsed, Marcie says.

And now we have to pop all their *gaudy bubbles of expectation*, Valentine says. Expose them for what they are. We're doing our bit for sober realism.

It's just nihilism, Ismail says. You're nihilists—all of you. And you want to destroy anything that might risk being something other than nihilism . . . You're death-dealers. You want something to worship, even in the form of not worshipping anything. Even in the form of *denigrating* everything.

Better anti-faith or whatever than *fake* faith, Marcie says. Than pretending to have faith. Than *willing* yourself into faith.

You don't say that to Simone! Ismail says. You act all pious around Simone! Why can't the Collective go to work on *her*?

The Collective admits Simone Weil is a wild card, Marcie says. The Collective admits that there are still surprises, even for us.

The Simone case needs further analyses, Valentine says. Your case, however, is more straightforward. You're one of us—

Which means you can't be Andrei Tarkovsky, comrade Ismail, Marcie says. You can't be all Russian and profound. Nor can you be Terrence Malick: some Catholic boomer star-child . . .

Marcie, suddenly sitting back. Closing her eyes.

Opening them again.

Okay—I have a plan, Marcie says. This is a stroke of fucking genius, I warn you. We could recapitulate the history of film. Remake some arthouse classics—really canonical stuff . . .

Far too hard, Valentine says. I mean, technically . . .

Yeah, but we'd do it *crappily*, Marcie says. As only *we* could. Look, it's going to be farcical, so why not embrace that? Go-kart Tarkovsky. Bargain basement Malick . . . Whatever we make will show the lie of art for what it is . . .


## 14

**THURSDAY MORNING.**

Walking Chorlton with Simone.

Wealthy people around here. Southerners on a civilising mission. Converting old bedsits. Repointing brick. Binning the double glazing, the plastic drainpipes, the fire doors. Planting trees and bushes . . .

Sometimes, some taste. They're improving the world. Making it better without too much fuss. Optimising the world for themselves, and so for the rest of us. Southerners know the secret of good middle-class life, and they're modelling the way we should live it . . .

But still the *unregenerated* wander the Chorlton streets. Meths drinkers . . . Addicts . . . Day-ghouls . . . Human shells . . . Street shufflers . . . Street ghosts—too weak to steal. Too weak to mug you, though they beckon to you from alleyways and try to lure you close.

Street soldiers, all testosteroned up. Death-starers. Solo gangsters, challenging you to look them in the eye. You have to look down. Have to look away; show nothing on your face. Lest you give offence and you're beaten to death. Lest you become a target for ultraviolence. Because you're not *pumped* like them. You're not looking for trouble at eleven in the morning.

And the Knaves. The Wild Ones. The *Unpredictables*. You never know what they want—whether they'll stab you or hug you. Friends? Enemies? It depends on what mood they're in. It depends on what mood *you're* in. Maybe you're saved if you can banter with them. If there's a to-and-fro. If you're as lively as they are. As *chipper* . . . But maybe they'll just stab you anyway.

Still there are maniacs abroad on the Chorlton streets. It's the Chorlton paradox.

There could come a blow from nowhere, as from fate. You could be down on the pavement, your head cracked open. You could be blue-lighted into A&E, head in a neck-brace . . .

## 15

**THURSDAY AFTERNOON.**

Through the old village green. Into the Ees.

It's our favourite place in the world, we tell Simone. The antidote to *everything*.

Meadows, opening out.

Piles of hay bales, covered with tyres. Plastic paint tubs. Cracked pipes.

The Ees is our gift to you, Simone. Or maybe you're our gift to it . . .

The Ees is a dump, Gita says.

Yeah, but it's *our* dump, I say.

It's like a giant landfill site that's broken the surface, Gita says.

It's a kind of *museum*, I say. Except it doesn't take care of its arte-facts—just lets them rot.

It's so *random*, Valentine says. No rhyme or reason . . . Who had the energy to dump that sofa here? You'd need a fucking crane. Or some friendly giant—Vortek, maybe.

Vortek's an *un*friendly giant, Marcie says.

It's like some flood carried it here, Valentine says. A tsunami that washed through all the homes, and swept everything out . . .

Wading through the ferns.

The Ees makes us fall silent. It imposes a kind of reverence. You don't want to talk too loudly. You don't want to disturb it. To wake it up . . .

You come to the Ees to lose yourself. To be forgotten. No one's looking for you. No one needs you. You're not *wanted* anywhere.

Where's that place the elves sail to in *Lord of the Rings*? Marcie asks. When they've had enough of it all?

The Western Lands? Valentine says.

That's a Burroughs novel, I say.

The Grey Havens, Ismail says.

The Grey Havens is where they sail *from*, not where they sail *to*, I say.

Well, that's what the Ees is to us, Marcie says. Every time we come.

Not for *me*, Gita says.

The woods, deepening.

Admit it—we're lost, Marcie says. You haven't got a fucking clue.

The whole point of the Ees is to get lost, Ismail says.

We should go back the way we came, Valentine says.

Except that's probably not the way back anymore, I say.

The Ees is . . . *anomalous*, we tell Simone. The laws of space and time don't apply here. There are weird spatio-temporal folds—strange pockets. A path that leads somewhere today will lead somewhere else tomorrow. Old safe places become impassable, and the route can be plain or easy, or impossibly confusing. That's how the Ees is.

And yet the Ees is the only freedom we know, we tell Simone. This is where we come to be away from our desks—away from screens. Out from under ceilings—out from behind closed doors. Out from all bounded spaces.

We come here to get lost, in the non-university of the Ees. And when we're most lost—when we're most tired of our starings-into-the-air, our dead-ends, our cul-de-sacs, our missed deadlines—that's when the Ees will bring us . . . somewhere.

Somewhere the Ees wants us to be, Ismail says.

What's the Ees *for*? That's what I want to know, Gita asks. What's it doing here?

Many have pondered that question, I say.

Many have gone mad by that question, Valentine says.

The Ees is not *for* anything, Ismail says. Maybe that's what saves it—that it's just abandoned. It's good for nothing . . . It's not just another leisure resource.

The Ees is a kind of commons, I say. It's for everyone.

For everyone who wants *toxic shock*, Gita says. The Ees is a dump, you guys!

It's in some legal Limbo—that's what I heard, Valentine says. It has some special status, which means it can't be developed.

They've tried to build things here though, I say. It's full of ruins.

There was a whole shantytown the crusties built after the Hulme Crescents were demolished, we tell Simone. All these self-builds and tree houses, like Christiania in Copenhagen. They declared the Ees a *temporary autonomous zone* or something. And they made that *Ees flag* . . .

Then there's a whole *paranormal* thing with the Ees, we tell Simone. Some say that there was an explosion, like the one over Tunguska. Others say an alien spaceship landed . . . Or there was a Roswell-style crash . . . Of course there's the question of why the aliens landed in Manchester. But why not Manchester?—they probably liked the music. They were aliens of *taste*.

And there are conspiracy theories about the Ees, we tell Simone. Some mini-Chernobyl research lab. A radiation leak . . . We're probably shortening our lifespans right now. Contracting strange forms of cancer . . . Acquiring weird superpowers . . .

They used to keep the Ees fenced off, that's what I heard, Marcie says. It was all barbed wire and watchtowers and army jeeps patrolling. Like East Germany.

So what happened? I ask.

It was all dismantled, Ismail says. They thought the best way to hide it was in plain sight—as some innocent woodland. No need for fences and dogs.

And there's the legend of the Room, we tell Simone. Passed down from All Saints humanities PhD student to PhD student . . . A place that grants all your wishes. It's supposed to be somewhere round here—no one knows exactly where.

But it's not like Aladdin's lamp, where the genie grants you three wishes. You don't ask for anything in the Room. The Room knows what you want deep in your heart.

You only get what you *really* want, we tell Simone. So you'd better not have *secret paedophile desires* . . .

Come on—the Room's just a story for big PhD students to fuck with the heads of little PhD students, Gita says.

The *apocalyptic* Ees is the best of all, though, Valentine says.

The Beast from the Ees will rise in the End Times and destroy the world—or Manchester, at least . . . That kind of stuff . . .

You know where the Beast is kept? Marcie asks. [Dramatic pause.] In the *Room*. We'll only find the Room once the Beast from the Ees begins its apocalyptic flight. On the last night of the world, in other words.

What's the use of getting what you wish for on the last night of the world? I ask.

Unless what you wish for *is* the last night of the world, Valentine says.


## 16

FRIDAY EVENING.

Michael's *welcome Simone* dinner party.

The Jesus pictures are just great, Marcie says. Not kitschy at all. I mean, they're still Jesus pictures, but there's no kitsch about them. I was brought up with kitsch Jesus . . . Carrying a lamb across his shoulders . . . Cradling a lamb . . . Holding his shepherd's crook, with lambs around his feet . . . There was a lot of lamb stuff. And Jesus was so Aryan . . . bright blue eyes . . . blond hair . . . Positively *Danish* . .

Have you seen icons before? Michael asks.

She would have done if she hadn't fallen asleep during *Andrei Rublev*, Ismail says.

It was so *black and white*, Marcie says.

Yeah, but you get Rublev's *Trinity* in colour at the end, if you stay awake that long, Ismail says. And all the horses rolling around in the grass.

Fabulous! Marcie says, inspecting another icon.

Jesus Pantocrator, Michael says.

Panto what? Marcie says.

Jesus the all-powerful, Michael says. The lord who is coming in power to put an end to this era.

I don't think of Jesus as *powerful*, Simone says.

Jesus puts worldly power in its place, Michael says. He shows how the earthly powers are already dethroned. How death is already conquered.

But that doesn't make him powerful, Simone says.

It's not power as a worldly authority, granted . . . , Michael says.

I thought the Bible said you weren't supposed to show graven images, Ismail says. I thought there was some basic distrust of vision.

Didn't someone see the burning bush? I ask.

Yeah . . . a burning bush—not *Jesus*, Ismail says.

What about the Book of Revelations? Valentine says. Wormwood fallen from the sky and so on. That's a vision.

There's Daniel and the beast from the sea . . . , I say.

And there's Ezekiel and his weird wheels, which is clearly about an *alien visitation*, Valentine says.

Visions in the Bible must be understood eschatologically, Michael says. In terms of the end of times, and the possibility of seeing God in the fullness of his truth and reality.

So they show what's going to happen? Ismail asks.

They show what will happen at the end of time, when everything will be made whole—every aspect of the cosmos, Michael says. When the past is recapitulated in Christ, summed up in him, taken over by him, transfigured in him. When the past enters the hands of God to be made new.

Beautiful, I say. Do you think . . . Do you think it could happen?

I think it *will* happen, Michael says.

What would be saved of Manchester, do you think? I ask.

The New Creation . . . , Ismail says. That's what I'd like to show in my films . . .

Typical artist-opportunist, Marcie says. Always thinking of your *projects*.

And what about icons? Ismail asks. What do they show? I mean, they're not visions, are they? They're not about the New Creation or whatever.

Why, then, is there an icon of Jesus on the Cross? I ask.

Simone, calmly: Because Jesus will be on the Cross until the end of time.

For all of time . . . That sucks, doesn't it? Marcie says.

And after that—after the end of time? I ask.

There is no end to time, Simone says.

We disagree, Michael says.

It's the world that is the Cross of Christ, Simone says. And it's in the world we remain.

But we can see through the world, Michael says. We can see eternity.

We can't see through the crucifixion, Simone says. And if the world is the Cross of Christ, then we can't see through the world at all. This is simply the place where God has divested himself of all power.

You reject the risen Jesus? Michael asks.

I reject your risen Christ sitting at the right hand of God, surrounded with the glory of angels, Simone says.

You'd prefer that the resurrection never happened, Michael says.

Simone, quoting: *Christ on the Cross: the greatest harm inflicted on the greatest good: if one loves that, one loves the order of the world.*

Sitting around the table.

Michael and Ismail bringing in steaming pans. Rice. Creamy chicken korma.

I haven't eaten proper food for, like, ages, Marcie says.

I don't know what proper food *is*, Valentine says.

You shall, cuddles, Michael says.

Ismail, filling our glasses.

And I'll bet this is really good wine, I say.

We don't know anything about wine, Marcie says. It's wasted on us.

Wine is never wasted, Michael says. I agree with the ancient Greeks: the search for truth begins around a table with a glass of wine . . . So let's toast. To truth!

To truth!

Of course, the truth is that ancient Greece was a slave society, Marcie says.

It was, Michael says.

The slaves worked so the rich could think, Marcie says.

There are no slaves here, Ismail says. Michael cooked this meal himself.

There were people who grew the rice, Marcie says. Who raised the chicken or whatever. Who harvested the spices and dried them.

That's why we sometimes say grace, Michael says. To give thanks for our food.

To thank *God*, not the farmers who actually grew it, Marcie says. Or the poor fucker . . . sorry, *people* . . . who harvest it. Or the folks who . . . who built this house . . . made the furniture . . . All of which makes it possible for you to bestow charity, Michael. Because that's what this is: *charity* . .

Charity tastes great, Valentine says.

Thank you, my *dear* Valentine, Michael says.

I just think this *symposium*, or whatever you call it, is part of the system, Marcie says. Real thought comes from the outside.

Allow me to try to justify myself, Marcie, Michael says. You see the candle at the centre of the table. Do you know what it stands for?

Let me guess: sweet baby Jesus, Marcie says.

*Marcie!* Ismail scolds.

The candle stands for the stranger, Michael says. The early Christians always kept a place at their table for the one who might arrive in their midst.

Who might be Jesus in disguise or something, right? Marcie says. Take it from me—Johnny's definitely not Jesus. And nor is Valentine. Have you seen his table manners?

Do you know the story of the Good Samaritan? Michael asks.

Where some guy helped another guy . . . , Marcie says.

Michael, unhooking an icon from the wall. Telling us its story. A Jewish traveller was beaten and left for dead by the side of the road. A priest came by, and did nothing. Then a Levite, and he, too, walked by. But then the Samaritan arrived. According to the customs of the time, the Samaritan had no obligations to those outside his own people. But he felt the pain of the injured man, and helped him. This was a parable that Jesus told when he was asked the question, *And who is my neighbour?*

The Samaritan was a nice guy, Marcie says. So what?

The Samaritan helped a stranger who wasn't part of his family or clan, Michael says. One human being chose to respond to another, and quite *gratuitously*—for no other reason than it was the good thing to do. That's what charity means.

So you're charitably feeding us all, like the Good Samaritan, Marcie says. That's laudable . . .

You suspect me of condescension, Michael says.

I don't like the power relations, Marcie says. I mean, look at you, with your big house—

A house that takes in all kinds of guests . . . , Ismail says.

Come on, Marcie, what could be wrong with that? I say.

On whose terms is your hospitality given? Marcie asks. It's like, Mr Bourgeois puts you up . . . Mr Boomer rents you a room . . .

The Good Samaritan is a story about the Incarnation, Michael says. If you believe, as I do, that the Lord became human in Jesus—that God became flesh—then you must also understand that human beings face one another in a new way. You can see the face of God in that of everyone you encounter. With Jesus, there appears a humanity of neighbours, a universal community no longer bound to family, place of birth or religion.

Words like *community* and *neighbour* have been emptied of all meaning..., Marcie says.

The candle at the centre of the table is my welcome to the neighbour, Michael says. To all of you—and to the first comer who may knock at the door.

Or who may break through the window, this being Manchester, I say.

All very impressive, Marcie says. But there are people out there who don't need your charity—or anyone's charity.

Here we go, Valentine says.

The mancunian lumpenproletariat, Michael, Marcie says. Have you heard of them?

Michael, shaking his head. Smiling.

They're out there, busying themselves, doing their runnings, Marcie says.

Doing their *what*? Valentine asks.

Dealing coke, crack, steroids, Marcie says. Fencing stolen stuff: sunglasses, leather jackets. Avoiding the benefits agencies and housing departments. Not being connected to any address. You can't tell them from petty thieves. In fact, they *are* petty thieves.

Admit it, Marcie: the lumpen are a myth, Valentine says. They're bedtime stories for bored, overmanaged PhD students...

The only people out there are the homeless, I say. Addicts and ne'er-do-wells. If we opened the windows now, we'd hear them screaming. Every night it's like Manchester's going down with all hands...

All these people beyond the reach of the so-called care system and the so-called mental health services and the so-called addiction services, I say.

Simone has just started working with the homeless, Ismail says.

I'm part of a direct-action charity, Simone says.

It's dangerous, Michael says. As I'm always telling Simone . . .

The guy who runs it has been stabbed, like, several times, Ismail says. They're all mad volunteers—not professionals. A bunch of Christians just go out there, into the night . . . There's no expensive HQ or overpaid CEO. Everything goes to the homeless.

Is it scary? I ask Simone.

Sometimes, Simone says.

How do you keep from despair? I ask.

I look into the faces of the ones I try to help, Simone says.

What do you see there? I ask.

A neighbour, Simone says. A sufferer who needs what I can give.

And how do you help? I ask.

I sit down beside them, Simone says. Listen. I might give them food, if they need it. I'll pray with them, if they want me to.

How do you cope? I ask. How do you go on knowing that there's such suffering?

By focusing on the suffering that lies in front of me, Simone says.

Simone, you actually give a fuck, Marcie says. It's stirring. I'm actually moved by what you say. I'm not some doctrinaire atheist, you know . . . I went to Catholic school, where we probably learned about the Good Samaritan, though I've forgotten all that now . . . Sometimes I want to do *wild kindly things*. But I only *want* to do them. I don't *actually* do them.

I can believe that there is such a thing as goodness, Marcie says. I can believe there are good people. I daresay you're a good person, Michael. You've made, like, an authentic chicken korma for us. And you, Simone—you work with the homeless, which is what we should all be doing. I can believe that goodness is better than anything, and that there are kind acts, *good* acts . . .

But goodness also means us sitting around our candle, eating and drinking together . . . , Michael says.

# 17

SATURDAY EVENING.

There's no *grandeur* to an All Saints party. It's never *about* anything. Never *for* anything. Nothing's supposed to happen. Just the usual drunkenness. The usual doping. More of the same.

It's barely even a party, for fuck's sake! An after-pub hangout, that's all. A back-to-mine do, nothing more. Nothing to see here, folks— just our old All Saints drinking games.

(Imagining a Victoria party. An old-style salon. Intellectuals sipping wine and discussing matters of the day. Exchanging bon mots. Wit. Probably listening to a string quartet.)

At least there's a new batch of MAs to entertain us.

Discussion. MA students are some of the few people of the world who actually look up to us.

Yes, but MA students are undergraduates with bells on . . . Just movers-through . . . Gone in a year.

MA students are creatures of the surface, splashing about in the shallows. They haven't done deep dives. They don't know how to hold their breath. They haven't sounded their PhD whale songs, all mournful and vast. They haven't plunged down into the deepest darkness.

MA students are still being taught. They still go to classes. They're still writing essays for their tutors. They haven't gone where no one's gone before. They haven't had to *reinvent philosophy all by themselves,* or whatever it is we're doing.

MA students are sweet in a way, true. Trainer-bra existentialists, starting uni all over again. Cute little life rebooters, who've freed themselves from the world *out there.*

I was never like that even as an MA, I say. I was never that *gauche.*

Sure you were, Ismail says. Pretty little Johnny Obadeyi, just moved back to the big city . . . All hopeful . . . taking your first puffs of salvia . . .

Valentine, thoughtful: They are *scrummy,* though, aren't they . . .

Fuck, yeah, Marcie says. Look at that one . . . Look at her tats . . .

Jesus, don't fall for her, Marcie, Valentine says. It's basically *paedophilia* . . .

She could be my fucking *muse*, Marcie says.

You'll be disappointed, Valentine says. You're always disappointed.


Climbing out to the roof (without Marcie.)

Helicopter noise. Helicopter searchbeam.

There are people being murdered all around us, we agree. High-speed car chases . . . Stabbings . . . Gang vendettas . . . Drug deals gone wrong . . .

And there are screams, too—we can hear them. Screams like daggers. Screams that *cut*. Screams that shred. Screams that tear the air apart.

And shouts. Shouts mixed in with it all. Shouts of triumph? Of joy? But how could there be shouts of triumph and joy? Who could be enjoying themselves out there? What pills have they taken?

Something *extreme* needs to go down, we agree. Something as great as the stupidity of the world.

It's going to happen! It's *got* to happen! They should bring on the flaming skies. Snap the night up like a scroll . . .

But it's coming too slowly, we agree. It's like they've dropped the bomb but it hasn't yet hit.

At least we're safe from the maniacs up here, Gita says.

Maniacs can climb, you know, Valentine says.

Maniacs can't be bothered to climb, I say.

Looking up at the sky.

Your old friend the moon, Johnny, Valentine says. Totally full.

Why is it called *the* moon? I say. I mean, it's just *a* moon, right? Earth's moon. There are loads of other moons.

It means it's the Man of moons, Valentine says. The boss moon. Just like the Rock's called *the* Rock.

*Da* Rock, I say. *Da* Moon. *Da* Man.

Why aren't there moon missions anymore? Valentine asks.

Because there's nothing up there for us, I say. It's fucking *dead*. Smoking.

Fuck the sky, Valentine says. Fuck it all. It's a giant satellite lane. They've basically stolen the sky, haven't they?

Agreement: The sky's been privatised. The sky's been financialised. It's a whole new asset class. The night itself has been assigned a value. The aerial commons is no more . . . It's being sliced up with heli-blades and drone-rotors . . .

*FUCK YOU, SKY!* Valentine shouts.

*FUCK YOU, SKY DRONES!* I shout.

*FUCK YOU, GENERAL SURVEILLANCE!* Ismail shouts.

We need UFOs, we agree—alien breakthrough. A show of alien strength. We need the equivalent of the *Phoenix Lights*. Some inter-dimensional spaceships appearing and disappearing.

We need to be abducted, Valentine says. We need to be fucked by aliens.

Speak for yourself, Gita says.

Marcie, climbing out through the window. Move up, fuckers.

Don't spoil the mood, Ismail says. We're very chill.

Guys—I've just been hanging with . . . *Ultimate Destruction Girl*, Marcie says. That's what I'm calling her.

Fuck *off*, Valentine says.

That's a really stupid nickname, I say.

I was thinking of Nihilation Girl, too, Marcie says. But it didn't have the—

Pretension? Valentine says.

You should have heard us talking, Marcie says. The heat death of the universe. The end of all things. Eschatology, in general. Biblical prophecy. The powers of the nightside. Chaos Gnosticism. The *Liber Azerate*. The Misanthropic Luciferian Order. The Spartakus revolt.

Wow! Valentine says. You're making *me* horny.

*Fuck*, she's cool, Marcie says. Makes Simone look like Little Miss Carefree. Makes the Dane look *cheerful*. Makes Vortek as peaceful as Gandhi . . . She's destined for prison. Her poster's going to be Blu-Tacked on a thousand study-bedroom walls . . .

You should've heard her, Marcie says. She's, like, an apocalypse native. Her generation take it for granted that the world's going to end. Apocalypse can't come soon enough for them.

Fantasy, Gita says.

Apocalyptic youth, guys, Marcie says. A whole generation of anti-Thunbergs, perfectly posthumous. For them, the end has already come and gone. They already know the truth—the eschatological truth. They're already living beyond the end of time, which you have to admire.

And her fucking *cheekbones*, Marcie says. Don't overlook their role in it all. And her *tats. Age of Kali*, on her forearm. *Kalki baby*, on her upper arm.

When are you going to see her again? Ismail asks.

I don't know, Marcie says. She disappeared . . . She didn't want to stand around at some shitty student party. Probably got better things to do . . .

I'll bet you scared her off, Marcie, Gita says.

She scared *me* off, Marcie says.


## 18

THROUGH THE EES.

Following the metal fence, running along the stream. To keep us out? To keep the Ees in?

There's supposed to be a crashed airplane around here somewhere, Valentine says.

There is *not*, Gita says.

Well, a crashed *helicopter*, then, Valentine says. It's like the Bermuda Triangle.

It's actually a crashed drone, I say. Vortek brought it down with his slingshot. He doesn't like surveillance.

Ismail, whispering: The Ees lets in those who've got no other hope left. Everything we need is here. Our freedom, our happiness. It's all here . . .

Big Ees raindrops, bursting on our skin.

We're lost again, Valentine says. You don't know where you're going again . . .

The only way's forward, Ismail says.

Forwards following *you*, I say.

We should follow Business Studies Guy, Marcie says. He's got an instinct. Lead us home, Business Studies Guy.

Business Studies Guy's more at home in the Ees than we are, we agree.

He's more trusting, I say.

He's more innocent, Ismail says. The Ees likes innocence.

We could only learn from Business Studies Guy's humility, we agree. His *silence*. One day, he'll come out with something as lapidary as Heraclitus. A perfectly formed profundity. A single sentence, that sums everything up and couldn't be said any other way.

Out of the mouth of babes, eh? Out of the mouth of a Business Studies student . . .

A slump in the woods. Our path collapsed. Which way to go?

Calling from above. A figure, silhouetted against the sun, beckoning us upwards.

Vortek, leading us over the ridge.

Look at Vortek, Business Studies Guy! See the bliss on his face! That's what Vortek's happiness looks like. It's dreamy. It's deep.

Vortek breathes differently in the Ees. Vortek even *laughs* in the

Ees. The Ees awakens the great Vortek soul. Sometimes he comes here just to lie in the meadow. It reminds Vortek of a Polish forest glade. Vortek's a man of the woods, at home in the woods.

The Ees is where Vortek will come when he's hiding from the police after his great act of terrorism. Vortek will become a wild man of the Ees, a legend, like Tarzan or something.

View of the deepwood.

That's where our tulpas live, Business Studies Guy. You probably haven't heard of them.

Business Studies Guy, shaking his head.

They're our doubles on the Ees. They're born on the Ees from leaves and twigs and moss and stuff as soon as we begin our PhDs. They wander the Ees trees and fields until we finish. Then—*pop!*—they disappear.

But we're not actually going to finish . . .

Are there Business Studies tulpas? I ask.

Of course not! Ismail says.

Victoria PhD student tulpas? Valentine asks.

Pah! Ismail says.

How about the lecturers: Do they have tulpas? I ask.

Come on—they can't even *see* the Ees, Ismail says. They walk their dogs round the lake, but don't realise it's here.

What do tulpas actually *do* all day? Valentine asks.

The opposite of what we do, Ismail says.

So, like, actually work? Valentine says. Actually write their dissertations?

Maybe they'd write ours, I say. That'd be something.

They, like, *un*work, Ismail says. They unravel whatever we write.

Probably not a bad idea, Marcie says.

Do the tulpas read things? I ask. How do they find out stuff?

They just work at forgetting everything we know, Ismail says. Returning it to oblivion.

Do they have tulpa laptops? Valentine asks. Tulpa supervisors? Weird.

Tulpas live in loss, Ismail says. They sleep in burrows all day, and wander the deepwood at night. Twilight's their time, and the hour before dawn. They're crepuscular, like cats . . .

So there's a tulpa Gita out there . . . , Gita says.

Sure, and she's, like, the opposite of you, Marcie says. Really open-minded and kinda mystical and not at all uptight.

And a tulpa Marcie who's, like, really kind and warm-hearted and not an über-bitch, Gita says.

Don't listen, den mom, Valentine says.

My great dyke heart accommodates all, Marcie says.

What do they live on? I ask. How do they survive out here?

The Ees is their mother, Ismail says. Do you think she'd let them starve?

The tulpas are probably watching now, Business Studies Guy. They're curious. You can hear them, if you listen. Shuffling about in the leaf-litter. You might be able to catch a glimpse of them, too— just out of sight. In your peripheral vision . . .

There are supposed to be *ghost tulpas*, too, Business Studies Guy. Trapped spirits. Ghosts of All Saints PhD students who never finished. Stuck in some kind of spiritual holding pattern . . . They'll only be released on the last day. The Day of Judgement. When God becomes the external examiner of all things.

# C H A P T E R    2

**1**

**EIGHT AM, MONDAY MORNING.** On the bus.

They're drawing us in. Flushing us out. They're making us *break cover*. Bringing us into the morning. They're exposing us to the full light, to full scrutiny.

Why bother with us? Don't they know what we can and cannot take? Don't they know what we can and can't *be*?

We came to uni to escape. Can't we be allowed to escape for a little longer? We came to uni so we could say *leave us alone* to the world. Why couldn't we be left alone for a little more time?

Don't they know that we're *dead* in the morning? That we essentially *lie slain* in the morning? Don't they know that we're not ready for human company in the morning—let alone the lecture theatre? Let alone *method class*?

Don't they know the risks they're taking? What they could do to us? Some of us have deep, deep mental illnesses! Some of us are actually *allergic to sunlight*!

Giving us no time to slowly wake up. No time to *adjust to the horror*. No slow walk to the café. No gentle macchiatos. No *civilised moaning*. No *general complaints*.

We should at least be given the chance to *voice our objections*. To air our grievances. We should at least be able to note that *this is not how it's supposed to be*.


All Saints.

Nine AM. Through the revolving doors into Alan Turing Building. Through the glass entrance lobby into the atrium.

Floors and floors of offices, all the way up to the highest floor (Philosophy's floor). To the skylight. To the false sky.

The vast central space. We should be grateful for this. Like St Peter's Square, with a coffee shop at the end.

But it's *enclosed* space. We're captives. We're sealed in! Shut up! This is our mausoleum. This calm, vast building. That says, *Trust me. Everything's going to be alright . . .*

As though there were nothing but the Alan Turing Building, and the atrium. As though everything were settled. As though everything were decided. As though there were nothing but the all-uni, the pan-uni. The technocratic uni. Totally sealed.

As though the end were not at hand. As though today were simply going to be succeeded by tomorrow. As though it were business as usual, and forever.

*Come, apocalypse!* we scream silently. *Come, destroyer of worlds!*


The lecture theatre, amphitheatre-style. Rows sloping down. As though something of *world-historical significance* were about to happen at the front.

So vast, the lecture theatre. Surprising that it hasn't got its own weather. Surprising that there aren't clouds forming up there. That there aren't *birds in flight.*

And no windows. No light getting in. They wanted a *total environment.* They wanted *total control* of the *total environment.* They wanted to control light. To control volume. To determine what should be seen and heard. To *set the parameters of the sensorium.* There should be no distractions. No gazing out . . .

Enter Professor Bollocks, mic'd up like some boybander. Professor Bollocks, all wired up, introducing himself calmly. *Can everyone hear?* Yes, we can hear; we can hear all too well! No arts of projection needed! No oratorial skills! No *lifting of the voice!*

The *auditory environment,* designed to *distribute sound evenly,* through a thousand invisible loudspeakers . . . The *Smart Auditorium*™, allowing the calmness and evenness of the voice to reach us all . . .

Professor Bollocks, clearing his throat. Professor Bollocks, doing some *housekeeping.* Telling us where the fire exits and assembly points are. Professor Bollocks, fiddling with the PowerPoint.

Let the PowerPoint not work, at least. Let Professor Bollocks not be able to log in, at least . . .

The lecture begins. It couldn't but begin. It was inevitable that it begin . . .

Title, spinning towards us (PowerPoint special effects): *Taking Control of Your PhDs. Oh God, oh God . .*

Professor Bollocks's voice, insistent. Professor Bollocks's dry and drowsy voice. Cover your ears! Shield your eyes!

You cannot not hear in the Alan Turing lecture theatre.

## 2

RUIN BAR, AFTER METHOD CLASS.

Slumped. Day drinking. Picklebacks all round, except for Simone with her spritzer.

Things are bad, we agree. Was method class actually worse than we thought?

It was what I thought it'd be, which is the horror, Marcie says.

What did you make of it, Simone? Ismail says.

Simone, shrugging. Awful.

You seemed busy, I say. Taking notes or something. And then you went to sleep.

I was *thinking*, Simone says.

Prove it, Valentine says. Show us you weren't just being some super-swot.

Simone's notebook.

On the cover: *Contradictions*.

Let me guess ... Something to do with God, Marcie says.

Everything in blue is from Weil herself, Simone says. Everything in red is my comments.

Inside, in blue: *It is impossible for God to be present in creation except in the form of absence*. In red: *The withdrawal of God. The nihil as the space of creation. As the real presence of the absent God.*

I like it, Ismail says. Very terse.

Some problems you can't think through—only contemplate, Simone says.

More blue: *The existence of evil here below, far from disproving the reality of God, is the very thing that reveals him in his truth.*

In red: *The absence of the good is the purest negative revelation of God.*

You don't really explain anything, do you? Valentine says. You're just adding contradiction to contradiction.

Reality's contradictory, Marcie says. I'm fat, yet I want to eat. Gita's supposedly gay, yet she's fucking her supervisor ...

You're supposed to *contemplate* the contradictions, not try and solve them, Simone says.

Like Zen koans, right? Ismail says. What's the sound of one hand clapping, and all that.

What's the sound of Marcie *wanking*? I say.

It's dialectics, Simone says. It's about opposites that correlate— that are brought together in their separation. God is love, pure love, spanning the distance, letting it *be* distance. But God also allows us to hold those contraries together.

So maybe Marcie's wanking corresponds with something really true and pure in heaven? Valentine asks. Amazing.

It's like, God's dead in this world, therefore God's alive in heaven, Marcie says. Wow, I can do dialectics. This world sucks, therefore this world's great. God's not in the toilet, therefore God's in the toilet.

Luther had a *great* vision of God while on the toilet, Valentine says. Luther had terrible constipation. There he was on the pot, and it was all revealed to him: the priority of scripture over tradition, of faith over works, grace over merit. The birth of the Reformation! Courtesy of the Holy Spirit himself, supposedly.

You have to go low to go high—clearly, Marcie says.

Which is why you're studying at All Saints, Simone: to be amongst the lowest of the low, Valentine says. It's a contradiction thing. You're hoping that the highest of the high might descend to save you . . .


# 3

## THE EES.

Escorting Business Studies Guy to the shroom fields.

You might not think of this as working, Business Studies Guy, but it is. It's research. It's mind-expansion.

There are shrooms here that don't grow anywhere else, Ismail explains. Something about the special terroir and the general dampness. The Ees is particularly conducive to shroom growth.

They look as toxic as everything else, Gita says.

The shroom grows *through* the poison, Valentine says. The shroom takes the toxins into itself and converts them . . .

These are the shrooms of life, Ismail says.

Each shroom has a mystical name, Valentine says. Starbright. Delacroix. Harbourmaster. Penitence. Shagribanda. Enter-Eller.

Shrooms make me spew, Gita says.

That's the sickness coming out, I say. The shrooms *purge* you of sickness.

The cure for every disease on Earth is here, if you know where to look, Valentine says.

How would you even begin to know where to look? Gita says.

Just ask him, Ismail says, pointing.

The Wizard, asleep among the shrooms.

He always turns up when you need him, I say.

He's turned up *dead* this time, Gita says.

He's still breathing, I say.

Prodding the Wizard.

No response.

He's probably visiting another dimension, Marcie says.

What's his story, anyway? Gita asks.

He began a PhD in the '80s, and got lost along the way.

He didn't get *lost*, Ismail says. *He found the Ees.* Which is altogether different.

They should give him an honorary PhD in psychedelic studies, Marcie says.

So he lives by drug dealing? Gita says.

He doesn't deal drugs, I say. The *world's* the drug. The Wizard deals in *antidotes*.

The Wizard, opening his eyes.

Hey, Wiz, Ismail says. Welcome back.

The Wizard, gazing at us, silently.

It takes a while to readjust to the lower plane, Marcie says. Explaining our plight.

We need to lose our way, Wiz! We need a brain holiday! We need a *blow to the dome*!

We want to leave consensual reality, Wiz! We want to see Ees UFOs! We want to wander the world in God-mode. With no clips. With all the power-ups. We want to open the Ees stargate! We want astral projection!

We want to scream into the night, Wiz. This is the day we want to—*snap*.

The Wizard, nodding comprehendingly . . .

Waiting for the shrooms to hit.

Why isn't it still the '80s? They just left you to get on with it back then. You met up with your supervisor in the pub every now and again. Your work might be read through, might be commented upon . . .

There wasn't training, in the '80s. There was no method class, back then. There were no *Annual Progress Reviews*. No completion rate targets. No progress assessment. No agreed workplan. No *professional development*.

You didn't have to finish on time, in the '80s. You could take ten years, if you wanted to. You could simply *roam the face of the Earth*. Like being unemployed, but with a little bit of direction . . .

## 4

**TUESDAY.**

Al's café.

The humanities PhD student needs a café, Business Studies Guy. The humanities PhD student need to get out of the house, to escape the study-bedroom. Life's not just you and a laptop—that's what the humanities PhD student should remember. You need a reminder of *wider life*. A sense that you're not alone.

So here we are, Business Studies Guy. Humanities PhD students one and all. Al's only customers, as always. The place all to ourselves, before the lunchtime rush (there never is a lunchtime rush).

The humanities PhD student likes to moan about the futility of study, Business Studies Guy. About the pointlessness of life. There's a whole art of lamentation, which only the humanities PhD student has mastered. The humanities PhD student is a *virtuoso* of the complaint.

Ringing changes on our misery is what saves us from misery, Business Studies Guy! It's good to be good at *something*, even if it's complaining that we're good for *nothing* . . .


## 5

**LATER.** Walking Chorlton.

Imagine being Victoria PhD students—*real* PhD students, Business Studies Guy! Where it's not a struggle just to be able to write. Just to get vaguely grammatical words down on a page.

Imagine being able to write proper prose, not a bunch of half sentences and jumbled notes, Business Studies Guy!

Imagine sitting at our laptops and *writing*, Business Studies Guy. Tapping away, without porn breaks every half hour. Without masturbation breaks. Without tea-and-biscuit breaks. Without staring-into-air breaks. Without going-for-a-wander breaks . . .

And writing—*actually* writing, Business Studies Guy! Writing, tumbling over itself, out of itself. Writing that knows only its own momentum, its urgency, its desire to go somewhere.

The happiness of writing, Business Studies Guy. Of writing discovering itself, following after itself. Writing for writing, because of writing. Writing, drawn back into its own birth—its own origin. That springs forth from its spring.

And reading—*actually* reading, Business Studies Guy! Reading the books that will keep us steady. Book-ballasts that hold us down. That stop us from becoming flibberty-gibbets. Whole oeuvres, like ships' anchors.

Oh, those hundreds of pages! Business Studies Guy. Oh, those heavy, heavy books! Months of work. Months to even *approach* them, armed with the right secondary texts . . . With the appropriate introductions . . . It's a trek! It's an expedition! You might never be seen again! They'll have to send out search parties!

You'll be hopelessly lost in the pages of the *Grundrisse*, Business Studies Guy. You'll have been last seen on chapter thirty-six of the *Logical Investigations*. There'll have been vultures sighted over you two thirds of the way through *The Science of Logic*.

## 6

**LATER.** Walking.

There are dangers in the afternoon, Business Studies Guy. There's such a thing as having *too much time*. It's like everything's opened too wide. Like the sky's too empty.

Don't stare into its depths, Business Studies Guy. Don't look directly at the abyss.

The humanities PhD student fears the afternoon, and is right to. You've heard of night terrors, Business Studies Guy? Well, these are *afternoon* terrors.

We're not made to live in this kind of openness. We're not made to float free . . .

It's as though we'd each become as vast as the universe, Business Studies Guy. Vaster . . . as if our atoms were scattered everywhere.

There's too much time: Haven't we always said that? Our days are open—infinitely so. They reach. They implore. They *ask*. It's like they're looking for something . . .

Dead days, when nothing's to be done . . . Vague afternoons, where nothing's to be written . . . Shells of days. Failure days. Cancelled days, with nothing sown, nothing reaped . . .

Time, sunk to its knees. Time, slumped. Time, forlorn.

Time you cannot reach. Cannot inhabit. Amnesiac time, that forgets itself—forgets *you*.

Blurred time. Blows-to-the-head time . . . Comedowns, crashes, awful slumps . . .

Time's question: that's what we know, Business Studies Guy. Time's search for eternity. Time's waiting. Until what? Until the end of time . . .


# 7

### EVENING.

Ruin Bar.

Another day done, Business Studies Guy. Another day gone. Hopes thwarted, hopes dashed, yet again.

Picklebacks, at last, Business Studies Guy. To soothe our troubled brains. To rouse us from our deathbeds. We'll ride the pickleback waves and forget our troubles . . .

We need to be helped to cross the threshold, Business Studies Guy. We need something to lift us from our melancholy. From the ruin of our efforts.

We've grown old with the day. We had dreams, ambitions in the morning. We were idealists in the morning. We'd *forgotten our stupidity* in the morning. But now?

We need to know that there's life after our botched and ruined day, Business Studies Guy. That we won't plunge down on the day's *Titanic* . . .

We need consolation for what we did not do. For thoughts we did not think. For passages unwritten.

We're tired of our brains (our so-called brains). Tired of thought, and the effort to think (our so-called thinking). Tired of ourselves, of our *solo efforts* (our so-called efforts). Misery wants company. We need to be with others who *understand our situation*. Who have known the same agonies, the same disappointments . . .

What solitude we've known! What loneliness! Just us and our so-called work, all day (all afternoon)! Just us, alone with our laptops! We need the hubbub of Ruin Bar around us, Business Studies Guy. We need conviviality! Human company!

So let's drink! Let's fill ourselves with beer! Let's slam down a pickleback at the bar before we even sit down!

This is our milieu: the bar, early evening, Business Studies Guy. Before we get incoherent. This is where we're at our best, the alcohol beginning to enliven us, to *warm up our blood*. When we're finding our second wind. When we're lifted from exhaustion—by what miracle? When despair can bloom . . .

You'll hear exhilarated talk, Business Studies Guy. You'll hear arrant fantasy. You'll hear drunken clarity—sense in nonsense, chaos in disorder. Drunken logic: there'll be a lot of that. Drunken *thought*. Great ideas that reveal themselves in drunkenness, and are forgotten straightaway.

*What did we speak about?* we'll wonder afterwards. *What did we say?* But it's not for us to remember.

# 8

## THE BUS STOP.

A homeless guy, asking us for money.

Searching our pockets. A few coins . . .

The homeless guy, moving on.

He's going to get fucking out of it, Marcie says. Good luck to him. I wish *I* was fucking out of it.

Does Manchester wreck people, or do people come to Manchester because they're wrecked? Valentine asks.

They come here to keep their appointment with wretchedness, Marcie says. To be wrecked. It's a destiny for some people.

He probably came straight out of some children's home, I say. He was probably abused or something . . .

Maybe he's a veteran, Ismail says. Maybe he broke up with someone. Lost his house . . .

He lives in Hell, I say. These streets are his Hell, and he takes stuff to forget that he's in Hell.

Simone would have seen the suffering Jesus in him, wouldn't she? Ismail asks.

Definitely, Gita says. *Tediously.*

She'd see a *neighbour*, Ismail says.

Do you think he expected the good, once upon a time? I ask.

Who—that guy? Gita asks.

He was a child, wasn't he? I ask. He was the same as anyone else. He deserved to live a happy life.

There are some people you can't help, Gita says.

There's something wrong with the world, I say. With the whole universe . . .

Because one poor guy's a drug addict? Gita says. Look, it's tragic— of course it is. But it isn't our fault. It isn't *anyone's* fault.

Shouldn't it be our fault? I say. Shouldn't we take it on as *our responsibility*? If we can't stop the horrors happening right in front of us—

. . . Then what? Gita asks.

. . . Then we're part of the horror, I say. We're *morally mediocre*, on top of everything else.

You want to play Good Samaritan? Gita asks. These people are addicted. They're mentally ill. They need, like, specialist help. Trained social workers. Stints in rehab . . .

Remember that homeless guy who was supposed to have helped people after the Victoria Station massacre? Marcie says. They crowd-funded him some flat. As if he could just move in and begin normal life. As if he could suddenly become middle-class! And what did he do? Trash the place and wander off . . .

The refusal of condescension . . . , Marcie says. Of the middle-class model of charity. Sometimes, the only thing you do is refuse. Just say no to everything offered.

In order to do what? Gita asks.

To live in truth, Marcie says. To say you don't want a helping hand into the abyss. That you don't want a leg up into Hell.

You can actually invest in the outcomes of the poor: Have you heard about that? Valentine says. *Social impact investment*: it's a new model of charity. Gathering data about people leaving care homes or prison or refugee centres. Then betting on whether they'll improve their life chances. Whether they'll stay away from sex work and hard drugs and find a steady job.

There are probably people betting on *us*, I say.

Will we finish on time? (Laughter.) Will we finish at all? (Laughter.) Will we make it into academic jobs? (Laughter.) Academic careers? (More laughter.)


## 9

### THE BUS TO UNI.

Five miles of irrelevance, Marcie says. Five miles of fucking purgatory. This bus is carrying us more deeply into mediocrity.

Was there, like, a bus to greatness? Valentine asks. Did we miss it?

There's no *gradient* to our bus-journey, Marcie says. We don't go up, we don't go down. There are no hills. Just the infinite plain, that's all. Just more Manchester, endlessly sprawling . . .

The mancunian plain was the bottom of a seabed, back in the late Devonian, I say.

It's no different now, Marcie says. Manchester's submerged, basically. The weather's heavy. The air pressure's twice what it is anywhere else. It's why everyone's so melancholy. It's why there's no *urgency* to this bus. The driver's as depressed as the rest of us.

Why don't we cycle instead? I ask.

Because we haven't got bikes, Marcie says. And if we did, they'd be stolen.

How about getting an Uber? I ask.

Too expensive, Marcie says.

Why don't we just walk, then? I ask.

Because it would take, like, forever, Marcie says.

I think you actually *like* being on the bus, Valentine says. You *like* moaning.

It's the *passivity* I can't stand, Marcie says. Look at us all, sitting in rows. Facing the same direction . . .

How are we supposed to sit? I ask.

*Pass*engers—the clue's in the name, Marcie says. We can't do anything. We don't move—we *are* moved. A bus is a mobile prison, basically . . . Rolling through the open prison of the world.

Traffic-jam Gnosticism, Valentine says. I've heard everything now.

I don't like being dependent, Marcie says. This is how they get us used to subjection. It's conditioning. It's a way of nudging us to *accept* everything. I'll bet it's a New World Order strategy, straight from Davos . . . The Man's deliberately trying to keep us down. To stop us dreaming . . . It's a psy-op. It's behavioural psychology. It's deliberate fucking *diminution* . .

What would Simone do on this bus? we wonder.

View it as a spiritual task or something, I'll bet, Marcie says. As some opportunity to live in contradiction.

She'd sit patiently, Ismail says. Obediently. Just waiting.

Waiting for what? I ask.

Waiting, in French, is *l'attente*, and *l'attente* means paying attention to, listening to, being present at . . . , Ismail says.

Looking at what? Paying attention to what? Being present at what? Marcie asks. The beauty of the mancunian suburbs? Endless rows of '50s semis?

Sure, Ismail says. Just ordinary things. The ordinary world . . . You can look at it all in perfect detachment.

In perfect *passivity*, Marcie says. In perfect obedience. That this is how it has to be. Just saying *yes, sir*, to the whole of existence. Just accepting the law of finitude. That everything we do is, like, *eroded and nullified in advance.*

Ismail, pointing his camera through the window. Filming.

Maybe the secret of life's out there, and we'll miss it if we don't pay attention, Ismail says.

Crap, Marcie says.


## 10

### THE ATRIUM, LOOKING OUT FOR ULTIMATE DESTRUCTION GIRL.

Why do we never see her? Why isn't she wandering about, like all the other MA students?

She probably can't stand the uni, Marcie says. She probably hates it more than we do. And she's right to. I'll bet she's really *pure* in her hatred. There's so much to hate . . .

Discussion. We're institutionalised—face it. Institutions exist to suck up life. To mop up life, spontaneity, anarchy . . .

And unis are the worst, we agree. Unis suck education out of every other sphere of life. Suck the capacity to think out of anything else we could do. Turn learning into bullet points and aims and objectives and learning outcomes and then sell it back to us as a bunch of bullshit credentials.

And it's no good complaining that unis have declined. It's no use trying to *reform* them. In truth, unis do exactly what they're supposed to do. They're *supposed to* discourage students from learning—from critical thinking. From independent thought. They're *supposed to* prevent questioning. They're *supposed to* busy everyone with routine bureaucratic tasks. That's what they're designed for.

And we're *typical* products of uni life. We're totally implicated. We've entrusted ourselves to a system. We've outsourced our freedom—our personality. Our *creativity*.

The Man's tangled us up in academic knots, that's all. He's drained us of poison. He's kept us defanged. He's completely separated thought from life.

What if *Mark E. Smith* had been captured by the university—if he'd breezed through a degree, an MA, a PhD and gone into academia? Would The Fall ever have emerged like Yog-Sothoth from rockabilly garage surf, from prole art animosity, from biker speed delirium, from M.R. Jamesean channellings?

What if *Ian Curtis* had gone on to technical college? Would he have ever found his baritone? Would he have sung of the *ultra-farce*—of the *desperate things on his mind*? Would he ever have discovered his *James-Brown-in-Hell* dancing?

What if *Morrissey* had written a poetry collection or two and become some tenured creative writing lecturer? What if he gave up on the General Strike of his life? On his *education in reverse*? On his sense that England *owed him living*? Morrissey would never have *given birth to himself*—never conjured some personal mythology of '60s *Coronation Street* stars, failed glam acts, obscure northern comedians and forgotten kitchen sink dramas.

What about *Happy Mondays*? What if, by some miracle, Bez hadn't gone off the rails and Shaun hadn't been dyslexic and they'd made it through school and college? What if they'd studied at rock school? At pop uni or whatever? What if they'd learnt to play their instruments? The Mondays were predicated on *not* being able to play properly. In *not* knowing what they were doing.

## 11

### ALL SAINTS LIBRARY.

Through the stacks.

Hector, our enemy! Hector, the turncoat! Hector, who was once one of us! The badminton messiah! Professor Bollocks's pet Disaster Studies student!

What's Hector doing here? What's with his *library turn*? Does he think it's a matter of working nine to five every day, at his laptop? Does he think completing a dissertation is all about hard graft and good attitude?

Hector seems to think he's a Victoria PhD student. That he's writing a work of analytic philosophy. That he can simply sit down and write his dissertation from start to finish.

Doesn't he understand that a PhD dissertation isn't something to be forced? That there are *spiritual risks* to doing a PhD? That there's a psychological price to the *passion of studious solitude*?

Doesn't he see that heaven loves postgraduates more than anyone? That we are creatures born in yearning? Vessels of infinite desire? That every part of our existence is prayer? That we strain, continually, against the universe of death? That we yearn for more, much more, than this world?

Doesn't he know postgraduates—All Saints PhD students—have faith only in the impossible: that we could actually complete; that we could actually bring our projects to term?

Doesn't he know that we cannot finish our dissertations by ourselves? That we need higher help. *Divine* help. From another order. From heaven up there. From the ranks of the choirs of angels . . .

Business Studies Guy, with a pile of books.

We see the excitement in you, Business Studies Guy. We remember what it was like, beginning our studies. Dying to the world—to your former life. Burning everything away—everything inessential.

The humanities postgraduate is *driven* to postgraduate life, Business Studies Guy. The humanities postgraduate must know themselves damned or they're nothing at all. The humanities postgraduate must have already reached the end of the world.

All the others are fooled but you!: that's what the humanities postgraduate knows. All live in falsehood but you! All others are compromised but you!

Vehemence! Keenness! The edge of a knife, whetted in starlight! What ardency you'll know! What solitary passion! The mystics have nothing to teach you. The stars themselves burn less brightly.


## 12

**WITH SIMONE AT THE CINEMA.**

Ruin Bar, after seeing Malick's *Tree of Life*—the extended cut (now with extra whirlwind).

It's a remake of the Book of Job, right? Ismail says. Jack O'Brien, the protagonist: J.O.B. See? See?

Woo, Gita says. So clever.

Except this Job lives in twenty-first-century USA, Ismail says. Except this Job's some architect who's lost in life, who doesn't know who he is or what he wants, and who lights a candle to remember the suicide of his brother half a lifetime ago.

Uh . . . Who's Job, anyway? I ask. I've forgotten everything about Job.

The faithful servant of God who loses everything in the Bible, Marcie says. His wife dies, his children perish, his house burns down and he sits there on a pile of ashes, scratching his sores with bits of broken crockery, wondering how God could do this to him.

It's a fair question, Valentine says.

It's the eternal question, isn't it? Marcie says. *Why me? What did I do wrong?* We always want to know *why*, even if there is no why . . .

That's because there aren't whys for that kind of thing, Gita says. Things just *happen*.

Job thought there was a why, Ismail says. He thought there had to be a reason for his suffering. And it's the same with the mother in *Tree of Life*, when she asks, *Where were you? Who are we to you? Why did you take my soul, my son?*

But they're God-believers, aren't they: Job and the mother? Gita says. They expect everything to be meaningful—to have some place in God's plan. But if you don't believe . . .

If you don't, all you can do is cry up to the sky, like a tragic hero, Valentine says. *Why, why, fucking why?*

That's a question that the Christian must ask, too, Simone says.

All the while knowing the answer, Gita says.

Faith isn't about certainty, Simone says. It's not about answers. It doesn't mean you know anything.

Job still has faith, right? Gita says. The Lord giveth and the Lord taketh away: that's what he says. He thinks the Lord, capital L, is real.

Job has faith that his question can be answered, Simone says. But nothing is certain for him. All he knows is that nothing in the world can be an absolute. Nothing by itself has any purpose; every good in the world is a false good. But it's only once you lose everything that you can reach out towards a good *beyond* this world.

Sure, if you're religious—if you believe in God, Gita says. The rest of us actually *like* it here.

Speak for yourself, posh girl, Marcie says.

Job has faith, which means he can't ask, *Why?* Valentine says. Not truly. Not from the depths of abandonment.

And what about Jesus on the Cross? Ismail says. Didn't he ask *why*? *Father, father, why have you abandoned me?*

Job and Jesus had faith in faith—let's call it that, Valentine says. They believed there was something to believe in, even if belief isn't easy. As for the rest of us . . . We're vulnerable animals. Miserable animals who thrash about in suffering. Who are born in pain, grow up, struggle, fall ill, suffer, cause suffering, cry out and die . . . Knowing that some other poor sap will be born to start the whole useless comedy over . . .

The funny thing is that God doesn't even *answer* Jack O'Brien's question, I say. One minute it's all crying and lamentations, the mother asking where God was when her son died, and next there's the creation sequence. We get the origin of stars and planets and the whole course of evolution . . .

And dinosaurs, Gita says. Ropey CGI dinosaurs.

The dinosaurs are there to show the birth of compassion, Ismail says. The predator spares the prey. The predator looks down and sees something to pity. Some . . . *creature* like him. Who expects the good, like him. Who wants to live, like him. Who cries, *Why?* too, in his own way. So the predator releases him and pads off down the river . . .

Wow, dinosaur mercy, Gita says.

And there's the suffering dinosaur on the beach, swaying in pain, Ismail says. He's asking, *Why?* too. He's sending up his dinosaur cry to the sky . . .

Come on, it's obvious—all that creation stuff and stars and planets are supposed to be an answer to Jack O'Brien, Valentine says. Because there's supposed to be some *great benevolent order*, right? That's the answer to Job's question: Things happen as they do because God made the world as it is. And God's fabbo, therefore the world's fabbo.

So why didn't God make a better world? Gita asks. I thought he was supposed to be all-powerful . . .

God made a *finite* world, Simone says. A world of order and limits, of . . . fittingness and proportion—

God made a fucked-up world, Valentine says.

—And I know sometimes it can seem cold and cruel and unforgiving, Simone says. I know it can seem arbitrary and full of chance. That it can seem to stand against us, to refuse our wishes and our will. But it's an orderly cosmos, not a chaos of forces. And even if order leads to suffering, that suffering is grounded in order—God's order.

Is that supposed to console us? Gita says.

See, I don't believe in order, Marcie says. I believe in hybrids—in miscegenation. The universe is drunk and disorderly at the best of times. Everything good is mixed up and queer. That's what lumpenness means.

So the actual *universe* is lumpen? I say.

The universe is random, basically, Marcie says. Unruly. Order comes out of chaos and returns to it. There's not some great tree of everything with us at the highest tip.

Ismail, looking upwards. I think I understand: The answer to Job, to Jack O'Brien in the film, is the order of the cosmos itself, he says. The question, *Why?* dissolves into what is. The only choice we have is whether to consent or not to consent. The only question is whether we can affirm everything as it is.

What about the heaven sequence? I ask.

Oh God—it's just fantasy, Gita says. All those people wandering around on the beach, forgiving each other in some giant group hug. It's worse than the dinosaurs . . .

No—it's a *vision*, Ismail says. It's eschatological. Jack O'Brien sees his mother consent to her son's death. *I give him to you. I give you my son*: that's what she says. She's seen the glory, the divine order. So she can forgive God . . .

It was beautiful—very beautiful, I say. Like the most wonderful fairy tale. If only it were true. I wish everything you believe could be true, Simone. I wish there was an answer.

I . . . I want to believe, I say. I want there to be a meaning to pain. I want to love the . . . *natural order* just as I love Malick's film. I want there to *be* an order. I want to believe there's a reason why we suffer and die. I wish I could consent to everything—fall to my knees and thank God for the *gift of existence*.

But I don't consent, and never could, I say. And if God existed, I could never forgive him. I don't believe that order and beauty are anything but lies. In fact, I don't believe in order and beauty. And I don't believe that joy soars over pain in some *perpetual Easter*.

I've known things—terrible things, I say. I've seen real evil . . . People talk about the banality of evil. The evil of pen-pushers, following orders, being good Nazis or whatever. But this wasn't banal . . .

People say that evil is merely the absence of good, I say. But I know better than that—I know goodness is only the effort to keep evil at bay.

The *horrors and the terrors*: I've seen them, I say. I've known them. And I see them now. I see a darkness. I see a fucking darkness, swallowing up the world. Putting out the stars. Eating up the sky. Devouring me and devouring us all.

God, Johnny . . . , Gita says.

I see a darkness—that's all I see, I say. And sometimes I can forget it, and sometimes I can't. *I see a darkness.* Sometimes it feels too thick, and that it's choking me. And sometimes . . . It lets me breathe.

# 13

## THURSDAY.

Gita and I, Beech Road Vintage.

Sitting at Gita's counter. Nothing happens here, does it? I say.

Not really, Gita says.

You just sit around doomscrolling? I say.

Basically, Gita says. And listening to tunes . . .

I thought you were busy doing real stuff in your real shop, I say. That you were always mending clothes and doing the window display and generally being out in the world.

The real question is why *you're* always here, Gita says. Haven't *you* got anything better to do?

This is where I come when I've got nothing better to do, I say.

To skive off working, you mean, Gita says.

Who can work in the afternoon? I ask.

But you don't get up before *eleven*, Gita says. And then you go to Al's café with the gang. And then you take the long walk home . . .

Yeah, well, I say.

It leaves a pretty small window for *actual work*, Gita says.

You have a very narrow idea of work, I say. You have to factor in contemplation time . . . Wandering-around-vaguely time . . .

See, that's what I hate about doing a PhD, Gita says. All this unfocused time. All this openness . . . I always feel I'm in someone's dream. That this isn't real, and I'm not real.

I thought you said working here made you feel real, I say.

I *work*, in inverted commas, in a *shop*, in inverted commas, Gita says. I don't feel *real*, in inverted commas. It's like I'm playing a role. Like it's all fake—like I'm not in focus. Can you actually see me? Am I here? Am I real?

You're real and you're fabulous, I say.

It's like I died long ago, Gita says. No—it's like I never lived. It's like death again and again and again. Yet I never actually *die* . . . God, I sound like you guys.

That's the loneliness of the long-distance PhD student, I say.

Do science PhD students ever feel like this? Gita asks.

Science PhD students actually have to do stuff in labs, I say. They

put on their white coats and get busy with Bunsen burners or whatever. And they're part of these big research teams. They're not just
sitting in a room on their own with a bunch of *fundamental books* for
month after month . . .

It's like the surface of my life is far, far above me, Gita says. Like
I'm sinking—like I've always been sinking. How much farther do we
have to fall?

You'll finish in the end, I say. You'll complete.

That's what Russell always says, Gita says.

I never want to finish my PhD, I say. There shouldn't be any such
thing as completion for important stuff. You can't just close things
down, can you? You can't just *conclude*—sum up your findings or
whatever. Maybe incompleteness is its own thing—a whole way of
life. Like, a spiritual state.

I'm going to have to start writing again, Gita says. I'm going to have
to see through my PhD. Because it'll send me mad, if I don't finish.
And it'll send you mad if you do . . .


## 14

**SCREEN TESTS ON THE EES.** Trying out the camera.

Magic hour, Ismail says. It's not yet dusk, not yet evening. No actual sun, even though it's still quite bright. There's just light, diffused
evenly. You get these really soft hues.

It's like everything's in suspense, I say. Like someone's pressed
pause on the world.

It's a threshold—that's how we should think of it, Ismail says.

The threshold of what? Valentine asks. What's supposed to happen?

Nothing's *supposed* to happen, Ismail says. But anything *could* happen—that's the point.

What, *literally* anything? Valentine asks. The Second Coming? An
alien invasion? World revolution?

*Potential*—that's the magic hour, Ismail says. A potentiality that will never exhaust itself. Will never be realised. That remains as a perpetual promise.

A promise of what? I ask.

The inexhaustible, Ismail says.

The inexhaustible what? I ask.

It's . . . utopia, Ismail says. It's youth that remains forever youth. It's a shimmering. Like, flashes from another life. It's hope incarnate. Hope now—not hope about the future. It's about what's here—right here . . . That's what I've always wanted to film. And instead . . .

It sounds like you need a session with the Collective, Marcie says.

Oh, not the Collective! Ismail says. Please not the Collective!

Marcie: Comrade Ismail admires cinema at its highest and holiest, comrade Val.

Valentine: Don't we all, comrade Marcie! Sometimes we want to watch films that open around us like a great cathedral. That let the holy silence resound. That ask the great questions without answers. Sometimes we, too, want to dissolve into absolute beauty, God knows . . .

Marcie: But we know such feelings are not for our kind, comrade Val, and it's no good pretending otherwise. We're not high-art types. We're not *Old Europeans*. We're not star-child Yanks raised in the '60s. Isn't that right, comrade Val?

Valentine: If only we could take ourselves seriously, comrade Marcie! If only we were capable of Old European high-mindedness! But our deflationary tendencies get in the way. Our anti-pretension *reflexes* . . .

Marcie: We admit it, we're drawn to arthouse, comrade Ismail. Which is perhaps our tragedy. We even *love* arthouse—can you imagine that? We know its power over us: the *arthouse spell*. The *arthouse susceptibility*. We distrust it in ourselves, comrade Ismail. We don't want it! We can't accept it!

Valentine: We know we can't measure up. We know we don't have the concentration span . . . *Arthouse guilt*: we don't want to feel that. The *arthouse shortfall* . . . Which is why we want revenge on arthouse— of course we do! Revenge on your *magic hour* and all that goes with it!

Marcie: No—don't cry, comrade Ismail. The Collective are firm, but never unkind. Our cruelty is tenderness—the *greatest* tenderness! We simply want to remind you who you are. That arthouse isn't available to you—isn't part of your repertoire. That your high-art dreams are inevitably *grotesque*.

Valentine: You have to see yourself for what you are: an ape. A high-art pretender.

Marcie: But we're not telling you to hang up your camera, comrade Ismail. You have to push on, in inevitable self-parody. There's no other option. It's just that you have to *own* your self-parody. To understand *that you can do no better.*

## 15

**EVENING.** Russell's house. Russell's family house.

Guys, take your shoes off, Gita says. Seriously.

The house of a Bataille scholar, Valentine says. I couldn't miss it. The house of a *Chorlton academic*.

Looking round.

God, is this where you get to live as an academic? A bit crap, isn't it? A bit *modest*.

See, the bourgeois are fucked, too. The bourgeois aren't exactly loaded anymore. They're not exactly unassailable. It's not as simple as *us and them*.

Where have they gone for the weekend, anyway? Marcie asks.

The Lakes, I think, Gita says.

A family break, Valentine says. Lovely.

A cat, winding round our legs.

This is Georges, Gita says. With an *s*. Who I'm here to look after.

Named after Georges Bataille himself, right? Marcie says. How cute.

That's terrible—that's a terrible sign, Valentine says. Like they think Bataille is a joke *chez Russell*. Like you could name a *domestic animal* after the *excremental philosopher* . .

Inside. The open plan.

A chaise longue, in William Morris fabric. A facing sofa, covered in throws. A faux-marble fireplace.

This is where they relax. This is where they're off duty. Where they watch TV or whatever.

Examining their bookshelves. Graeber, Klein, Kingsnorth. Macfarlane's book on the underearth. George Monbiot. Eco stuff. They're right-thinking. They're concerned about global matters. They're people of conscience, not destroyers, like us. They're *good global citizens*. They don't want to let the world go down . . .

Marcie, lying on the chaise longue.

Valentine and I, on the sofa, feet on the coffee table.

Guys—take it easy on the furniture, Gita says. Don't just plonk yourself down.

Oh, come on, why did you invite us? Marcie asks. You want to see this place wrecked. You want to hear our *anti-bourgeois venom*. You want us to fuck things up. You want us to *unleash the hatred*. You've brought the *real* Batailleans into his home—the real wreckers of civilisation—to raid their drinks cabinet. Actually, I'll bet they don't even *have* a drinks cabinet . . . I'll bet lecturers can't afford drinks cabinets anymore . . .

Valentine, opening cupboard doors, looking for booze.

Marcie, stroking Georges-with-an-S.

There's half a bottle of wine in the fridge, Valentine says.

They said I was welcome to that, Gita says.

Very generous, Valentine says, swigging from the bottle. Very fucking Bataillean.

This house is cool, Ismail says, filming. Check out this pot stand. And really dope pots. And a food processor. And a *coffee bean grinder*. And a *salt pig*. And a mortar and pestle that don't match.

Not matching is the new matching, Valentine says.

And this dresser's authentically vintage, isn't it, Gita? Ismail says. It's authentically distressed. It looks like it's been in the family for fifty years . . .

I'll bet Russell's wife is the one with all the taste—what's her name?

Vera, Gita says.

*Vera*—she even has a cool retro name, Marcie says. You and Vera must have a lot in common.

Do you think Vera knows about you and Russell? Valentine asks. Do you think she turns a blind eye, French-style, so long as he's discreet?

Gita shrugs. Maybe.

She just thinks you're safely dykey, right? Marcie says. You have her fooled.

Jesus, Vera mustn't be able to compete, Valentine says. You've got the dyke thing going on and the posh thing and the subaltern thing. It's a triple whammy.

Marcie, examining the family photos. A smiling Bataillean, she says. His smiling Bataillean wife. The Bataillean kids. It's charming. Do you think he reads them *Story of the Eye* at bedtime?

Does this seem like the house of someone who believes in the disaster? Marcie asks. I'll tell you one thing: The senior lecturer of Disaster Studies doesn't live a disastrous life. The senior lecturer in Disaster Studies gets by *quite comfortably*.

Marcie, lying back on the sofa. Fucking domesticity, she says. Cosiness! Shoot me if I ever get settled! Houses are counterrevolutionary. Russell and family are counterrevolutionary. Even purring is counterrevolutionary, Georges-with-an-S. Did anyone ever tell you that?

## 16
### FRIDAY.

Al's café.

Contemplating at the alkies.

Don't you think they have a *grandeur* to them? Ismail says, filming. A lyricism?

It's early in the day, I say. They haven't got abusive yet.

They've got the right idea, Marcie says. They're on strike from life. Look at them.

Maybe we should go on strike, too, Ismail says. Maybe we should take a day off.

Our whole life is a day off, I say.

No, I mean a *proper* day off, Ismail says. When we wouldn't even *try* to work. Like a holiday or something. Like the Sabbath . . . See, that's our problem. We spend the day trying to work and failing to work when we could have just relaxed instead. It's the PhD student predicament.

We haven't got self-discipline, I say. I haven't, anyway.

Nor do I, Valentine says. God, I think I've reached *peak* procrastination. No one could be better than me at *putting work off*.

Look, at least we procrastinate about *work*, I say. At least it has some relation *to* what we're supposed to be doing . . .

So what? Valentine says.

It means we're pointed in the right direction, I say. It means we have some *orientation*.

It means we always fail, Valentine says. Over and over again.

Look—we shouldn't expect to be workhorses, Ismail says. We have the slave mentality, that's the problem. Seriously—we should take some time off. Like, *become worthy of our indolence*, rather than feel ashamed of it.

So what are we going to do? I ask.

*Nothing*, Ismail says. We're going to learn to do nothing.

I can't *imagine* doing nothing, I say.

And yet what do you actually do all afternoon? Ismail says.

Prevaricate, I say. Procrastinate.

Go out for pointless errands, Ismail says.

Watch porn, Marcie says.

*Nothing*, in other words—except you're ashamed of it . . . , Ismail says. Don't you think procrastination is a *sign* of something? Maybe we just haven't learnt what it's *for*. What our distraction *means* . . . Don't you see: We have to reevaluate doing nothing. *Affirm* it.


## 17

**BADMINTON PRACTICE.**

Working on Business Studies Guy's *fast-twitch muscle fitness*. Working to develop his *contractive strength*.

We need to develop his *lunge*. His *explosive jump*. We need to make sure nothing tears when he leaps . . .

Patter steps: Business Studies Guy, running on the spot, very quickly. Scissor steps: Business Studies Guy, bouncing on the balls of his feet, very light. Business Studies Guy, sprinting on the spot. Snapping his knees up as fast as possible . . .

My God, you're good! We have to wipe away tears. You remind us of Hector in his heyday! That precision . . . That *discipline* . . .

Badminton's a farcical sport—that's why we love it, Business Studies Guy. No one takes it seriously; no one follows it. Which is why we take it seriously. Which is why we follow it.

And you're our secret weapon, Business Studies Guy. You're how we're going to win the Manchester Postgraduate Badminton Cup . . .


## 18

### THROUGH VICTORIA UNI CAMPUS.

A proper campus. All redbrick muscle. All on a vast scale. A magnificent scale. All Solemn. All Serious.

Great crouched buildings, each as though closed around a secret. The secret of History. The secret of Politics. The secret of Medicine. The secret of Physics.

This is where you're taught Substantial stuff—*real* stuff. Not trendy bollocks. Not *Disaster Studies* . .

And the vast library, too great for you to contain in a gaze. Too vast to take in all at once. Knowledge incarnate. Redbrick Certainty. And it's open till midnight, and probably beyond.

And the Victorian Gothic centre, like the Houses of Parliament. All upthrust—all filigree. All reaching aspiration.

Old Manchester wanted to show it could do Civic Pride. That it could do Magnificence. The old industrial city wanted to show it was as good as anywhere else . . .

Victoria, for the pretty bright. Not Oxford- or Cambridge-bright, it's true, but significant minds nonetheless. Victoria, for those who know their way around the library. Who are on their way to decent jobs . . .

Victoria, where you come to study traditional subjects in a traditional way. Where intellectual life isn't magpie-ism—isn't Theory pick-'n'-mix.

This is where you belong, Gita. This is your kind of campus . . .

Marcie: Why did you transfer to All Saints? Were you tired of being an overachiever? Did you want to fail for a while? To *self-sabotage*? To disappoint your parents for the first time? Was it a *late-adolescent rebellion*? Did you want time off from being a swot? Was the time right for a *new university fly-by*?

Why are you so mean? Gita asks.

Valentine: You should find yourself a nice set of Victoria PhD students to hang out with. You wouldn't get this kind of shit from them. The Victoria PhD student neither takes the piss nor has the piss taken out of them.

But I actually *left* Victoria—I came to All Saints, Gita says. Doesn't that mean anything?

Marcie: Sure, you wanted to join the *Disaster Studies ragamuffins*. You wanted to hang with the *philosophically damned*. It's the equivalent of running off to join the circus . . . We can see the appeal. There's a bit of life to us, right? We're crabbed . . . Cruel . . . Twisted in upon ourselves. That's what makes us more interesting—as *cases*. It's what gives us inner lives . . . sick lives, true. But inner ones . . .

Oh God, you're just getting going, Gita says.

Valentine: But our charms will fade. We're going down. Sure, things are going our way, for the moment. We've got our scholarships. Conditions seem favourable. The wind's blowing in the right direction. It feels as if we're not actually *doomed*, although of course we *are* actually doomed. It feels as if we won't have to kill ourselves, although we inevitably will have to kill ourselves.

Marcie: We don't expect to live long lives. We're not expecting things to go well. But don't worry—you're not going to be swept down the plughole with us . . . You've got deep middle-class survival instincts. You'll bounce back. You'll find some job in publishing, or fundraising for some private school.

Valentine: And when someone asks about your PhD, you'll say, *It was something I always wanted to do. I'm glad I did it. I was a bit lonely. And the people were fun, but kind of a bit weird. A bit intense . . .*

Marcie: *They were all so tortured—they were all really sadistic or something*, you'll say. *They actually liked being mean to each other—*

*really mean. And they were always talking about philosophy in this really overinvested way . . .*

Have you finished yet? Gita asks. I'm not listening, you know.

Valentine: We're in steerage in history's *Titanic*. But you belong to the upper decks. Sure, the world's going to end for your kind, too. But it's going to do so in *comfort*.

Marcie: Anyway, there's one consolation: you'll never love these philosophical books as we do. You don't *need* philosophy in the same way.

Valentine: You don't come from the intellectual gutter, which means you'll never know the intellectual stars. You'll never look upwards in awe at the great works of European philosophy. You'll never see them through working-class eyes. You'll never know their distance; the full contradiction that is their separation from us.

Marcie: Which means they're just dead books to you. Dead books by dead authors, and none of it about anything.

Valentine: Which means you don't know *Desire*, either. You aren't Claimed—called by what you're not. You're not saturated by *infinite philosophical eros . . .*

Which means I'm entirely free of your weird mixture of self-abasement and grandiosity, Gita says. And I'm rather glad about that.

It's dialectics! Marcie says. It's contradiction! Totally Simone Weil.

Past the History of Art building. Past the School of English building.

We shouldn't even be *on* this campus, we All Saints types. We're bad examples. Look at us, brazenly crossing the grounds. Loud-talking. Hyena-laughing. Irreverent. Lacking the requisite *respect*.

There are probably Victoria postgraduates watching fearfully from the windows. They should come down to the pavement and join us. We could swallow them up in our roving festival. We'd could infect them with *St Vitus's dance . . .*

We should topple some statues, at least. Pull down some plinthed worthy, raised above us in the classical style. Storm the humanities building, piss in the marble foyer. Scratch the wood panelling with our keys. Smash the framed photos of some *bourgeois eminences . . .*

Why are they letting us through? They should at least try to get rid of us. Where are the security guards? They're probably tracking us on CCTV. There are probably cameras swivelling to follow us. But they're doing nothing. They're letting us walk through. They've essentially abandoned the campus to the barbarians.

Unless this is a deliberate ruse. Unless it's being opened deliberately, just as Russia exposed itself to Napoleon's armies after torching the fields. After evacuating the countryside. Half of Napoleon's troops starved to death . . . The other half died of obscure diseases . . .

Or is it that Victoria knows we're no threat. That we'll burn ourselves out. That our laughter will stick to our throats . . . That we're totally overawed by its bullshit Victoriana, despite our bravado. By gothic revival Manchester, rampant, rearing. And even by its vast '60s blocks—so civic. So responsible—as if Serious Things were going on here. As if Matters of Significance were being taught and researched . . .


## 19

VICTORIA UNIVERSITY LIBRARY.

Walking Business Studies Guy through the stacks.

*Books*, Business Studies Guy. Not *précis*. Not *intro guides*. Not *textbooks*. Not pseudoscience Business Studies papers. Books, *real* books, old and new.

Look at their bindings, Business Studies Guy. Their weight. They're real. They're substantial. They have history. Old date stamps. People have read them before you. Maybe people will read them *after* you. Actually, they probably won't. No one reads anymore . . .

You've got a lot to read, Business Studies Guy. You're going to need a whole anti-business deprogramming. A whole de-Business-Studies-ising bibliography.

Read, Business Studies Guy! Read the greats! Climb every mountain! One peak after another, Business Studies Guy! Break your head against Laruelle! Crack your skull on Bergson! You don't know you've read Simondon until you've actually *drawn blood*!

And you'll have to make a stab of learning languages, Business Studies Guy . . . Do better than we miserable monoglots . . .

The joys of reading, Business Studies Guy! The books we've opened (even though we haven't opened that many)! The pages we have read (even though we haven't read that many)!

To experience the unfolding of a masterwork for ourselves, Business Studies Guy. To be a face moving over its pages. To say, *Let there be reading*. To part the pages like Moses, the Red Sea. To let our gaze follow its lines like the children of Israel, the pillar of fire.

The sense of co-discovery! Co-exploration! That no introductory guide could give you, that no Idiot's Guide could convey. Of reading *with* the book! *Beyond* it! As though it *continued* in us, and we were its true sons, true daughters—its true nonbinary legatees. As though we could continue its writing, stream forwards with it, caught in its flow, propelled by its rhythms . . .

We've wanted to lower ourselves in obscure oeuvres, like archaeologists into a tomb. We've wanted to be fathoms-deep, among arcane writings. We've wanted to read thinkers half-lost, half-forgotten in the murk. Wanted to tour great thought-systems, consigned to oblivion.

We revisit scholarly disputes no one recalls. Affairs of dust. Abstruse debates, figures, names. We've wanted to scuba dive around the great wrecks of thought. Among great drowned beasts. Through arching thought-skeletons, picked clean by fishes.

We've tasted paradise, Business Studies Guy, and know everything else is bitter. If we seem to hate everything, it's only because we've loved so many things. If we appear to say *no* to so much, it's only because we've said *yes* so many times.


## 20

### BAR HYPOTENUSE, JUST OFF THE CAMPUS.

This is where Victoria PhD students drink.

I don't think they *do* drink, Valentine says.

They sip at something, Marcie says. A small glass of white wine. Half a weiss beer.

God, it's so clean, so clinical. Everything is so glistening. It's kind of *sterile*. It's all straight lines and cleanliness. Ruin Bar may be fake, but at least it has filthy corners . . .

And there's nowhere to *smoke*. They presume no one smokes. Not even on the steps outside . . .

And there's too much light! There's light everywhere. These big windows. It's like an airport terminal . . .

And the bar staff are, like, *fembots*. All vocal fry and *sangfroid*. Lacking all the northern social skills. They've never even *heard* of picklebacks.

And where is everyone? A few students tip-tapping their laptops . . . Victoria lecturers, talking funding bids over herb teas. We've brought the battle to the enemy. But where is the enemy?

A bar for *numbed androids*. A quick-drink-after-work place. It's a smoothie-post-squash place. A refresh-and-pass-through place. Not a journey-to-the-end-of-night boozer. Not a secret-of-the-universe-at-the-bottom-of-your-pint-glass joint . . .

Do you think anyone's ever had an idea here? Do you think anyone ever *thought* anything?

Victoria PhD students don't actually think, we agree. They just apply rules. They're content with pure formalism. Pure logic.

They're busy with calculation—with *quantified management*. With positivities and their manipulation. Professor Bollocks would *love* them.

There's never any *vagueness* for the Victoria PhD student. Never opacity. Never any lingering, pausing, hesitation. Never driftwork. Never *empty contemplation*.

They've never *failed* in their thinking, Victoria PhD students, that's the problem. They don't know themselves as failures. *Doubt*—entirely unfamiliar. *Madness, too.* They've never thought themselves as *channelled by demonic forces*. They've never suspected they have some kind of *brain disease*.

They've never struggled for words, unlike us, Victoria PhD students. They've never battled to string a sentence together. They've never been at a loss for language. Don't trust a PhD student who can *explain what they do*. Who isn't groping for words . . . Who isn't stuttering like Moses . . .

And Victoria PhD students know nothing of the *hatred of the world*, we agree. They know nothing of *all-disgust*. Their thoughts aren't full of destruction. They don't live in a universe they reject—that has no legitimacy in their eyes.

*A critique of all existence*: Victoria PhD students feel no need for that. They're not on the side of *antinomian lawlessness*. Of *anarchist outbreaks*. Of the *new aeon*, shattering in. They're entirely foreign to *ecstatic nihilism*. They don't want to *set fire to the cages of the world*.

Victoria PhD students don't need hyperbole—our *arts of exaggeration*. They never want to talk in *CAPITALS*. With exclamation marks! But that's the only way to talk! The only way we can reach what we have to say!

We're more stupid than they are—of course. We're more idiotic—by necessity. But it's a *massive* idiocy. It's a sky of idiocy, moving. It's a whole moving sky, alive with the highest, wildest thoughts.

## 21

THE EES, WITH SIMONE.

Grand steps, leading down to a pool. Like something left over from a country estate.

A perfect spot. Laying out our picnic. Opening Tupperware boxes. Plates and cutlery for everyone. Napkins. Plastic tumblers.

Can't believe Michael sent you out with leftovers, I say. It's a proper *meal*.

Last night's dinner, Ismail says. Curry's even better the day after.

Sipping bottles of beer.

You're happy there, Simone? I ask. You're happy at Michael's house?

Simone, taking off her glasses. Rubbing her eyes. I am.

Michael thinks Simone needs feeding up, Ismail says. He's always making sure she eats.

Michael's kind, Simone says.

I think there's an ulterior theological reason behind it, too, Ismail says. Michael thinks you're too much of an ascetic. He calls you a *zelotos* . . .

. . . And I call him a hedonist, Simone says.

Michael places great faith in the good things of life, Ismail says. Too much faith, you probably think, Simone.

I have no objection to the good things of life, Simone says.

Except you think they aren't *absolutely good*, Ismail says.

I place my faith elsewhere, Simone says.

I think this aloo gobi might be absolutely good, Marcie says.

People who talk of the absolutely good are just a fancy kind of nihilist, Valentine says. Nothing in the world's good enough for you. So you declare the world valueless: that's the intellectual move. And it's one step from that to Gnosticism . . . to the idea that there really is some absolute source of value, beyond the corrupt and disgusting here-below . . .

Guessing what each other would wish for, if we found the Room.

I'll do Gita, Marcie says. Russell's hand in marriage. The breakup of his family. Turfing Vera out . . . That, or being properly queer.

And I'll do Marcie, Gita says. Being *really* lumpen, not just pretend. Like, actually not giving a fuck about the morrow. And definitely not doing a *PhD* on the lumpen.

I'll do Johnny, Ismail says. Just hanging out like this in the sun forever, hoping that the day would never end.

That's actually true, I say. How did you know?

Valentine would wish for some *complex religiopolitical martyrdom*, Ismail says. Or for some crazed world-annihilation—for some hyper-death to shatter down from the sky . . .

You got me, art boy, Valentine says. And you, obviously, would make some spurious art-wish. To make the most pretentious film of all time or whatever.

What would Simone wish for? we wonder. More exalted suffering? More charity? More agape? More love of the neighbour?

I don't think it's a matter of wishing or wanting, Simone says.

You wouldn't, Valentine says.

Why do you have to make everything so serious? Marcie asks.

You asked me, Simone says.

We *did* ask you, Val says. Carry on, Simone.

Wanting things for yourself is the problem, Simone says.

Why shouldn't we want things for ourselves? Marcie asks. Why do we have to be selfless?

Because you want to be a saint, Valentine says. I understand that. I want to be a saint, too.

The saints are those who match their will with God's, Simone says. They're not perfect—they're human just like we are. But they show us what it means to live a Christian life—that it really is possible.

Saints live by their own lights—that's what I know, Valentine says. Saints look for a way of living while renouncing being someone,

91

Simone says. They give up positions of power and sovereignty. They no longer seek might and self-assertion. Decreation—that's their task.

*De*creation? Valentine says. I thought the act of creation was supposed to be *good. Let there be light* and all that . . .

Decreation means detaching ourselves from our will, Simone says. Wanting nothing for ourselves, nothing from power . . .

Jesus just gave himself up to power, didn't he? Ismail says. He didn't fight. He yielded to the tyrants.

Yes, but God was behind Jesus, backing him up, Gita says.

But Jesus never used the power he had, Simone says. During his arrest he said he could have summoned twelve legions of angels, had he wanted to.

So why didn't he? Gita asks.

Because he didn't want to compete with the powers of this world, Simone says. Which meant the powers were stripped of the one thing they have: the power to vanquish. The worst tyrant wins no triumph when the enemy voluntarily gives himself up.

Is that what decreation means: giving yourself up? Gita asks.

Decreation means loving the will of God, Simone says. Submitting our will to his so that it might be done in us.

But that's how you bring back power and sovereignty all over again, Gita says. Except it's now *God's* power and sovereignty . . .

God is neither powerful nor sovereign in this world, Simone says.

But God *made* the world, supposedly, Gita says.

Only by renouncing power, Simone says. Have you ever read the Kabbalists? Isaac Luria?

Heads shaking.

Once, only God existed, and he was everywhere and everything, Luria writes, Simone says. God was all in all. There was nothing but God.

But then God limited himself, Simone says. He opened non-

God in God, so that he wasn't all there was. And our world opened there where God was not. Our world, governed by necessity that God set in motion.

So why couldn't God make a better world? Gita asks.

Because this is a world of limits, Simone says. It had to be, if it was to be a world without God; if it was to be ordered.

So God abandoned us to the world . . . , I say.

God withdrew—which was the madness of God, Simone says.

Madness?! I say. Is God mad?

God madly limited his powers—who knows why? Simone says. He constrained himself. Tied his hands behind his back. God madly made a world that stood apart from him, in which he could not act.

But what he made was imperfect, I say. It wasn't worthy of his love.

Why pray to a God who can't do anything? Marcie asks.

Why pray to a mad God? I ask.

Because that's *our* madness, Simone says. That's the madness in which we answer God. We're mad to ask for the absurd, the impossible—but that's what we ask for. We're mad to think we can cross the distance between us and God—and yet that's what we desire . . .

## 22

### IN THE NIGHTCLUB QUEUE.

Marcie, inspecting Gita's lifetime Paradise membership card.

I didn't know you could even *get* a lifetime membership card, I say.

It's, like, *laminated*, Marcie says. It's built to last.

How much was it? Valentine asks.

I'm not saying, Gita says.

I'll bet it cost a couple of hundred quid, Marcie says. I'll bet only a handful of suckers fell for it.

Don't you think it's a bit excessive? Valentine asks.

You'll probably save money on it in the long term, Gita, I say. If you came here, like, fifty-seven times. Seriously—do you anticipate coming to Paradise when you're fifty-three? When you're sixty-five? Do you think it'll still be open in, like, 2063?

I think you're *investing* in being queer, Marcie says. Like you can just posh-girl your way into it. Like you can just buy the keys to the kingdom. Do you think you'll get a certificate or something if you put in your lesbian hours?

Was it, like, adopt-a-club? Marcie asks. I suppose it was worth it for a sense of *belonging*. For the sense that you'd finally discovered *your people*, now and forever. The only place you feel truly at home, etc.

Have you been able to discover the *real you*? Marcie asks. Something to let you say, *So that's who I was all along* . . . ? You want the queer truth, Gita—but there is no truth. You want the queer conversion that's going to make your life okay—but it's not going to be okay. *Nothing's* going to be okay . . .

Leave her alone, guys, Ismail says. I hate all this queerer-than-thou crap.

Marcie's jealous because you're so fucking cute, I say.

I'm saying you can't just *decide* to be queer, Marcie says. It can't be a *choice*. You have to *be* queer. Fuck it, I've never even seen you on the women-only dancefloor, Gita. You stay on the *mixed floor*. The *queers and their pals* floor.

Why are you fucking Business Studies Guy, if you're so queer, Marcie? I ask.

See that's the thing: *I* fuck *him*, Marcie says. And I do so *queerly*.

It's not like you're anyone's great favourite here, Marcie, Ismail says. You just hang out on the stairwell, setting people against each other.

Anyway, your lifetime Paradise membership card isn't getting us *in* any faster, is it? Marcie says. The bouncers aren't exactly beckoning us to the head of the queue.

## 23

**LATER.**

The night bus home.

Sitting on our seats downstairs. Sitting where we'll draw no trouble, downstairs. Sitting on the front seats, close to the driver, minding our own, eyes down, catching no one's wild eye . . .

Sitting downstairs, close to the front, so that trouble can go upstairs, to the back of the bus, away from us. Sitting downstairs, safe (we hope) from anywhere trouble might go.

We're peaceable people. We don't want trouble. Keep us from trouble. We've survived the night so far. Can't we get through this part of it, too?

Ah, but we're mortal! Vulnerable! Our flesh bruises. *Cuts!* Our flesh is ready for blows! . . . We're exposed on every front! Open to violence!

We're not made for public transport! We weren't formed to go out among the *mancunian public*!

We don't want to be watchful! Don't want to be vigilant! We're tired of all the fight-or-flight! We're weary of all that primitive stuff! We're not tough people—we're not bare-knuckle fighters! We're not skilled in the *mixed martial arts*!

The night bus, riding on. The night bus, descending through all the circles of Hell.

Only scavengers out there, in the darkness. Human hyenas, hunting in packs. Shoals of human piranhas, ready to strip you to a carcass.

Only the human Elements, slipping and sliding. Human Forces, materialised from the night. Only wraiths—the undead and addicted. Junkies, circling the death-drain.

Only strangers to sleep. Night-wanderers. Nightmares . . . Only midnight shufflers—scraps of the night loose in the night. Feral types. Ambushers. Only waiters-in-darkness. Nightcrawlers, with sharpened teeth, tooled up for trouble.

Why does the bus have to stop? Why is it obliged to pull up at bus stops? If only it could just cruise through the night. Ride right through . . .

Hell could burst in—does no one realise? Hell could be admitted through the bus doors. Hell could bust its way on without a ticket.

There could be stabbings—just like that, very sudden. Beatings . . . We could be caught up in some drug war. Gangs with beefs, with revenge in mind, charging through the bus. Tooled up—testosteroned up.

The bus driver's face in the mirror. The bus driver in his booth, behind plastic. Drive on, driver. Drive us fast, driver. Drive us through Hell and out the other side.

Drive *dark*, driver. Turn off the lights. Cloak the bus, so we attract no attention. So we can drive on unnoticed. Make this a *stealth* bus, driver. A black-ops bus . . .


## 24

### BEECH ROAD VINTAGE.

Valentine, flicking through a biography of Simone Weil.

Her parents called her *Simon* or *son number two*, apparently, Marcie says. She signed letters to her parents, *your respectful son*.

I always thought Simone Weil had a real *trans energy* about her, Ismail says.

She dressed like a man, kinda, I say, looking at the photos.

She was *aromantic*. It was to signal her aromanticism, Ismail says. To show she was out of the game.

Does our Simone desire anyone, do you think? I ask.

Sure she *desires*, Ismail says. But not people. Remember what Plato said about the ladder of eros. There's erotic love for bodies, and you transcend that. Then there's an eros for orderly structures—for laws, for maths, for systems—and you transcend that. Then there's an eros for the beautiful as such, as the visible manifestation of the Good, capital G. The principle of order, in other words.

So Simone's beyond bodies, I say. Simone's beyond maths. She's ascending all the way towards the True and the Real . . . It's Gnosticism again, right?

Plato came before the Gnostics, Ismail says.

Plato despised the world and looked beyond it—it's basically the same idea, Valentine says.

Just like you guys despise the world and look up to Simone, Gita says. Just like you think she's better than the world or whatever. Just like you want to think of her as untouched, unsullied, safe from harm . . .

Something has to be, I say. There's got to be something better than all the shit. Better than *us* . . . It's like everything has cancer. Like there's cancer in existence. It's like cancer *is* existence. And she . . . she's the cure . . .

There is no cure, Valentine says. There's only . . . intensification. The way through cancer is more cancer. We have to go *through* the cancer.

Good ol' self-loathing, Gita says. Where would you be without it?

It isn't really self-loathing, Marcie says. It's the loathing of everything, ourselves included. It's a loathing of the *conditions of existence.* Of the great joke of the world. Which is worse because the world doesn't even know it's a joke.

Simone wants to be a saint, Valentine says. She's making a last stand. Demanding meaning. Demanding the conditions of faith.

You can demand all you like, but it doesn't make it real, Gita says.

You can become pure demand—that's what matters, Valentine says. Pure intensity. Simone wants to be a saint. She wants to *shake the bars of this world.* She wants to say that this isn't enough. *Faith*: that's what she calls it. But it's really just an attempt to live the truth. To testify to the truth with her entire life.

What truth? Gita asks. That there really is God? That Jesus is real?

We live in a world of lies, and we are made liars, Valentine says. We live in the world of death, and we're made dead. We live in a world of meaninglessness, but for Simone, there's a *meaning* to meaninglessness. That's her dialectics.

God's dead, right? Gita says.

God's dead, God's absent, God does not exist, but for all that . . . , Valentine says.

It's negative faith, isn't it? I say. That's what Simone talks about. Negative theology, where you can say nothing positive about God. Not even that he exists.

How can you be religious and trans, anyway? Gita asks. Aren't you supposed to believe in a cosmic order, if you're Christian? Where, like, everything is in its right place?

She sees transition as a correction, Ismail says. To *restore* order. Just like you'd treat some . . . imbalance.

It's about refusing all the forms of power, of domination, I say. What she was saying the other day about decreation. About voiding the self. Being a witness for non-power. Emptying herself of every thought of her own . . .

So she thinks she can be free of power just like that, Gita says. By some kind of fiat.

She's freeing herself of power, I say. It's a process. That's why she only ever says she has faith in faith.

She's the trans messiah, Marcie says.

The trans messiah—sure, why not? I say. Living, like, in contradiction to the world. Against all earthly power . . . There's so much evil in the world, there must be something good. There's so much ugliness around us, there has to be something beautiful. There are so many lies, there must be truth. Even if you can only speak of it negatively. Even if you can only say what it's not.

So you're all in love with Simone, basically, Gita says.

She's living a . . . *personal apocalypse*, that's what I admire, Valentine says. She's sacrificing herself in the name of a trans new heaven and Earth. A queer New Jerusalem . . .

Yeah, really beautiful, Gita says. But why would you transition into a nun?

Because that's how she wants to be seen, Ismail says. How she wants to be *desired* . . .

But she doesn't want to be desired, that's the point! Gita says. She's asexual! She wears nun-shoes!

It's about how she wants to be desired by God, Ismail says. How she wants to realise God's will.

Saint Simone, beloved of God, desired by God, Marcie says. Saint Simone, dreaming of God's cock. Of being given head by the fucking godhead . . .


## 25
### SUNDAY.

The Ees.

A clearing.

A long-sunken basin. Water, ankle deep. Stranded columns . . . What was this, a swimming pool? No: an underground reservoir that's been exposed, somehow. The columns would have supported a ceiling . . .

Recreating the last scene of *Nostalghia*.

Explaining things to Business Studies Guy. Gorchakov, this despairing Russian type, has promised to walk all the way across a drained pool carrying a lit candle. It's supposed to be an act of faith . . . It's supposed to save the world or whatever . . . Come on, it's a Tarkovsky film—these guys believe in this sort of stuff . . .

And it's supposed to be filmed in a single shot, in a single take. Tarkovsky was trying to *enter the domain of time*, he said. He wanted to portray an entire human life in one shot, from birth to the moment of death.

You're supposed to convey *messianic temporality*, Ismail says. Time, beside itself. Time, in excess of itself. Time, intensified. Time that yearns and waits. In which what is awaited is nothing other than waiting . . .

Business Studies Guy, donning his Russian-style long coat. Business Studies Guy, lighting his candle. Business Studies Guy, beginning to cross the reservoir.

The candle flame, guttering. Business Studies Guy, sheltering it in his coat. Walking.

Go, Business Studies Guy!

The candle, fizzling out.

Business Studies Guy, going back to the beginning.

Business Studies Guy, relighting his candle. Setting off again.

It's kind of moving, I say.

It's kind of *boring*, Marcie says.

The candle, going out.

Business Studies Guy, starting again.

He looks so serious! I say. What's in Business Studies Guy's head right now? What's he thinking?

He's repenting for his Business Studies sins, Ismail says. And there are many of those.

The candle, going out.

This is a farce, Marcie says. (Shouting) *GET ON WITH IT, BUSINESS STUDIES GUY!*

You're ruining the mood, Ismail says.

Business Studies Guy, starting again.

Business Studies Guy, shielding the candle with his hand. Walking backwards to protect the flame . . .

Business Studies Guy's persistent, I'll give him that, I say.

He's feeling it, Valentine says.

Come on, save the world, Business Studies Guy! Save *us*, for God's sake . . . Look at us . . . Don't you think we need help?

He's nearly halfway across . . . , I say.

*YOU GO, SALVATION BOY!* Valentine shouts.

*DO IT FOR ARTHOUSE!* I shout.

*BOR-ING!* Marcie shouts. *BOR-ING!*

The candle, blown out.

I think we distracted him, I say.

Okay, he's not going to save the world, Ismail, Valentine says. I think we have to accept it.


## 26

EVENING. The Nehmet Kadah, with Michael.

They treat him like a god here. Just *bring food*, he says—and they do. The restaurant is bringing out its best in stainless steel serving bowls.

The proprietor, introducing the dishes. Explaining them. Everything's off-menu. Michael never wants anything to do with a menu.

This is Michael's milieu. A bit of grandeur. A bit of magnificence. We're not ordinary people, in Michael's company. This is not a drunken, red-eyed curry-house scramble. We are to Eat. Dinner is an Occasion.

A whorl of dishes. Chef's specials. Home cooking, almost. Our cutlery's better than at any other table. Our plates are larger. The poppadums are crispier. The rice bowl's piled higher. The dishes are more various. The napkins are cloth, not paper. We're drinking Natarajan beer, not Cobra. And there's a proper candle at the centre of the table. Only mancunian gangsters are treated as well as this.

This is a feast! Forget the petty economies of life! Forget concern for the morrow! This is conviviality! There's gladness abroad! Great-souledness rules! General expansiveness! We're not bit players anymore. Our lives have been lifted onto a grander stage. We're all as maharajas at the Nehmet Kadah...

And Simone, among it all. Simone, with everything happening around her. Happy with it. Caught up with it. Glad to be part of the Occasion, with a plate full of food.

Evil: that's our topic, my dears, Michael says. The nature of evil—its source, its essence and what can be done about it.

The true evil is that we live untrue lives, Marcie says. We're part of the middle-class lie.

And what lie is that? Michael asks.

That the world is going to continue as it is, which it obviously isn't, Marcie says. The middle-class have no conception of what's coming.

And what *is* coming? Michael asks.

The end of all things, Marcie says. The hour's getting late, right?

Unless our symposium is about what comes after the end, Michael says.

Like your icons, Ismail says.

... And there's the class exploitation, of course, Marcie says. Don't forget that. The usual class war, which is also a race war...

Do you think Raj, our host, is exploited? Michael asks. And his sons, who run the place? Or the chefs who work in the kitchen?

Maybe not Raj, or his family, Marcie says. Maybe not even his chefs. Maybe not even the people who clean the kitchen or load the dishwasher. It's the system that's evil. It's the Man. It's the fakery of the Man's world.

But you believe the world is going to pass away, Michael says.

I hope it's going to pass away, Marcie says. But in the meantime, we should reject it all—the whole thing. We see through the lies—even the lies of *good food* and *good company*...

Do you reject the chapli kebab? Valentine asks.

I like the chapli kebab, Marcie says.

Do you reject... Natarajan beer? Valentine asks.

I'm actually planning on having several more bottles of Natarajan beer, Marcie says.

Would you reject, like, the body of Ultimate Destruction Girl with an *I Love Marcie* tattoo? Valentine asks.

I didn't say I was *perfect*, Marcie says. I'm not some kind of saint . . . Maybe I'm stupid or something . . . But I have a stupid question: How can we feast while others starve? How can we drink when others are thirsty?

That's how the real Simone died: She wouldn't eat more than the rations of French prisoners of war, Ismail says. She starved to death.

She starved *herself* to death, Valentine says. Pure masochism. She was in love with death, which I thoroughly understand.

You're not going to starve yourself to death, are you? I ask Simone.

Michael, refilling Simone's glass with lassi. My earthly mission is to keep Simone alive for as long as possible, he says. But come now, Johnny—you've barely said a word. This is a symposium—everyone has to talk. What is evil? Are *we* evil?

I saw a man being beaten on the street today, I say. It was a turf war, I think. A punishment beating. Maybe he was from some rival gang. Maybe he was selling something he shouldn't somewhere he shouldn't. Maybe it was some kind of warning to others, like, *don't fuck with us.*

He was down, curled up, foetal, I say. And he was surrounded by this horde of maniacs kicking him fast and hard. Kicking his kidneys. Kicking his head. Rattling his brain around his skull. They'd done it before. They were practised. It was, like, a really *efficient* beating. It wasn't even personal . . .

Yesterday, I saw this homeless guy screaming, I say. Just standing in the middle of the pavement, screaming and hitting himself. Striking at his own face with his fists. *His own face* . . . What life must he have led? What happened to him? What was he seeing? Hallucinating?

What had he *taken*? Gita says.

His scream wasn't a cry for help, I say. It wasn't a cry of outrage. It was, like, the uttermost of desperation. The emergency of everything. A scream to God to end it all *now*! To stop it all *now*! For the world to be destroyed—all at once, *right now*! A scream that was the whole agony of existence. And it wasn't a new scream. It was ancient. It was the oldest scream in the world . . .

But life can't be reduced to misery and suffering, even if it seems that misery and suffering are all around us, Michael says. You see, I think the antidote to evil is right here—in the way we're eating together. There is a goodness of succour—of these marvellous dishes, prepared for us by our marvellous hosts. There's a goodness to being guests of Raj and his family, just as there's a goodness of hospitality.

But the goodness can't hold the horror back, I say. Not forever. It's waiting out there. It's in the streets. In Manchester . . . Tell everyone, Simone. You understand, don't you? The fragility of it all . . .

I can't begrudge the hospitality of the Nehmet Kadah, Simone says. Who wouldn't enjoy themselves, sitting here being brought the most wonderful dishes?

But you have another perspective . . . , Michael says.

All temporal things are impermanent, Simone says.

Yes, I say. *Yes.*

So we shouldn't value anything that's going to end—that's, like, finite? Valentine says. Fuck that.

So what are you saying: seize the day or something? Gita asks.

There's this moment right now, Valentine says. What's happening right here. Raj's saag aloo! Raj's beer! I don't know about anything else. Tonight we'll be drunk, and fuck tomorrow! Which means that the finitude of the poppadum, or whatever, isn't a *major* issue . . .

Michael: I would say we enjoy this food not because we lack anything, nor even because we're hungry (although we might be that); not because it's nutritious (although it is that, too); nor even because it's fulfilling a need (which it certainly is) but because it's *good*.

Only *relatively* good, Simone says.

That might be the case for the great mystics, but it's not a general recipe for life, Michael says.

I don't seek a *general recipe for life*, Simone says.

You see life in terms of what it lacks, Michael says. But I understand it in terms of what we are *given*: the warmth of Raj's hospitality, the way we're sitting down together, pursuing truth . . .

The Moment—the fucking Moment, Valentine says. These are poppadums of the Moment. This is lassi of the Moment . . .

We don't live in moments, Simone says. We live in time.

We *explode* time! Valentine says.

Time is necessity in its purest form, Simone says.

Time reveals itself in the explosion of necessity! Valentine says. Time is freedom! Time is *lumpen*—isn't that right, den mom? But you deny all that, Simone. You see it as part of the mechanism. As the grinding of gears. As lack, loss, powerlessness, evil.

A mechanism that God set in motion, Simone says.

Which goes to show that you're a Gnostic, Simone, Valentine says. You hate this existence—don't try to hide it. You hate time, which is why you talk of the mark of eternity. You hate the world, which is why you talk of the good and the beautiful. You hate human helplessness, which is why you talk of divine grace. The difference is that we hate the world and call it hatred. You hate it and call it *love*.

I hate nothing, Simone says.

You hate the world, Valentine says. Don't pretend.

There's evil in the world, but there is a greater good outside the world that balances it, Simone says. There's hatred, but there's a greater love that we can let act in our place.

We have to love the world with *God's own love*, Simone says. To know a love that loves *through* us. A love that we *are*. That is and was our deepest identity all along . . . And that lets us accept everything,

105

all things, without reservation. To love even *suffering*. Because the love of the world is the love of God. And because all things in existence speak of God somehow.

You *want* the world to be disgusting! Valentine says. You *want* it to be totally free of justice, mercy and goodness! You *want* to see it as *sheer blind mechanism* ... Everything but death is a lie for you.

Simone, speaking deliberately: I believe that there's an inner limit you have to cross. Where you offer no resistance to God—where you're in perfect transparent continuity with him. And that's when you can desire everything that happens because it's part of the order of the world.

That's when you accept your total *passivity*, Valentine says. That's why you think you can't do anything to change things.

But we *can* change things, Simone says. God can't feed the hungry—but *we* can. God can't comfort the poor—but *we* can. Our role is to bring God and the creation face to face. God can say *I* in us, act in us, through us. Until we have nothing of our own to say or do.

And that's our sacrifice, Simone says. That's our decreation. *Compassion*, in a word. Compassion in which God becomes a person. *Me*. When God's love passes through me like light through a pane of glass.

# C H A P T E R 3

**1**

**MONDAY MORNING, ONCE AGAIN.** Monday morning, come round again. Time to lift the lid from our coffins again.

*Bring out your dead!* the university's calling. *Bring out your gloomers! Your doomers! Bring out your ruined! Bring out your botched!*

*Bring out your recluses!* All Saints is calling. *Bring out your nocturnals! Bring out your insomniacs! Bring out your still-drunk-from-the-night-befores! Bring out your still-stoned!*

And here we are, in the obscenity of the morning. We're owls in daylight. Robbed of sleep. Robbed of oblivion. Forced to open our eyes.

Our morning selves, before the caffeine has hit. Our morning nonselves, before we've pulled ourselves together.

We haven't woken up. We're still dreaming. Still have sleep in our eyes . . .

Will someone switch off the light? It's too early for light. Too early to be out of doors . . .

We're owls in daylight. Morning-blinkers. We're dazed! Stunned! We can't even remember who we are . . .

Nine AM, Alan Turing.

A nine AM lecture: They know our weakness! Our Achilles' heels! They want to disarm us! They know how to destroy the humanities mind!

The nine AM thing is a show of strength. The nine AM start is a flexing of muscles. It's there to demonstrate the uni *means business*! To show who holds the power! It's a deliberate disciplining of the postgraduate hordes!

Nine AM, in Alan Turing. Nine AM, in the *total environment*. The building's like a generation starship, carrying us through darkness to some faraway planet. We're passengers, nothing more. We're drones. We're all but cryogenically suspended . . .

They have us lulled. Quietened. Even *awed*, in our own way. Even *dwarfed*. The uni's steering us through the darkness . . .

Descending into the lecture theatre. Finding our seats in the lecture theatre.

Here we all are, in the belly of the beast, the great calm beast. In the digestive tract of the uni. Here we are, being broken down—metabolised. The great uni stomach is doing its work.

We're being digested, slowly. We're being processed. We're an input that's being turned into an output. Without our even noticing it . . .

Fantasies of civil disobedience—of a mass storm-out. Of some PhD General Strike—some Postgraduate Spring.

Daydream: If we rushed Professor Bollocks, all at once . . . If we stampeded . . . Or if we simply stamped our feet and hollered . . . If we cried, *no! no! no!*

Why are we so cowardly? Why are we so passive? Look how many of us there are!

But there's something *inevitable* about method class. A kind of *morning fatalism*, which compels us to subject ourselves to this— to let ourselves be destroyed. The same thing that prevented Oscar Wilde from fleeing to Paris before his trial.

We *want* the horror, in some sense. We *want* to be appalled. We *want* our dread confirmed. We came here for horror, and we want nothing but horror.

There's no point resisting. Nothing for it other than to fly directly into the storm. Just fix our eyes on the monitors. Just accept that it's happening.

Professor Bollocks, on the danger of PhD mission drift. Of going off-course. Of drifting. (*But that's what doing a PhD is, Professor Bollocks: mission drift. Losing your bearings. Knowing the futility of bearings. That's what we're doing a PhD for . . .* )

Professor Bollocks, on the importance of tracking our time-usage. (*We don't want* to budget our time, *Professor Bollocks. We don't want* to invest time where it matters! We *want* to spend time! We *want* to burn it off! We *want* to set fire to time—*our* time!)

Professor Bollocks, on the need to self-monitor. (*We're not our own Stasi spies*, Professor Bollocks. *We're not informants on ourselves. We're not going to be our own secret police.*)

Professor Bollocks, recommending we give ourselves *permission to make mistakes*. (*We're not going to reward ourselves as good servants of the Man, Professor Bollocks. We're not going to acknowledge the progress we're making as* obedient methodologists. *Self-punishment instead! Self-loathing instead*!)

Professor Bollocks, advising us to find *an accountability buddy*. (*That's not why we hang out, Professor Bollocks. It's not about* outcome-focused study.)

Marcie's panic noises, like bat squeaks. Valentine, saying calming mantras. Repeating the words, *Gilles Deleuze*, over and over. Me, clicking my heels together. Saying, *There's no place like home.*

Business Studies Guy, pay attention for us. You're on. Jot down some notes. Keywords, to use in the exercises . . . because there are bound to be exercises . . .

## 2

## ST PETER'S SQUARE.

No one's around, we notice. No one in the streets.

Shops without shoppers. No footfall, nothing. Are we the only ones who see it?

The afternoon shows us the secret of Manchester. The truth of the world. That it's all ended. It's all hollow. That there is no real economy, not anymore.

Suspension. Fate hasn't been allowed to play out. The inevitable hasn't been allowed to be inevitable. The crash wasn't allowed to come. The end hasn't been permitted to end.

This extend and pretend . . . This *economy of nihilism* . . . How's the Man doing this? How's he keeping it all so-called going? What's holding back the breakdown? The devaluation of all currencies? What financial chicanery? What blizzard of money-printing?

The breakdown's coming—everyone knows that. The great global debt default. Behind the scenes: total kleptocracy. The Man, buying up every physical asset. Collateralising all predictable income streams. Controlling all land, all water, all minerals, all means of production, all animals, all plants, all food, all energy, all information and all human beings in the world . . .

And for us, in Manchester? The interregnum. The lull before the breakdown. Before the floodwaters rise.

Which is why they're rebuilding Manchester as a Smart City, as a Surveillance City. Which is why they're readying the tech to track us all. To analyse our data. To apply *predictive analytics*. Which is why they're learning how to shape our thoughts, our feelings, preemptively. To bring us under total control *before we find out what's going on.*

This is just the lull before full Implementation. Before the gear shift. For the moment, the city's as numb as we are. As dissociated as we are. As lost as we are . . .

Manchester, lost in Manchester. Manchester, trailing behind itself in Manchester. The mancunian unconscious, still alive. Old Manchester, amputated Manchester, still dreaming in its freefall.

Decades as a backwater. Decades left to rot. Left to fester. And only music to show for it. Only the music, as testimony. Only its musical martyrs to sing the truth of Manchester through blackened lips . . .

Waterstones.

Grandeur. Air. Great stairwells.

Whoever buys books here? How can this place keep going?

Three-for-two books. Calm books. Unperturbed books, with forever before them. Resistanceless reads. Styleless books, serenely themselves. Books of the new nothing. That say nothing, add nothing to nothing. Smoothed-away books, like rocks in a river.

Books for our cells. Books about prison, about life in our prison world, all the while pretending that it isn't prison. Learning-to-love-your prison books. Prettify-your-cell books. Admiring-the-view-through-the-bars books. The joy-of-wanking-in-your-prison-cell books . . .

Where's *posthumous* fiction? Where's the poetry of the *already dead*? Where are the books that begin with the end—that start with defeat? Where's the literature of *perpetual disaster*?

Upstairs.

Agreement: it's amazing there even *is* a philosophy section. My God, look at them. *Medical Nemesis*, just there on display. *Humiliation of the Word*, on show to the afternoon. *Things Hidden Since the Foundation of the World*, there for anyone's gaze.

They're too available. Too obtainable. They're right here, exposed to the air! To the light! To *casual interest*! As though they were books like any others! As if they weren't prison breakout manuals!

Lying there. Impotent! Fallen! Good for nothing! Pointless! Simply left to the afternoon! Stranded in the afternoon! To browsers: To afternoon moochers: It's cruel. Mockery!

It makes philosophy even more irrelevant, in a way. It makes a *display* of its irrelevance. The fact that anyone can read these books. The fact that they're just open to anybody, in paperback, with introductions, with shiny covers.

The desire to gather them in. Shelter them. From the eyes of others. From our *own* eyes. It's bad enough that we read them, let alone anyone else!

## 3

### POST CLUB, THREE AM.

Hector's house. The house of the apostate. The great betrayer.

Calling up. Coo-ee, Hector! Let us in! It's your oldest compardres! It's us!

No answer. Hector's probably had an early night. He'll probably be up with the larks to study tomorrow.

Rattling the front door.

We're not leaving until you let us in! We'll wake up all your neighbours!

The door opening a crack.

Then a little wider.

There he is: *Hector.*

You have guests, Hector! Old friends! For the first time in ages! It's time to revive your arts of hospitality!

We're hungry! We've been dancing all night! What do you have to drink? To smoke? Bring out the best for your guests!

Whip us up picklebacks! What do you mean you've forgotten how to make one?

How many pickleback nights did we have, Hector? How many nights drinking together after badminton, back in the day?

This is a reunion, Hector. It'll be just like the old days, when you were part of our crew. Our glory days, back at the beginning of our PhDs! When we'd first got our scholarships! When we were just happy not to be *out there*!

When we thought we'd be able to write our dissertations *just like that*! That one sentence would simply follow another . . . Give unto another . . . When the Alan Turing atrium was a space of sheer possibility. When our supervisors were as gods to us . . . When every guest speaker was a revelation . . . We didn't even call Professor Bollocks *Professor Bollocks* back then . . .

Our PhD youths! Who we used to be! All innocent! Fresh-faced in our studies! But we couldn't remain in the days of postgraduate heaven. There was a fall—a terrible fall. There was a Realisation, capital R. Our mediocrity—our failings. The *academy's* mediocrity! The *academy's* failures!

Which you denied, Hector! Which you couldn't cope with! There's a pain to mediocrity—no doubt. None of us want to contemplate our stupidity—of course not. But you can't simply *deny* your mediocrity. You can't pretend that you're *not* stupid. You can't delude yourself that you'll finish your PhD on time, in three years, under the personal guidance of Professor Bollocks. Or that you can complete your PhD at all . . .



# 4
## TUESDAY.

The bus to uni.

Do you ever wonder whether things can continue as they are?

Valentine asks. Whether something's *got* to happen, from the sheer pressure of *nothing* happening.

I'd settle for a bus crash, just for the novelty, Marcie says. I'm sure I could get off on it sexually, like a J.G. Ballard character . . .

You have to understand the *ideological function* of the bus, Marcie says. It's designed to rub our noses in the ordinary. It's perpetually reminding us of the reality principle. It wants us to think this is all there is.

This *is* all there is, right? I say.

You've fallen for it, idiot, Marcie says. *Nothing changes. The same is the same. The bus is the bus.* This world, this whole way of life, was inevitable. There could be no other outcome. All of history and, dare we say, natural history, was leading here. It couldn't be prevented. That's what bus rides tell you.

What about the lumpen—do they get buses? Valentine says.

They *hijack* buses, I say. They mug people on buses.

Petty crime's all they've left, now *lumpen life has been criminalised*, Marcie says. Now it's *total fucking control* . .

You'd be terrified if one of them got on this bus, I say. You'd be cowering like the rest of us.

Maybe they'd recognise you as one of their own, Valentine says. Is there a secret lumpen password or something?

The tragedy is how I *could* have lived, Marcie says. My people are semi-criminal. I'm from genuine lumpenstock. We're *loveable rogues*—only some of us aren't that loveable.

We eat the wrong things and drink the wrong things and order too much take-out food and belch in the streets, Marcie says. We're obese and unfit and probably not going to live very long. We're a public health hazard.

We don't have the dignity of the poor, Marcie says. We're, like, human vermin. *Rats*, basically . . . We're in and out of prison for pointless, petty offenses. But we'll survive the collapse . . . We'll be out looting—*stealing* . . .

So what happened to you? Ismail asks.

Catholic school, Marcie says. I got a scholarship.

A tragedy! Valentine says.

They thought they were saving me from the streets, Marcie says. Freeing me from my *class destiny*. But it was no better than kidnapping. What I could have been!

A minor drug dealer, I say. A backstreet pimp . . .

I fell into their *deferred gratification traps*, Marcie says. Into their *zombie institutions* . . . I gave up the imperative of the Now. Of wanting it all right away and damn the future . . . And now look at me—sitting on the bus with you saps . . .

## 5

THROUGH THE ALL SAINTS NON-CAMPUS. Through the city, where its buildings are scattered. There's no heart to All Saints, not really. No place to say: this is where All Saints *is*.

All Saints, indistinguishable from the city. All Saints buildings, running right up to the street. No cloisters, no inner courtyards. No statues of worthies in shady groves. No Victorian leafiness. No *retreat from the world*, on the All Saints non-campus.

All Saints buildings are what they are—all obvious—all *there*. They're all glass and steel. All light, streaming through glass. You can see right through them. There are no All Saints secrets. No All Saints introversion. It's all on show. All sheer visibility.

As though there were a Weilian *dialectics* to All Saints, to the almost-entirely-Business-Studies uni. As though the absence of depths, the absence of shadows, attested to greater depths, to deeper shadows.

The unregenerated city: that's what we see in All Saints's steel and glass. The city buried in the city. The counter-city. Undevelopable . . . Unredeemable . . . That returns like a curse, in All Saints's steel and glass.

The atrium, on the lookout for Ultimate Destruction Girl.

Make your great mating cry, den mom, Valentine says. Shake the foundations.

No point—Ultimate Destruction Girl's not here, Marcie says. She's too good for this place.

The whole design of this building... The way it lets us see its workings ... The way it's all on display ... The way we can watch these students going up and down the stairs ...

The way it doesn't hide its nothingness. It doesn't cover up its void. The way it shows that there's nothing but absence—the void where a university should be.

Students in sportswear, up and down the stairs. Don't they know what's being done to them? This is the only taste of freedom they're going to get! This is all they'll know of independent life!

Because what's waiting for them when they graduate? Care work—bathing-old-people work, at best. Gig work—picking-up-dogshit work, at best. Or they could just let themselves be sex-trafficked to pay off their student loans. Offer up their adrenochrome to be harvested ... Sell their internal organs ...

They might as well have *DOOMED* written on their foreheads. Or *FUCKED*. Or *KILL ME NOW*.

And us, contemplating it all. We PhD students, waiting for our supervisorial appointments, waiting for reading groups to begin, waiting for Research Forum, looking out over it all.

We should set an example. Show the undergraduates how people of integrity actually live, which is to say *die*. Leap from the eighth floor, all the way down the tiled foyer. Destroy ourselves, before we're processed to death! Take our own lives, before we're *spiritually killed*! Preemptive suicides, before we have to go back *out there* ...

First floor, Business. Second floor, Business. Third floor, Business. Fourth floor, more Business. Fifth floor, the same ...

And the other floors? The business social sciences, *basically*. Business

Sociology. Business Linguistics. The *business humanities*, in essence. Business English. Business History . . . And, at the very top, on the eighth floor: *Philosophy*, from which Disaster Studies sprung.

That's where they had the idea, the European-style thinkers, employable only in new-uni Philosophy departments. That's where Russell, Professor Sentinel and Professor Moribund came up with it: the rebranding of philosophy—*continental* philosophy—as *Disaster Studies*. *The Centre for Disaster Studies*. A cunning move, though it sounds like a joke. A clever ploy, though it sounds like self-parody. It's a *unique selling point* for All Saints Philosophy. A brand identity. A way of increasing recruitment. Of securing a power-base. Of putting *All Saints Philosophy* on the map . . .

What well-meaning dean approved this? Who actually gave it the go-ahead? Did they believe Philosophy could be brought into the fray, could be put to *applied ethical work*? Did they think Philosophy could be made to show its relevance to *real-world problems*?


# 6
## EVENING.

Valentine's birthday.

Gita and I, outside Marcie and Valentine's flat.

Into the chamber of horrors, I say, knocking at the door. Wait till you see *this*, Gita.

Here's the all-but-hetero couple, Marcie says, opening the door. Here they are, Val: a pair of breeders, come to wish you a happy birthday.

Do you guys actually know what to do? Valentine asks. Do you know what goes where?

We're not actually fucking, I say. We're not actually *anything*.

Heterosexuality is so reassuring, Marcie says. Glad to know there are a few of you left. Well, you can help repopulate the Earth when the time comes.

Wow, this place is so dark, Gita says. Do you ever open the curtains?

No, Valentine says.

And it's so *damp*, Gita says. It's practically aquatic.

We were going for a sort of *sodden nihilism*, Marcie says. Like a Chinese wet market.

And there's a mural, kinda . . . , Gita says.

It's the headless guy from Acéphale—you know, Bataille's secret cell, Valentine says.

It looks like the Acéphale guy drawn by a child with a felt tip, Gita says.

And there are cock drawings, too . . . , I say.

Valentine was drunkenly developing a cock theory one night—with illustrations, Marcie says. Using every available surface.

It was a *Gesamtkunstwerk* thing, Valentine says. Like Wagner.

Wow, Bayreuth in Gorton, I say.

And a pentagram . . . , Gita says.

We had Weep round, Marcie says. We were trying to conjure some ancient mancunian gods. Open another dimension.

And is that a real noose, hanging from the ceiling? Gita asks.

A noose covered in glitter, Marcie says. And Christmas lights. It's a disco memento mori.

Marcie, switching on the lights. The noose, flashing.

Very festive, I say.

God, now I can see the mould, Gita says.

The Wizard thinks it might be sentient, Valentine says.

He thinks *everything*'s sentient, I say.

Inspecting the mould.

We think of it as accidental gardening, Marcie says. Like, indoor gardening.

It's growing into something rich and strange, Valentine says.

Or just strange, Marcie says.

Tell Gita about our livestock, Valentine says.

Oh yeah—there was this two-headed rat, Marcie says. Like in that James Herbert novel.

It might be hyperintelligent, Valentine says. It might be planning to take over the world.

I think it might be the Man's rat, Marcie says. I think it might be a spy for the Man.

We called it Deleuze/Guattari, Valentine says.

We haven't seen it since, Marcie says.

This is the sort of place you'd hold someone hostage, Gita says. Or confine sex slaves.

See, we have the horror where we want it, Marcie says. Where it can be seen. The horror's, like, all out in the open.

This flat is *honest*, if nothing else, Valentine says.

There's something so, so wrong here, Gita says.

So wrong it's right? Marcie asks.

So wrong it's *WRONG*, Gita says. In capitals.

Understand this place and you'll understand us, Marcie says.

That's what I'm afraid of, Gita says.

A present for Valentine.

What do you get for the guy who hates everything? I say.

Valentine, opening it.

A vintage Arab strap, Marcie says. One careful owner, it said on eBay. We all saved up.

Actually, we just found it on the Ees, I say.

Probably discarded by Russell, Marcie says. Do you recognise it, Gita?

How does it actually *work*? Valentine asks. What's the mechanism?

You fasten it around the cock and balls, idiot, Marcie says. It maintains your stiffy . . . Not that you have problems with *that*.

Thanks . . . very thoughtful, Valentine says. I'll save it for old age.

Manacles, attached to the wall.

Is that where you lock up Business Studies Guy? Gita says.

Props for Valentine's sex-cam adventures, Marcie says. For his on-line sluttery.

And is that, like, a stalagmite rising from the floor? Gita asks. And a stalactite, above it? I thought they took thousands of years to form . . .

Geology's, like, sped up here, Marcie says. And evolution.

*De*volution, more like, Gita says. Degradation. General decay.

Ismail, arriving with cake.

Your real present's baked into this, I say. The Wizard's best.

There's enough for all of us, Marcie says.

Mouthfuls of cake.

So, twenty-five today, birthday boy, Marcie says. What's it like?

I feel *old*, Valentine says. I feel fucking posthumous. I'm losing my appeal. No one will want to fuck me anymore.

You're just moving on to another phase of male beauty, I say.

I was an ephebe and now I'm a has-been, Valentine says. See, my problem is I've missed the perfect moment for death. The moment that would have made sense of it all.

There was a moment? I say.

Sure, Valentine says. A personal pinnacle of youth and beauty. Look, the young should die young. Do you know what Mishima said? *I never look at a beautiful boy without wanting to douse him in petrol and set him on fire.*

Which reminds me, Marcie says. Here's a little something . . .

Valentine, unwrapping a poster-sized photo of a severed head.

It's a meditation image—for your wall, Marcie says.

Fuck—Mishima himself, Valentine says. I don't know what to say, den mom. Thanks . . . *Thanks!* You know his story, don't you guys? Genius author, ultranationalist, had his own private army. Finished his world-changing masterpiece on the same day that he stormed the Japanese army HQ, took some general hostage, gave some speech about emperor worship and then committed ritual seppuku with his young lover. May 2, 1970. *One should work on one's suicide all one's life*—that's what he said.

And there's his severed head, Marcie says.

Gross, Gita says.

So you're supposed to meditate in front of it? I ask.

On the practice of joy before death, Valentine says.

Mishima doesn't look very joyful, Gita says.

He thought there's a love of life which can say yes to death, Valentine says. That there's a death you can live as the highest life. He thought we shouldn't just live on by default. That our hearts shouldn't just continue to beat. That we shouldn't take too many breaths . . .

He rehearsed his death over and over in his fiction, Valentine says. In films. In his romantic relationships . . . He wanted to crown his life's work with some *magnificent terrorist act*. To make his whole life cohere, before he fell into old age. And that's what he did . . .

You could do the same, Marcie says. You could kidnap the uni president or something. Give a speech to the postgraduates at method class, exhorting them to *rise up*. Swan-dive from the top of the atrium at the pinnacle of your beauty . . . Come on, how much longer do you have to leave a beautiful corpse?

# 7

## WEDNESDAY.

Al's café.

God, another day in absurdistan, Marcie says. I'm so tired of *raising myself from the dead* each morning.

It's hardly the morning, I say.

I'm sick of the *daily resurrection*, Marcie says. I hate adding futility to futility.

Maybe this is it, Valentine says. We've been falling up to now, and we've reached the bottom. There's nowhere further to fall.

No—we're still falling, I say. We just don't notice it anymore.

How did we get like this? Marcie asks. I mean, what happened? We're beyond fucked up.

*Solitude, despair, clichés, incommunicability are the product of the inner solitude of the bourgeoisie*, Valentine quotes.

But we're not actually bourgeois, Marcie says. We're not middle-class. We're from the ghetto, right?

Doing a PhD is still a very middle-class thing to do, Valentine says.

Our problem is that we *expect* things to happen, Marcie says. We despair because we hope, which is totally middle-class. Hope means you actually expect something's going to save you. You believe things might actually *change*, despite all signs to the contrary.

So we shouldn't hope? Ismail asks.

Hope's a luxury, Marcie says.

And we shouldn't despair? Ismail asks.

Despair just means the absence of hope, Marcie says. We have to free ourselves from the hope-despair axis.

How? I ask.

Lumpen existence, Marcie says. The lumpen way of life . . . The lumpen never despair. And they don't hope, either. They don't look ahead. They don't defer expectations. They simply live in the moment.

I thought they were busy ducking and diving, Ismail says. That must take forethought . . .

Cunning, sure, Marcie says. The ability to improvise. But it's about responding to the moment, not bourgeois planning. Looking out for . . . opportunities.

Sure, to mug people, Gita says. To break into houses.

**8**

REALLY, YOU SHOULD KEEP AWAY FROM US, BUSINESS STUDIES GUY. We should beat you away from the humanities. We should be a cautionary tale. Living warnings. There's no future for us, as humanities PhDs . . .

Forget all the new things you've learnt, Business Studies Guy. You'll readjust. Your perspectives will narrow again—it's okay. You can still read Scholem as a hobby. Leaf through Kafka on a business flight. Your humanities studies will be something to add to your CV under *interests and hobbies*. A curio for an interview or ice-breaking session. *Tell us one really surprising thing about you . . . Something no one knows . . .*

*(I've read the gloomiest books in the world. The darkest books. Books of utter dread, utter torment, that howl out in the world's night.*

*I've read the most joyful books. Wild with yea-saying. With affirmation. Books that tell you how to overcome yourself. To create yourself. To experiment with wild intensities and flows. With energies, speeds, lines of flight.*

*I've read the most revolutionary books. That advocated setting the world on fire. That claimed the world is on fire.)*

Sure, you'll think of us one day, when you're riding one of those glass elevators, Business Studies Guy. You'll remember with a smile something from your *holiday in the humanities* as you cross the threshold of a corporate atrium. Some lines from Karl Barth's *Romansbuch* will come to you unbidden at a marketing team away-day . . .

For a time, you'll keep a few books from the old days on your shelves. But how many house-moves will *Écrits* survive? How long will you continue to cart *The Omnibus Homo Sacer* around? How long before *Difference and Repetition* is bagged up for Oxfam?

# 9

THURSDAY.

Al's café.

Marcie, with a pile of books.

Valentine, flicking through the top one. *A Cultural History of Masturbation*. I suppose if you're going to be wanking all day, you might as well learn something about it . . .

The next book. *Sympathetic Wank Magic*. Valentine, reading the back cover: *Actualising your desire through onanism. The entire contents of all time and all space, while experienced in a masturbatory fantasy, actually coexist in an infinite and eternal Now.*

Wow—wank metaphysics, Valentine says. *Imagine yourself into the feeling of your masturbatory wish fulfilled. Appropriate it, claim it, use it. You possess the masturbatory power of intervention—the power that enables you to alter the course of your future.*

You could use wank magic to get your dissertation to write itself, I say.

Believe me, I'm trying, Marcie says.

*Masturbation Theory*, Valentine reads. Looks highbrow. Wow, it's really dense. There's a whole chapter on *communist wanking* . . . Lenin disapproved, apparently. Onanism was verboten in the era of blood and iron. Masturbators were to be shot on the spot for *slowing the revolutionary tempo* . . .

Wank Studies is clearly the next big humanities thing, I say.

Sure, after they milk Disaster Studies dry, Ismail says.

*Onanism in Art*, Valentine says. Ah—*pictures*! Cleopatra, wanking with a hollow gourd full of bees . . . A twenty-eight-thousand-year-old dildo from Swabia . . .

*The Joy of Self-Pleasuring*—what's this? I say. A wanker's *Kama Sutra*? Turning the book upside down. I didn't even know you could *do* this stuff . . .

## 10

ISMAIL AND I, DISCUSSING SIMONE.

What does she do all day?

She and Michael talk, Ismail says.

And what does she say?

She can be quiet sometimes, Ismail says. She just listens . . . I think she's happy to let him talk. Just to let it wash over her . . .

Do they have discussions?

Sometimes, Ismail says. They disagree on a lot of things. Simone's too polite to say that much. But she indicates her disapproval, which Michael finds very amusing.

But they agree on so much, too . . .

He believes there'll be an end to time, which makes no sense to her, Ismail says. He believes in universal salvation. In the immortality of the soul. In divine providence. She doesn't speculate about those things. He believes in the centrality of the resurrection. Whilst she insists the Cross comes first.

When it's warm, they take tea in the garden, Ismail says. They do it with real ceremony.

I always think of Simone as solitary, I say. As up in the peace and calm of her room, meditating in silence.

I think she gets up very early to write, Ismail says. Then she comes down to relax. Sometimes, she taps away at the computer in the front room, answering emails and stuff, when Michael's having a nap on the couch. Simone's there, doing her thing, when he's in deep discussion with his friends.

I'd like to watch her work, I say. Like, writing things. Reading things. I'd like to watch her without her knowing. I'd like to be a spiritual voyeur. Simone in prayer . . . Simone, on her knees, offering up her soul . . . I don't think there could be anything more beautiful . . .

# 11

## GITA AND I, AT RUSSELL'S.

The open plan.

How come you hang out so much here? I ask.

I'm keeping Georges-with-an-S company, Gita says. He gets lonely. And besides, I like playing house.

Vera's paintings on the cupboards. Hummingbirds. Roses. Vera's framed nature sketches on the wall.

You can't loathe her, can you? She's pretty cool.

She's very creative, Gita says. She teaches fine art at All Saints. She wrote some memoir.

Maybe you'll feature in her next volume, I say. *The Other Woman.*

I think there have been plenty of *other women*, Gita says.

She's expressive, he's intellectual, I say. I'm sure they're *great* company as a couple. The life and soul of the academic set.

She's spiritual, too, Gita says. She's a Quaker.

And he's some dirty Bataillean—it's perfect, I say.

This place makes me feel so *random*, Gita says. Like I don't exist.

Because you don't have all this middle-class stuff? I ask.

It's more than that, Gita says. It's like we're . . . tourists of life. We're too old to be students, really. There's something grotesque about it. We're like overgrown children. I mean, we should be adults. Adulthood's supposed to be, like, a time of purpose. A time of getting stuff done. When you stride forth into the world. When you make your fortune or whatever, like Dick Whittington. And instead? Cat-sitting in Chorlton . . .

But what a cat he is! I say. Georges-with-an-S is the king of cats!

If I owned a house like this, I'd just close the door on the world, Gita says.

If I owned it, I'd sell it and go on adventures, I say.

What kind of adventures? Gita asks.

I'd travel, I say. I'd become a citizen of the world.

Where would you go? Gita asks.

I don't know . . . I'd hole up somewhere cheap, I say. Djibouti, maybe. There was a guy from Djibouti in the Home.

Your children's home? Gita says.

He ended up at a young-offender's institute, I say. He was a good guy. He made me laugh . . .

How long were you in care, anyway? Gita asks.

It was only supposed to be temporary, I say. That's what they said. While my mum couldn't cope. Turned out she could never cope.

What happened to her? Gita asks.

She died while I was in the Home, I say. She starved herself to death. Depressive anorexia.

Poor Johnny, Gita says.

Sure, poor me, I say.

I'll bet you get tired with me sharing all my existential shit, Gita says.

I feel the existential shit, too, I say. The point of a Philosophy PhD is to articulate the angst you feel about doing a Philosophy PhD . . .

How come you're not fucked up? Gita asks. *More* fucked up, I mean. What saved you from a life on the streets?

Reading, I guess, I say. I had this cool teacher who leant me inappropriate books. Genet's *Thief's Journal*—that was one of them. I read the first sentence, and closed the book and said to myself: *This is it. This is the book I've been waiting for.* Which is exactly what Genet said to himself when he read Proust.

I even led a life of crime like Genet, I say. Me and the guy in the Home from Djibouti—Abdallah—used to go out shoplifting. We used to call it *buying*, with heavy emphasis. Did you *buy* anything today? Wink wink. He got caught one day, when we were at the mall. We'd nicked all these batteries to, like, sell on. We ended up at the police station. They didn't charge me, though. I wasn't old enough. I just said, *I don't know,* to everything they asked me. Then the people from the Home came and picked us up.

Anyway, Abdallah ended up in a remand centre, I say. He killed himself in the end.

Fuck, Johnny, Gita says. Your life . . .

Outside, smoking.

Power-washed slabs. The original outhouse, all preserved, with a slate roof, with a cast-iron gutter. Neatly stacked logs. Chairs, table and an umbrella, folded away. A squat chiminea, on little clay legs.

They've probably spent countless nights out here with *compatible couple friends* around the chiminea, I say. Cocktails and a laugh when the kids are in bed . . . Is that what you'd like: sitting next to Russell, laughing at his anecdotes?

I don't care about Russell anymore, Gita says. I want to change my life. Everything about it. But I probably won't, will I . . .

Do one thing: split up with Russell, I say.

Okay . . . That I can do, Gita says.

Do it now, I say. Text him now.

Okay, Gita says.


## 12

### FRIDAY.

Al's café.

Fuck, I'm hungover, Marcie says. I don't think I have a *pulse* anymore. My heart's actually stopped beating. Al's macchiatos are doing nothing for me.

Yeah, it takes four macchiatos to get me high now, Valentine says. I have to basically replace my blood with caffeine.

Ismail, putting cube after cube in his macchiato. Sugar rush, he says.

Do those still work for you? Valentine asks. *Lucky.*

I need something stronger than a fucking macchiato, Marcie says.
You should try the foametto—it's new on the menu, Valentine
says. Even stronger than a ristretto. Just a *film* of coffee—nothing
else. Just foam. You lick it off a plate. It's for the hardcore.

Marcie, hand up. Calling out to Al: Foametto please.

Al, looking puzzled.

Valentine, laughing: I made it up, idiot.


## 13

### AT THE BUS STOP, WITH SIMONE.

Valentine, waving to the alkies.

Look, they're waving back, he says. They recognise us.

Do you think they're allies? I say. Are they actually on our side?

Come on—they're rejecting *deferred gratification*, Marcie says.
They'll have no truck with moderation. They're not working for a living. That takes courage.

*Dutch* courage, Gita says. Look at them drink . . .

They're drinking against the bourgeois, Marcie says.

They're drinking against the technological system, Valentine says.
It's a refusal of means-ends reasoning.

It's totally means-ends: they're drinking to get drunk, Gita says.
To destroy themselves.

They're drinking to destroy the bourgeois in themselves, Marcie says.

It's a kind of sacrifice, Valentine says. Deliberately wasting time.
Deliberately fucking yourself up. Saying, *Fuck you, I don't want this
world.* And everyone despising you. And you, shouting abuse back . . .

I think the alkies are shouting abuse at *us*, I say.

Bellowing: *SHE-MALE! TRANNY!*

Bastards! I say.

No—don't respond, Ismail says. Don't dignify it.

Simone, rising. Crossing the road.

What's she doing?

Simone, among the alkies.

That's what we should have done months ago, I say. We should have gone over and introduced ourselves . . .

They would have despised us for it. See, we haven't got the touch.

We could have asked them about their favourite tipple. About their favourite swearwords. Their favourite homophobic insults . . .

They seem to be getting along, we agree. They're offering Simone their white cider, very precious for an alkie. She's refusing. Sensible woman. You can't drink white cider for breakfast . . .

They're talking. Simone's going from one to the other. She's learning their names. Their stories. I think they're still coherent at this time of day, just about. They're not yet completely off their tits . . .

They're shaking hands. They're welcoming Simone as one of their own. They were shouting at her a minute ago . . .

Simone has the touch, Valentine says.

That's what you can do if you believe in stuff, Ismail says. If you have a mission. People can see it in you—even the homeless. It's absolute sincerity—vulnerability.


## 14

### RUIN BAR.

We know how important the lecturers are supposed to be to us, Business Studies Guy. We know we're supposed to talk about them, ponder them, speculate about their every move.

We know we're supposed to learn from their example: to observe their bearing, their way of talking, their very *gestures* (heads cocked querulously, fingers pressed into an arch . . . ).

We've heard what academia used to be like, Business Studies Guy. We know about the old days of the university, when lecturers would go to Research Forum ready for a dust-up. When they'd roll up to presentations with their game faces on.

Postgraduates would *inwardly thrill* when lecturers sniffed blood. When they'd gang up and move in for the kill on a visiting speaker. (That poor sap who couldn't pronounce the word, *ineffable* (ineff-a-tible, she said); that unfortunate who said that Socrates gave *no positive definitions* (what a howler! Hadn't he read the *Laches*?)) . . .

We heard about the old machismo! It's probably still like that at Victoria. That's probably how they do things in analytic philosophy . . . But it's all meek and mild at All Saints now. The stakes are low. No one draws blood—no one's offended. Discussion's no longer a matter of life and death.

It's all speaking hushedly, in an academic whisper, Business Studies Guy. It's all thanking you for your talk and thanking you for your question and thanking you for your thanks. It's no wonder we're bored, Business Studies Guy. It's no wonder we're jaded . . .

## 15
EVENING.

Walking to the Weep party.

The Weep house, standing on its own. Bars on all the windows.

Weep bought it when it was totally dilapidated. It was some down-and-out hangout. The council were selling off houses for a quid back then. Weep run it as a gothic Airbnb. Goths come and stay here from the four corners of the Earth. It's a hotel for vampires, basically. Weep are, like, landladies for the end of times.

At the door. We're early. Anything before three AM is early, when it comes to a Weep party.

Whispering the password.

The door, creaking open. Severina Weep, in a shroud. Merryn Weep, beckoning us in.

Inside.

Give your eyes time to adjust, Business Studies Guy.

Heavy black velvet drapes. Black lava lamps. Black candles, with black flames. How do Weep do that?

Taxidermy. A stuffed duck in a bell jar. Mounted animal heads.

Assorted international goths, standing round the punch bowl.

Sipping Weep's black punch. It's strong! Strong!

Collapsing into sofas.

Admiring the high Weep ceiling. The fine Weep cornicing. Glorying in the marble Weep fireplace . . . In the flock Weep wall-paper . . . In the framed Weep sigils. *PRFSSR BLLCIKS S DD. MTHD CLSS S DSTRYD.*

A Weep party is very chill, Business Studies Guy. Very Xanax. Like an opium den.

The Dane, next to us, under a velvet throw.

The Dane is drunk, Valentine says.

The Dane *is* very drunk, I say.

He's been Dane-drinking, Marcie says. It's how they weather the long Danish winter, when it goes dark at two in the afternoon. When you basically won't see the sun again until the end of March.

Valentine, in his best David Attenborough voice: *The heartbeat lowers. All signs of vital life diminish. The Dane has disappeared into the burrow. The Danish soul is resting.*

Vortek, scowling at some business PhD students.

Who let them in here? Valentine asks. How did they know the password? Vortek will *eat* them.

Maybe Weep brought them as snacks for Vortek, like crickets for a pet python, I say.

Loud, posh voices.

A bunch of Victoria PhD students, moving through the room. Weep invite strange people. Can't they see they don't belong here?

They're so *tall*. Like giants. Look at them—they're actually graceful. They have long necks and long fingers. They're, like, a different species.

Feast your eyes, Business Studies Guy. Those Victoria guys actually have prospects. They're not steerage-class PhD types, like us. They're the managerial classes at study . . .

Yeah, but they're doing analytic philosophy PhDs, Valentine says. They're fatally bored, but don't know it.

Well, they haven't even been bothered to dress up—they haven't made an effort. You can't wear cricket jumpers at a Weep party. You can't swish about in culottes . . .

Inspecting jars along the wall.

Are these foetuses? I ask.

Jesus—they are, Valentine says. They're all deformed.

A real conversation piece, Marcie says.

Business Studies Guy, tapping at a bell jar.

Look at this one, Valentine says. It's a tiny person, curled up.

It says *homunculus* on this tag, Marcie says. What's one of those?

Me, reading from my phone. *A golem-like miniature of a human being. Generated by alchemists as servants . . .* It tells you how to make one. *Collect sperm, bones and bits of hair and skin, and lay it in the ground encased in horse manure for forty days . . . Drink cum from the final ejaculations of a hanged man.*

Nice, Valentine says.

It's supposed to have sharp little teeth and wild eyes and be very hard to discipline, I say.

It's dead, right? Gita says.

Of course it's dead, Marcie says. It's pickled.

I swear its eyes are opening, Gita says.

133

How could they be? Valentine says.

They are, Gita says. Look.

Eyes looking out at us, full of sadness.

We're hallucinating, right? Marcie says.

It's some trick, Valentine says. It's animatronics.

It's an art-piece, Gita says.

It's a party piece, I say. Made just for tonight, to spook us.

It looks a bit like Ian Curtis, Valentine says. Do you think it's his unborn brother or something?

The homunculus, eyes closing again.

That's right, homunculus, go back to sleep. Don't wake into this dreadful world.

Another bell jar.

It's a miniature Professor Bollocks, Marcie says. Looks very like him.

What's it made of? I ask. It's all waxy.

Like a voodoo doll, right? Valentine says.

How come Weep haven't beheaded it? Gita asks. Or stuck pins in it at least . . .

They're planning something, I'm sure . . . , I say.

Another jar. Murkiness. A floating sphere.

Reading the label.

An authentic Derrida testicle, supposedly, Valentine says. There's a lively trade in continental philosophy relics, I hear.

I think Weep *make* the relics, I say. As an extra source of income.

Well, they made the wrong relic, Marcie says. No one reads Derrida anymore. Now, if it was a *Deleuze* bollock, that would be different . . . Or a Meillassoux bollock . . .

Meillassoux's still alive, idiot, Valentine says.

Which would make it even more valuable, Marcie says.

The back of the house.

The garden.

Torches stuck into the grass.

Marcie, in an urgent whisper: I can't fucking believe it. There she is. Don't look.

Who? we ask.

There—next to Bitcoin, Marcie says. My future wife: Ultimate Destruction Girl. *Fuck*, those cheekbones. They're cheekbones from the Steppes. I'll bet Ultimate Destruction Girl's *Cossack* or something...

Look at her: the beauty of destruction, Marcie says. The last beautiful thing before the end ... No—she *is* the end. The world's ending tonight. The stars will go out as soon as I take her hand.

Bitcoin's moving in, Marcie, Valentine says.

Marcie, scoffing. He's probably telling her how they'll survive the apocalypse. About his luxury bunker. She won't be impressed. Ultimate Destruction Girl doesn't want to survive. She'll be happy to go down with the ship—at the prow of the ship, arms outstretched. With me holding her and singing *Heaven Knows I'm Miserable Now* ...

Go and talk to her! Valentine says. Before it's too late! Bitcoin's going for it! Wow her, Marcie! Tell her about your plans to build a war-rig, once you learn to drive! About your ambition to live like what's-her-name in *Fury Road*! Tell her about all the disaster-thinkers you've studied! And that you'll hold her in your arms as the bombs fall around you! Tell her only a *fully operational Scouse Überdyke* can save her now!

Bitcoin, leaning over Ultimate Destruction Girl. Ultimate Destruction Girl, letting herself be kissed. In full view of us all! What indecency! What a lack of taste!

Comforting Marcie. Walking her away. Never mind, den mom! Don't cry, den mom! There's nothing for it but to plunge into the darkness of the Weep rooms. To lose ourselves in their *house on the borderland* ...

Wandering the house. Wandering dark rooms, dark passageways, dark nooks and crannies.

Passing occasional *international goths*. One or two Business Studies students. A clutch of bewildered MAs, quite out of their depth ...

Rooms and rooms. Some carpeted, muffled; others echoey. Some claustrophobic, tunnel-like, cave-like; some vast—high-ceilinged, reverberant.

Sudden openings, as if the house were unfolding through some reverse origami; as if we were in a maze. And sudden closings again—channellings, compressions, leading us on.

Disorientation. How long have we been wandering? How long have we been lost? We're beginning to forget who we are. Who we were, before . . .

An opening. Are we outside? No, still inside—in the cavernous inside. So where's that breeze coming from?

The *portal* . . . We've heard rumours about this . . . Weep's experiments in *interdimensionality*. They're trying to summon this eleventh-dimensional entity called LAM. In capitals.

What are they going to do with LAM, when he arrives? Marcie asks.

Make him write their dissertations, Valentine says.

Anything to avoid real work, Marcie says.

More wandering. More darkness.

This is the failed PhD night. The night of the hulks of unfinished dissertations. The night of student-ghosts who *ran out of time*.

The night of wasted words! Of junked drafts! Of keystrokes in the void! The night of blind alleys! Of rabbit holes! Of ghost-chapters, written and discarded!

The night of PhD-insomnia! Of nights without sleep! Of thoughts without thinker! The night of black, blind universes! Of failed universes where no Big Bang ever banged!

We're losing our boundaries. We're changing places with the night. We're porous—infinitely so. The night, exploring us. The night's inside us, and we . . . Where *are* we?

Fear. Weep have us trapped. We're in a bell jar of our own. We're being exhibited, next to the Derrida bollock, next to Prof Bollocks's voodoo doll. The tag reads: *failed PhD students*.

Oh God—don't do this to us, Weep! There's an innocent amongst us! Business Studies Guy doesn't deserve this! He's young—*young*!

And then, all of a sudden, we're somewhere again.

The entrance to the Weep basement.

Is this where they've brought us?

It's like the portal to Hell, Marcie says. They've probably got the Beast from the Ees trapped down there . . .

Down the steps.

Darkness alive. Streaming and pooling. Gathering and loosening.

Different *tones* of darkness. Different consistencies, thicknesses, viscosities.

Are there colours darker than black? *Apparently* . . .

But now light, of sorts. Now a distant glowing radiance.

And sound. Music—growing louder.

And now the central chamber, lit by strange glowing globes (are those shrooms?).

Weep, at their keyboards, before a small audience of international goths.

It's Weep, doing their Nico thing. Doing full-on death-trip electronica.

It's Weep's death-disco. Slow, slow, slow.

It's so heavy. It's hypnogogia, man. What are they playing?

A drone. *The* drone. God's drone. From before the universe began.

The lightless universe—before protons, electrons. Just sound waves pulsing through plasma.

Confusion. Hubbub . . . No regular pulse. Not even *time*, as we know it.

Force fields . . . Energy fields . . .

Destruction, without there being anything to destroy. Ruination, before there's anything to ruin . . .

The not-nothing, but not something, either . . . The not-nowhere, but not anywhere, either.

Low-end turbulence. Sub-bass shockwaves. Drum spits. Ricochets. And now bits of light: flickerings. Glitches, becoming beats. Scratchings, regularising. There's a pulse. There's beginning.

And now melody. Now a tune of sorts. Randomness, taking form. Order, emergent.

Recognition. We know this music. It's a song—a decelerated song. This is *Ceremony*, slowed down five hundred times.

And now the Dane, pressing the Scandohorn to his lips. Now the Dane, all breath, playing the sound of the wind over the Scando-fjords. Now the Dane, playing Danish shepherding songs; Danish *kulnings*, like you hear in Tarkovsky's *Sacrifice*.

*To be or not to be*: that's the Dane's question. *Not to be*, says his Scandohorn. *Never to have been.*

Now the Dane, playing his mourning song. His life-lament. Danish *tungsind*. As sad as a Viking burial. As sad as Kierkegaard on the cliffs of Gilleleje . . .

The Dane, playing the fallen. Playing the utter-dark. The billowing ice-wastes. The frozen sorrow of life. The snowbound sadness of being . . .

Look, the Dane's even made Weep weep. Merryn Weep, tears in her eyes. Severina Weep, eyes crystalline.

## 16

**RECREATING TARKOVSKY'S *NOSTALGHIA TODAY*.** The flooded church scene.

The culvert.

I think those are cave paintings, Ismail says.

Of cocks? Valentine asks.

Graffiti on the walls. *TRUE LIFE BEGINS AT THE POINT OF NO RETURN. I AM THE INSURRECTION, THE HATRED AND THE FURY. LIVING LIFE ONE NIGHTMARE AT A TIME. ALL THE DOORS ARE OPEN BUT THERE'S NO WAY OUT.* Not your usual Northenden boys smut.

Descent. Voyage to the centre of the Earth.

Fallen bricks. Running water. Wet shrooms, growing in darkness.

What's that slurping sound? I ask. Something's eating something.

God, everything's covered in slime, Gita says. Everything's *glistening*. It's all sticky. There's stuff, like, drooling from the rocks . . .

The perfect spot, Marcie says.

Setting up the camera.

This is the brief: Gorchakov—that's you, Marcie—is drunk, Ismail says.

Oh good—I can do drunk, Marcie says, unscrewing her hipflask. Pickleback, anyone?

Ismail, preparing Marcie. Gorchakov's full of impossible longing, an absolute desire for the presence of the divine. For transcendence— for the vertical—and not just the high indifference of the sky.

Gorchakov's looking for some constancy, a centre from which to act, Ismail explains. In the midst of a world that goes wrong every time, where love and serenity do not last.

Gorchakov's overwhelmed by the sense of the *futility of human endeavour*, Ismail explains. The sense that our path can only lead to destruction. He's nostalgic for a vanished state of harmony . . . for a wholeness of existence.

Just think of old Liverpool, Valentine says. The Liverpool of your distant girlhood. Sofas on the front lawn . . . tinnies in your hand . . . swearwords on your lips . . .

Me, singing *Ferry Cross the Mersey*.

Marcie. Fuck *off*!

Come on, den mom—think deep European *Weltschmerz*, we say. You're overseas, in exile! You miss your wife and children! You yearn for the motherland! The Russian chernozem!

Me, singing *We'll Never Walk Alone*.

Marcie. You *fucking fuckers*. I'm trying to get into my role.

Now you have to stagger towards the camera, reciting something profound, we say. Give us some French prose-poetry philosophy stuff, den mom. Something *profoundly European*.

I don't know anything *profoundly European*, Marcie says. Except *Frère Jacques*. Does that count?

Okay, we need a prop . . . Your character's carrying a book, den mom, we say. Did anyone bring a book with them?

Valentine, opening his manbag. *The Writing of the Disaster*: the foundational text of Disaster Studies.

I carry it everywhere, Valentine says. I don't understand a word.

Ready to shoot? Ismail asks.

Lights, camera, action.

Take one. Marcie, stumbling into frame, looking glum. *Frère Jacques, Frère Jacques, / Dormez-vous? Dormez-vous?*

Enough! Ismail says. Shut up!

*Such* a fascist, Valentine says. Quite a turn-on, actually.

Take two.

Marcie, staggering, stumbling, sloshing through the puddles. I'm doomed. *Doooomed!*

That's too much, Ismail says. Too theatrical. This is supposed to be *Russian* drunkenness. It's more interior . . . more tortured . . .

Take three.

Marcie, staggering, jumping in puddles.

This isn't *Singing in the Fucking Rain*, Valentine says. This is arthouse, den mom! *ARTHOUSE!*

She looks kind of constipated, I say.

Okay, Marcie—this isn't working, Ismail says.

Let Business Studies Guy have a go, Valentine says.

Shrugs. Why not?

Take four.

Business Studies Guy, staggering into frame. Business Studies Guy, reciting: *Late is early, near is far; we are neither ahead nor be-*

*hind. Shining solitude, the void of the sky . . . It is the dark disaster that brings the light.*

He can do it! Valentine says. By God, he knows it by heart!

And the echo makes Business Studies Guy sound really profound, I say.

Business Studies Guy, reciting: *Straight roads, eternal, under a scratched-out sky. The void of the future. The void of the past. Keep watch over absent meaning. Voice of no one, once more.*

That fucker, Valentine says. He has the edge on us.

Business Studies Guy, reciting: *The lapse of time. The unbridgeable interval. The retreat of the cosmos. The secret escapes; it is never circumscribed; it makes itself boundless.*

He's going to become some great philosopher, isn't he? I say. Some great European-style prose-poetry philosopher, with all the languages . . .

Don't forget that we nurtured you, Business Studies Guy, Valentine says. Den mom basically suckled you. She actually *gave birth* to you . . .


# 17

## BAND NIGHT, AT TWISTED WHEEL.

First bands: Junk DNA (sort of DC punk stylings). Deaths of Despair (keyboardy new wave soundalikes). Xombies of a Lesser God (hardcore soundalikes) . . .

Rock school bands, playing rock school music. They're all tribute acts, basically. They're reenactors. Pop simulacra. Heritage rocksters. The whole thing's in quotation marks . . .

More bands: Moss Side Gnostics (they're actually from Withington). Obsidian Mirror (a prog band from Hyde). The Lucy Balloon (landfill indie). Trailing Ash (more indie). The Ingrates (still more indie). The Goats of Wrath (indie squared) . . .

This music isn't Necessary. It doesn't *have to exist*. It doesn't know the disaster—doesn't *feel* it.

It knows nothing of running out of time. Of running out of air. Of death a thousand times over. Of death and then death again. Of cosmic corruption.

It knows nothing of *NOTHINGNESS* in capital letters. Nothing of *ARDENCY*. There's no *becoming* here. No trafficking with chaos.

There's no *anarchy* to this music. No nihilation. No hatred. It's not close to the *lumpensprung* . . .

No one would live or die for *this* music. No one would sell their soul to the devil to make *this* music . . .

Unferocious music. Unangry music. Music unmad, unfurious, un-queer, unhating. Corporate alternative. Verse-chorus blandishment watered down and down.

Entertainment music. Diversion music. Music to distract you while they thin out the herd. While they implement the new reality. While they intensify the *staggered democide*.

And worse: *mass hypnosis* music. *Mass formation* music. New World Order music, about the uselessness of resistance. Part of some plot to *weaken youth*. To keep us in infancy. To revel in indie sad-boy helplessness.

It's not even mancunian, this music. It doesn't *taste* mancunian. It didn't grow from the mancunian terroir. This is Smart City music, about everything but *this* city. This is music for the Sectors. For the fifteen-minute neighbourhoods.

Knowing nothing of *mancunian despair*. Of *mancunian melancholy*. It's oblivious to the *mancunian black sun*. To outbreaks of *mancunian evil*. To mancunian evil massing like clouds.

With no memory of the *great* mancunian music. That groaned for redemption. Lifted itself to be blessed. Waited for the touch of God on its fevered brow. For the kiss of God on its febrile forehead.

No trace of great mancunian music, soaring in its despair.

Touching despair's roof. Touching despair's sky. Rising against gravity. Rising—touching the sky. Raising its cry. Falling back . . . Mancunian music, breaking itself against the prison-sky.

## 18

### SUNDAY.

Gita and I, Beech Road Vintage.

Enter Valentine and Marcie.

No wonder no one ever comes in here, Valentine says. There's nothing *in* this shop.

There's a worldwide shortage of vintage, Gita says. They're actually running out.

I thought there'd always be old things, Valentine says.

Vintage stops at the end of the '80s, Gita says. Big shoulders, structured suits, power dressing, etc. There aren't any vintage styles after that. There's no post-'80s look. It's just pastiche or *clothing solutions*.

This is a nostalgia shop, Valentine says.

It's a nostalgia for vintage shop, I say.

How does it get by without any customers? Valentine asks.

Because the Man approves of vintage shops, idiot, Marcie says. Because the Man likes *local colour*, a bit of funky alternative life. The Man likes to play-pretend edgy. The Man likes somewhere to mooch around on a Sunday.

The Man would like a *profit*, I would have thought, Gita says.

Ask yourself who funds Beech Road Vintage, Marcie says.

No one funds it, Gita says. It's just a shop.

With no customers? Marcie asks.

So it's a front? Gita asks. Come on, I know the owner—Lorna. She's not *the Man*. She's sound.

But is she the *real* owner? Marcie asks. Is she the one who's actually behind the scenes? I'll bet Topshop or someone keeps this place afloat. They probably pay Lorna a stipend, or secretly cover half her rent. Just like Amazon subsidises all these old bookshops.

Because the Man likes a thriving local ecology of shops, Marcie says. He likes cute little businesses. He loves good pesto and good pasta. He's into a bit of crate-digging—he approves of Alt Vinyl. He wants to add to his collection of vintage tees, so he likes this place, too. And he likes our kind being round here. Mavericks. Creatives...

Yeah, but we hate the Man, I say.

The Man loves being hated, Marcie says. He likes *pushback*. It tickles him. See, the Man's already got world domination. That's easy. But he wants a bit of countercultural life, for the moment at least... The Man likes to *play alternative* just like Marie Antoinette liked to play shepherdess...


## 19

NIGHT, AFTER RUIN BAR.

Me, visiting Gita's house.

Your room's so *big*, I say.

It's the old drawing room, Gita says.

I don't even know what a drawing room *is*, I say.

The best room in the house—where they'd bring guests to impress them, Gita says. Victorian England was all about tiny social gradations.

It's so *cold*, I say. It's going to take ages to warm up.

Gita, throwing over a quilt. Wrap yourself in this.

There was a charity that made quilts for us when I was in the Home, I say. I loved mine. I always thought if I could hang on to it, then everything would be okay. So long as my quilt wasn't lost, I wouldn't be either.

God, Johnny—your life, Gita says.

Admiring Gita's Chinese screens. Admiring her scarves and silks.

Admiring the peacock feathers in a jar. The various *objets d'art*. The rails of clothes . . .

You've made a home in Manchester, I say. You've found all this cool stuff.

It's flea-market stuff, Gita says. Vintage stuff.

You're a curator, I say. You're saving all these things from oblivion. They'd all be forgotten if it wasn't for you.

Someone else would have bought them, Gita says.

But they wouldn't have put it all together like this, I say. You're wasted in philosophy. You should design interiors for tosser London billionaires or something. There's got to be money in it.

You're taking the piss, Gita says. I'll bet you despise the domestic, like the other guys. I'll bet you think it's something real thinkers aren't concerned with. Like it's just so much frippery—triviality— far beneath the philosophical mind.

Gita's music.

Of course it's *classical* music, I say. It would have to be classical music. And this is *classical* classical music. Like, Mozart or something. It's not even all fracturedly modernist. It's not even discordant. It's not something Adorno would write about. I'll bet the SS would have listened to this stuff in their spare time . . .

Stop channelling the other guys, Gita says, pouring wine. It's tedious.

And it would have to be wine, I say. I'll bet you have the best wine . . .

Don't go all faux street urchin on me, little orphan Johnny, Gita says. You know what wine is.

Inspecting Gita's bookshelves.

You should burn some of your sitting-on-the-fence books, if you really want to go full-blown *European*, I say. Fuck Rorty! Fuck *Habermas*! There are certain books you should have on your bookshelf, Valentine would say, and certain books you shouldn't . . .

Oh, do piss off, Johnny, Gita says.

Des Forêts, Roger Laporte . . . Imagine—you actually read French, I say. You can just, like, open a French novel and read it . . .

You can pick up French—it's not that big a deal, Gita says. If you guys spent half the time actually trying to learn things rather than complaining about *not* knowing them . . .

The thing is I've always thought I *deserve* being able to read in French, I say.

So take some lessons, Gita says.

I'd like to write a book one day, I say. Not something academic.

What would you write about? Gita asks.

All this, maybe, I say. Gita Mukherjee and her Chinese screen and her antique washstand and her peacock feathers and her Indian miniatures and the infinite expanse of her floorboards in her freezing drawing room slash bedroom . . . I'll write about her full-length mirror and her chamber music and her wine and her books in French . . .

Are you sure you aren't taking the piss? Gita says.

It's still fucking freezing, I say.

Get into bed, if you like, Gita says.

Gita's futon. Under the duvet. Under layers of blankets.

Gita, climbing in next to me.

I warn you—I'm a couple of glasses of wine away from making a pass at you, I say.

That . . . wouldn't . . . be . . . a . . . good . . . thing, Gita says.

Why not? I say. Why—*really*—not? Don't you see—this might be a chance.

A chance for what? Gita asks.

For the same not to be the same, I say. For one day not to follow another. For the inevitable not to be inevitable. For cog not to be locked into cog . . . Wouldn't you like to think that we're on the brink of something? That something's about to happen?

You sound like Ismail, Gita says.

Let's get drunk, I say. Let's let the drink decide.

Let's *not*, Gita says. I'm tired of blundering into things. I'm sick of mid-twenties relationships where no one knows what they want, where friendship becomes love and love becomes … . what? That's your twenties, right—trying out romance. Getting it wrong. Because there's still time for fuck-ups, supposedly. Because it's not got all *urgent* yet.

You apparently get very self-reflexive in your mid-twenties, I say. Talking about being in your mid-twenties is a sign of being in your mid-twenties …

See, we're all so *clever*, aren't we? Gita says. We're clever about everything … We shouldn't just play with our lives—that's all I know. We shouldn't play with the flame of life. We can't just go from lover to lover …

Valentine does, I say.

Valentine's a slut, Gita says.

More wine.

It's all okay for you because you'll have an actual girlfriend—one day, at least, I say. Whereas I'll have … I don't know that.

Have you ever had a *proper relationship*? Gita asks.

Like, where you live with each other and stuff? I say. No.

Or even where someone calls you their *boyfriend* or *partner* or whatever? Gita asks.

Shaking my head. How about you? I ask.

Sure … there have been … people, Gita says.

Guys? I ask.

Guys—not gals, Gita says. So nothing real.

What about Russell? I ask.

Russell doesn't count, Gita says. Russell was my last heterosexual hurrah … Look, I came to Manchester to find out who I was—what I wanted. And then I got waylaid …

Didn't we all? I say.

I think we *like* failing at romance, Gita says. Maybe that's what we have in common.

Maybe we just want to be outside romance for a bit, I say. Just . . . contemplating the *possibility* of romance rather than *doing* anything. It's a postgraduate thing . . . Just like we're outside of real life, contemplating the possibility of real life . . .

I've always thought it'd be simple when you met the right person, Gita says. That everything would, like, flow.

See, you're basically pre-Relationship, capital R, I say. You'll only make sense in your Relationship-to-Come. And everything prior to that will have been the before-times. Your whole life in Manchester will have been a period of uncertainty and confusion. You won't even remember any of this—not really. *It was a bad time for me*, you'll say. *I didn't know what I was doing.*

What about you, Johnny? Gita says. You'll find someone. You'll shack up with some fella.

I want to be no one at all and nothing at all, I say. Just disappear.

That's not what you want, Gita says. I don't believe it. Stop saying those things.

Never mind me, I say. I'm used to this cruel old world.

What do you *want* in your heart of hearts? Gita asks.

You, maybe, I say.

Stop it, Gita says. Come on—*tell* me.

How am I supposed to know what . . . I . . . want? I ask. Maybe I'm not *even* gay. Like I'm not *even* straight. I'm not *even* anything . . . I don't know . . .

# CHAPTER 4

**1**

METHOD CLASS.

Monday morning again! Opening our eyes again! Knowing ourselves alive again! The curse of time again! The fact there's always more—again!

Even to have opened our eyes. Even to have opened the curtains. Even to *be outside* . . .

We don't want this. We want nothing of this world, the early-morning world.

We're late-morning wakers. We want to sidle into the world when it's calmed down after rush hour. After all the commuters. After the school-run. We want nothing to do with the busyness of the morning.

Why get us up this early? Is it some kind of experiment? Some act of cruelty? Is it a psychological trick? A method of torture?

They're deliberately destroying our morning. They're deliberately lifting our rock. They're deliberately poking us with sticks. They're deliberately removing us from our comforts. From our morning rituals.

Don't they know how close to insanity we are? Don't they know we're sensitives? That we're weak vessels? That we're mini Hölderlins, pocket Sarah Kanes, Georg Büchners in training? Don't they know that we might just *snap*?

Unless that is the point: to destroy us, psychologically. To finish us off. No—to compel us to finish *ourselves* off. To make us do it to ourselves. To tidy away our own mess. To negate our negation . . .

How *blithe* the Business Studies PhD students are! How cheerful! They're all but whistling! They seem to lack any sense of the *indecency of good cheer*, especially at this time in the morning. They don't see that their brazen happiness displays *a basic lack of understanding of the situation in which we find ourselve*s.

False PhD students among us. Aims-and-objectives students, bullet points students, among our body. Do you think they'd even pass the Turing test? Search their eyes—what do you see? Has the light completely gone out? Are there horrific moments of self-awareness?

A screaming inside . . . Eyes open in alarm . . . In blank horror . . . *Help me*, on the lips . . . But it's too late to help. The only thing for it: a clean break. A quick death. A mercy-killing. If only it were legal . . .

Hope. Perhaps there are *Marrano philosophers* amongst them. Secret philosophers. Humanities types in hiding, who dare not speak their name, reading *From Cult to Culture* under their Business Studies desks. Humanities types, driven underground. Driven to disguise themselves. Who applied for Business Studies scholarships so they could hide among the braindead.

There are probably secret signs. Ways of communicating like Polari or Pitmatic. Ways of signalling a secret interest in Vaneigem or The Invisible Committee.

But no one's signalling to us, not today . . .

## 2

### BADMINTON PRACTICE.

Working on Business Studies Guy's *explosive start*. On the speed of his *first step and push off.* The badminton *Ursprung*. Nothing more important.

Business Studies Guy, in front defence stance. Trunk upright, head upright, knees flexed. Stepping towards the right forecourt, then pushing back to the stance. Stepping towards the left forecourt, the right midcourt, the left midcourt, etc.

Trying to conceal our excitement. Perhaps badminton's the only thing that isn't farce, Business Studies Guy. Or it's so farcical that it isn't farcical anymore—one of the two.

Either way, winning the Manchester Postgraduate Badminton Cup is the way we'll lift farce into seriousness—into *farcical* seriousness.

## 3

### LIFE AT MICHAEL'S, ACCORDING TO ISMAIL.

Michael, bringing in bags of food whenever he goes out: lavash bread from the Arab grocery, dolmades and olives from the Greek one; black loaves of Polish bread; German pumpernickel. Sending Ismail out to the supermarket with forty quid: *Bring back things for an amazing salad, my dear.*

Buy-in feasts at the weekend. Fish 'n' chips on Saturday night. Kleftiko, from Kyria Tina's. Takeaways from the Nehmet Kadah. And when money comes, we all go out to dine. Michelangelo's on the high street—a whole fish each, sliced open. Renos's, for meze plates that keep coming all night until you're completely stuffed . . .

And does Simone go? I ask.

Sure she does, Ismail says. You know Michael—he insists. Anyway, she likes it—you can tell. Though she always chooses the most austere thing on the menu . . .

Ismail, describing visitors on short and long orbits around Michael's house. Different monks and sets of priests. Father Kallistos, from Wales. Two nut-brown Copts. And scholarly callers: a translator, consulting on his rendering of the Vedas. A disappointed ex-PhD student in dispute with Victoria Uni.

And old friends: a former nun and her autistic son. A Ukranian Catholic priest, lodging for a while to learn English. An AA-member Nebraskan, gorging on three-litre bottles of Coke and whole roast chickens.

And where does Simone fit in? I ask.

Simone's part of it, Ismail says. She's woven in. Just like everyone's woven in at Michael's. Everyone has their place.

How come Michael knows how to live? I ask.

He just loves things happening around him, Ismail says.

Imagine having friends like that . . . , I say. Will we ever have friends like that? Will we ever have *old friends*?

# 4

**OH GOD, WHY ARE WE GOING TO A VICTORIA PHD STUDENT SOIREE?** Why are we walking the streets in the direction of the Victoria PhD student soiree? Why are we essentially *leaving Manchester* to go to the Victoria PhD student soiree?

Agreement: We'll have to be *magnificently drunk* when we arrive at the Victoria PhD student soiree. We'll have to be gloriously berserk, as though we'd drunk a hundred macchiatos and a hundred picklebacks, when we step through the door into the Victoria PhD student soiree.

Why did they think to invite us—*us*—to such a function? Don't they know that we've been raised beneath black skies? That we're all but *suicide bombers*? That we're the kind of people who form *terror cells*?

Don't they know we're full of bad news—*diabolical* news? That we bear the *negative revelation*? Don't they see it in our eyes: that we're *final*, somehow? That we've been to the end and back?

Don't they know how we *burn*? How fast our hearts beat? Don't they know we're full of *monstrous dreams*? That we have histories of *divine violence*?

Don't they know we're too *raw* for polite company? That we've gone all buckled and warped—all bent out of shape? That we've turned strange—that we've turned each other stranger? Don't they know there are no *rounded personalities* amongst us? That we've no *breadth of character*? Don't they know that we're just obsessions and fetishes and strange compulsions?

We're *beasts of the lower classes*. We come from outside—from the wasteland *out there*. We're creatures of the ruins, and the ruins are our destiny. But perhaps that's why they've invited us: to see what creatures of the ruins look like.

Drinking on the bus.

We need to settle our nerves. To make it all more natural.

We're not going to get pissed, right? I say.

Maybe we should, Valentine says. It'd make it easier. We'd feel less awkward.

We shouldn't get pissed, I say. We shouldn't live up to the stereotype.

Maybe they're getting pissed, too, at the thought of our coming, Valentine says.

They don't give a fuck about our coming—that's the point, Marcie says. We're local peasantry. We're nothing to them.

So why have they invited us along? we wonder.

They just want a bit of All Saints rough, we agree. A bit of fresh, working-class blood. For the novelty. To satisfy mild curiosity. To have a *slightly different kind of evening*.

They need us—they need our *life*, we agree. The bourgeois want to

153

plug into lower-class electricity. They're bored of themselves. They're tired of *middle-class mildness* . . .

Well, they've unleashed the chaos now, we agree. They'll regret it. We'll destroy their fucking place. We're wild, compared to them. Barbarians! Fanatics! We all but foam at the mouth!

We've lost the run of ourselves, we agree. But then we never *had* the run of ourselves, not really. Why did they think they could awaken the forces of destruction? Why did they suppose they could *poke the monster in the eye*?

The thing is, they're probably *harder* than we are, we agree. They probably did tae kwon do at school or something. They're probably training for the coming prole riots. They'll probably put us all in chokeholds . . .

Through Fallowfield. Through Withington.

Manchester's opening out. Manchester's becoming civilised. There's no one scary on the bus. No maniacs in sight. No police helicopters flying overhead. No police car sirens. And the sky isn't orange anymore . . .

Why don't we move further out? Why don't we begin again, out here?

Because we couldn't afford it . . .

Where are we going? Why are we bothering? The Morlocks should never consort with the Eloi. The underground shouldn't mix with the overground.

Class anxiety. Didn't Marcie herself confess to *wine embarrassment*, back at the off-license? Didn't she say she didn't know what wine to buy? That she had no idea what was good or bad? *Marcie—embarrassed!*

Mustn't we hate the Victoria PhD students for making us feel like that? For making Marcie—*Marcie!*—feel awkward. Marcie's a force of life . . . Den mom's tremendous . . . They should be afraid of her. Should cower before her. Should want to placate her. Make offerings . . .

Fuck it, they should kneel before *all* of us, the Victoria PhD students! Before our natural anarchy! Before our unfittingness with the bourgeois world! Before our lack of manners! Our crudenesses! Before our *appalling formal education*! Before the vastness of our ignorance!.

We're twisted beings! Forced in upon themselves! Contorted! Full of hatred and ultra-hatred! Wasters and ne'er-do-wells! Witless! Immature! Developing serious addictions!

The Victoria PhD students were actually born to academia, not like us. They're probably from old academic families. Breeding-lines of brilliances. Intellectual life always surrounded them. Radio 3 burbled by their cradles.

They probably grew up surrounded by Penguin Classics, the Victoria PhD students. Art reproductions of the Old Masters. They're at ease with Culture, capital C, just as they're at ease with their old furniture. With the old names. Oh, *Browning*... Oh, *Meredith*... Like old teddy bears. Like comfy sweaters.

They're probably used to the *finer things in life*, the Victoria PhD students. To William Morris wallpaper and open fires and reclining on chaise longues and taking long country walks.

They probably know all these bits of poetry, the Victoria PhD students. Can quote things off the top of their heads. They're probably witty. Bon mots for every occasion ... Aperçus ... They're not barbarians like us. They're not *puerile*. (What's it like, not to be puerile?)

They probably speak other languages, like, effortlessly—from childhood—the Victoria PhD students. That they're not struggling to *learn on the fly*. That they don't even *need* for their scholarly work. They could read continental philosophy in the original, if they wanted to, the Victoria PhD students. If they *deigned* to. If they were even interested in continental philosophy, which they're not.

They're not drawn to wild European ideas as we are, the Victoria PhD students. They don't feel the pull of the crazy continental stuff, of the can't-get-over-the-death-of-God stuff, of the using-big-vague-words-like-*nothingness* stuff, as we do. They're guardians of all the so-called intellectual virtues, the Victoria PhD students. They know how to debate—how to put forward an argument. They don't take everything *personally*, like us. They're not all *touchy*.

They haven't been *malformed by the attempt to think*, the Victoria PhD students. They've not been pulled in strange directions. They don't feel rushes of ecstasy, nor the undertow of despair. They've never been essentially *scared for their sanity*.

And they didn't have to fight their way into the academy, the Victoria University PhD students. They didn't have to turn their backs on everyone they knew. They didn't have to become *weirdoes of the century* to their friends and families. They didn't have to essentially *renounce their social class* to pursue their studies, the Victoria PhD students. They didn't have to all but take *elocution lessons* to be able to utter a fucking word.

They're sensible people, the Victoria PhD students. Calm people. They're not overwhelmed by the *thirst for annihilation*. They're not calling in their hearts for the *grace of destruction*. They don't look up at the sky in dread and horror. They don't think of their lives as weeping sores. They don't whisper the word *apocalypse* to themselves over and over.

Didsbury. Alighting.

Is this where the Man lives? we wonder. It must be.

White man's country, right? Straight man's country. Cis man's country . . .

But it's so *pretty*, I say.

Of course it's pretty, Marcie says. The Man likes pretty.

The legendary Didsbury calm. The legendary Didsbury prosperity.

The pavements are wider out here. More room to walk, to think, to contemplate, out here. The sky's bigger—broader.

And there are *trees*. Mature *Didsbury trees*. Exhaling oxygen into the *Didsbury air*. Where else would the Victoria PhD students live? How far we are from Trouble! No one to fear here! No meths drinkers, addicts, day-ghouls! No human shells, just about alive! No street soldiers, testosteroned up! No death-starers! No human wolves assessing you—weighing you up at a glance!

You don't have to scan the shadows, likes soldiers on patrol. You don't have to be afraid of the dark.

You could just sink into yourself, if you wanted to. Forget where you are. Daydream, drift.

You couldn't roam like this in any other part of Manchester. It's like having the freedom of the city . . .

Calm streets. Sober avenues.

This is where the *professional intellectuals* live. *London Review of Books* reviewers. Radio 4 contributors. Lecturers who write for the so-called general public, by which they mean the *Didsbury* public.

This is where they make good on their fee-paying educations. On their prestigious-university undergraduate studies. This is where they'll reach full *Didsbury maturity*, full *Didsbury wisdom*. This is where they'll unfold all their potential.

Because they'll have time to think in these safe and sober streets. The leisure to think—the calm. They won't be foamers-at-the-mouth like us. They aren't wild conspiracy theorists. *Measure*—that's what they'll show. *Balance*—considering things in the round, from all angles.

Undisastrous thought. Unapocalyptic thought. Things-have-always-been-this-way thought. Things-will-always-be-this-way thought. Untroubled thought. Unruffled thought. Unhating. Unextreme.

They're not *thinkers of our times*, the *Didsbury intellectuals*. It's not a permanent state of emergency for them. They're not gasping for intellectual breath. They're not reeling from intellectual blows.

They've not been driven mad, the *Didsbury intellectuals*. They're not screaming in the head. They're not running barefoot in the head. *Didsbury intellectuals*, defusing every culture-bomb. Making things safe for the rest of us. *Didsbury intellectuals*: framers. Contextualisers. *Didsbury intellectuals*, reassuring us that everything can be thought, discussed, explained, and calmly . . . That everything can be written about in full sentences, not telegraphic bursts . . . That there's no need for a single exclamation mark! never a single ellipsis . . . That nothing will ever have to be said *IN CAPITALS* . . .

Coming closer. What's our strategy going to be? How are we going to deal with the soiree? Are we ready for light conversation? Nibbles?

Don't get too comfortable! Too drawn in! Don't eat their vol-au-vents or whatever! This is enemy territory! This is their terrain! They're used to this! This is what they do every day! This is *their* reality, not ours . . . !

Should we keep tight-lipped? Dignified? Like noble savages? Just nod sagely when we're spoken to? Appear as though we're in possession of significant wisdom?

Just so long as we don't live up to the clichés, I say. Like, what they expect of us. So long as we aren't total barbarians . . .

But we *are* barbarians! That's how we should act: *barbarously*! We shouldn't disappoint. We should live up to our reputations. We should do our bit for the class war. Throw their vol-au-vents around the room. Climb on the table and go all death chimp. Scoop up handfuls of food and just pelt the fools . . .

I hope we can dance, Valentine says. I hope they know that *proles wanna dance*.

I don't think you dance at a soiree, Marcie says.

Will we have to make small talk? I ask. I know these things are all about small talk. Where you discuss skiing or whatever.

Yeah—microhumiliation stuff, Marcie says. That's where the class system really operates.

Jesus—I've got stage fright, I say.

Fuck that, Valentine says. I feel defiant. I feel *angry* ..

I wish we were drunk—properly *fatalised*, I say. I wish we were as red-eyed as werewolves ...

Their house, all lights on. People sitting outside, smoking.

God, they're so *tall*, Valentine says. So healthy-looking.

Is it too late to bail? Too late to head for home?

Gita, waving from the front door. Where *were* you guys?

After. Walking to the bus stop.

Fuck, Marcie says. Fuck.

We were played, Valentine says. We were *duped*.

I think they liked you, Gita says. I think you did your bit for All-Saints-slash-Victoria-PhD-student relations.

Sure—they thought we were *colourful*, Marcie says. As though they were at the zoo or something.

They're like the royals on tour, Valentine says. They take it all in their stride. Like nothing human is strange to them ...

I hate the way we were given the spotlight in turn, Ismail says. Permitted our little idiosyncrasies—our little turns. It's containment. I mean, they even had *you* cowed, Marcie.

They made me feel like a fucking *impostor*, Marcie says.

See, if we were really lumpen, we would have started a fight, I say.

Which we'd *lose*, Marcie says. Those posh boys learn boxing at school.

Yeah, but we'd fight dirty, Valentine says. We'd bite and stuff. We'd foam at the mouth like rabid dogs.

If we were truly lumpen we wouldn't have gone in the first place, Marcie says. Just robbed the place. And burnt it down to destroy the evidence.

They weren't actually rude, Gita says.

They were disdainful, I say. They were all but tittering at us.

I actually thought they were being *nice*, Gita says. I don't see why you guys have to get so hysterical.

It's what they do to us, Marcie says. It's what class war looks like, Gita—centuries of it. It's microaggression after aggression! It's microassault and battery!

Why do you have to be so sensitive? Gita asks.

My God, don't they know how much we hate them? Marcie says.

Or even *that* we hate them? Valentine says.

There's so much ferocity in us, we agree. They should have felt afraid, like the Romanovs before Rasputin. They should have known terrible deeds were afoot. That there was *wild divine violence* on the horizon. They should have felt some augury of the end—of their murder. They should have known that we were their gravediggers—*spiritually*, if not actually.

Gravediggers?! Valentine says. We actually *deferred* to them.

*I* didn't, Marcie says.

You were bowing and scraping like the rest of us, Valentine says. Typical working-class fascination with aristos and pseudo-aristos.

We were gauche in a thousand ways, we agree. We embarrassed ourselves . . . We made things worse . . . Why did we have to tell them about Vortek's terrorist plans? About Valentine's human sacrifice plans? About den mom's faith in lumpen non-plans? About our futile resistance to the Man?

And then there was *Gnosticism*. Why did we have to bring up Gnosticism?! When prophecy fails, apocalypticism arises—that's what we told them. And when apocalypticism fails, Gnosticism comes to stand at the door . . .

We spoke of our ur-disgust. Of our *all*-disgust, and they looked at us, nonplussed. We told them about divine self-hatred. About God as sacrilege. About positing God only to murder him anew, and they looked at us, nonplussed. We told them that God exists only in his death, his expulsion, his violation, and they looked at us, nonplussed.

We spoke of the death of Man, of decreation and destitution, and they looked at us, nonplussed. We spoke of the necessity of forgetting, of thoughts out of use, of philosophy left idle, and they looked at us, nonplussed.

We told them of our desire to write of the illimitable *as* the illimitable. To know dissolution *as* dissolution, and they looked at us, nonplussed. We told them how we wanted to *un*write with our writing. To *un*study with our studies, and they looked at us, nonplussed. We told them we wanted to seize upon study itself. To write of the *time* of study. The time of learning. We told them that the time of study must also be the study of time, and they looked at us, nonplussed.

And we began to feel nonplussed ourselves! We began to doubt ourselves! Second-guess ourselves! Judge ourselves! Think ourselves wrong! They made us hate ourselves, when we should be hating *them*.

And the way they *sipped* their drinks . . . They're not guzzlers, like us. They weren't looking to *drown themselves in alcohol*, like we were.

It wasn't *emergency* drinking. *Desperation* drinking. They didn't drink because they needed the antidote—and *fast*.

They weren't *apocalyptic* drinkers, like we are. They weren't *eschatological* drinkers. They didn't drink because they're thirsty for the end, and the end never came.

They weren't waiting for the drunken *Kairos*—for the drunken Moment. For the Moment they'd miss *because* of their drunkenness.

They didn't decide to *meet us in alcoholism*, which would be true hospitality. They didn't try to reach out to us through inebriation. To heal the All Saints/Victoria divide through deliberate hangover-manufacture. By following *pickleback logic* with us to the end of the night . . .

Revenge on the Victoria PhD students: that's what we need. Victory! To reset the agenda! To move the debate onto another plane!

161

Marcie will have to take up badminton again, quite clearly. She'll have to reenter the fray, win the Manchester Postgraduate Badminton Tournament. There's the honour of All Saints to think of . . .

## 5

### ON THE EES.

The forgotten church. Nearly overgrown. Sinking under the earth . . .

The church is being rewilded, just like the rest of the Ees . . .

It doesn't smell too good, we agree. It smells like shit . . .

*Pigeon* shit, I say, peering through a window-grille. There are pigeons inside, flying about.

I think this is *actually* the spot where God died, Valentine says. He couldn't stand the smell of pigeon shit . . .

The church is being reclaimed, we agree. The Ees has taken it. The Ees is working its changes. Soon, the spire will fall. The stained-glass windows, shatter. Waves of earth will bury everything. St David's, or whatever it's called, will become a crypt, a stone space underground. A catacomb open only to earthworms and moles . . .

The church, given over to oblivion. With no memory of its rituals. No memory of God. The church, forgetting itself. What it was for. What worship was. What the Cross was. The church, where darkness and silence worship themselves.

## 6

### THE FORGOTTEN GRAVEYARD, ALMOST COMPLETELY GROWN OVER. Names too faded to read.

They should have buried Ian Curtis here, we agree. And Mark E. Smith. And Tony Wilson. They should carry Morrissey here and lay him down when the time comes.

This is where everyone great should end up: in the forgotten graveyard. Because they can rest in forgetting, too. Because their grave-stones can be reclaimed by Ees peace, by Ees silence ...

Do you think our families would prefer us dead? Like, *safely mourn-able*? We wouldn't be such a problem anymore. So hard to work out. To talk to. To be with. Wouldn't it be easier for them if we were already dead and buried, and they could carry flowers to the gravestones?

And the uni would prefer it, too. We wouldn't be a problem for method class to solve. We wouldn't need instruction in the arts of study. We see it in our minds' eyes: our names, read out solemnly at graduation. A candlelit vigil, just for us. Dignitaries, leading a procession through the campus. The uni president herself, giving a speech. *The best and the brightest ... Following their passions ... Making a difference ... Believing in themselves ... Future academic leaders ... Addressing the most urgent societal problems ...* Each of us, awarded an honorary doctorate ...

# 7

## THE FORGOTTEN RECORDING STUDIO.

It's atmospheric, Valentine says.

It's derelict, I say.

No one's been here in a very long time, Ismail says.

How can you just abandon a building? I say. Doesn't anyone own it?

The Ees owns it now, Ismail says.

Blackened walls. Remnants of a fire. Crumpled beer cans.

A drinking den for Northenden boys.

Walking gingerly. Looking out for needles.

This is mancunian heritage, we agree. It's like Sun Studio. It's like Graceland. This is where Martin Hannett worked the mixing desk. It's where mancunian music became *world-historical*. There should be a memorial, not some giant tree growing through its middle ...

This must be where Joy Division demoed *Ceremony*. Four days before Ian Curtis hung himself . . .

And where New Order demoed *Movement*, a couple of months later. They'd come to Eschaton in all humility. They'd come, wondering whether their band could go on. And Martin Hannett, laughing at them. Martin Hannett, telling them they were *shit*.

Their frail, fragile sound. So weedy. So vulnerable. Recording *Ceremony* again, faster this time, with Barney singing. With Barney, before he could really sing.

And still mourning Ian Curtis. And still feeling his loss. And not knowing what they felt. And not knowing how to grieve. Still young—much younger than we are. Still not knowing their greatness . . .

(And isn't that our dream, too—that we might be great? That we, too, might stumble into greatness? That greatness might be our birthright after all? That greatness might enfold us in its wings?)

Before *Temptation*. Before they discovered sequencers. Before they built their own synths. Before they went to the disco. Before *Blue Monday* . .

Just drink up the ambience, Valentine says.

There's the theory that sound never dies, Ismail says. It floats around forever. So if you listen in the right way, we would hear *Ceremony* on the day it was first recorded.

If you *shroom in the right way*, more like, Marcie says. Maybe the Wizard could help . . .

# 8

REMAKING *STALKER*.

A rest-break.

Weep, eating some of Michael's leftovers.

Marcie and Valentine, taking a nap on the banks of the tiled pool. Business Studies Guy, recumbent on a low island, hand trailing in the water.

Ismail, dressing the set. Carefully placing in the pool: a packet of condoms, half covered in sediment, a dartboard, a gimp mask, two algae-covered shuttlecocks, a rusty sex toy . . .

Wandering into view: a dog. A black dog, coming down to the water . . . wading through the shallow pool.

She looks so *intelligent*, we agree. Her face is so alert. Her fur so burnished . . . lustrous. She's so lithe, so graceful. She's positively aristocratic. She must have *some* pedigree . . .

An Anubian Alsatian, Ismail says, marvelling. A Russian breed. Tarkovsky had one . . . He always has these dogs just *materialise* in his films . . .

So she's a Tarkovsky dog, straight from Russia! She's Tarkovsky, basically, in dog form—isn't that right, T-dog?

T-dog, looking at us curiously.

She should be our spirit animal, we agree. Our spirit seer. She's arthouse on four paws. A canine witness for *lofty spiritual seriousness*.

Do we charm her? Do you think she appreciates us? Does she have a working-class sense of humour?

T-dog, padding back into the mist.

Uh . . . She's off, guys, Valentine says. She's given up.

Who blames her?

## 9

### EVENING.

Gita, accompanying me on my rounds in Langford Hall.

Stairs up and down. Winding corridors. Kitchens, every now and again. Bathrooms, with vast bathtubs. Heavy firedoors. Fire regulations on big round stickers.

I can't believe you actually know your way round here, Gita says. It's all the same.

Not to the initiated, I say. Anyway, I like taking the most obscure, circuitous routes.

What are we supposed to be doing, anyway? Gita asks. What are the duties of an *assistant warden*?

Checking up on stuff, I say. Making sure everything's calm. That no one's here who shouldn't be. That no maniacs are trying to break in.

It's noble, Gita says. You're holding back the chaos.

And I've got to make sure the students are okay, I say.

Do you have to tell the students off? Gita asks. Do you act all stern?

They're fine, mostly, I say. They vape, play on their consoles . . .

With you watching over them, Gita says. You're the guy behind the scenes, unthanked, unnoticed . . .

Gita, reading out the door numbers.

Doesn't the fact that the students are just passing through bother them? Gita asks. The fact that they're just another wave of undergraduates, and that there'll be another wave of them coming next year . . .

I don't think they mind, I say. They like living here. All their needs are met, basically.

But this place is so impersonal—it's so *indifferent* to them, Gita says.

Yeah, but they're indifferent to the hall, too, I say.

God . . . No one knows how to *live* anymore, Gita says. Do you ever feel that? Like we've lost the arts of life . . . It's like the new halls they're building—have you seen those? Student pods stacked upon one another, with everything built in: bed and bathroom, microwave, games console, flat-screen TV. Student living solutions, with everything the modern student supposedly needs . . . At least this place has some atmosphere . . .

Downstairs.

A big framed photo of the current students.

Who are the hotties this year? Gita asks. Anyone take your fancy? Me, shrugging.

Oh, *this* guy's nice, Gita says. He's very pretty. He looks as sweet as you. Maybe you'd just cancel each other out . . .

Photos of the warden and her staff.

There you are, smiling out, Gita says. Johnny Obadeyi, one of the crew. What are the other assistant wardens like?

Nice, I say.

I'll bet you're a real favourite, Gita says. I'll bet they all love you. You're so meek and obedient and sweet . . . I'll bet you take on extra shifts . . . I'll bet you're really flexible about providing cover . . .

Sure, I say.

You know you're just another postgraduate assistant warden to them, don't you? Gita says. You know they have no idea who you are. You're *replaceable*.

I like that idea, I say.

I couldn't stand it, Gita says.

Because you're a prima ballerina, I say. You want to be the centre of everyone's attention.

Whereas you want to be the centre of *no one's* attention, Gita says. You *like* being a ghost.

I like the hall best in the holidays, I say. When all the undergraduates have gone home, and there are only a few foreign students floating about. I like the silence. I like the sense of space—the empty vastness. Your soul, like, *expands*—hovers in the nothingness. You *are* the nothingness, and the nothingness is you . . .

God, this place has really let you *come into your own* in some strange way, Gita says. You're actually at home here . . .

The Junior Common Room, by the refectory.

Armchairs. A table for flyers. Pigeonholes for mail. The hall noticeboard, with a poster for the Samaritans. *Whatever you're going through, a Samaritan will face it with you.*

The closed metal shutters of the bar.

It's open two evenings a week, I tell Gita.

I'll bet it's *lively*, Gita says.

There's a Hall Ball every year, I say. The Junior Common Room turns into a disco.

An *institutional* disco, Gita says. Like something you'd hold for mental patients. Sad, sad, sad . . . God, it really *smells* institutional, too. There's a real *eau d'institution* . .

And it's so *still*, Gita says. I'll bet everything's been exactly where it is for years. I don't believe anything has ever happened here. I don't believe, like, the '60s touched Langford Hall. I don't think *Madchester* could have reached it . . .

Peering through the reinforced glass of the refectory doors.

So you actually eat communal dinners? Gita asks.

Sure, I say.

*Institutional* dinners . . . , Gita says

And institutional breakfasts, I say.

I can just imagine it, Gita says. The clatter of plates and trays. Chairs scraping. Taking your seat with the other assistant wardens. Eating soggy toast. Making conversation.

Free board and lodging, I say. Comes with the job.

Sad, Johnny.

Not so sad, I say.


## 10

### WEDNESDAY.

Al's café.

There's a 70 percent chance we're living in a simulation—that's what they say, isn't it? Valentine says. That we're inside some app.

Some really crap app, called *Postgraduate Wankers*, Marcie says.

What do you think you're doing in real reality? Ismail asks.

Playing with myself, Marcie says.

So this is all your wank fantasy? Valentine says. Ismail—filming everything as usual. Johnny, writing *THE APOCALYPSE IS DISAPPOINTING* in the window condensation?

Reckon, Marcie says.

It's not much of a fucking wank fantasy, is it? Valentine says. Us sitting at Al's café. You've got to have better fantasies than *this*.

Maybe it's just *my* dream, actually, Marcie says. You guys are just recurring dream characters.

How do you know it's your dream and not, say, mine? Ismail asks.

Because it's all about *my* life, Marcie says.

Maybe it's someone else's *dream* about your life, Ismail says.

Don't fuck with my head, Marcie says. Not at this time in the morning.


## 11

RESEARCH FORUM, WAITING FOR THE GUEST SPEAKER, SITTING AT THE BACK AS USUAL.

To think, we used to sit at the front, Business Studies Guy. We used to want a *ringside view*. We'd all but sit in the lap of the guest speaker. We'd lean in, keenly taking notes. And then, in the Q&A, we'd listen in admiration to the All Saints lecturers, to Professor Deathly, Professor Earwig and co., with their long and complex questions...

We're old, Business Studies Guy—terribly old. We've seen every possible guest speaker. We're heard it all before—every position-taking; every thought-move and counter-move. We're tired of the theatre. We're jaded. We're past our prime.

We know we PhD students are supposed to *transfuse the uni's blood*, Business Studies Guy. We know we're supposed to be cute, like baby animals. We know we're supposed to be light relief: *the university at play*, all chipper and jolly, full of a bumbling freshness, keen to be among the grown-up lecturers. We know we're supposed to ask *postgraduate-appropriate questions* when guest speakers visit (guest speakers have to treat us gently . . . ).

We know we're here to be *petted*, essentially, Business Studies Guy. To be mini-mes—to remind lecturers of when they were gauche and keen and eager. We know we're here to be rubbed gently under the chin. To make up the background at departmental events, or when they take guest speakers to the pub. We know we're supposed to *disappear discretely* when lecturers go off for dinner. (No one would invite us. No one would pay for our meals . . . )

Postgraduates only exist in the plural, Business Studies Guy. There's supposed to be a haze of postgraduates at research fora and symposia. Sometimes lecturers might deign to talk to us, to join us for a smoke, to chat at the bar. We know that they might enjoy our youth, might hatch little infatuations—even little *affairs* (think of Gita). But we know no academic would ever bring one of us on their arm to a departmental party . . .

We're will-o'-the-wisps, in the end, Business Studies Guy. The lecturers are glad we're here. They nod to us as they pass. They know our faces, even if they don't know our names. But we're hardly the kind to hold on to.

We've grown too old, Business Studies Guy. We're not fun-sized any longer. We're not hatchlings. We don't look up to lecturers as we used to. We avoid their eyes. We don't want to be seen. We sit at the back. We're too old to be cute. We've become sullen, even aggressive. We're not going to ask any keen, puppyish questions. We're not looking to ingratiate ourselves with anyone.

Are we ready to fledge, Business Studies Guy? To make our way into the world? Not that, either. We don't want to stay, and we don't want to go. We remain on the threshold, like overgrown adolescents . . .

## 12

(THE DREAM OF WRITING A NON-DISSERTATION, WHERE THE NON- IS IN NO WAY
PRIVATIVE. *A dissertation not made of arguments but contradictions . . .
Inconsistencies . . .*
*Fractured syntax. Ellipses. Trailings-off. Never keeping to the point.
A record of irrelevancies. Insignificant events on insignificant days.
The stupid things we've said . . . The ways we've wasted time . . .
A non-dissertation, loyal to non-finishing. To incompletion. And
then submitted to God, the ultimate external examiner. Left in the
grass of the Ees, to be read by the sky . . . )*


## 13

THURSDAY.

Al's café.

Are we getting more depressed or less? we wonder. Is it getting better or worse?

Worse, Valentine says.

Yes, he's probably right . . .

So we haven't reached rock bottom yet? Things aren't yet on the turn for us?

I actually *long* for rock bottom, Marcie says. At least I'd be sure of something. At least there'd be firm ground.

Discussion. We've got *too much time*, that's the problem. There's always time to fill. Always the dissertation to write. Always stuff to be read. Life goes on and on and on . . .

Who let it happen? Who gave us all this time to waste? We should be working. Should be put to hard labour. Should be on a chain gang or something. Anything to stop this *dissolution*.

Are we actually supposed to be alive? Is this actually *it*? Will we be back here tomorrow and the day after that? Just as we were here yesterday and the day before that? All this time, and look what we're doing with it. Sitting here talking about meaninglessness and the fucking void, like every other continental philosophy PhD student who's ever lived . . .

Existentialist musings, a hundred years too late . . . Death of God piety . . . *Angst* piety . . . indigestible philosophies that we don't believe in . . .

Our crazed apocalypticism . . . The vast stupidities at work inside us . . . Our sense of how it is. How it must be. Of the inevitable inevitable. Of fate's fucking fate.

Disgust! Self-disgust! We never wanted to live. Nobody asked us. We weren't consulted. We were just thrown into the mess, and asked to make sense of it. Asked to make meaning all by ourselves. Asked to struggle *against the archons* all by ourselves.

All we see are dead people. All we see is death—even in the mirror. We're the end of something. Of some dreadful process . . . Some long degradation . . . We're chasing our tails. Living on the scraps of life thrown to us, like dogs. Lost in sloth, anomy, overwanking . . .

Isn't this just typical postgraduate self-hatred? Haven't we simply *internalised the hostility of the world*?

But maybe our kind *should* be hated, we muse. What do we actually contribute? The world doesn't need us. Our kind should have been bred out years ago. What happened to the survival of the fittest? Evolution, like, fucked up. We're *transcendentally useless* . .

Valentine, standing. Right, work time, he says. That's my talking-shit quota filled for the day. Back to the fortress of solitude . . .

Oh, come on—I don't think we've moaned quite enough yet, Marcie says.

I can feel the caffeine roaring in my veins, Valentine says. I think I'm going to write epochal things today.

No you don't, Marcie says.

No . . . I don't, Valentine says.

## 14

ON THE BUS. At the bus stop.

Why isn't it moving? Ismail asks.

A man, shouting outside. Shouting and shouting. About what? About drugs. About dealing. About corruption . . .

*That* guy, I say. He's like the terror of Chorlton. A care in the community case. *Fuck*—he's getting on.

The madman, coming past the booth. Not swiping, not paying.

The driver, not looking at him, wanting no trouble.

Silence on the bus. Fear.

The madman, coming up the aisle, slowly. Looking right into people's faces, very closely.

What's he looking for? What does he want?

And terrible anger in his face. Contortion. Knots.

How can anyone be that angry—that scary? How can anyone be that *pumped*?

Passengers, looking straight ahead. Not reacting. Not doing anything, hoping he might go away.

The madman, looking into faces. So close, so close.

The bus, unmoving, engine on.

The bus driver, sitting. Has he pressed a panic button? Is someone texting the police?

A woman, crying. Saying quietly: *Please go. Please go.*

The madman, looking into her face. Looking.

And across the way, a mother shielding her child's face.

Simone, rising. Simone, *rising*!

What's she doing? Where is she going?

No, Ismail whispers.

Simone, approaching him.

The madman, much taller than she is.

Simone, standing in front of him.

173

The madman, looking at Simone. Looking into her face.

She's saying something to him, I think. Whispering something...

It's hard to hear... We can't see... not from this angle...

And suddenly: the madman, turning. The madman, heading down the aisle. Back past the passengers. Past the driver. The madman, out the doors. The madman, going down the street...

A three-in-the-afternoon miracle. An 86-bus-to-uni miracle...

Simone, sitting back with us again.

*God*, Simone, I say. *God*.

You saved the bus, Ismail says. Not that anyone seems grateful.

Why isn't anyone cheering? I ask. Why isn't anyone saying three cheers for you?

Because that's the law of the bus, Marcie says. Even miracles don't mean anything on the bus...

Everyone's in shock, Ismail says. I'm in shock...

Why didn't we all just band together? Valentine asks. Rise against him? Like, we were many and he was just... *one*.

Because he's a maniac, Gita says. He was lawless and he was pumped.

Imagine what it's like to be in that kind of rage all the time, Ismail says. At perpetual boiling point...

He can only get away with it because no one can be as aggressive as him at three in the afternoon, Valentine says. Notice how he chooses his battles. He doesn't go after *real* drug dealers, just randomers on the bus.

I don't get why we have to be frightened like this, Gita says. Why's he allowed to roam around? Someone should be looking after him. He should be in hospital, not out on the streets...

Did you know you'd save us, Simone? Marcie asks. Did you know you had *special powers*?

I don't have any powers, Simone says.

You made something happen, Marcie says. Like, against the grain ... Against the ancient evil of the world.

You looked into his eyes and soothed the beast, Valentine says.

It was like the *Second Coming*, Ismail says.

I don't think the first coming ever actually reached Manchester, Marcie says.

You should get an OBE or something, Valentine says. A fucking sainthood ...

You should be famous, Marcie says. You're the maniac whisperer. You disarmed the most violent man in Manchester ...

I spoke to him, that's all, Simone says.

What did you say? I ask.

That I'd pray for him, Simone says.

He needed that, I say. He wanted to hear that.

And there you were before him, Ismail says. Your face. Your eyes. Your vulnerability ... It was like a face-of-the-Other Levinas thing ... A *thou-shalt-not-commit-murder* kind of thing ... You woke up his innocence. You made strength ashamed of what it had become. What could he do but leave?

It was like a scene from Robert Bresson, Ismail says. Jeanne's forgiveness of the pickpocket. Marie's caring for Balthazar. The old woman's tenderness with Yvon in *L'Argent*, regardless of his crimes ...

Don't arthouse it, fucker, Marcie says.

It was a three-in-the-afternoon miracle, Ismail says. An 86-bus-to-uni miracle ...

What was he looking for? Gita asks. Why was he peering into everyone's faces?

He was yelling something about drug dealers outside, Marcie says. He probably believed he was doing something righteous, Ismail says. That he was serving some *higher cause*. He probably believed himself to be a paladin of the good, scouring the city for wickedness . . .

It's like Socrates said: *No one knowingly does evil*, Ismail says. Wrongdoing is always a perverted form of the good. The madman wanted to do good. This was his way of doing good . . .

Look, he's a paranoid schizophrenic—clearly, I say. He probably hears voices telling him to do terrible things—to spread as much fear and confusion and dread as possible. My mum used to hear voices, like, every hour of the day.

The voices want to destroy you, I say. To turn everyone against you: your friends, your family. To have you all to themselves, which is when their work *really* starts . . .

They're pure evil, I say. They lie and accuse and deceive and you can't even think straight. *Why are you so stupid? Why are you such a fool? Everyone hates you. Your friends hate you. Your parents hate you . . .*

And the voices always pick on weak people, I say. The people who deserve it least. The ones who've already suffered the most . . . Who are already lonely. And they just make them lonelier.

And he's probably on some dreadful medication that's destroying his nervous system, I say. He's probably in and out of locked wards . . .

They should have kept him in, Gita says.

How are your prayers going to help, Simone? I ask. Do you think you can drive back the demons? Do you think you can cure him? That you can exorcise his evil?

I don't know, Simone says.

What's prayer supposed to do when there's so much suffering in the world? I ask.

I fear for that man, Simone says. I despair over what his life has been—that he's had to live that way. But I hope for him, too. And I'll pray for him, because prayer is an act and expression of hope, even if it is also a cry of despair.

I'll pray for all those who hear voices, who are made to harm themselves, Simone says. Who are alone—utterly alone—even as they walk through crowds. I'll pray for those we fear even as they, too, are afraid. Who terrify us because they are themselves terrified.

I'll pray for those who drink to deaden themselves, Simone says. To drown out the voices they hear. I'll pray for those who end up in holding cells and mental hospitals. Who are confined and dosed up and turned loose again.

I know who these people are, Simone says. I meet them on the streets. I know they are the weakest, and that the voices target them because of their weakness. I know they've come from the children's homes, from the Forces. From broken relationships.

I know the street drinkers and the drug addicts, Simone says. I know the ones to whom the voices come. I know them and I'll pray for them and I'll hope for them. And I'll pray for you, Johnny, even if you think it'll do nothing.


## 15

UNKNOWN PLEASURES TOWERS.

On the way up to Bitcoin's party.

Rumours that this party's a kind of *test*. To see who Bitcoin wants to take into space. He wants smart, groovy people with him. Who'd be a laugh. Who'd entertain him. Who'd be his court jesters on Elysium.

Maybe he wants to restart the human race up there, Valentine says. Maybe it's about selecting breeding pairs.

Forget it. I'm not breeding, Gita says.

That's what the Man wants: to keep the population down and manageable, Marcie says. Which means we should found a big gay dynasty instead. Using your womb.

Using *yours*, Gita says.

The lift, rising.

Manchester's so flat, we agree. An infinite plain. You can see all the way to Alderley Edge. To the Pennines . . .

We're higher than everyone. We're above the clouds—above the fog. Above the struggles of the poor. You can't hear the screams from here . . .

The thirtieth floor.

*Great* vantage point to see the future riots, when everyone works out their pensions are gone. To toast the supersoldiers, wired into their battle suits. The militarised police, with their precision rifles. The new robot dogs, with mounted energy weapons. Well done, chaps . . . Keep the serfs down . . .

And when it gets too scary, you can just whistle up your helicopter and zip off to your bunker. Fuck it, the whole penthouse can probably detach and zoom off into low Earth orbit.

Inside.

Done out like a space-age '70s bachelor pad. Circular sofas, like in Francis Bacon paintings. Very *shagadelic* . . .

Alvar Aalto hanging chairs. Former Haçienda bollards. Former Haçienda cat's eyes in the floor.

All this *mancuniana*. All these old Haçienda fixtures and fittings. In the penthouse of some billionaire. Is this where everything cool's going to end up?

There they are: our hosts. Bitcoin and Ultimate Destruction Girl, sitting round the firepit.

Look at them: the Elon Musk and Grimes of the PhD set, Marcie says. Ultimate Destruction Girl's like Bitcoin's consort.

What have you got to offer by comparison, Marcie? Valentine asks. Supposed street smarts. Alleged telekinetic powers. An in-depth knowledge of Spartakus and Bogdanov and other forgotten Bolshevists. Your ability to act out the entire October Revolution with hand puppets . . .

Shame she never saw you play badminton . . . , I say.

You can't rival a *helicopter courtship*, Valentine says. He's probably flown Ultimate Destruction Girl up to see the Northern Lights . . .

I can't believe it—Ultimate Destruction Girl's given up destruction, Marcie says. She should hate all this. I mean, Bitcoin's so uncool.

Maybe there's more to him, I say. Maybe he's some kind of superhero. PhD student by day, Batman by night. Bitcoin is his Bruce Wayne persona. He's only a pretend-buffoon.

And who's Ultimate Destruction Girl in all of this?—that's the question, Valentine says. She's hardly Little Miss Suicide Bomb.

She's wowed by his millions, I say. Or by his spiel about the marvels of blockchain. About cryptocurrencies saving the world.

She's just another MA student power-fucker, Marcie says.

I'll bet Bitcoin told her they're going to be kings and queens of Elysium, in some space-station garden paradise, with trees and running water, Valentine says. He told her they'd wait out global extinction up there. Rule space. And then they and their descendants will return to Earth in hundreds of years' time . . .

Wandering.

A fish tank wall, like a slice of ocean. Clown fish. Anemone. A mini-ecosystem.

Rainer Maria Dillwood, The Torn Curtain and Originary Ron, puffing on a hookah.

Animadab Jones, Hannibal and Nostradamus on the dance-floor with the MA students. And there's Fox Piss, doing his famous limbo dance.

The jacuzzi. Weep and the Dane, bubbling away. We thought they'd be trying to conjure up aural residues of Joy Division. To, like, remote-view the past of Unknown Pleasures Tower . . .

Vortek in the VR studio, headset on, punching, ducking blows, parrying empty air. Getting all his violence out in *good virtual fun*.

He's no longer a one-man terror cell, we agree. No longer a man of the wilderness. A Polish superwolf. He's forgetting his deep ecology. He's no longer working his way up to an *anti-tech terror attack*.

Looking through Bitcoin's library.

Books, real books. In their original language. In plain, sober covers. Suhrkamp Verlag. Gallimard. Books—not *précis*. Not *intro guides*. Not *textbooks*. And pristine. Not destroyed by annotation—by marks in pencil and marks in pen, by marks over marks, and highlighter over all. Not sticky, not mangy. Collected works, in sober editions . . .

Heidegger's *Gesamtausgabe*, Valentine says. Complete—all hundred and twenty-five volumes, *auf Deutsch*.

Oh, the irony, Valentine says. Bitcoin doesn't even read German.

Nor do we, I say.

The complete Adorno. Forty-seven volumes . . .

Why does he want this stuff? Valentine asks.

Blanchot galleys, in a display case. Exercise books, propped open. Blanchot's notes, all neat on quadrille. Blanchot first editions, with handwritten dedications.

*Friendship is the truth of disaster. You know mine.*

*Thinking of the goal we share.*

*It seems to me that in these distressing days, something has been given to us in common, to which we must also respond in common.*

Blanchot photos, ultra-rare . . . Blanchot as a baby, already looking like himself. On the deck of a boat as a young man, dancing a jig. Standing by a roadside, tie flapping in the wind. Sitting, smiling, in front of his bookcase.

And what's Bitcoin doing here—that's the question. Why All

Saints? Why study? Why a PhD? Why Disaster Studies? He's got enough money to do whatever he likes . . .

It's a cover—that's what I reckon, Valentine says. Bitcoin's here to spy on us. He's been sent to find out what Disaster Studies is all about. He's probably working for MI6.

Like MI6 would give a fuck about us, I say.

I reckon Bitcoin's probably *funding* Disaster Studies, Marcie says. And our scholarships. Do you think All Saints came up with the money for the Centre all by itself?

Bitcoin's too stupid for that, Valentine says. I'll bet it was Bitcoin's dad.

Papa Bitcoin endowed Disaster Studies—that figures, Marcie says. He threw the university a million or two to fund all our scholarships. We were all brought here for the sake of Bitcoin Jr. To provide him with an intellectual milieu. An authentic humanities PhD scene.

At All Saints? I say.

Sure—Bitcoin needed stupid playmates so he wouldn't feel inadequate, Marcie says. Look, Papa Bitcoin is part of the Man's cabal, and the Man's got his finger in every pie. It's all clear: Bitcoin wanted to play at being a PhD student, just like Marie Antoinette wanted to play at being a peasant. And here we are: his stupid playmates.

So the Man funds Disaster Studies, Valentine says. It makes sense.

But why—why does he bother? I ask.

To buy off the opposition, Marcie says. To keep us under control.

But why bother with us? I ask. We're hardly a threat, are we?

I think it must be entertaining, watching us groping about, Valentine says. Our fumblings. Our stumblings . . . Each down their own rabbit hole . . .

The Man must have better things to do, I say.

Maybe the Man wants us to discover his secrets, Marcie says. To study him. To lay bare his *disastrous operations*.

But why? I ask.

Speculation. It could be a psychopath thing. Psychopaths feel compelled to leave clues, to fuck things up a little. They want to be caught—just so someone can appreciate their brilliance . . . So the Man's letting us get to the heart of the problem. Our scholarships are about seeing how far we can go—whether we can work it all out by ourselves . . .

So he's watching us?

*Someone's* keeping tabs.

Russell? Prof Bollocks?

Higher than them. It's beyond the uni. There are probably nano-drones, watching us uncover the technocratic slash neo-feudalism system . . . The intelligence-services-slash-big-tech system . . . The banking-slash-debt-enslavement system . . . The bionet-of-all-things system . . . And the Man at the centre, pressing all the buttons . . .

It could be a data-gathering thing. The Man wants to pick up on our patterns of thought. To detect new trends, to feed the algorithms. He wants the countercultural response to the coming end. He wants the humanities reaction to the disaster. The Man wants to know what we know. What we *sense* . .

Agreement: The Man likes humanities colour. He likes our little ecology. The flora and fauna of the All Saints coral reef. He likes to snorkel through shoals of PhD student youth! He likes the octopuses' gardens of our dissertations.

This is a PhD student reality show for him. He's watching with his popcorn, Deleuze/Guattari on his lap. Enjoying our cute little story arcs. Will Business Studies Guy escape Marcie's clutches? Johnny and Gita: will they, won't they? Will Valentine actually jump from the eighth floor of the atrium? Will Vortek go divine-violence crazy and hold the uni president hostage before committing ritual seppuku?

Another theory. Maybe the Man wants to tap into *apocalyptic energies*. The anarchy that's released at the end, like helium from undersea vents. From the melting permafrost. Maybe there's such a thing as *disaster energy*, like solar energy. That's what the Man's trying to harness. He wants our *disaster vitality*. The life of our dying. That's why we've been brought here . . .

The Man and his cronies are just waiting for us to do away with ourselves, prettily. For our entertaining little suicides. Our cutesy auto-deaths. They'll probably share them like they share puppy and kitten videos . . .

Sure, we're in the crosshairs, but we're too cute to shoot right now . . . Anyway, we're not a threat. There are priorities elsewhere.

Depression. Every anti-Man thought we've ever had: sponsored by the Man. Every anti-Man sentiment we've expressed: Man-funded. Man-underwritten.

We're part of the disaster—the Man's disaster, the controlled disaster.

The Man sponsored continental philosophy: Isn't it obvious? Just like he funded Abstract Expressionism. Like he funded *Encounter*. The Man *owns* continental philosophy. And critical theory. And cultural theory. And *queer* theory. The Man's won. The Man's on his victory lap. It's actually *too easy* for the Man. He's frustrated. He wishes we'd put up more of a fight. He wishes there were some *meaningful resistance* . . .

And isn't this exactly the doomy kind of conversation the Man likes to hear? He loves our apocalyptic chat. He's tickled by our doom-talk. We're the equivalent of disaster go-go dancers . . .

Unless there's a *deeper* disaster. Like, God's disaster—true apocalyptic disaster. A disaster that brings the new heavens and Earth. A disaster that plays itself out of the hands of the Man.

In what do we place our faith? The end. What do we long for? The end. Because it will be truth—even as it's the *deadly* truth. Even as it *murders* us. And that will be part of the truth: our murder.

The disaster as truth—as the last true thing: Isn't that we believe in? As our last judgement, which is to say our *death*. What could be truer than that?

Maybe the Man knows it's coming: the true disaster, the disaster as truth . . . Maybe his efforts are all about holding it back: our *apocalyptic hit*, our *apocalyptic ecstasy*. Restraining it . . . Preventing it from ever reaching us.

But we're playing a greater game. We're playing a *divine* game. Maybe *God's* game . . .

Heading out.

Distraction: free swag, on a suspended table. Party bags of coke. Little packets of cocaine, one for each of us.

Should we?

They've got our names on them, Gita says. How thoughtful . . .

I'll bet it's really pure, I say.

Bitcoin probably flies it in himself on his private helicopter, Valentine says. Direct from Colombia.

But isn't it just what the Man wants us to do: to snort his coke? Marcie asks.

Gita, snorting.

The rest of us, snorting.

Jesus, this stuff's strong, Valentine says. It's like the Man's own coke.

It's like mainlining ten macchiatos, Marcie says.

It's like fire in the blood, I say. Flames along the synapses . . .

I think I'm actually having a heart attack, Marcie says. The Man's murdering us . . .

We should see it as a heart *liberation*, Valentine says. I'll bet this is how our hearts are supposed to beat: as fast as a hummingbird's. This is how you know you're alive.

I feel so *alert*, I say. I don't actually feel dissociated for once. I don't feel *numb*.

I'm actually thinking things, Valentine says. I'm actually *concentrating*. I feel so precise. Like I could do really complicated logic.

Everything's so bright, Marcie says. So sharp—so in focus. I can see everything like it's hi-res. Like it's high definition. It's all clear, for the first time. There are no shadows, nothing hidden.

I've never been as awake as this, I say. I think I could shoot laser beams from my eyes.

I can see my whole dissertation, Valentine says. I've planned it all in my head. It took, like, one second. I didn't have to think—I just *intuited* it. I downloaded it from God. I could start typing my dissertation now and finish it by sunrise . . .

Data—that's all I can see, Marcie says. Data—raw data—from all the sensors, actuators, surveillance cameras. Data, updating in real time, instantaneously, all at once. From every source.

I actually think I could speak *Latin*, Ismail says. In fact, I'm only going to speak Latin from now on.

I don't want to be human anymore, I say. I'm more than human. My name is no longer Johnny. It's Klaatu.

*Veni, vedi*, Klaatu, Ismail says.

I see things as the Man sees them, Marcie says. Data, for the dashboard. For predictive analytics. Data, to be harvested, managed, sold on. Data about our emotional lives. Our hormonal lives. Our endocrinal lives.

They should give me a lectureship, right now, Valentine says. They should make me a full professor. I should be running the university. *All* universities . . .

I see how they'll transform us, Marcie says. I see the nanobiosensors in our eyelids, in our throats. I see smart-blood slopping through our veins. I see self-assembling nanobots in our bloodstream transmitting information; receiving it.

I see the capture of all human behaviour as *concrete data points*,

Marcie says. I see direct cortical interfaces. I see bioelectronics, embedded in our tissues. I see genetic, biological, biometric, mental and emotional infostreams.

I see where it's going, Marcie says. I see what they're planning. I see DNA wars. I see them fucking with the genome. I see GM human beings. I see implanted memories, thoughts, dreams. My God, they haven't even *begun* their work on us . . .

## 16

### SATURDAY.

Remaking *The Sacrifice*.

Explaining the scenario to Business Studies Guy. Alexander (that's you), a lecturer in aesthetics, haunted by apocalyptic dreams and visions. World War Three breaks out (or looks like it does; it could all be happening in Alexander's head . . . ) and he offers up everything he loves—his family, his house, his intellectual life, his own sanity—in exchange for God returning everything to how it was before.

The most serious film in the world, the Collective agree. The most seriously arthouse of all seriously arthouse films! A film with a world-historical mission! That takes itself entirely seriously! And that *we* take entirely seriously, that's the thing. That *we* love, entirely seriously, for its seriousness!

Which means it's the film *we're least entitled to remake*, the Collective agree. Which means it's the film we *have* to remake—to defile. We have to sacrifice *The Sacrifice*! The supposed world-historicalness of *The Sacrifice*! The high-artiness of *The Sacrifice*! The high-humorlessness of *The Sacrifice*! Even as we love *The Sacrifice*!

The desire to *despoil The Sacrifice*. The desire to desecrate the things that move us so desperately, that make us ashamed to be ourselves. The desire to laugh at all seriousness. And in the name of *the English reality principle! English realism! English anti-pretension!* Because we want to punish *ourselves*! To correct *ourselves*! Because we want to sacrifice our instincts at their highest and best!

We're destroyers! the Collective agree. Murderers! Of *ourselves*, first and foremost. And so we should be! So we deserve to be!

We're dead, but at least we know we're dead! the Collective agree. We're defeated, but at least we know our defeat! We're puerile, but at least we know our puerility!

That's why we live in truth even as we live in falsehood, the Collective agree. That's why we never lie. That's the merit of our self-hatred. Of our eternal auto-horror.

We come from the apocalypse, to do the work of the apocalypse, the Collective agree. We're here to show the fakery. We already live in the ruins—the *real* ruins.

We parody parody, the Collective agree. We deepen the farce, which is why our bad faith is faith. Why our madness is sanity. Why our evil is goodness. We're fulfilling our eschatological role . . .

Climbing the Ees mound.

The afternoon moon, like the ghost at the feast.

What's the moon actually *for*? we wonder. What does it do? All day, all night?

The way it doesn't even turn. The way it doesn't rotate. The way it's locked in orbit, just dumbly going round . . .

The same face of the moon, expressing—*nothing*. Communicating the great cosmic message: *nothing*. Just a surface to be struck. To be bombarded. Just a blast zone. An impact zone. The moon, being pounded into ever-finer dust . . .

Funny no one goes up there anymore, Ismail says.

What—to the moon? Marcie says. Why would you bother? What would be the point?

They all went mad on the moon, I say. That's the great secret. The astronauts all underwent *irreversible psychological damage*, which is why they stopped the Apollo missions. You know what Neil Armstrong *really* said in debrief? *The eternal silence of infinite space terrifies me.* He never uttered another word about the so-called moon landing. He was fucking terrified and became a total alcoholic.

They should have left the moon alone, I say. They should never have gone there . . . Crawling all over it . . . Playing *golf* for fuck's sake. Golf on the moon! . . . Bounding around . . . Planting their fucking flag . . . Claiming ol' Luna for the USA or whatever. The *hubris* . . .

What's actually on the dark side of the moon—the side we can't see? Gita asks.

More moon, idiot, Marcie says.

And is it really dark? Gita asks.

Only because we can't see it, Marcie says.

# 17
## SUNDAY.

Al's café.

I'm tired of coming to Al's, Marcie says. I mean, shouldn't the word *café* conjure up more than this? Shouldn't it echo with the great coffee houses of Vienna? Or the Parisian left bank? . . . This isn't even a real macchiato. This is Al's *idea* of a macchiato . . . Call this a fucking crema?

It looks like Al *spat* on a coffee, Valentine says . . . Just like this is Al's *idea* of a bagel, Marcie says. And Al's *idea* of a carrot juice. And this is Al's *idea* of a café. No frills, right? Just right for scummers like us . . .

# 18
## WALKING CHORLTON.

So many big houses. So much prosperity. The middle-class world is a wall against us and our kind.

But it's so *lifeless*, we agree. No one's on the streets. Children aren't playing. People aren't sitting out . . .

They've retreated inside, really. The middle-class are indoor people. They've become domestic. They're *domesticated animals*. They have their comforts: g-'n'-ts and Netflix and new recipes from Ottolenghi. And everything they want is just *brought* to them. It's all delivered to their door.

They're basically *happy*, the middle-class (a *mediocre* happiness). They basically think everything's okay, and that it will continue to be okay (a *mediocre* confidence).

The Man's rewarded them—up to now. The Man's smiled upon them. Their kind has been allowed to prosper. To turn in their circles. To reproduce. (But their children: cutting themselves without knowing why; dissociated, without knowing why; starving themselves, without knowing why; completely saturated with despair, without knowing why . . . )

The middle-class, voluntarily compliant (though they don't know it as *compliance*). Happily obedient (though they don't know it as *obedience*). The middle-class, outraged by what they're supposed to be outraged about. Loving what they're supposed to love.

Sure, the middle-class have their *frontier myths*—their approved outlaws. The middle-class have their culture heroes, unbound by bourgeois rule. Who *smoke*, for God's sake. Who fuck who they shouldn't. Who drink themselves to death.

They have Mark E. Smith coffee table books in the big houses, the middle-class. Ian Curtis's lyrics book, reproducing his handwriting. Hundred-quid New Order LP boxsets. *Mr Maracas*: Bez's memoirs, signed. Shaun Ryder's *Bumper Book of Crack Anecdotes*.

But they're the pillars of the world, the middle-class. They're administrators of the world. They're the willing workers—the good managers—who keep it all propped up.

They don't believe in *evil*, the middle-class. They don't believe in malevolent forces, in demonic possession. And they don't believe in *wild Dostoevskian goodness* either, the middle-class. They don't believe in lawless revelation, in antinomian faith—in the chaotic good that irrupts in miracles. They don't believe in the theophany that leaves only scorch marks.

They'll never know our world-alienation, the middle-class. Our world-rejection! They'll never know our *apocalypticism*! They'll never see the world in an eschatological light! *Destruction* will never be a safe word for them, the middle-class! Nor *antinomian*! Nor *eschaton*!

But their turn is coming, the middle-class. Their pensions are being raided. Their debts are being repackaged and rolled up and resold. Their savings are being inflated away, the middle-class . . .

And they'll have absolutely no instincts to guide them in the coming horror, the middle-class . . . They'll not know what to do when their world falls apart . . . They'll just stand around open-mouthed, the middle-class, when the world collapses all around them.


## 19

**AFTERNOON.** The China Garden, for dim sum. For *a dim and a sum*, as Michael calls it.

Afternoon extravagance. In honour of what? In honour of everything. In honour of *life*!

A dim and a sum: the best way to defeat the afternoon. The best way to wrestle down *afternoon melancholy*.

A dim and a sum around the round table. Around the rotating thingy. With jasmine tea and sake. A dim and a sum, high on jasmine tea and sake . . .

And they know Michael here, as they know him everywhere. As someone who'll order *the entire menu*. As someone who'll bring a bunch of guests to sit around the table . . .

What are we doing to discuss today?

Politics!

Politics, Michael says. Meh.

It's all very well for you to say that, Marcie says. Your generations are the ones who fuck . . . who screwed it up for the rest of us.

You may be right, Michael says.

And you had all the hope, too, Valentine says. You had the '60s, you bastards.

We *did*, cuddles, Michael says.

You could dream of a total transformation of the world—that the revolution was really possible, Valentine says.

But that was the problem, Michael says. We expected too much.

Politics is a house of lies, Marcie says. Party politics is just a wrestling match. Left and right don't mean anything anymore. That's how they hypnotise you: left then right, right then left. With their hypnotist's watch . . .

There is no legitimate political order, or social order, Valentine says. There's no legitimate order at all. Which means there can be no positive political expression. The only honest form of politics is destructive—*apocalyptic* . .

We need something to *shatter* politics, Valentine says. All the false goals and false debates; all the false parties and false elections: the whole procedural apparatus . . . It has to be destroyed. We need transcendence! Need some blow from without!

See, I love reading about the early church, Valentine says. About the Christianity of the catacombs, back when they thought Jesus was about to return and judge the world . . . They thought the End Times were imminent . . . They knew the world had to descend into Hell . . . That the power of evil was intensifying . . .

They were waiting for a mercy-killer, Valentine says. For a world-smasher. They knew the Incomprehensible needed to be brought onstage . . . Something utterly beyond human understanding. That would change the rules of the game. That would change the game itself . . .

But you're forgetting the rest of the story, my dear, Michael says. Yes, the Christians of the catacombs were waiting for Christ's return and the fall of Rome. But that was so a great reversal would occur—so the weak would shame the powerful and put an end to violence.

But only in the New Creation, Valentine says. Only once the world had been destroyed . . .

And in the meantime, in this world, they gathered as friends— as *equals*, Michael says. Servants and masters broke bread together. Each took the other as a neighbour. Loved God in one another, trusted each other. *Agape* superseded *ethos*; this was a new self-chosen life.

So we have to go back to the catacombs—is that what you're saying? Marcie asks.

Proudhon says it best, Michael says. *To be governed is to be kept in sight, inspected, spied upon, directed, law-driven, numbered, corralled, indoctrinated, preached at, controlled by creatures who have neither the right nor the wisdom nor the virtue to do so.*

Which is to say we have to be suspicious of power—of the idolatry of politics, Michael says. We have to understand that political institutions are not there to make our societies embody justice, freedom or love—merely to ensure that the world remains liveable.

I'm not sure it *is* liveable, Marcie says.

As for the rest, it's a matter of *agape*—of the love of neighbours, Michael says. Of what moves from face to face, mouth to mouth, hand to hand . . .

You're an anarchist, Michael, Valentine says.

I *am* an anarchist, cuddles, Michael says. Christ was an anarchist. He didn't trust politics. He wanted no part of earthly authority and hierarchy ... He knew that those who take power will perish from it. That the best is very easily corrupted into the worst. But now I want to hear what Simone thinks ...

There's a *spiritual* order to which we should aspire, Simone says. The whole order of the universe: the harmony of all the orders that make it up. And politics should be a part of that.

As the microcosm in the macrocosm? Ismail says. Like the ancients thought?

There's a larger whole in which we can live and move, Simone says. That can give ... *dimensionality* to our lives. That can ... redefine our moral and spiritual horizons.

Come on, there's no such thing as *political harmony*, Valentine says. There's no way of organising things that isn't more managerialism. Politics is the problem—

Politics is perfectible, Simone says.

Ha! Nothing's perfectible! Valentine says. The only answer from politics is more politics.

There are better and worse political systems, Gita says.

Politics—what we know as politics—is a smokescreen, Marcie says. Elected politicians are just middle management. They're functionaries. The decisions are made for them.

It's the Man who's pulling the levers, Marcie says. He's laid his eggs in the deep state, the deep uni, the deep church, the deep everything, like a parasitical wasp. He's got the politicians, the tech and pharma billionaires on his side. They're summoned to the big conferences, to Davos and the rest, for the Man to advise them about the long plan, the multigenerational plan.

Like some James Bond film? Gita says. Talk some sense into her, Michael.

Who knows—she might be right, Michael says.

It's *Brave New World* stuff, I say. Technocracy stuff. The kind of thing about which the Unabomber corresponds with Vortek.

Rewriting the genetic code . . . Reprogramming the *human operating system* . . .

See, only now does the Man have the means to realise the oldest political dream, Marcie says. Only now can he exercise his *hideous strength*. The digital grid's ready. The digital gulag. The all-seeing eye's in fucking place. The Man's omniscient, practically . . .

So we're fucked, I say.

If we can't defeat the Man head on, we can still *sidestep* him, Ismail says. Maybe there's a way of *seceding*—of going *under* the state. Of declaring independence from the Beast. It's like those Alpine valleys that have their own currency, that are all low tech—using mechanics, not electronics. They write stuff on paper—no emails. They homeschool their young. It's like those parts of Mexico that just do their own thing, regardless of what the central government tells them.

Anarchism, Michael says. Precisely.

It's like the lumpen, staying out of sight of the middle-class world, Marcie says. Keeping to the shadows, untracked, off-grid. Knowing how to hide. Having no permanent address. Letting no records be kept of their movements. But they'll pour out of the underground when the time comes . . .

Yeah, to scavenge the bodies, Gita says.

# C H A P T E R  5

**1**

**MONDAY MORNING.** It's happening again. Manchester's been turned up-side down again. They're shaking out all the humanities PhDs from their beds . . .

Again! Again! They're flushing us out. They're making us break cover. They're bringing us into the morning. They're exposing us to full light, full scrutiny.

It's like the census in Nazareth. They want to count us, All Saints's finest! They want us present in person! They want us in a lecture theatre, all of us! Facing forward! They want to see the *bloodshot whites of our eyes*—at nine AM! For a nine AM start!

So here we all are, blinking in the morning. Having to get up, like regular people. Having to come in, like ordinary people. To commute in on the bus, like the common run of humanity. On the bus, and sitting next to fellow commuters on the bus. Sipping our takeaway macchiatos on the bus . . .

The lecture theatre.

Above us: the great projector, doing its work. Above us: beams of light through the air.

It's like a planetarium. There should be a light show. A pseudo night sky in the darkness.

It's a false cosmos, built by a false demigod. How will we break out? How will we shatter the *prison universe* and escape?

And there's Professor Bollocks at the front. As far away as a performer at a stadium gig . . .

The PowerPoint title, dropping down towards us: *TIME MANAGEMENT.*

Rising rage. Tired anger. Not this topic . . . Anything but this topic . . . Is he actually going to couple the word *time* with the word *management*? *TIME! MANAGEMENT! TIME! MANAGEMENT!* Within the walls of a uni! As if Henri Bergson never existed! Nor Martin Heidegger! As if Deleuze had never formulated the three syntheses of time!

Is he actually going to talk of the *management of time* in front of us? As if it were a topic like any other? As if it were possible simply to conjoin the words *time* and *management*? . . . *TIME MANAGEMENT! MANAGEMENT TIME!* Only the Man himself would bring these words together. Only the Man himself could fail to see it as a *total contradiction.*

Whispered in our hearts: *Don't you understand that a PhD is essentially a stay on time, Professor Bollocks? A holy pause, before we plunge over the waterfall? Don't you remember what it said in the Book of Revelations: that there was silence in heaven for about half an hour?*

Whispered in our hearts: *Don't you see that PhD students dream only of the messianic era, Professor Bollocks? Don't you realise that we're all feathers on the messiah's breath? Which is why we're immortal, in our way. Why time's undivided for us. Why our lives will be one long mad spree of time . . .*

Whispered in our hearts: *The future's already escaped, Professor Bollocks. The future's flown. The future's light. We squander time (what is called squandering), Professor Bollocks. We waste time (what is called waste) only to give time back to itself. Only to let time be.*

Whispered in our hearts: *We only know about suspended study, Professor Bollocks. About studying left idle. We only know about unlearning, Professor Bollocks. About ways of getting lost. Errancy: that's our specialism. The displacement of ends. The uncoupling of potentiality from act.*

Whispered in our hearts: *We know nothing* of success conditions, *of* progressive understanding, *Professor Bollocks. Of the idea of* culminating judgement. *We're foreign to* self-motivation, *to* self-directed action, *Professor Bollocks. To* self-management. *To* self-realisation.

Whispered in our hearts: *Don't talk to us of* transferrable skills, *Professor Bollocks. Of* economically manageable skillsets. *Of the* needs of the market. *Don't even mention* measurable outputs, *Professor Bollocks!* Productivity; professional accreditation! *No more, Professor Bollocks! No more!*

Whispered in our hearts: *We need* errancy *class, not method class, Professor Bollocks. We need to learn the arts of* self-divestiture and self-decompletion. *Decreation: that's our aim, Professor Bollocks. We want to become saints—humanities PhD saints, totally decreated . . .*

Whispered in our hearts: *We're time's celebrants, Professor Bollocks. We're time's fools. We're time's lunatics, time's drunkards. We allow time to languish, Professor Bollocks. We unchain time from its end, its purposes. We allow time to take its time.*

Whispered in our hearts: *We're founder members of the Time Protection League, Professor Bollocks. Of the Methodology Liberation Front. We're launching the Campaign for Postgraduate Drifting here and now . . .*

## 2

**ANOTHER RUIN BAR EVENING.**

Can we still get drunk? Is this still drunkenness? Can we still depend on it: drunkenness? Or has even our drinking become hollow now? Has even our drunkenness become parodic? Does it just echo in vain with every other night we've spent drunk?

Drinking for nothing. On a night that marks nothing—no Saint's Day, no Feast Day. Our *festival of insignificance*. Our *nobody's-wedding*. Our celebration in the void . . .

Our drunkenness changes nothing—we know that. We drink when we're allowed to drink. We go to method class; we leave method class. We're being broken in. Method class is working . . .

We lament! We wail! We raise our two fingers to the Man! But Ruin Bar's where the Man wants us to be. Our railing at the Man is really a kind of paean to the Man. Our despair at the Man only *celebrates* the Man. His infinite power! His limitless reach!

There's tonight and our rebellion, but there will be tomorrow and next week, and next Monday morning. We're drunk, but there'll be the hangover, and the rest of our lives as hangovers . . .

Ruin Bar changes nothing. It's a timeout. A compensation. It's built into the rhythm of the week. Admit it: we're obedient. We follow the accepted rules of getting out of our skulls. And we'll be right back in our skulls tomorrow . . .

## 3

**TUESDAY.**

Al's café.

Hungover. Serotonin-depleted.

Are we supposed to be alive? Marcie says. Is this actually *it*? Every day's more impossible than the last. It can't go on like this.

Yes it can, Valentine says. Yes it will.

This is the deadest I've ever felt, Marcie says. Is there anything stronger than a macchiato? Like, some forbidden coffee, only for those in the know? Coffee you'd just *sniff*? Coffee you'd just *mainline*?

You should get Al to make us *Greek* coffee, Valentine says. Tell him to really pulverise the coffee so it's like powder. So it gets into your bloodstream more easily.

You should get Al to give us a coffee *enema*, I say. It hits quicker that way.

Why not do a fucking line? Valentine asks. A leetle bit of coke . . .

Coke makes me think everything I write is fucking intergalactic, Marcie says. I'd lose all quality control.

Like your quality control is world-renowned, I say.

We should go natural, Valentine says. We need a *natural* stimulant . . . Ask the Wizard for something. Maybe there are some righteous shrooms that could help us.

Shrooms lay me out, Marcie says. I can't write *shit* . . . There's got to be some microdosing solution.

Or what about a shot of *adrenaline*? Valentine asks. Can you buy a syringe of it on the black market, do you think? And smash it down through the rib cage. Pump it straight into the heart à la *Pulp Fiction* . .

Face it: nothing's going to help, Marcie says. It's just you and your stupidity, now and forever.


4

ISMAIL, QUOTING:


I met this guy named Ding Dong. He told me the whole Earth is going up in flames. Flames will come out of here and there and it'll just rise up. The mountains are gonna go up in big flames. The water's gonna rise in flames. There's gonna be creatures running every which way, some of them burnt, half their wings burning, people are gonna be screaming and hollering for help.

# 5

## ALL SAINTS STUDENT WORK-IN-PROGRESS EXHIBITION.

*Plaqueism.* Artists, explaining their art. Made to become their own explicators—their own critics. Because no artwork means anything all alone. And art must *mean*, just as everything has to *mean*. Everything has to have a message. And a message needs a messenger.

*Plaquery.* No time to linger over the artwork. No time for contemplation. We'll just have to cut to the lesson of what it's *about*. What it's *actually saying* . .

All this Theory, capital T . . . All this pretension . . . Art, made to set out its stall. To make its case. To tell us why it should claim our attention. Why we should regard it as *important*. Plaques, flagging the appropriate *social justice credentials*. To show that the correct political moves have been made . . . to reflect our virtues back at us . . .

Our exhibit. Our video art.

*Tarkovsky Parodies*: That's our title? Valentine says.

We didn't agree to that, Marcie says. You've given too much away. You're taking out the sting . . .

Ismail's plaque: *A critical interrogation of high arthouse seriousness, of the piety of the long shot and le temps mort . . . Drawing on the 'low' traditions of music hall and vaudeville . . . Pantomime Tarkovsky . . . Deflationary working-class humour . . . Deliberate amateurism . . .*

Outrage. You should have let the film speak for itself! You're justifying what we're doing in *their* terms! You're explaining it in the language of the *bourgeois enemy*! You've framed it for them—done all their interpretational work. You've excused yourself, basically. You've actually said sorry. Never explain, Ismail! Not to these bastards. Never account for yourself!

Our film, looping.

Footage of Business Studies Guy, as Ivan from *Ivan's Childhood*, wading through the water meadows. Under enemy fire. Dream-sequences of horses and orchards and cartfuls of apples . . .

Footage of Business Studies Guy as Andrei Rublev, pondering life in the mud. Deep-focus camerawork. Us in the background, playing peasants in the mud. Vortek, as a Mongol invader . . .

The other bits. Footage of us shaving Business Studies Guy's head, to play *Stalker*. Footage of Business Studies Guy as Ignat from *Mirror*, building a bonfire in the yard, setting it alight. Footage of Ismail himself as Kris Kelvin from *Solaris*, washing his hands in a stream. Letting the rain sprinkle on his face. Collecting some soil in a metal box . . .

Well, it's less artwanky than the other stuff, Valentine says.

Less artwanky perhaps, but it's still art, Marcie says. It's still tainted with *artism*.

Come on, guys—it's just art, Gita says. This is what art does.

Yes—exactly—it's *just art*! Marcie says. It's still art!

But you guys think that art's dead, right? Gita says. What does it matter?

A lumpen 'no' to arthouse is still arthouse, Marcie says. A lumpen pisstaking of arthouse is yet more arthouse. The film is a 'no' and not yet a 'yes'. But what would it mean for a film to be a 'yes'?

You need to tap directly into the *lumpensprung*, comrade Ismail, Valentine says. Let film gush forth from the *lumpensprung*. No more self-awareness! No more references to the history of film!

You need to make film *without* making film, Marcie says. To shoot off film from life like some fire-arc, some solar flare. As though filmmaking were an accident, not a career. A by-product . . . Something just done for laughs. Because—*why not?* Because—*no reason* . . .

You should be the director who's *forgotten* film, Valentine says. Who doesn't know what film *is* . . .


**6**

PHD NON-COMPLETION STORIES . . . PhD horror stories . . . The things big PhDs always warn little PhDs about. Like some tacky TV show: *When PhDs Go Wrong*.

Minds unravelled, Business Studies Guy. Minds torn apart. Ruined PhD students, left for dead at symposia . . . overwhelmed by total intellectual inadequacy. By their sense of being nothing but impostors.

PhD students thrown to examiner wolves, Business Studies Guy. Told they were useless. That they'd got it all wrong. Told to rewrite their dissertations, and then rewrite them again.

*Blocked* PhD students, Business Studies Guy, ghosts of their work. Unable to write, yet unable to do anything else. Suspending their studies for year after year. Students battered in the storms of their supervisor's whims. Their supervisor's *moods*. Torn down and built up, over and over again.

Students drawn to PhDs because they want to be defeated, Business Studies Guy. Because they want to fail, and hadn't failed sufficiently yet. Because they need to fuck up and hadn't completely fucked up already. For whom doing a PhD, the highest academic qualification of all, is really a fancy kind of suicide . . .

Former students, returning to the uni like revenants with *unfinished business*, Business Studies Guy. With revenge to take. With stories to tell of gaslighting, of menticide. Of thought-crimes. Of philosophical vendettas.

Failed PhDs, on distant orbits, Business Studies Guy. Rarely seen.

But returning, sometimes. Turning up at conferences, unbidden. Unwelcome. To guest speaker visits. Fearsome! Half mad! Unkempt! Dirty-fingernailed! Full of old and complex grievances! You see academic staff shudder and turn their heads. Oh God, not *him* again . . . Oh, not *her* . . .

Living hard-luck stories, Business Studies Guy. Living warnings. Who were set off course and are never coming back. Who've spent years in the darkness, thinking of nothing but their humiliation. Fisher Kings and Queens, looking to be regenerated by that which destroyed them. Drawn back to the uni in *twisted hope*.

# 7
## EVENING.

Gita and I, walking to the off-license.

A man in the alleyway, beckoning to us. A bedraggled man, a broken man, beckoning, *come, come*.

What does he want? I ask.

What do you think he wants? Gita says. Come on, Johnny.

Gita, pulling me away.

Walking.

It's like he couldn't be *bothered* to mug us, I say. He couldn't be *bothered* to jump us with a knife.

Do you think he was in any state to mug anybody? Gita says.

We were supposed to follow him into his alley and just turn ourselves over, I say.

He was pretty far gone, Gita says.

It's weird—I *wanted* to go to him, I say. I *wanted* to go down his alley.

Pure death wish, Gita says.

I almost went, I say. If you hadn't have been here . . .

No wonder you've been mugged so many times, Gita says.

Did you see how he came towards me? I say. Like he *recognised* me.

He wanted to part you from some cash, that's all, Gita says.

I could have helped him . . . , I say. I could have given him some money.

You're skint, Johnny, Gita says. And he would only have spent it on crack.

His face was an abyss, I say. You could fall into a face like that.

Years of addiction, right? Gita says. Very sad.

But that face . . . , I say. It was showing something. *He* was showing something. Is that what Simone means when she says only those who know the lowest degree of humiliation . . . only those who've lost all standing, dignity, humanity . . . Only those people don't lie?

I think we can safely assume crack addicts are liars, Gita says. And muggers. I mean, what do you think he'd have done to you if you'd followed him down his alley?

We're supposed to engage with evil and brokenness and disaster, I say. That's our vocation: that's what Simone says. To take evil and turn it to the good . . .

What are you going to do: give all your earthly possessions to that junky? Gita says. What would that accomplish? It's almost *indulgent*. His situation is a product of all kinds of complex social problems. Of some terrible upbringing. Of cheaply available crack cocaine. How can any of us change that?

Nothing at all! I say. Nothing does any good! Of course it doesn't! Nothing does anything . . . We know that. But we know too much! *Nothing ever changes! It can't change!*: That's always our excuse! But it's not enough . . .

God, you always have to out-nihilise everyone, Gita says. You always have to make it *our fault*. Which it might be collectively—as a society—but not *individually*.

We have to die to ourselves in compassion, according to Simone, I say. We have to be decreated. To love the helpless with God's own love.

I don't know what those things mean, Gita says.

*Evil*—pure *evil*: that's what's that poor wretch shows us, I say. The evil done to him, who was once a child. Who once expected good things. The . . . pure evil of the world.

There's no such thing as *pure evil*, just like there's no such thing as *absolute good*, Gita says. It's systemic. *Political*, if you like.

We should . . . *pray* or something, I say. We're corrupted . . . Do you know how they found Ian Curtis when he died? Hanging, kneeling, as though he was in fucking *prayer*. Not just dangling from the clothes rack, but bent over, the palms of his hands pressed together. That's how we should pray: *dead*. Already dead. Because we haven't done enough.

It's like you're living in your own personal Dostoevsky novel, Gita says.

We're supposed to decreate ourselves, according to Simone, I say. Supposed to follow the will of God, wherever it leads us. But the will of God would have led me straight down that alley. If I'd followed my . . . instinct or whatever, if I'd just let myself be vulnerable, I would just have headed into darkness to be stabbed . . .

But that's what Simone does every day on the streets: be vulnerable, I say. Be mortal. Deliberately expose herself to all kinds of violence . . . It's like some kind of death drive. It's like she *wants* death.

Isn't that what Valentine always says? Gita asks.

Perhaps what Simone calls compassion is just a way of inviting death, I say. Perhaps Simone wants to be killed, unconsciously. And so do I. And that's what I saw in the crack addict's eyes: my death. My murder. And that's why I wanted to follow him: Or is that just *my* sickness, *my* misunderstanding, *my* Gnostic version of what Simone calls compassion?

Is God a killer after all? I ask. Is God just a name for the desire to die? Or . . . or is there something else? Something real and good and true? . . . We need a Word. A Word from God. Why can't he say anything? . . . *Fuck* . . . We need help. We need the sky to fucking open. But it won't open. It doesn't open.

I need someone else to see me—*look* at me, I say. I need to look into someone else's eyes—*Simone's* eyes . . . And she'll burn away my death. And I'll burn away the death in her . . .


## 8

WEDNESDAY.

The atrium, eighth floor.

The Alan Turing building is getting bigger—it must be. It's actually *growing*.

It's vast enough to have its own weather. I'm surprised birds aren't circling up here . . .

The vast central space. To give us—what?—a sense of awe? A space in which the spirit might rise? Might spread its wings, as in some faux cathedral?

Serenity. So much light and air and space. Light everywhere. The air, flooded with pearly whiteness.

As if the afternoon could be tamed. As if it could be made benign. As if afternoon anomie could not reach us. Afternoon entropy. As if we could be protected forever from the *madness of the day* . . .

Skylight light. Fake sky, not real sky. And shouldn't the sky always frighten the PhD student? Shouldn't it always be a reminder that work is impossible? That indetermination is all? Shouldn't every PhD student be essentially *afraid of the day*? Shouldn't the sky always be a *revelation of erosion and nullity*?

## 9

**SINGLES PRACTICE.**

Ismail versus Business Studies Guy.

Ismail's serve: high, defensive, dropping vertically into rearcourt.

Business Studies Guy's reply: a slice drop shot, skimming the net.

Ismail's feint, very subtle . . . Business Studies Guy, sent the wrong way. Thrown off-balance. Business Studies Guy, replying late—very late, straight to midcourt.

Recovery. Business Studies Guy has Ismail's measure. He knows Ismail's a *runner*. He knows Ismail likes the open-court game. He knows Ismail wants to manoeuvre him out of position.

Business Studies Guy, pinning Ismail down. Hitting *through* Ismail. Smashing into forecourt, giving him no angle. Business Studies Guy, restricting Ismail's game, narrowing the direction of his returns. Never getting caught up in a rally.

Ismail's frustration. Ismail's mistakes.

An easy victory for Business Studies Guy . . .


## 10

**THURSDAY.**

Al's café.

Well, what's happened since yesterday? Marcie says. Anyone had any adventures? Is there anything to report?

Things are exactly the same as yesterday, Valentine says. Today *is* yesterday, basically. As it will be tomorrow. The boredom's become a bit deeper, that's all. The mundane is a little more mundane.

And as usual there's nothing to talk about except having nothing to talk about, Marcie says.

Isn't that always the case? Valentine says.

Fuck it, we're so *meta*, Marcie says. We don't live directly. We talk too much about our situation to actually *be* in our situation. We're not really *here*.

I don't want to be *here*, Valentine says. Here's a shithole.


## 11

### ON THE BUS BACK FROM UNI.

Our time's coming to an end, Business Studies Guy. You can't stay on at the uni forever, we know that.

There'll come a time when we'll simply be too old for any *realistic academic prospects*. When too much time has passed since we did our PhDs.

Decency will demand that we can no longer style ourselves as would-be lecturers. That it will be *better for everyone* if we no longer attend research fora or day symposia.

Soon enough, we'll have to bow our heads and *accept defeat*, Business Studies Guy. We won't be able to show our faces at reading groups or academic conferences.

Inevitably, we'll have to understand that we can't hang out on the eighth floor of the atrium anymore. That we'd simply embarrass everyone. All the lecturers would look at us as if to say, *What are* they *still doing here?*

No one will want to contemplate our failure, Business Studies Guy.

Before long, it will be generally assumed that we'd be better off *out there*, away from the uni, doing whatever it is that people do *out there*, away from the uni. Soon, the general consensus will be that it would be kinder to cut us off entirely. So we can make our own lives *out there*, rather than fight over scraps of teaching with up-and-coming PhD students.

And it will be obvious then what should have been obvious all along: that we were *academic passers-through*, that's all, Business Studies Guy. That we were *uni traversers*, and no more. Comets, through academic skies, just that ... Stones skipped across uni waters ... And we'll know that it's time to head back out into the outer darkness from whence we came.


## 12

### ISMAIL'S ROOM.

Ismail's *Andrei Rublev* film poster. The icon of the Trinity, as appears in *Mirror*.

Ismail's Bruegel reproduction. As featured in *Solaris*. In *Melancholia*. The most arthouse painting of them all.

Everything in your room is, like, an arthouse quotation, Valentine says. I daresay *you're* an arthouse quotation.

Too bad you haven't got one of those iron-framed beds, like in Tarkovsky films, Marcie says. Your futon really doesn't make it. And it's a shame the plaster isn't coming off the walls, for the full Tarkovsky effect...

Ismail's journal. Written on the front: *Notes of a Cinematographer.*

Marcie, reading:

> *Everything happens when we're not looking.*

> *Show things as seen from the corner of the eye.*

> *Paths petering out. Detours to nowhere. Time pockets, like air pockets.*

You're almost convincing.

> *Nothing matters more than this. Nothing matters less than this.*

*A film that's always being made. A film we live inside.*
*That contains our entire lives.*

*No narrative. No build. Let the film go. Release it. To*
*discover—what? To find—what?*

This would be profound if you *actually* were a filmmaking genius, Marcie says. To think: you have the *look* of some arthouse genius, you have the *bearing* of an arthouse genius, you write about your work as though you *were* some arthouse genius, but you're not *actually* an arthouse genius.

*Theology of Cinema*—a new subsection, Marcie reads. This sounds more interesting . . .

*Believing in creation—an apocalyptic statement about*
*the future. Why? Because the creator will one day win a*
*final victory over disorder and chaos.*

*The collapse of the world into its own destruction. Passing*
*over into a New Creation and the resurrection. Anakeph-*
*alaiosis: recapitulation. The recapitulation of history.*

*The coming kingdom of God is already present, hidden*
*in the world. Already working in the world. Show that.*

As I suspected: you've gone Christian, Marcie says. Or you're *pretending* to have gone Christian, to give your filmmaking more depth. A cunning move. A *cynical* move! But you don't get to be Robert Bresson that easily.

Ismail, setting up the projector.
I don't know why I bother, Ismail says. Why I expose myself to this.

Because we're your friends, Valentine says.

Because we're the Collective, Marcie says.

Because we'll keep you *honest*, Valentine says.

I'm warning you—there's nothing new, Ismail says. I haven't filmed anything extra. I've been going through the archives, that's all. Everything I've shot . . . And I threw the Tarkovsky stuff in there as well. I warn you: It's very rough—and it's silent. I've still got to put a soundtrack over the top . . .

Footage of Marcie, demonstrating *anal breathing*. Held for a moment.

Jump cut. Footage of Gita, busy with a window display. Another moment.

Jump cut. Footage of Vortek, stripping off on the banks of the Mersey. Diving in. Three seconds. No sound.

The most gorgeous sight I've ever seen, Valentine says.

Cut. Footage of Vortek, pissing in the Ees. A moment.

Do you know he's supposed to have the word *disaster*, in Polish, written on his schlong? Valentine says. Of course you can only read it when it's, like, tumescent.

Footage of our hunt for the famous *Ees yeti*.

I think Marcie made up the Ees yeti, Valentine says.

Footage of yeti footprints in snow.

Where did those come from, then? Marcie asks.

Footage of my first talk at the PhD seminar. My maiden voyage. The camera, panning across the room.

There's the young Gita in the audience, newly transferred from Victoria, Marcie says. A *most* respectable aspiring dyke.

Footage of Weep on the Ees moor. Weep in direct daylight. They couldn't have been too keen on *that*. Footage of Weep in the long grass. In their velvet dresses. They weren't dressed for a ramble, were they? They were actually dressed *against* a ramble. They were sartorially *anti*-ramble . . .

Footage of us dowsing. Trying to detect the secret rivers that run beneath the Ees. Val had a real gift for that.

Footage of me, trying to lasso an Ees pony. Failing to lasso an Ees pony...

Footage of a ritual burning of analytic philosophy books ... Footage of us in our *apocalyptic animal masks* for Weep's end-of-times party...

Each time, quick. Each time, silent—crude. With a shaky camera. With jump cuts. With under- and overexposure.

Footage of a robin alighting on Business Studies Guy's hat. Footage of a butterfly, fluttering into frame; Business Studies Guy, dancing with it, following it. And the butterfly landing in his outstretched hand.

Ismail: Well? Do you like it?

We haven't told you to stop, have we? Valentine says.

In rapid transition: footage of Marcie, getting her *COCK LIFE* tattoo along her bicep. Of Valentine, getting his *FULL OF HATE I WANT TO KILL* tattoo on his shaved chest...

Footage of a *Mark E. Smith appreciation journey* to Prestwich. Of Mark E. Smith's semi, up for sale. Of his favourite pubs: the Woodthorpe, the Red Lion, Foresters. His favourite offie: *Bargain Booze...*

Footage of the baboons at Manchester Zoo. Footage of Valentine's impressions of the baboons at Manchester Zoo.

Come on. guys—you wanted something lumpen, right? Ismail says. You wanted lumpen energy... It's about the way we are together. Like, our natural anarchy. Our skylarking. It's about our *friendship*... These are bits of life saved from the Man. These are bits of *lumpen life*. I'm showing our *lumpen revolution*. Our *Songs of Innocence*.

Footage of Weep's favourite sigils (no vowels: written in the past tense—as if what they asked for had already come to pass): *BBLN'S FLLN. BLD N FR.* Footage of Valentine and Marcie playing the Situationists' Game of War. Footage of The Torn Curtain in hospital, selling his kidney to fund his writing-up year.

Discussion. Ismail's showing our *youth*. Youth that remains forever young—inexhaustibly young. Youth that just passed through us, borrowing our lives . . . Youth's supposed to be wasted on the young, right? But what if youth just *is* the wasting of youth? Youth's idling? What if youth's about what *laughs* between us?

General agreement: Ismail's film has *something*. It's not obvious artwank. It's got animal spirits. Approval: Ismail should continue his project.

## 13

### GITA'S ROOM, WINDOW OPEN.

Those screams, Johnny, Gita says. They're so loud—so close.

It's lawless out there, I say. They've given, like, free reign to the mad.

Are all mancunians mad? Gita asks. Where are the un-mad people? Are there any left?

Listening to the ocean of misery. The ocean of suffering. Manchester's a great churning ocean of violence and chaos and horror. And it's never going to end.

Listening to the forever war of Manchester. Violence repaid with violence repaid with violence. Gang wars without cease, without mercy. Tit-for-tats. Petty revenge. Endless beefs. Ceaseless screaming misery . . .

Listening to Manchester's thrashing. Manchester's boiling. Manchester's screaming.

Everyone's going mad. They're going mad from Manchester . . .

## 14

### FRIDAY.

The Alan Turing building.

The inaugural Disaster Studies conference.

Lecturers from far and wide, come to discuss the disaster.

Wow, they've really disastered the place up . . .

A giant projection on the wall: a winsome suicide bomber. A waif of destruction, on the edge of detonation. It can't be . . . it *is*; the cheekbones are unmistakable: it's Ultimate Destruction Girl herself. *Great* disaster branding.

Disaster Studies banners, with the *winsome suicide bomber*. Look at the Disaster Studies conference packs, with the *winsome suicide bomber*. Look at the Disaster Studies tote bags, with the *winsome suicide bomber*.

Publishers' stands, with publishers' reps, full of Disaster Studies enthusiasm. New Disaster Studies series from Polity, from Rowman and Littlefield, from Routledge, from Edinburgh University Press. *Contemporary Thinkers of the Disaster* . . . *New Advances in Disaster Studies* . . . *Renewing Disaster Studies* (but Disaster Studies is still very new . . . Disaster Studies has just been born . . . ).

Lecturers, browsing Disaster Studies books. Lecturers, reading Disaster Studies blurbs.

Surveying the scene.

Attendees from far and wide. Visitors from overseas. From mainland Europe. From the distant US . . .

Young would-be lecturers, just finished their PhDs, looking to make contacts, looking to impress. All dressed up. All *on*. Sporting their name tags . . .

Seasoned professors, with nothing to prove. Senior lecturers, on a weekend pass. In carnival spirits . . . Looking to flirt. Looking for intrigue. Looking for scandal. Looking for one-upmanship. What's the collective noun? A *gossiping* of lecturers. A *bitching* of lecturers. A *jockeying* of lecturers . . .

Then the grandees. Very Important Academic People. Like, a different *race* to us. Thronged. Courted. Fussed over. Top of the tree in the new disaster star-system . . .

And now Russell's welcome speech. And now Russell, talking about the Disaster Humanities ... *a burgeoning multidisciplinary field* ... *the most urgent and difficult of questions* ... *world-catastrophe* ... *the endgame of civilisation* ... *the question of the future survival of humanity* ... *the wrecking of the biosphere* ...

There's life in the disaster, apparently. They've turned the end of the world into an academic fuel. They've given nihilism a funky new name. They've rebranded *world-despair*.

The end of the world, the end of everything, folded in upon itself. Turned into an opportunity. A gravy train.

The French had already picked the disaster up and dropped it. The French, ahead as usual, had published a few books with *désastre* in the title, and moved on. But we Brits, we Anglophoners, really know how to *wring the rag dry* ... How to build a whole Disaster Studies infrastructure. How to make *disaster hay* at our so-called unis ...

It's a gold rush! It's a feeding frenzy! To be among the first to publish on the subject. Among the first to set the disaster agenda! Everyone will have to quote you! You'll be invited to keynote at the new disaster conferences! Asked to examine disaster PhDs! Peer-review disaster book proposals!

Disaster's on the up! The disaster's there for the taking! It's kinda trendy, kinda *new uni*, but that doesn't matter. Oxford and Cambridge wouldn't touch it, but that's okay.

If only we were more ambitious! More careerist! The disaster could be the making of us. It could launch us. We might actually get an academic job ... Ah, but we're truer to the disaster, in our failure. We're *actually* disastrous ...

Postgraduate panels.

Contemplating PhD students from other unis. They're actually *into* it. They're actually *enjoying* it. They're here to make an impression! To curry favour! To forge connections!

And we're here, too.

An All Saints MA student panel. A paddling pool panel. Not yet the open sea, for them. Beginner's armbands, for them. Giving ten-minute taster papers. Maiden voyages. And all of them as cute as baby penguins . . .

Ultimate Destruction Girl's paper. Something about something. Sentient AI. Machine sex. Fully automated luxury communism. Who cares? *Marcie* Cares, capital C. Marcie's asked a question . . . Marcie's showing *interest* . . .

Ultimate Destruction Girl, confused. Ultimate Destruction Girl, discomfited.

But now *Gita's* asked a question. Now *Gita's* showing how it's done. Appreciative . . . Tender . . . And Ultimate Destruction Girl, blooming as she answers. Smiling, eyes widening.

Bitcoin, looking jealous . . . Marcie, looking jealous . . .

Afterwards.

Gita, straight up to Ultimate Destruction Girl. *Shameless.* Gita, leaning in. Cuteness meets cuteness. Gita, playing the older-sister student. *Really fascinating how you . . . Loved it when you said . . . You were so right about . . .*

And U.D. Girl, flattered. U.D. Girl, running her fingers through her hair.

Gita and U.D. Girl, orbiting one another. A binary star system of cuteness. U.D. Girl's cute vintage dress. Gita's cute vintage dress. It's almost too much.

And Marcie, hovering behind. Marcie, all desperate. Marcie, unable to get *close* . . .

And Gita and U.D. Girl, off, away, leaving us all behind. Gita and U.D. Girl, escaping together, arm in arm . . .

Afternoon.

*Our* turn. All Saints PhD students' turn.

A tiny room. A projector. Bottles of water.

Very grown up. Very career-y. Very professional.

Twenty minutes each on our research projects. To an audience of each other, basically—and Ultimate Destruction Girl, come to watch Gita. And a couple of duty-bound members of academic staff... Valentine, on *deicide*—the murder of God. Marcie, on antinominalism. On living life in the *opposite direction*. Me, on Modernist *Gnostic resurgence*. On the eternal return of evil. Ismail, on the anarchic breeze. On messianic shifts—sudden, catastrophic. Gita, on queer apocalyptic (with Ultimate Destruction Girl watching closely. Mouthing *wow, wow, wow* ...).

Late afternoon.

The conference keynote.

Professor Hélène Lagonelle, Paris VII. Imagine it: a real Parisian... A real Parisian, come to our crappy campus! Come to All Saints...

A former supervisee of Sarah Kofman . . . A graduate of the École Normale Supérieure . . . Dressed in high French style (pinstripe suit, noir vibe) . . . Speaking fluent English . . . Speaking better-than-us English...

Thoughts from Paris! From unimaginable Paris! From in-another-universe Paris! You mean there really is a place called Paris? That you can actually *come from* Paris? From *France*? Does France actually *exist*?

No doubt Professor Lagonelle finds the very idea of Disaster Studies hilarious. No doubt her colleagues have told her all about the pathetic UK continental philosophy scene, but she wanted to see it for herself.

English monoglots, paraphrasing high French thought. British bumpkins, aping *École Normale Supérieure philosophy* . . .

We're what happens when European philosophy goes wrong. When it's gone off. Gone *decadent*.

217

We're, like, idiot twins of real philosophers. Of real *European* philosophers. Of real *continental* philosophers. Cut off from our mainland. In our own weird niche.

We're developing strange characteristics. Like fish trapped in caves, whose eyes have de-evolved. Who've lost their pigmentation. Who've, like, atrophied.

We've set up our idiot shrines, with our versions of the great thinkers. Idiot-Heideggers. Dunce-Deleuzes. We're venerating our icons. Repeating their vocabulary. We've made our cargo-cult version of the European greats.

Some growth between paving stones that someone forgot to spray: that's us. Stunted thinkers. An inbred outpost. Weeds, wild weeds, left to grow unchecked, untrained . . .

A by-product: that's us. Uintended. Not supposed to exist. Like mould grown on something in the fridge for months and months. Like a film of scum on European philosophy.

Someone should just *hose us away*! Someone should just *power-wash us away*!

Evening.

The day over at last.

Everyone to Ruin Bar . . .

Drinking. Drinking more.

The melee. The mix-up. MA types, talking to grand ol' keynotes. PhD students, becoming *strangely fascinating* to faculty . . .

Academic seething. Academic swarming. Conference bacchanalia.

Lecturers, trying small talk. Trying chat-up lines. Lecturers, out for the night, out of the study, away from books. Lecturers, out in the world, abroad. Not disembodied after all. Not scholar-ghosts, unused to daylight.

The unsociable, socialising. Study-recluses, out on the town.

Thought-albatrosses, walking clumsily on land instead of soaring in thought.

Big names, who'd be mingers anywhere else, drawing thought-groupies . . . Postgraduate nothings and no-ones appearing as beauties. As crush objects. Chatted up. Taken seriously. Listened to, which they'd never be normally . . .

And there are Gita and Ultimate Destruction Girl, hand in hand. There are Gita and Ultimate Destruction Girl, kissing a little . . .

Marcie, in horror. Marcie, staggering from the bar. Marcie, like a great galleon, sinking with all hands. Tragic! Operatic! *Woman down! Woman down!*

We've never seen Marcie's bowing out—leaving the field of battle. But here she is, laying down her arms. Here she is, *abdicating*. What will we do without our Boudicea? Without our Amazon queen?

Don't collapse here, Marcie—not outside Ruin Bar! Not in the mancunian gutter! The mancunian sharks are circling! The mancunian vultures are hovering! The mancunian ecosystem knows what to do with the wounded!

Bundling Marcie into an Uber. Sending her home. Off she goes, defeated . . . (Marcie—*defeated*?! She should never be defeated!)

A thinning of the crowd. Soon, the bar will be closing. Soon, they'll throw us all out.

Stray older lecturers, wanting to party with the postgraduates. Up for a night out.

Stray older types, who have a pass for the weekend. Who are off childcare duties. Who are a hundred miles from home and wanting to relive their youth . . .

Disaster Studies luminaries, turning to us. Editors of famous learned journals, seeking our guidance. Conference keynoters, consulting *conference kids*.

We're not shy and awkward anymore. We're not Insignificants

anymore . . . We're mancunian spirit guides. Mancunian Virgils and Beatrices. We're lumpen leaders. Because we know the city, if nothing else.

Time to blossom. Time to spread our nightlife wings.

Sure we'll lead the way, if they can keep up . . .


Uptown. To the centre, with crowds of mancunian youth. Young and alive, with mancunian youth. Moving with the moving streets, with mancunian youth . . .

Is this what the revolution will be like, moving together like this? Everyone heading in the same direction, irresistibly, irrevocably . . .

Divinity on the march! Liberty or death! The coming truth, incarnate! The general will, irrepressible—*fateful*! A new dawn of humankind!

Our conference guests, falling away one by one. Our conference followers, lost in the crowds. Picked off by scavengers, probably. Mugged in alleyways, probably. Who cares? They're Manchester's now.

They wouldn't have liked where we were going. The door staff would never have admitted them . . . The music would have been too loud . . .

Proles wanna dance! Proles wanna dance away the conference! Proles wanna dance away the academy! Proles wanna dance away the world!


## 15

**VISITING MARCIE.**

She's grieving, Biblical style, Valentine says.

What, like rending her garments? I ask.

As good as, Valentine says. She's gone all King James Bible. She's cursing, ancient prophet style. It's full-on Catholic despair. She's like a tragic heroine. She's raging against God. Demanding explanations from the heavens. Well, from the ceiling. From the damp . . .

She's just passing through the six stages of grief, right? Gita says. First, numbness and denial—

There wasn't much of that, Valentine says. It was howling from the start.

—Then anxiety and panic— Gita says.

No—just howling, Valentine says.

—Then bargaining and control— Gita says.

Howling! Valentine says.

—Next, frustration and anger— Gita says.

Howling like a jet engine! Valentine says.

At least she's getting it all out, Ismail says. At least she's expelling her inner demons.

I think Marcie *is* an inner demon, I say. And an outer one.

—The next stage: depression and despair— Gita says.

Something to look forward to, Valentine says. Actually, I think there'll just be more howling.

See what you've done, Gita? I say. I hope Ultimate Destruction Girl was *worth it*.

I actually feel great, Gita says. Marcie deserves what she fucking gets. I feel like I've achieved something in my life. Ultimate Destruction Girl aka *Jen* is hot, hot, hot. And all *mine*.

Marcie's room. Den mom's den . . .

Marcie, turned to the wall, like someone who's decided to die. Don't give up, Marcie . . . We need you, Marcie . . .

Marcie's favourite snacks, piled up on the floor. Wasabi nuts and biltong. Oreos and Twizzlers . . .

No appetite, Valentine says. I've left them to Deleuze/Guattari.

How are we going to cheer her up?

We should get Business Studies Guy to sing *Ave Maria*. It's quite lovely. Or there's his Bronski Beat medley . . .

Should we play *Ceremony*, or would that send her over the edge?

The *grandeur* of Marcie's suffering. It's *depth* . . .

This is grade-A misery. This is real Father-why-have-you-deserted-me stuff. This is legit alone-in-the-garden-of-Gethsemane despair.

Marcie, knowing true abandonment. Marcie, knowing God's silence. Marcie's struck by anomie, by *taedium vitae*, by the longing for death . . .

I think it's, like, catatonia, Ismail says.

How can you tell? I ask.

Ismail, working through an online checklist. Not responding to other people or their environment. Check. Not speaking. Check. Blank stare. Check.

She's actually breathing, right? Gita asks.

Just about, Valentine says.

Is she awake? Gita asks.

I don't know, Valentine says. Her eyes are closed.

Can she hear us? Ismail asks.

Calling: Marcie . . . Marcie . . .

No response.

Now what? Gita asks.

Speculation.

She *needs to die*—spiritually at least, Ismail says. Marcie needs to collapse into her own destruction—her own personal apocalypse—so that something new can be born.

A new Marcie . . . imagine that . . .

Maybe she's just *depressed*, I say.

She's in the grip of a *Grundstimmung*, Valentine says.

A what?

It's from Heidegger, Valentine says. A grounding attunement. A profound mood that reveals everything as it really is. Like Hölderlin's holy mourning or whatever.

*Holy mourning*: Is that what Marcie's feeling? The fugitive gods . . . The divine default . . . The interval between the old gods and the new . . . Does it look like a metaphysical despair? Like *religious* despair? We should say a prayer or something.

Ismail, reading: *Christ, be with me. Christ before me. Christ behind me. Christ in me. Christ above me. Christ in the heart . . . Flood our souls with your spirit and life so completely that our lives may only be a reflection of yours . . . Shine through us. Show us how to seek you. We were made to seek you.*

It's from *To the Wonder*, Ismail says. Terrence Malick's film. It's when Father Quintana recovers his faith. It's modelled on what happened to Mother Teresa. She felt deserted by God for most of her life. She thought that God had turned away. There was just silence, and the silence didn't fill with God's Word. And then, one day . . .

She heard it again, I say.

Exactly, Ismail says. Just like in the film.

There's a Celan poem that says, *Pray, God, we are coming*, I say.

So? Valentine says.

He's asking *God* to pray, I say. To *us*.

Do you think God should? Ismail asks.

He could put an end to all the terror and the pain and the suffering just . . . like . . . *that*, I say. He could cure Marcie in a moment.

God's not about manipulating events like some magician, Ismail says . . .

I wish he would, I say. I miss Marcie.

Agreement. We should hold a vigil. We need to accompany den mom through the darkness. It's going to be a long night . . .

Sending Business Studies Guy out for liquor.

Looking through Marcie's bookshelves. Just *Bating: An Onanism Memoir . . Wank Yourself to Riches . . Positive Masturbatory Visualisation . . .* A real collection . . .

Me, reading:

> *Guided masturbation alone is the means of your prog-*
> *ress, of the fulfilling of your dreams. Your masturbatory*
> *fantasy is the instrument—the means—whereby your*
> *redemption from slavery, sickness, and poverty is effected.*
> *It is the beginning and the end of all creating.*

That was from *Secrets of Guided Masturbation* ...
Wacko, Gita says.
Me, reading:

> *Form a mental image, while masturbating, of the person*
> *you desire. Concentrate your attention upon the feeling*
> *that that person already loves you. Visualise the picture*
> *in your consciousness.*

That's from *Masturbatory Magick*. Quite a title.
Discussion. Is wanking always selfish? You'd say so, wouldn't you? Is there such a thing as *decreative wanking*? Of wanking for world peace? Is there such a thing as charity wanking? A wanking for the Other? For the widows and the orphans? It can't all be about you, can it?
A tear, running down Marcie's cheek.
See what you did, Gita? Valentine says. See how you broke Marcie?
*There is no unhappy love*: that's what Benjamin said, Gita says.
Benjamin killed himself, Valentine says.
That was because of Nazis, not because of *unhappy love*, Gita says.
Inspecting Marcie's badminton trophies. Den mom in her whites. She and Hector, holding medals. They really swatted their way out of the ghetto ...
Inspecting her *complex European women* pin-ups. Olga Kurylenko from *To the Wonder*. Thingy from *Mirror* ... Women with com-

plications. And depths. Who speak lots of languages. Who'd tremble as Marcie kissed them.

Inspecting the damp patches on Marcie's walls.

Ah, if only these walls could talk, I say.

They'd say, *I'm sick of watching Marcie wanking*, Valentine says.

Simone, arriving. Simone, sending us out of the room. Simone, closing the door. Simone, in a one-to-one with Marcie.

Sitting, drinking, remembering the Manchester postgraduate badminton tournament last year. Marcie and Hector, so *fast*. Like they played in bullet time . . .

But it was more than that. They were noble, in their way. A *dirty* nobility, granted. Didn't they break the leg of a Victoria PhD student (and badminton's a non-contact sport)? Didn't a Business Studies student end up swallowing the 'cock?

Always a tension between them. Hector wanted to win. Hector was always energised. Hector always had a strategy. An ambition . . .

But Marcie never thought ahead, never strategised, was never concerned with victory. Her playing was too wild for that. It was like she was greater than the game. *Better* than it, in some sense.

Marcie was a badminton-trickster. *Non serviam*: that was her motto. That's why they could never have put her on Team GB. That's why she could never be part of the world of *medal targets*.

That's why it was inevitable that she would deliberately *throw the contest*. That was why, after coming through the rounds, she lost it for them—deliberately lost the Manchester postgraduate badminton tournament for All Saints.

She turned up drunk. Dishevelled. She could barely hold her racket . . . Marcie was staggering about the court, swearing. She couldn't actually return a shot.

She picked a fight with the referee. Swore at their opponents. Shouted at the crowd . . .

No one could understand what was happening. Wasn't she at the pinnacle of her game? Wasn't she half of the greatest partnership Manchester universities badminton had ever seen?

But we understood what was going on. We knew she'd had enough. *Triumph is for the duped*: that's what Marcie was thinking. *Victory is debasement.* So she sought a victory over victory and the fetish of victory.

And yet she seemed to come to, for a while. It was like Drunken Master, in the films. For a few marvellous moments, Marcie reached a *sober* drunkenness. She *became* the racket. She *was* the 'cock. Badminton was, like, a divine sport. Marcie was a four-armed deity. It might as well have been Vishnu himself playing...

Remembering it: Marcie, helping them fight all the way to match point.

Hector, all concentration . . . Marcie, four foot behind the tee and square on . . . Hector, shifting his racket grip . . . Marcie, facing down the funnel, sending the 'cock arching over the heads of their opponents . . . The 'cock, about to drop straight down to the rear left court . . . The winning point . . .

And then what happened?

The *swerve*—the legendary swerve. The all-anyone-could-talk-about-afterwards swerve.

The 'cock, suddenly jolting, as though jerked in midair. The 'cock suddenly *out*—over the line.

How did it happen? What intervened? How were the laws of nature broken? Telekinesis? Quantum unpredictability? Divine intervention? Demonic interference? Was the 'cock possessed? Was Marcie?

A lost point. Game to their adversaries. Game to Victoria . . .

And Marcie, seemingly happy about the anti-miracle. Bowing to cheers from the Victoria bleachers and boos from the All Saints ones. And Hector, storming off, disgusted.

Simone, emerging.

So how did it go, Simone? Valentine asks. Is Marcie going to recover?

I don't know, Simone says.

Did you ask God for help? Ismail asks. Did you intercede for Marcie? Did you ask for her to be given strength?

She's been given all the strength she needs, Simone says.

Our wake. Simone, gone home.

Sipping picklebacks round her bed.

Valentine, telling us about the *Sea of Trees*.

It's a forest in Japan, near Mount Fuji, where everyone goes to hang themselves. The trees are really tightly packed together, with really knotted roots. There's barely any sunlight, and it's totally still. You just wander off the path, pin up a suicide note, tie a noose to a branch, climb up and let gravity do the rest. Simple . . .

You've got to be absolutely certain you want to die, Valentine says. If you leave the path and change your mind, it's like a labyrinth. GPS systems don't work. Nor compasses. Nor phones—there's too much iron in the soil. Lost people starve to death in the Sea of Trees.

They've put up all these surveillance cameras to stop the suicides, Valentine says. And there are patrols, looking to intervene. And there are all these suicide prevention signs. *Talk about your troubles. Don't keep them to yourself. Your life is a precious gift from your parents. Think carefully about your children, your family.* It doesn't stop them, though.

Discussion.

Didn't the Golden Gate Bridge used to be a hot spot for suicide? Then they put some mesh net beneath it.

There's some Chinese bridge that's the number one suicide spot in the world now. The Chinese are killing themselves in droves. The Man's been *very* busy over there . . .

Do you think this is cheering Marcie up? Ismail asks.

Maybe den mom wants to be taken to the Sea of Trees, we agree. Maybe it's time. Or maybe we should throw *her* off a bridge . . .

Could just phone DIGNITAS. They might have a home delivery system . . .

Quiet, everyone! Ismail says. I think I heard something. I think I heard Marcie.

Silence.

Marcie, whispering: *Antichrist.*

Antichrist? Is that what she said? What's it supposed to mean?

There was that Lars von Trier film where she cuts off her clitoris . . . , Valentine says.

Jesus! Gita says.

The Antichrist is the *opposite* of Jesus, Valentine says. You take everything Jesus is and reverse it.

Marcie, whispering again: *Antichrist.*

Antichrist?! Den mom's gone apocalyptic.

Den mom was *always* apocalyptic.

Den mom's gone *more* apocalyptic.

What's the Antichrist got to do with anything? Valentine asks.

The Man . . . , Marcie whispers. The Man is the Antichrist.

The Man is the Antichrist: Is this what Marcie's come back from Hell to tell us?

Marcie, stirring in her bed.

Gathering round.

Marcie, whispering for a third time: *The Man, the Antichrist: the same.*

Is that all we're going to get out of her?

# CHAPTER 6

**NEXT AFTERNOON.**

Victoria library café.

Gita, Ismail, Valentine and I, sharing our Antichrist investigations.

Me, reading from my notebook. The word *anti-* can mean against or opposite of, but also in place of, apparently. The Antichrist substitutes himself for the real Christ before the Second Coming.

He's the false messiah, in other words, Ismail says.

Me, reading on. *Aims to destroy the work of creation, to nullify the redemption, and to cancel every trace of good on the Earth. Seeks to overturn and pervert established order.* [Sounds like you on a bad day, *Valentine*, I say.] *Associated with various Biblical figures, including Behemoth and Leviathan, the little horn in Daniel's final vision, and the dragon of the sea in Revelations.*

There's more, I say. *A malevolent angelic power. An apocalyptic messianic adversary. A persecutor of the faithful. The arch-blasphemer. Perverts the law through deception.*

A baddie, then, Gita says.

Definitely a baddie, Ismail says. A regular supervillain. Everything wicked concentrated into one person.

Valentine, reading from his notebook: *His head is as fiery flame: his right eye shot with blood, his left eye blue black. His fingers resemble sickles.*

What's to be gained by calling the Man *the Antichrist*?: that's what I want to know, Gita says.

There's such a thing as the *evil of order*, Valentine says. As the evil of the *system*, which is what the Man's been trying to impose all along. It's the usual story; it's how history works: one power grab after another, to gain control of everything. Babylonian Man, Roman Man, Chatham House Man, Bank of International Settlements Man, Trilateral Man, Davos Man; and it's the same every time . . .

The Man always fails, Ismail says.

But the Man's reach is greater, I say. This is global. He has the tech, right? The whole digital-financial nexus . . .

One guy having all this power?! Gita says.

It's not about *one Man*, Valentine says. It's about a *system*—an oligarchy. A kind of *mafia*—of these connected interests who struggle against one another, have internecine wars, but who ultimately work together. Like human predators, pursuing their agenda. Like a wolf pack, advancing its cause. Steering the world but keeping out of sight.

The ruling class, you mean, Gita says.

It's not as simple as that, Valentine says. This isn't just about class. It's a religious thing. We need *political theology* to understand this.

Ismail, reading out a quote:

> This great evil, where's it come from? How'd it steal into the world? What seed, what root did it grow from?

Who's doing this? Who's killing us, robbing us of life and light, mocking us with the sight of what we might have known? Does our ruin benefit the Earth, does it help the grass to grow, the sun to shine? Is this darkness in you, too? Have you passed through this night?

There's no such thing as the Great Evil, capital E just like there's no Good, capital G, Gita says. There are good acts and bad ones. There are decent people and corruptible people who go along with bad things because it's the easiest thing to do. And maybe there are some *really* bad people who had really fucked-up childhoods or whatever. And perhaps there are some *really* good people who are kind and so on. But that's all.

Michael always says that evil has been beaten, essentially, Ismail says. That evil was destroyed by Jesus on the Cross. The thrones, powers and dominions have been stripped of their pretensions and now the kingdom of heaven's revealing itself, bit by bit, person by person . . .

Come on—there's been an awful lot of evil since the crucifixion, I say. It's been *largely* evil. And it's, like, spreading. Don't you feel it all around you?

The final evil, the evil of the Antichrist, is supposed to lead up to the Second Coming, Ismail says. Just before Jesus returns to rule the world, there's one last surge. It's like in horror films, when you think the monster's dead, but it isn't. That's the final energy of despair . . . It's the recapitulation of all evil. It's all the horrors of history returning . . .

You guys just worship the horrible, Gita says. Venerating the Man's supposed *Satanic greatness* . . . Pretending he's some demonic monster: it's just the flipside of Simone worshipping Goodness, capital G. Turning it into something sublime. Except you bow down before Evil, capital E . . .

How *sensible*, Gita, Valentine says.

If you analysed the system properly—if you laid out its structure, its lines of force—then maybe you'd find a way to fight it, Gita says.

You can't analyse evil, Valentine says. You can't break it apart. You need a language that acknowledges its integrity, its depth, its omnipresence . . . That's what den mom meant . . . *The Man is the Antichrist.* She's right. The Man *is* the fucking Antichrist. Only religious language has the gravitas . . . has the *dimensions* . . . to let us talk about these things. Because evil really does have a capital E.

Maybe it's sending us mad, but maybe we have to go mad. We're the last theologians, and perhaps the *only* theologians, Valentine says.

Agreement: We're theology's rodeo clowns! Theology's jesters! Theology has become the preserve of lunatics—that's us! Theology's suffered a blow to its head—*our* blow! Which is why the word, *Antichrist*, has fallen to us . . .

A text from Marcie. Meet me at Jackson's Boat.

A miracle: Marcie's *risen.*


## 2

**JACKSON'S BOAT, ON THE OTHER SIDE OF THE MERSEY.** Fellow diners, on evenings out.

Marcie, entering. A round of applause. She's resurrected herself. On the third day, she rose . . .

Carbs, Marcie says. Chips! Crisps! Bring them to me!

Marcie, eating.

Agreement: Den mom seems *taller* somehow. Den mom's changed. She's risen, changed. There's a *seriousness* about her.

Marcie, dabbing her lips. Pushing away her plate. I had a vision, she says.

A vision?!

Marcie, looking into the middle distance. It's nearly here—what we've been waiting for all our lives, she says . . . We've never understood who the Man really is . . . We've never understood the Man's plan in its true dimensions . . .

He's rich—of course, Marcie says. So rich he's beyond the economy, which is just for peasants. *Power*: that's what he wants. He was born into power, but he wants more. He wants what every tyrant has ever wanted. But we knew that, too.

What we never knew was his *fear*, Marcie says. The Man's terribly afraid.

Of what? we ask. Of who?

The future—the open future, Marcie says. Time itself. Anything he can't control. He's afraid because of the limits to his power. He fears what's coming.

For a long time, the Man wanted only to be able to save himself and his family, Marcie says. Escape to an underground bunker when the trouble came. To an orbiting Elysium. Or he dreamt idly of nanobot upgrades to his body, allowing him to live forever. Of uploading his consciousness to some silicon platform. You know—all that biotech Frankenhuman bullshit.

But that's not enough for him anymore, Marcie says. Because he knows that if civilisation collapses, it doesn't matter whether he's uploaded himself or not. It doesn't matter where he's escaped to. That's why he's afraid. He knows there are limits to his power. That he can't manage everything. Which makes him even more dangerous.

He's afraid of us—the people, Marcie says. He's afraid of financial collapse, and of the people rising up. The banking system's broken (the Man was the one who broke it). Everyone knows the debt can't be repaid. The whole economy, a façade. Central banks, battling the debt crisis by printing money—by taking on even more debt. The repo market, going mad. It's going to implode at any moment.

So the Man's busying himself with the last cash grabs, the last land grabs, the last asset-stripping before the final collapse, Marcie says. He's buying up everything—all land, all property. The economy's going landlord-owned. The financial-creditor class—the Man himself—will own everything.

The plan is total creative destruction, Marcie says. A Year Zero reset, Jacobin-style. A new financial transaction system to replace the banks: that's what's coming. And a new global security system, to manage the transition. Biometric IDs for all. The digitalisation of all interactions. A new transnational governance system, so the Man can satellite-control us from afar like livestock.

*Benevolent tyranny*, which will no doubt be followed by *benevolent genocide*, Marcie says. By *benevolent culls*. To reduce the human herd to a manageable size.

Sure, we know this stuff, we tell Marcie. The whole remake-the-world-as-rat-maze thing. The whole Satanic-aristocracy-with-a-slave-population thing...

The question is how the Man's going to bring in the new system, Marcie says. How's he going to stage his coup d'état? What's going to allow him to take absolute power?

Uh ... mind control? Some MKULTRA thing? Stirring up some crazy war? Some panic about terrorism? Some fake UFO invasion?

Fear, Marcie says.

Fear, sure, the oldest weapon. But fear of what?

[Dramatic pause.] *Chaos*: that's what I saw in my vision. The Man is going to wield chaos against us. Reawaken the atavisms. The chaos gods. The screaming gods. The blind gods. The gods of nothing but horror. The Man's going to destroy all security and safety.

Discussion. We know how that'll work. The Man could start a war. Plant some false flags. *Terror* attacks—a powerplant explosion, knocking out the energy supply. A *natural disaster* of some kind—an earthquake or tsunami. Or a *digital* disaster. A so-called *cyberattack*. They could turn off the internet. Suspend all comms. Set off some bomb in a major transport hub. Blame the Russians. Or whoever else is enemy of the month. Civilisation is fragile, right? Break the supply chain and starvation is only three days away . . .

The aim is to make us desperate, Marcie says. To leave us starving in the dark, all comms down. So that we'll turn to the Man, screaming for help. So we'll cry out from the chaos: *Save us, save us.* And then the Man will step in to quote unquote *save* us . . . The *digital gulag* will be ready . . . The social credit system, fully prepped . . .

Go den mom! Fear is the weapon, as it always has been—we know that. Which is why we've been pummelled with fear-based messaging for years. Why our brain chemistry's changed so we've become *addicted* to fear, to our own powerlessness. And now the Man's going to ramp it up . . . The Man wants an apocalypse—*his* apocalypse. So he can bring about *his* salvation. Yes! Yes!

So that's why the Man's the Antichrist, den mom? Okay, we get it.

No—I haven't got to that bit yet, Marcie says. There's more. I haven't got to the Vision.

Okay, den mom—the Vision! We want to hear about the Vision!

I saw chaos—a sea of chaos. A flood. But there's something else. This is weird shit, right. Are you braced?

We're braced.

I found myself in a high place, Marcie says. By some . . . portal. Some opening in space-time. At the threshold of a different reality or whatever. It was dark—terribly so. Blacker than black. And there was all this smoke . . .

I heard these scratchings, Marcie says. Rustlings. Mumblings in the dark . . . Muffled shouts . . . There were screams. Cries . . .

And then I saw it: some, like, *android*, Marcie says. Some machine-deity, not living, but *functioning*. Not looking at anything, but *scanning*. Taking it all in, without love, without feeling. So malign and so intelligent.

Some psychopath cyborg. Some empathyless biomachine, Marcie

says. Some *optimising* robot, that hates the world as it is. That hates life as it is. That wants to make us evil.

I thought: *That's the Antichrist*, Marcie says. *That's the Demiurge. The false messiah. That's the one who's going to bring a false new heaven and Earth. Who's going to enclose us all in the prison world. In the cosmic fucking tomb.*

I saw a face, shrivelled up, Marcie says. This grimacing *hobgoblin* . . . Looking straight at me. Full of anger. Full of mocking rage. And it opened its mouth to scream. Not in pain—but in *glee*. Because it took glee in pain—in *all* pain. Because it thought pain was a *joke*.

And it was descending towards me, screaming. I thought to myself, *I give up*, Marcie says. *You're stronger than me. I can't stop you. I can't resist.* And instead of being frightened, I sent out, like, waves of love. I thought, *I don't want to die in a state of fear, but in love.* I thought, *Everything's so colossally, inexplicably fucked. But there are things I love on Earth. There are people I love* [does den mom mean us?]. *I have friends* [she really *does* mean us—aw!]. *I feel a great power of love, of friendship* [we love you, too, den mom!].

And I thought, *This is the face of evil, all the evil of the coming world*, Marcie says. *This is the face of the militarised police. Of robot dogs. Of no-knock SWAT teams. Of zip-zap energy weapons. Of weather-weaponry. Of nanobots in our blood. Of facial recognition systems and digital lip-reading systems. Of machine-learning systems and sentient AI.*

I thought, *You can do what you like, but you will not win*, Marcie says. *Because we have what you don't have: love. Because you don't understand anything good, anything gratuitous. Because we're not just wild biological machines, misprogrammed and out of control. Because we're never going to be predictable and content. Because we're not going to become a domesticated species. Because we're not going to be managed like cattle.*

I thought, *We're going to find the paths that lead from soul to soul*, Marcie says. *We're going to discover new forms of autonomy, of dwell-*

*ing, of self-organisation. New ways of being outside and against. New refusals. New modes of secession.*

And then the face changed, Marcie says. There was this luminous porcelain mask over light, just light. So beautiful. But she—I want to call her *she*, even though you couldn't tell its sex—saw me. Looked at me, like she was surprised. Intrigued, even.

Then she *smiled*, Marcie says. And it was the most beautiful smile in the world. You should have seen it, the smile. It was playful—even erotic. She wanted me to come to her—to come closer.

And then I saw something else, Marcie says. Us. All of us, exactly as we are, and yet different. *Taller* than we are, maybe. Happier than we are. And yet exactly who we are.

And there was a light shining behind us, Marcie says. Through us. Total radiance, just shining through. And we were smiling. There were beatific smiles on our faces. We were walking in some wide space. The Ees—it was the Ees. We'd laid claim to the Ees. It was ours.


## 3
### LATER.

Walking through the Ees. Sombre, reflective.

Marcie's vision! She had a vision! Do you think a Victoria PhD student ever had such a vision? A Business Studies PhD? Marcie had a vision. A theophany! What does it mean?

That we're not just saboteurs. Not just destroyers who don't want the world to last. Not just wreckers who want to go down with the ship, and to scuttle all ships.

That we're not just the last postgraduates, the postgraduates of the end and the very end, who study only the conditions of the impossibility of study.

That we're not just philosophy's temporary insanity . . . Before it comes to . . . Before it wakes up, scratching its head. We're not just philosophy, amnesiac. Philosophy, bewildered. Philosophy, half-demented . . .

We're Serious, capital S. We're like Christians of the catacombs, looking forward in expectancy. Explorers. We're rangers beyond the given world. We're burning minds. Minds on fire. Minds that might not have long to burn . . .

We've seen through the world—*this* world. We know the truth—the apocalyptic truth. First, the Man's false messiah, with its false prophets, its soft robots. Then the *true* apocalypse. *Our* apocalypse, *God's* apocalypse. First the apocalypse of the Antichrist, of the false reset. And then the apocalypse of the anti-Antichrist, of the great awakening.

But how to bring it about, the true apocalypse, the New Creation? How to show that we're not dead after all—not defeated after all? That we're not too stupid, too marginalised, too lost, too scattered . . . That we've already won—that we're already immortal? . . . That we've touched eternity . . . That it's right here, between us . . . In our laughter . . . In our skylarking . . . In our general fuckery . . .

Agape is the weapon. Friendship is the weapon. Life, everyday life: that's how we'll resist. We'll live our everyday lives. That's the way the Man won't reach us, won't defeat us. Our last stand of fools, in all our foolishness.

We are not negligible—*because* we're negligible. We're not nothing—*because* we're nothing. We're not stupid—*because* we're stupid. We're blessed *because* we're unblessed. We're saved *because* we're unsaved. No one's ever expected anything from us—which is why everything's to be expected of us . . .

And this is how we'll slip free of the Man, escape the Man. This is how the Man can never track us, never herd us, even as he tracks us, even as he herds us. We're the indestructible who cannot be destroyed. (And we will be destroyed. There will be destruction.) We're the murderable who cannot be murdered. (And we will be murdered. There will be great culls.) We're the governable who cannot be governed. (And they will try to govern us. They'll try to enslave us.) Ismail, turning to us. I know what the film should show. *Us.* I'll make an apocalypse of *us.* Of our ordinary lives. Of our everyday lives. But made eternal.

Our lives, Ismail says. What we were. Who we've been. But who we will be, too. Our *eschatological* lives. Our after-the-Man's-apocalypse lives. Icons of ourselves in the perfect future. Looking back at us on the screen. Waiting for us to catch up. To run towards them in heaven.

I'll show our youth—our eternal youth, Ismail says. I'll show the ones we were and who we will be again. Anti-Antichrists. Anti-Satanists. I'll show the eschatological everyday. I'll show that the kingdom of God is already here. I'll show the lumpen as the children of God. As who we are at our best. At our youngest. On the youngest of days . . . Do the Collective approve?

Yes, we approve!

Marcie, do you approve? Ismail asks.

I think we're beyond the Collective now, Marcie says.

Light, vast light, ahead of us. As though there were a football stadium, lights shining out. As though the Ees were on fire. But it can't be, not in this drizzle . . .

Perhaps there's been a plane crash (but we heard nothing. We heard no crash . . . ).

Has a spaceship landed? Are aliens back for another *roadside picnic*? Is a spaceship taking off? Has Bitcoin tempted Ultimate Destruction Girl to head offworld?

Is it the secret Ees military? Are they testing out some strange new weapon?

Is it a natural phenomenon? Is it the Ees's own, private aurora borealis? Is it some kind of *electrical storm*?

Perhaps we're being shown something. Perhaps it's some kind of *theophany*. Perhaps it's the light behind Marcie's mask-woman. The Ees, from the point of view of redemption . . . of the messianic kingdom . . . The Ees, in its multidimensional glory . . .

Sending Business Studies Guy off to scout.

Business Studies Guy, crawling through the undergrowth.

Business Studies Guy, returning. Eyes wide. Beckoning.

Following Business Studies Guy towards the light.

An opening in the woods.

Shrooms, glowing. Hundreds of them, in the undergrowth.

Glowing?! They've never done so before. Is it part of their life cycle in some strange way? Is it a once-every-hundred-years thing?

They look like *brains*, Valentine says.

They're, like, throbbing with light, I say. Pulsing. There's a rhythm . . .

Searching on my phone. *Fungal bioluminescence is a result of decay* . . . , I say. Shrooms glow as they rot, basically. It's some weird chemical process. Fox fire, they used to call it . . .

Imagining other bioluminescent creatures, unknown to science. Luminous deer. Brilliant slugs. Glowing homo lumens, our cousins—hairless, pale-skinned, communicating in hoots . . .

We're being shown something—an Ees secret, Ismail says.

Stuff glowing—so what? Gita asks. Things just *happen* here. One thing and then another and it doesn't add up to anything.

Rejoinder: Forget things adding up! We need waywardness! Unpredictability! We need to go where there are no paths—that's how we'll escape the Man!

We need to crack open our skulls! Ventilate our brains! A shroom trepanning! Only glowshrooms can save us now!

All of us, glowshroom-munching.

Lying in the grass.

The moon, as usual.

No one should be able to face the moon, I say. No one should be able to look it in the eye. It should be like staring straight at the sun—unbearable. The moon should drive you mad . . .

What about the stars? Ismail asks.

The stars are just dots, I say. They're far away. Anyway, at least they're burning. At least they're *destroying themselves*, albeit very slowly. The moon just hangs there, doing nothing. It's a corpse in orbit.

Idle conversation. Would we go to a moonbase if we were invited? Like they'd invite humanities PhD students to the moon!

We could be philosophers in residence or something. Ismail could make a moon film.

It'd be so *gloomy*. No trees, no grass. No running water. No blue sky. Stuck with all those positive-thinking astronauts.

We could see Earthrise.

That would be interesting for, like, one day.

We'd just depress our fellow moonbasers. We'd bring them down. They'd end up shoving us out of an air lock.

Valentine, wandering off. Calling out from the darkness. I'm pissing light!

We look.

An arc of golden urine.

And you guys are, like, glowing, Valentine says. It's like you're lit up from within. It's like you've swallowed glow-sticks.

So we are . . . It's true . . . And Business Studies Guy, burning brightest of all.

Maybe we'll get special powers . . .

Valentine, pulling out his copy of *The Writing of the Disaster*. Reading by the light of Business Studies Guy. I'm sure the answers are here, Valentine says. Blanchot can tell us what to do . . . Only French prose-poetry philosophy can save us now . . .

Flipping through the book.

All these fragments . . . It's like a fortune cookie thing . . . , Valentine says, throwing the book to me. Pick one at random and read it out.

Me, reading:

*It is not you who will speak; let the disaster speak in you,*
*even if it be by your forgetfulness or silence.*

Any the wiser? Valentine asks.
Shaking my head.
Gita, reading:

*It is only inasmuch as I am infinite that I am limited.*

God, I wish I'd stuck to analytic philosophy, she says.
Me, reading:

*The cry, the voiceless cry, which breaks with all utterances,*
*which is addressed to no one and which no one receives.*

That's the scream, I say. Blanchot knows about the screams . . .
Valentine, reading:

*To think the way one dies: without purpose, without*
*power, without unity, and precisely, without method.*

Without *method*, Valentine says. Did you hear that?
I like the way he just *says* stuff, Ismail says. It's like the opposite of a
dissertation. *Not* defining his terms. *Not* stating aims and objectives.
*Not* summarising his position—or even *having* a position. *Not* having chapters or subchapters. Or an introduction. Or a conclusion. Or
a method, probably . . .
It's exactly the opposite of a plaque, or some introductory book,
Marcie says. Nothing explained. Nothing contextualised. Laid out for
idiot readers . . .

Yeah, but it's hardly *How to Defeat the Antichrist in Ten Easy Lessons*, Valentine says.

Marcie, reading:

> *In common we have: burdens. Insupportable, immeasurable, unsharable burdens.*

Gita, reading:

> *I am not indispensable; in me anyone at all is called by the other—anyone at all as the one who owes him aid.*

Business Studies Guy, beginning to fade.

Me, reading:

> *Between the disaster and the other there would be the contact, the disjunction of absent meaning—friendship.*

Marcie, reading (just able to make out the words):

> *It is in friendship that I can respond . . . a friendship un . . . un . . . shared . . . without reciprocity . . . friendship for that which has passed leaving no trace . . .*

The relation to the other is disastrous: that's what this book argues, Ismail says. It's a break with what we know. With earthly order.

Like Simone . . . , I say.

Is Simone disastrous? we wonder.

She *dresses* disastrously, Gita says. Those nun-shoes . . .

. . . And there are disastrous friendships where what you have in common is, like, sharing the disaster, Ismail says.

Discussion, in the darkness.

That's us, right? Full of shared Man-hatred! Shared capacity for nihilation! Shared suicidalism! Shared desire for it all to end! Shared *nihilism*!

Only it's not nihilism, *because* we share it. *Because* we speak of it together. Saying we're utterly dead *means* we're not utterly dead. Saying we hate everything means we don't hate everything . . .

But Blanchot's not writing about what's *shared*, fools, Valentine says. It's not all cosy reciprocity. It's a *one-way* relation he's talking about. Something unilateral, that just breaks in. Like . . . a new aeon. Some epiphany. The fucking Kairos. Like the divine absence. Divine nonbeing . . .

Blanchot's writing about the other person as the unknown, as the Other, shattering all horizons, Ismail says.

Like God? I ask.

Like *death*, Valentine says. He's writing about the death of the other. It's like Acéphale . . . Like Georges Bataille and pals, meeting in the woods. Trying to start a new religion on the brink of World War Two.

See, Acéphale was all about the dying Other, capital O, Valentine says. To avert fascism or whatever. Bataille volunteered to be sacrificed as part of some secret rite in the forest. To let himself be killed. And then the legend of his death would spread, like some kind of contagion . . .

And, like, defeat fascism?! Gita says. Nutter.

Of course he was a nutter, Valentine says. All visionaries are nutters . . . See, this is how we could beat the Man: human sacrifice. Offering ourselves up as drones of capitalism.

We're hardly that! Gita says.

As pieces of human capital—Valentine says.

Or that, either! Gita says.

As makers of profits for the social impact market, then, Valentine says. As a resource for the coming technate.

Isn't some crazy suicide movement exactly what the Man wants? I ask. You know how he thinks. We might be cute, we might be diverting, but we're taking up space. We're breathing air that isn't ours. We're a drain on so-called vital resources.

Sure: we're pollutants! Valentine says. Toxifiers! *Waste*, basically! Who should clear up our own mess. Clean up ourselves *as* mess. It's a question of *hygiene*: that's what the Man thinks, in the end.

So aren't you just playing into it? I say.

This is about *sacrifice*, not waste disposal, Valentine says. About *burning up* all the questions about social use, about making a positive contribution to the northwest economy or whatever.

There's a . . . practice of joy before death, Valentine says. A way of lighting ourselves from the fire of the apocalypse. Of offering up ourselves as sacrifices. Burning up forever. Bringing life to its peak—its sacrificial peak. That's what we want. To live our lives as pure offering, pure gift. To the glory. To the roaring.

Becoming fucking angels of death, Valentine says. Saying, death to the Man, and life to us! Saying yes to life in death, by crucifying the Man. By driving the Man out of ourselves . . .

And I *volunteer*, Valentine says. Kill me! Sacrifice me! *The height of death*: that's what I want to attain. A way of *communicating* through death. Composing my death as a divine work—as perfect poetry in action. It's a way of becoming a saint. Of becoming a sacred being—living in the truth . . .

Can't you just kill yourself? I ask.

Someone else has to do it, Valentine says. Otherwise it won't have the full sacred effect. It won't be, like, *divine violence*.

See, ideally, I'd host a whole farewell banquet, samurai-style, Valentine says. Drink plenty of sake. Then I'd sit down and write my death-poem in one stroke. Which is going to begin: *The sky gives zero fucks*. Sort of a haiku. Then I'd take a sword from a special tray. Bow in silence to you, my witnesses. Put the tip of the blade to the left side of the belly. Stroke my stomach three times. Thrust in the blade and tug it to the right.

But I'd have to have a second to strike off my head at the same moment I sliced into my belly, Valentine says. He'd stand just behind me, aiming his sword at the nape of my neck, where it connects to my right shoulder. You'd need someone good. Someone who wouldn't lose their composure. One blow—that's all it should take. Without spattering blood unduly. Without letting the head roll too far forward, or in an unintended direction. That was Mishima's problem: his second wasn't up to the job. Poor Morita slashed and hacked, slashed and hacked . . . Left a right fucking mess . . .

And where are you going to get a decent second? I ask.

I thought I could train up Business Studies Guy . . . though I'm not sure there's time, Valentine says.

So one of us has to stab you? I ask.

Someone has to do it, for full ritual effectiveness, Valentine says. For it really to work.

Are you serious? Gita says.

It's a rite, Valentine says. My death could be the ritual crime on which you could build a whole religion. Imagine it: the religion of the dead postgraduate . . . Of course it would be a religion for PhD students, first of all. For those who are strangers in this world . . . Who have given up their old lives, their old friends, to come to study . . . Who bear the apocalyptic seed . . . But then it would spread . . .

This is the way to destroy the Man, Valentine says. To have done with his endless disaster. The Man would have it that we're useless fucking eaters—that we're the surplus population, barely productive, barely consuming. The Man wants the transition to the neofeudal order—for elites and their servitors only. The rest of us will be fodder for social-impact investing. For data-generation to enrich the algorithms. And then—the cull. Depopulation.

246

Well, sacrifice is how we lay hold of our uselessness—*use* it, Valentine says. Incandescent nihilism! Sacred violence! Religious fucking suicide! Ecstatic fucking martyrdom! In the same act: destruction and creation! Death and birth! The end and beginning! The ultimate fuck-you to the Man ... Of course, I'll need a volunteer. I need someone to ... you know ...

You're only saying all this because you know no one will actually volunteer to sacrifice you, Ismail says. It's pure posturing. The usual bad faith ...

Fuck—what are we *actually* going to do? I ask. Where's the resistance? We are the resistance, right? Ismail says.

There'll be no resistance from the likes of us—just total takeover, I say. A total solution, encompassing everything. Putting chaos in order—the Man's order. That's why they've made us so passive—so stupid. So inured to powerlessness. That's why we've been processed, for generation after generation ... This is the endgame. The Man's moving all the pieces into place.

We need divine help, Valentine says. We need an anti-cataclysm to save us. We need something greater than *the Man stroke Antichrist's* disaster. *Our own* disaster: that's what we need. We need *divine violence*, whatever that is. We need a violence of destruction that is really a violence of creation ...

We need real transcendence, right? Valentine says. We need *help*. A miracle. The fucking Other, shattering in ...

# 4

BEECH ROAD VINTAGE.

I'm happy, Johnny, Gita says. I'm actually happy.

*Happy* is the most inane word in the English language, I say.

It's amazing when you feel your life's going somewhere, Gita says. When your life just figured out how to get good.

And now you're going to sort *me* out—I know how it works, I say.
You're one of those *smug* lovers. You're going to give everyone advice so
you can *spread the love*. All the world needs now is love, sweet love, right?

I'm actually trying to stop being so introspective, Gita says. I hope
it doesn't make me a shallow person ...

So you share all your angst with *Jen* now? I ask.

Angst's a thing of the past, Gita says.

How about your PhD blues? I ask.

I'm actually reading again, Gita says. We're, like, working together.
She's writing essays, and I'm reading Lukács. In the same room. At
either end of the table.

How romantic, I say. Studying *à deux*.

And sometimes, we have these *study breaks*, Gita says. Like *hot* breaks.

Don't tell me, I say.

You should see her other tats—her *secret* tats, Gita says.

Me, with fingers in my ears: La la fucking la.

This is what life can be like, Johnny, Gita says. Outside the uni.
Outside the PhD. Love! Real love! Romantic love! Forget your *infinite philosophical eros*. Forget your *passion of studious solitude*. This is
*real* eros. It's real passion.

I can't imagine it, I say. I don't know what it means.

You're like some monk, with your studies, with your student hall,
Gita says. Well, fuck that. *Do* something. Make a move.

On who? I say.

Come on, you know, Gita says. It's obvious.


## 5

*(DREAMS OF SUMMER. Skylarking. Skywalking.*

*No meetings—our supervisors, away.*

*Summer reading. Summer writing. Ladybirds crawling across our
pages. Using leaves as bookmarks. Brushing pollen from paper.*

*And summer, opening to receive us. The halls of summer, widening. Great archways in the air.*

*Peace. Great peace. The vast sky, turning through us.*

*And Manchester, hot. Manchester, undamp. Unheavy. The lid of clouds lifted... Blue skies. The great blue eye of summer. Summer's trance. Dazed-working. Sleep-working. Sleeping upright at our keyboards, writing.*

*The Earth is stupid. The sky is stupid. And we're stupid, too, in the hot air...)*

## 6

**NEWS: HECTOR'S SUBMITTED HIS DISSERTATION.** He's ready to be examined. He's submitted?! How's that possible?! He began at the same time as we did! Has he handed in his full hundred k? Could it be any good? In any way competent?

Finishing your PhD on time! Handing it in on the deadline! So Hector had an iron will after all ... So Hector had the intellectual virtues after all ... So he was actually disciplined after all ...

Hector, of all people! Hector, who never excelled in his research fora papers. Who surprised no one in his conversations in the pub. Who wowed no one with his questions to visiting speakers. But he had the *discipline*, apparently. The powers of organisation, allegedly. He was a secret workhorse all along, supposedly.

Next, he'll be publishing articles. Next, he'll end up with an academic job! He'll find some crappy temporary lectureship, and leave us all behind.

If only we'd come into the library every day! If only we'd foregone Al's café! Ruin Bar! If only we'd simply got our heads down! If only we'd stopped masturbating! Prevaricating!

If only we, too, had given up parties and dissolute living! If only we, too, had shaped ourselves into dissertation-athletes!

If only we'd paid attention at method class, like him! If only we'd taken copious notes, like him!

Our dissertations, so far from being ready to submit! ... Our dissertations, dead from the first ... stillbirths! Tumours! Aneurisms! Blood clots!

Our dissertations: absolute stodge! Lard! Fatbergs in the sewer! Vats of liposuction! Drain-blocking sludge to be dissolved with super-toxins!

Our dissertations: marshes. Swamps. Sinking into themselves ... Pulling everything into the mire ...

But Hector's done it! Hector's submitted! Hector's finished! Hector's completed!

What's his secret? Professor Bollocks has probably been feeding him secret method tips. Like, insider dissertation-hacks ... Hector's probably been taking special vitamins. Bespoke supplements. Guarana! Ginkgo! Maybe it's performance-enhancing drugs! Steroid injections! Maybe it's *brainfood*! Blueberries! Oily fish! Pumpkin seeds! Maybe he hired a *dissertation trainer*, similar to a personal trainer. A *dissertation psychologist*, the equivalent of a sports psychologist. A PhD coach!

He's left us behind—far behind. He's left us in the dirt, scratching our heads ...

But, of course, Hector's yet to have his viva. He's yet to get through his oral exam. He'll face his internal and external examiners soon enough. And not everyone passes. Not everyone gets their doctorate. There's hope yet ...


# 7

## BADMINTON.

The doubles game is the pinnacle of badminton, Business Studies Guy. And there was no partnership greater than Marcie and Hector.

Remembering who they were. Their old partnership: mutually defining. Mutually supporting. Mutually dependent . . .

They needed each other, complemented each other . . . They delimited each other. Yielded to each other. They let each other fit . . .

Hector, balancing Marcie's wildness, Marcie's abandon; Marcie, complementing Hector's reliance on technique, on precision. Hector was Apollo to Marcie's Dionysus. Hector was the *clarity of intelligence* to Marcie's *fire from heaven* . . .

Fury and serenity. Wildness and control. Rage and splendour. Held together—brought together. As if they kept the world in cosmic balance . . .


Stretches on the court.

Marcie and Business Studies Guy, working together for the first time.

Marcie and Business Studies Guy, taking on Weep—no easy gig. Weep are surprisingly lithe for goths. You'd have thought black velvet dresses would be a hindrance . . .

Merryn Weep—a high, floating serve, very elegant.

Marcie's reply: a smash, crosscourt.

Severina Weep, moving from rearcourt to midcourt, covering the side. Merryn Weep, making room for Severina. Moving over to the adjacent side, lobbing the 'cock into rearcourt. But Business Studies Guy's *there*. Business Studies Guy's *fast*. A dink smash, very wristy.

The game. A pattern, emerging. Weep are *touch players*. Tricksy players. They're forecourt and midcourt players. They're senders of tumblers and spinners over the net.

Strategy: Marcie, hitting flat midcourt moves down the sides. Hitting at Weep, both of them, crowding them, keeping them under pressure. Forcing lifts rather than touch shots . . .

Win to Marcie and Business Studies Guy . . .

A good start.

## 8

MANCHESTER ZOO, IN THE RAIN.

Wet camels. Wet spider monkeys. Wet wolves, pacing about.

All these depressed animals. The monkeys aren't even wanking. They're not even pelting us with their own shit.

Did no one tell them they're supposed to be here for our delight? That they're supposed to caper about entertainingly? I mean, it cost enough to get in.

What are you supposed to do in a zoo, anyway? Marcie asks. What's it *for*?

I think we're supposed to learn things about ecology and stuff, I say. I think we're supposed to read all the plaques.

There are enough of them, Marcie says. This place is plaque Hell. Fuck, if I wanted to read I would have stayed at home.

Conservation plaques. Disappearing-habitat plaques. The-natural-world's-essentially-finished plaques. Making-us-feel-guilty-for-existing plaques.

It's, like, *doom zoo*, Valentine says. This place is pretending to be Noah's ark, saving all these creatures from catastrophe. As if these were the last animals. The last of their kind . . .

God, I wouldn't like to be conserved *like this*, Ismail says.

Agreement: We're conserving them according to the same logic that lets us wipe them out. It's just the other side of murder.

Penguins. Tigers. All listless.

They know their recreated ecological niches are fake, we agree. They know this isn't real rain forest, isn't real savanna.

They're appalled at being on show. At being watched. They don't want to be exhibited. They don't want to be explained. To be *edifying*.

They don't want the human gaze. They're embarrassed to be found like this. They're self-conscious—and animals should never be self-conscious. That's the beauty of animals usually: that they're not self-conscious. That they have some natural niche.

There used to be that gorilla who'd, like, regurgitate his food and eat it again, I say. Spew and eat, spew and eat . . .

*Substitute activity*: that's what it's called, Valentine says. When zoo animals engage in distractions to maintain a proper level of stimulation. Like the tiger that rubs itself raw against the bars of its cage. Like the hyena that fucks its waterbowl. Like the chimps that roll over and over in their own shit. Like the birds that invite you to preen them, and then nip at your fingers. Like the overfed monkeys that stretch out their palms, begging for food.

Animals, following us with their eyes.

They expect something from us, Marcie says. They're looking to us for liberation. Do they think we can help? We can't help, baboon! Don't look to us, wallaby—we've got problems of our own!

Animals staring through plastic. Asking implicitly, *Why? Why? Why?* Asking, *Why life, why bother?* Asking, *Why anything? Why nothing?*

## 9

### EDITING.

Footage of Business Studies Guy, busy in the library. Innocence, reading. The first morning of the world, reading . . . Like dewdrops in God's morning, reading. Have you ever seen anything so beautiful? . . .

Footage of Simone, in her room. Of Simone, brushing her hair. And now Simone, looking into the camera. There she is, looking. At what? Towards what? Us, in the future. Her viewers, in the future. Who she smiles at because she doesn't care about film, because she's *better* than film, and she wants us to know that there's something better than film, better than art . . .

(And that's what our film knows, too: that there's something better than film, better than art . . . )

253

A close-up of Marcie's street-urchin face. Of Valentine's death-ephebe face. Of my innocent's face—my holy idiot's face.

Scenes from a larger life . . . The last free days . . . Arpeggiated images, all in a rush . . .

It's, like, an *inadvertent* film, we agree. The film made while trying not to make it. When we were busy with everything else. It's an *effortless* film, that made itself in the margins.

*Fast* film, not slow film. Fleet film. *Slippery* film—*laughing* film, alighting on *that* moment and then on *that* one. Film that shows life, shimmering. Light-on-water life: Flashes-of-paradise life:

# 10
## ISMAIL, QUOTING:

*I had a dream. In the dream, there was our world, and the world was dark because there weren't any robins and the robins represented love. And for the longest time, there was just this darkness. And all of a sudden, thousands of robins were set free, and they flew down and brought this blinding light of love. And it seemed like that love would be the only thing that would make any difference. And it did. So I guess it means there's trouble till the robins come.*

# CHAPTER 7

## 1

THIS, THE BIG ONE. Method class awayday, off-campus, at the Tony Wilson Centre.

A whole day . . . morning and afternoon . . . They're going deep. Every kind of psy-ops. They'll reframe us, or try to. They're using advanced menticidal techniques. Mass formation.

A method class awayday. Away from what? From the atrium. From All Saints. There'll be fewer distractions. So they can really *ram the lesson home.*

This will destroy us. Or make us stronger. Why do they always *overreach*? Don't they see that they might push us too far? Don't they understand the psychic forces they might unleash?

We're close to madness: that should be obvious. This could be the one thing that pushes us over the edge. This could be, like, our super-hero origin story. The beginning of our *Humanities Suicide Squad* . . .

Marcie, as *Wanking Cleopatra*. Valentine, as *Captain Hustler* aka *Superfuck*. Ismail, as *The Mystic*. Vortek, as *PhD Thing*. Me, as the *Orphan Knight*.

We'll take on the super-baddies with our special powers of macchiato drinking and pickleback sipping. We'll smash the system with general prevarication and wank-talk . . .

Castlefield.

This part of Manchester used to be a total ruin. They've brought it back from the dead. They probably should have left it dead.

But there are still dead zones out there. Fenced-off scraps of *terrain vague*. Of, like, unofficial countryside. Still-unregenerated warehouses, trees growing from their roofs.

As if they had to keep an authentic patch of ruin in the city to set off the rest . . . As a foil to the regeneration . . . As a reminder of antagonistic energy. Of ghosts that still haven't been exorcised. Of a zone that is unprogammable, unanticipated, unprescribed, unmodelled . . .

Plaques, making the case:

> *An urban wildscape. A spatial state of exception. A superfluous landscape, ready for provocations, proposals and engagements.* [Pure artspeak! Oh God!] *Marginal, abandoned, unproductive, empty; yet also free, available, yet to be engaged.* [100 percent artwank! Nauseating!] *An experimental utopia. A land of latent potentials. A prefigurative solution, full of unaccomplished possibilities . . .* [Which they've killed, just by saying it.]

A terrible *literalism*. A terrible rendering-explicit. Everything explained, framed, contextualised. No ambiguity allowed. No vagueness. No ellipses, trailing off forever.

Everything *stated*, without irony, without play . . . Everything made to market itself, to give up its silence. Everything has to make a case for itself—for its claim to our attention—in declarative propositions . . .

The Tony Wilson Centre. A reclaimed warehouse. A conference venue. A training centre. All exposed brick and glass. Photos of Factory acts and others on the wall. One-offs. Manchester eclectica. There's Vini Reilly (delicate riffage; depressed scintillation). Cath Carroll (wildcat anarchy). A Guy Called Gerald (rattling jungle psychedelia). Buzzcocks (anti-apathy; love song rebirth). Magazine (angst-energy; riff ferocity; Dostoevsky as a band).

Obvious acts, unobvious ones. Bands less important than their record sleeves. Manchester miracle-makers. Joy Division themselves . . . New Order . . . The Mondays . . . In whom Tony Wilson believed. Who Tony Wilson championed.

Music that wasn't just entertainment. That couldn't be kept in the entertainment box. Music dreamed for us! Lived for us! Loved for us! Hated for us! Died for us! And that's what Tony Wilson understood.

Didn't he found Factory Records (a conceptual work of art, high-finish sleeves, Baskerville typeface)? Didn't he open the Haçienda (a tax write-off, a pleasure palace, a cocktail bar)? Wasn't he first to show Joy Division on Granada TV (Ian Curtis, desperate, staring; music turned outside-in)?

Come back from the dead, Anthony H. Wilson, northern visionary, haute bohemian, Chairman of the North, fosterer of tricksters and heretics! Reclaim your city! Batter back the regenerators! Reopen the cracks—the crevices! Bring back dole culture! Reawaken the lumpen! Their time is now. They're needed. Help them bring about the apocalypse from below . . .

Tony Wilson Centre facilitators, welcoming us. Showing us to our tables. It's a world café–style day. It's an *ideas-jamming* day. With big pads of paper and markers bearing the Tony Wilson Centre logo . . .

The sense that our facilitators are not quite human. That they're not quite right. Who trains the trainers? Who facilitates the facilitators? Who manages the managers of souls?

Must be *human programming* at work. *Biometric control.* Mind-wiping, probably. Who knows, even *demonic possession.* They're under the deepest hypnosis. Is there a way to reach them? To break the trance? Will they suddenly scream: *Get out! Escape! For God's sake!*

Questionnaire. Multiple choice. A personality profile. We're choosing As and Bs and Cs . . . We're supposed to be learning our *strengths* as researchers . . . The qualities that *drive* us and enable us to *engage at our best.* That might *enhance our performance and energy at work.* That might help us identify *overdrive risks . . .*

*(But we engage through our weakness, Tony Wilson Centre facilitators. We work by flailing. We work by losing control—by losing all hold. We're at our best when we're at our worst. We're vandals! Destroyers!)*

We're supposed to be sharing *strengths of execution* as dissertation writers. Do we have *efficient, well-ordered systems* for working? Are we sufficiently focused on *results*? On *self-improvement*? On how might we take *independent action to make things happen*; to achieve *clearly determined goals*?

*(But we execute nothing, Tony Wilson Centre facilitators. We improve nothing, let alone ourselves. We're ruiners! Despoilers! Mockers of achievement! We're vague-o-nauts! Day drifters! Brain-foggers! Cosmonauts of the afternoon!)*

We're supposed to be probing our *critical-thinking strengths* as up-and-coming academics. Are we sufficiently *oriented to detail*? Do we focus on the future and *take a strategic perspective on issues and chal-*

*lenges?* Do we use *critical decision tools* (SWOT analyses, impact-effect grids, decision trees, etc.)?

*(But we think from failure, Tony Wilson Centre facilitators. From ineffectiveness. We think from the ruins of our plans, of our analyses. The disaster as thought; thought as the disaster: Hasn't Blanchot said it all? Strategy: What's that? Tactics: a foreign language.*

*Thought flourishes in darkness, Tony Wilson Centre facilitators. Thought is a matter of inefficiency—of lags, delays, obscurities. Thought is delinquent, or nothing at all.*

*Thought needs chaos, Tony Wilson Centre facilitators. To dive down into the waters of chaos like a garnet. Thought needs to plunge into the first things, the chaotic things. Into rough-and-tumble. Into whirr-warr.*

*And into the last things, too; into what comes after, Tony Wilson Centre facilitators. Scattering. Dispersal. The impossibility of either beginning or end. Thought is about the interminable, the incessant, and the eternal return of the interminable and the incessant . . . )*

Wanting to rub our foreheads on rough brick. Wanting a rogue planet to blast into ours. Wanting a series of plane crashes right onto our heads. Wanting to be devoured by a *Dune*-style sandworm. Wanting an earthquake to swallow the city. Wanting bombs to rain and rain.

Weren't there once whole generations of PhD students for whom this would be intolerable? Unthinkable? Weren't there noncompliants? Refusers of this kind of thing?

They were day-wanderers. Thinkers of the open hours. Did they ever complete? Of course not! Did they ever finish? No, and again no! Because they knew that it wasn't about efficiency, about answers to questions. Because their studies *were* their lives—their whole lives. And life was vast. Life was a series of greater skies, greater questions.

And they were part of the old Manchester, unregenerated Manchester. They were part of the amputated city, left to its dreaming. They were part of the ignored city, left to go fallow. Left to be forgotten.

In which they could be lost. In which they could float off into the afternoon, unafraid. In which they could wander abroad. Sign on. Sing the song of absence.

Dropouts. Voluntary departers. Seekers after nothing in particular. Sidesteppers. Remote viewers. Far-seers. Rangers of the infinite. They'd have no truck with any of this . . .

## 2

### TUESDAY.

Beech Road Vintage.

I don't understand contemporary youth, Gita says. Like, the MA generation.

You're talking about Jen, I say. Go on, then—tell me about Jen.

She's into *gaming*, Gita says.

You told me that, I say.

No, she's, like, *really* into it, Gita says. It's what she *does*. It's what she talks about.

Kids today, eh? I say.

She wants to be some games designer, Gita says. Do games art or something.

Sounds ambitious, I say. Sounds like she'll get on in the new economy. She'll leave the other humanities types in the dirt . . . Go with it, Gita. Maybe you'll learn something.

I didn't envisage my life going in this direction, Gita says. In, like, a *gaming* direction. Have you ever *gamed*?

I used to play *Uni Massacre* a bit, I say.

Have you ever been around gamers? Gita asks. Have you ever *dated* a gamer? If there's one thing I've learnt, it's that I'm really not into gaming . . . And Jen's a complete *stoner*. She's always smoking stuff. Like, in the middle of the day. And I swear she's got some fentanyl habit.

At her age? That's impressive, I say.

She's so woozy all the time, Gita says. I hate woozy.

We can be pretty woozy, I say.

We're *existential*, not woozy, Gita says. And we're existential from life, not from fentanyl . . . Jen, like, takes pills, smokes and plays apocalyptic video games. And that's about it. I ask her how she is, and she says, *Just zoomin'*.

*Just zoomin'*: That's what it says on her face tat, isn't it? I say.

On one of them, Gita says.

You should get a matching tat, I say. Get down with the kids.

She's got *Bitcoin* written on her inner lip, Gita says. God! . . . And I have to hang out with all her MA student friends . . . All this romance is just throwing me back on myself. I'm questioning who I am. Fuck, I like *old things*, Johnny. I like *real things*. I like dinner parties. And *conversation* . . . Are you supposed to be bored by your lover?

I don't think so, I say.

I thought it'd be enough to just be in her presence, Gita says. Just to lie there together, all enchanted . . .

You look very pretty when you're wistful, I say.

I'd have things to tell Jen, if she were interested, Gita says. About interiors, say. About Mughal miniatures. About the aphorisms of La Rochefoucauld or Indian classical dance . . . I've got a lot to give. But she doesn't have any *curiosity*. She's not interested in anything that isn't virtual. She doesn't want to browse antique shops. She doesn't like anything from before *2018* . . .

How about her robotic dancing—does that turn you on? I ask.

Now you're taking the piss, Gita says. She's a child—a very pretty child, but so . . . *what*?

You're pretty enough, I say. You don't need another pretty.

I *am*, aren't I? Gita says. I *don't*, do I? I really just want to be appreciated.

You need someone who can look after you, I say. Who makes you the centre of their attention.

Exactly! Gita says.

You need someone to take you up, I say.

*Fabulous!* Gita says.

You need a champion! I say. A cheerleader!

Gita, reflecting. We're still learning how to live, aren't we? she says. It's embarrassing, learning how to live in your mid-twenties. But maybe that's what your mid-twenties are about: learning how to live. Making these mistakes. Believing you're one thing and discovering you're another . . . God, I'm almost *embarrassed to be alive* . . . Why are we such romantic fools, Johnny?

I wouldn't know, I say.

Come on, you must have been in love, Gita says.

I half thought I was in love with *you*, I say.

Which definitely makes you a fool, Gita says.


## 3

WATCHING BUSINESS STUDIES GUY, READING IN THE LIBRARY.

The books, half afraid of him. Of the light-beams from his eyes. The books, not expecting readers. Not expecting to be opened, let alone read, here in their dark corner of a library of a low-league-table university. They wouldn't have minded just dreaming away a couple more decades in darkness, before being dumped in the library skip . . .

But the books are trembling now. The books are fearful and hopeful—both at once. A thrill, passing through them. They know the burning gaze of Business Studies Guy will scorch their pages. They know the *messiah of reading* has come, who'll burn them up entirely.

## 4

THE EES. Through the tall grass.

Vortek, coming out of the forest. Falling into step with us.

Small talk with Vortek.

So is your real name actually Vortek? I ask.

Silence.

Is it true you were in a Polish boyband? Valentine asks.

Silence.

I heard you were basically raised by wolves, Vortek—is that right?
Marcie says. And that you didn't speak till you were twenty-one . . . It
would account for a lot.

Silence.

But you correspond with the Unabomber, don't you? I say.

Vortek, nodding.

Do your wolf-howl, Vortek, Marcie says.

Vortek, howling into the wood.

An answering wolf-howl from the darkness. Several wolf-howls.

What the fuck?

Trouble.

Battle-stations.

Crashing.

A bullet whizzing by.

Someone's *shooting* at us.

Northenden boys! Who else!?

Business Studies Guy, fallen.

Man down! Man down!

Kneeling by Business Studies Guy. A flesh wound. He's hit in the
thigh. They missed his vital organs. Thank God!

Business Studies Guy, lying in the ferns, quietly bleeding.

He can't walk, I say.

We could leave him there, Valentine says.

For Northenden boys? Marcie says. For the Ees wolves?

Improvising a tourniquet.

Another bullet. Another. *Whizz. Whizz.*

Business Studies Guy, stoical. Silent through it all. Will he ever play badminton again?

Vortek, in full war-face. Vortek, tying on the *bandana of destruction.* Vortek, moving off through the bushes, strangely silent. Vortek, taking the battle to the enemy. Those poor Northenden boys . . . They have no idea what they've unleashed . . .

Vortek's been reading up on medieval torture. He'll want to try stuff out. He bought a bunch of thumbscrews from eBay . . .

The *pain* they'll know. The *agony* . . .


Later. Vortek's hideout in the deepwoods.

A punch bag, salvaged from some rubbish tip.

Rings, hanging from the tree-branch roof for *complex aerial exercise.*

Are those really shrunken heads? Shrunken *Northenden boy* heads? Don't ask!

Field medicine. Vortek, dressing Business Studies Guy's wounds.

What care! You can really see the nurturer in Vortek.

Later. Vortek, reading from his Unabomber letters. *It's out in the open. They're not sneaking up on the herd anymore. They're breaking in the new system. Everything's lined up—every major logistical element. It's not enough to own everything; they want to take possession and control of living things in their essence. They want totalitarian control at the cellular level.*

Daydream: Vortek and Business Studies Guy, falling in love. Vortek, saved from his Unabomber fantasies. From his solitariness. Vortek, building a log cabin for them both in the woods. Vortek, becoming some kind of lumberjack, in a checked shirt and braces. Growing a great beard. Business Studies Guy, as a woodcutter's wife in a cute little dress, frying up some righteous shrooms for supper . . .

*Will Business Studies be fit for the Manchester Postgraduate*

*Badminton Cup?*: that's the question. Will he be fit for the Manchester Postgraduate Badminton Cup?


## 5

**WEDNESDAY.**

Editing.

Footage of shroom days on the Ees. Of hunts for the god-shroom. Footage of kite-flying days. Of Ees hangover days.

The film's a gospel of instants. The trail our lives have left. Why *these* details? Why not?

No plot. Nothing linear. The film explains itself. Is its own explanation (its non-explanation).

*The speed of life*: that's what the film's about. This is art that's forgotten it was art.

The way it's held together—that's what counts. Its rhythm, its velocity—that's what gives it form. Like a spear thrown through time, that draws time with it. Like the white horse that gallops through history and that *is* history . . .

Ismail's notebook:

> *The apocalypse of creation—creation fulfilled. Universal salvation.*

> *The kingdom of God: the transformation of each instant into the last hour.*

> *Eschatological logic. Every act, every human proceeding, should be carried out in relation to the coming kingdom.*

Footage of Valentine in his gimp mask. Footage of the Mersey, bombing along—muddy brown, imperative. Footage of the Dane, cross-legged, in yoga pose, lips to the Scandohorn. Footage of me, tootling on my melodica.

Who will we have been?: that's what we're looking to discover. Who were we, in Manchester, if we weren't just lost; if we weren't just blown into the air like dandelion seeds? Was there a place for us on Earth after all?

Proof of the utter contingency *and therefore* the utter necessity of our lives. Proof of the utter unimportance *and therefore* the utter importance of our lives.

Footage of Vortek, fresh from hunting, with a brace of Ees rabbits. Footage of the Wizard on a shroom-hunt, flies buzzing round his head. Footage of us all wading through waist-high ferns, like explorers in the new world.

## 6

**DOLEFUL AT RUIN BAR.**

Business guy, on crutches.

Horror of the world. Horror of what's *out there*.

Only now do we dare remember the horror of our lives as they were, Business Studies Guy. Only now we've been given a little distance.

Only now can we see the world as what it was: *unendurable*. Only now can we call it by its proper name: *damnation*.

Only now do we know it for what it was: our daily destruction and self-destruction. Only now can we understand that our lives would have led *directly to suicide*. That we are in effect all but *suicide survivors*. That we're more or less *post-suicide*.

We're post-everything, Business Studies Guy. We're *after*. God, how many times have we died? How many times must we keep on dying?

We've been playing dead all our lives, Business Studies Guy. No— we've *been* dead all our lives. We're just a little less dead for the time being because of our scholarships. We've been let off *utter death* for a few years . . .

But we mustn't think we've escaped, Business Studies Guy. We mustn't think we've left the world behind. This is a *reprieve*, that's all. We'll be *out there* again, and quite soon.

We'll be cast out of the uni, Business Studies Guy. The gates of academia will be closed to us. We'll no longer walk the campus as of right. We'll no longer be able to knock on our supervisor's doors. We'll no longer look out over the atrium. And who will we be then?


# 7

## ALDERLEY EDGE.

God, you really look the part, Marcie, Valentine says. You're really working the country gentleman look. Very tweedy. Like Gertrude Stein in Cheshire.

Did you think you were going hunting or something? I ask. Did you want to fit in with the locals?

Why are we here, anyway? Gita says.

For a Lovely Day Out, Valentine says. To get it together in the countryside.

To lose it altogether in the countryside, more like, Marcie says. I'm really not one for the *Cheshire idyll*. I think I actually need industrial decay to feel at home. I don't feel comfortable when a place isn't radioactive. If there's no nuclear waste lying about—if there's not a *vastly increased chance of catching cancer*, it's not for me.

I mean, what's the countryside actually *for*? Marcie asks. Nature doesn't do it for me. Whenever I see, like, nature's greatest hits on TV—sperm whales leaping out of the water, algal blooms from space, a crouching wolf-packs ready for the kill, fish in rushing shoals and all that—I just yawn. And it's the same out here. All I can think is that we're a long, long way from civilisation.

I thought you hated civilisation, I say.

It's all relative, Marcie says.

What's Alderley Edge the edge of, anyway? I ask.

Some ancient impact crater, I think, Valentine says. Where the meteor struck that wiped out the dinosaurs.

It's kinda desolate, I say. Is this where Myra Hindley and Ian Brady buried the bodies?

That was the *moors*, idiot, Marcie says.

I can't believe we came out here specially, Valentine says. It really builds up your expectations. See, we never expect anything of the Ees. It's just *there*.

Valentine, trying to yodel.

Shh—you'll cause an avalanche, Marcie says.

But there's no actual snow, Valentine says.

There's scree, Marcie says. Maybe it'll roll down and bury us.

Ascent, for the famous Alderley Edge view of Manchester.

I think the air's getting thinner, Valentine says. It's the altitude. I feel a bit dizzy.

Sheep, baaing at us.

You could make a great porn film out here, Marcie says. Like, *rural porn*. Ever fucked a sheep, Valentine?

Here we are: at the peak. At the crater's rim. The city, far off, blue. The new tower skyline. Gimmick buildings. Let's-pretend-Manchester's-prosperous buildings. Penthouses . . . Helipads . . . Manchester, gone vertical. Manchester, with sightlines to all the other vertical cities . . .

Manchester's so open to the sky, we reflect. The whole *mancunian plain*, so vulnerable. Death from the sky: Couldn't it come at any moment? Aerial bombardment . . . Missile strikes . . .

Time another meteor smashed down. Time another supervolcano erupted. Wiped everything out.

Truth, that's what we want. The destruction of Manchester (*this* Manchester). Manchester's real ruins.

The disaster's not death, but the postponement of death, we agree. The disaster's not the End, but the fact that the End hasn't come. That the cycle isn't complete. That Manchester's still standing...

Following the path.

An overhanging boulder, very mossy. A wet trickle from its base.

Merlin's well, Ismail says. It's supposed to have miraculous healing powers.

What was Merlin doing at the Edge? I ask.

What are any of us doing here? Marcie says.

This is probably where they perform ritual magic, Valentine says. Human sacrifices...

In Cheshire? Gita says.

Why not? Valentine says. That's how they keep themselves entertained out there, the mancunian elite. There was that fat MP—what was his name? And Jimmy Savile, of course—he was a DJ in town. Raiding the children's homes for victims. A bit of ritual Satanic abuse to keep them busy on dull countryside nights...

I'm sure they're boring bourgeois, just like anywhere else, Gita says.

The higher up you go, the more perversion there is, Valentine says. It's quite deliberate. Our rulers are selected for their sociopathy.

Why? Gita asks. By who?

The psychopaths at the top, Valentine says. The evil ones. The global predators. Anyway, if you're not a paedophile at the beginning, they'll make you one. They'll give you the keys to the city, once they have a control file on you. They'll give you access to the secret levels, but there's a price. They're real Satanists, some of them. They have all these weird rites and rituals.

I thought you were into rites and rituals, Ismail asks. I thought that's what you were writing about.

Georges Bataille and co. weren't actually *fucking children*, Valentine says. Face it: there's a whole nest of vipers out here.

Thirty-third-degree masons or whatever. *Eyes Wide Shut* types. Who knows, lizard people.

You make the countryside seem very exciting, Gita says.

Well, *something* must be happening in those big houses, Valentine says.

Marcie, passing round her hip flask. Swigs for all.

The Man actually has big plans for the countryside, Marcie says. He's buying it all up. The countryside will be closed to all but the elite. And the city will be a rat-maze for scummers like us. We'll be stacked up in high-rises on Universal Basic Income—the Man's version of charity.

At least we won't have to go to work, I say. At least they won't have to pretend that there's anything for us to do. Just let AI get on with managing things. We'll be given welfare, no questions asked.

Oh, sure there'll be questions—there'll be all kinds of questions, Marcie says. *Are you being a good citizen? Do you engage in antisocial behaviour? Are you ever critical of the government?* And if you are, they'll just switch you off. Because they control all your interactions.

Step out of line, do anything wrong and you'll lose your benefits, Marcie says. They'll freeze your bank account. They'll cut off your cash flow. Your electricity. They'll kill-switch your vehicle. You won't be allowed to travel.

Yeah, but everyone will have all this *time*, Ismail says. There could be some cultural renaissance . . . They'll probably lay on free arts-and-crafts activities. Creative writing . . .

Sure—to control us, Marcie says. To keep us busy. Just so long as we don't *question* anything.

They'll let us register as students, like, forever, I say. Everyone will be doing infinite PhDs, to be studied over a lifetime . . .

Sure, PhDs in which you can't question anything, which means they're not PhDs, Marcie says.

Cheaper to keep us dumb, Valentine says. They'll probably just flood the city with some new opiate . . .

Cheaper still to cull us all, Marcie says.

Cheaper still to get us to cull ourselves, Valentine says. Why bother with all these *useless eaters*?

The Man needs some peasants to serve him, I say. He needs a serf class to keep things going.

The Man will have AI, Marcie says. As for the rest of us . . . he might want to keep a few sterilised specimens, a few slaves, a few servitors . . . But not, like, billions of us.

The train back into Manchester. Back to Piccadilly.

The train on its viaduct. The raised railway to the centre.

We're heading back in. We're being enclosed again. We're being lost again, among the vast buildings of the centre.

Stations: Cheadle Hulme, Levenshulme. What are these places? What do they mean to us? What are we doing here? Isn't it entirely random, our being here?

The whole of Manchester. So arbitrary. So contingent. Why, but why not? Why anything, but why not anything?

How can we make sense of our life here? How can we bring the city—the whole city—into our lives? The whole mancunian plain? How not to be lost—*more* lost? How not to be forgotten? How to reclaim the city as our home? How to say, *we will have lived in Manchester*?

## 8

**BEECH ROAD VINTAGE.**

Now what, Johnny? Gita says. What's your excuse? You're disturbing me.

Are you actually *writing*? I ask.

Don't tell anyone, Gita says. Don't tell Marcie.

271

Wow—you're working on your dissertation—I can't believe it, I say. Is this a post-Jen thing?

Jen? Who's Jen? Gita says.

Don't pretend, I say.

Why do we have to make romantic mistakes? Gita asks. When does all that stuff stop? Shouldn't it be easy? Tell me it'll all be easy one day . . .

It'll be easy one day, I say. I'm lying.

God, how many times do you have to go through this to find someone right? Gita asks. How many trial romances do you have to have? Is this how it's going to be, over and again?

I prefer you like this than all smugly in love, I say.

It's just addiction, isn't it? Gita says. You get addicted to someone. And then . . . *de*-addicted. All these blind animal mechanisms. You have all these *epic feelings*, and for what?

We're the dupes of our hopes, Gita says. We hope to be something other than fools, and here we are: fools. We wake up in the morning, hoping it will be different, but in the end it's just the same. In fact it's even more the same than it was before. The world is the world is the fucking world. And we are exactly who we are. And fuck-all changes.

Very Morrissey, I say.

Well, Morrissey has it right, Gita says. Fuck, Johnny, do we always have to compromise? Are our expectations too high? I thought Jen and I were going to set up home—just close the door on the whole horrible world. I thought it'd be the two of us forever, in a self-enclosed universe we'd never have to leave . . .

So you agree that we're *Mangelwesen* now? I ask.

Mangel-what? Gita asks.

It's German for something *radically deficient*, I say. For being outcasts from the natural order. *The most orphaned children of nature*: that's what Herder calls us, I say. We're not, like, *for* anything. We don't have some natural niche, like animals. Our birth is always a monstrosity or error.

Is that what you wish: that you'd never been born? Gita asks.

*Perish the day I was born*: that's what Job said, I say. *Natus est denatus*, right? Being born is the same as being dead already. We're monstrous *Mangelwesen*, and everything else is a lie.

Don't drag me into your sad little world, Gita says. Some of us have hope for the future . . . Some of us actually have *plans* . . . See, I've decided I want this phase of life to be over. I want to leave all this behind. I'm actually going to *finish* my PhD.

*Such* determination, I say.

A hundred good days—that's all I'll need, Gita says. A hundred good days, and I'll be *done*. Actually, I think I'm going to shave my head. Get ascetic. Go running every morning and then crack open the laptop . . .

Woo! I say.

You'll do the hundred-day thing, too, right? Gita says.

What, you want to be *accountability buddies*? I say. *Very* methodology class.

Come on—we can breast the finish line together, Gita says. No languishing.

I actually *like* languishing, I say.

We can shave our heads together, Gita says. Become storm troopers of work . . .

I don't want to become a storm trooper of anything, I say.

I'm going to quit working here, Gita says. Give in my notice . . . And you should stop wandering about all afternoon.

That's who I am: a wanderer in the afternoon, I say.

You're too happy being a ghost, Johnny, Gita says.

What's the magical thing that's supposed to happen when we complete, anyway? I ask.

Things will be clear again, Gita says. We'll know who we are and what we're supposed to do.

I don't think there's anything we're *supposed to do*, I say. We don't have to *do* anything or *be* anything—that's the point. We're *Mangelwesen*.

Speak for yourself, mangel-boy, Gita says.


## 9

### THE ATRIUM.

Hector's oral exam. Hector's viva, in an office with *EXAM IN PROGRESS* posted on the door. And all of us waiting to hear the result.

Imagining the scene. Introductions—his internal examiner. His external examiner. Handshakes. Hector, taking his seat. Professor Bollocks, sitting nervously behind him. Keeping watch over his protégé. Willing him to succeed.

Hector's examiners, sitting across from him, copies of his dissertation open before them. With annotations. With Post-it notes on significant pages. With comments in the margins . . .

Did Hector have a couple of macchiatos beforehand? An energy drink? Did he have a shot of pickleback or two to boost the mood? A line of Bitcoin's coke?

How will he be coming across: Frantic? Maniacal? Deranged?

A first question, to put him at ease. A loosening up, before the real discussion begins. Before the *formal defence of the thesis* . . .

And now the questions come. Involved questions. Complicated questions. Questions with sub-questions. With questions stacked inside questions like matryoshka dolls.

And Hector, taking notes as they ask. Hector, trying to buy time with his note-taking.

What's going on in his head? Dissociation? Does he seem to be floating above his body, looking down? Does it all seem to taking place at an immense distance?

Is Hector having self-destructive thoughts? Is he contemplating cutting himself, injuring himself, knife pressed to the flesh? Is he thinking of throwing himself out of the window, if only the windows opened that wide?

Or is Hector coming into his own for the first time? Concentrating as he's never concentrated before . . . Foregoing our fools' bricolage. Our pick 'n' mix of European thought . . . Is Hector summoning up all the intellectual virtues? Opening up some thought-gate . . . Pulling thoughts through—divine thoughts, greater-than-him thoughts. Downloading them directly from God.

Later. Comforting Hector in Ruin Bar.

Failure! Well, near failure.

Hector should be out for a meal with his examiners. He should be being toasted by his supervisor, by Professor Bollocks himself! He should have already have phoned his parents in triumph! WhatsApped everyone! Updated Blurt! Ordered a new debit card with *Dr* before his name!

And instead? Referral. Which means rewriting.

Hector's been instructed to *fundamentally rethink his dissertation*. He's been told there were *basic problems in the presentation of his argument*. That there were *serious concerns about the quality of his scholarship*. He'll have to restructure the entire thing, from the ground up—rewrite whole chunks. How long will it take him—another year? Two?

Commiseration. You've had your comeuppance, Hector—your life lesson. Your limitations have been shown to you. What you can and cannot do. The game you should not try to play.

Did you really think you could just *finish your dissertation*, Hector? Did you believe you could simply *hand in your work on time*?

Did you imagine that you would be able to *complete a PhD in philosophy*? Impossible, Hector! Delusion! Three years could never be enough! PhDs, for our kind, are about the illimitable! About keeping the unknown before you! You're never going to end, Hector. You're just like us. Except you were even more stupid than the rest of us! Because you actually believed you could finish! You actually thought you'd complete!

Sure, you wanted to turn towards the European sun, Hector. You sensed it, the warmth and light of the European sun. You craved it, Continental thought, Continental Philosophy, without understanding it. You wanted to play, like us, with big, vague words like Being and Nihilism and Godhead.

You wanted to stay warm, that's all, Hector. You wanted to feel the rays of the European sun on your face, and who blames you? We all wanted that. That's why we began our PhDs.

And you wanted to *write*—to complete a dissertation, Hector. And you believed yourself to be in the last phase of your dissertation, to be coming to an end. The last lap!

You felt the momentum, Hector. You wanted to finish your writing in a single sweep, a single gesture. You weren't lost anymore. You knew what you were supposed to do. There was light on the horizon.

And you thought you'd finished, Hector. You thought you were done! You thought there could be a limit to study! You thought you could put the interminable behind you, but the interminable lay ahead of you. You thought you could step over the limit, but the limit had instead become illimitable.

The hubris, Hector! The overconfidence! It's not even tragic! It doesn't even rise to tragedy! It doesn't get there! It's *comic*, Hector! It's farcical! It's the farce of the universe!

Toasting Hector with picklebacks. You're one of us, Hector! No better, no worse! You'll be swept down the drain with us! You'll swirl down our plughole!

All of us, in unison: *ONE OF US! ONE OF US!*

Hector, staggering out of Ruin Bar. Stumbling down the towpath. Toppling into the canal with a great splash. Was it intentional? A suicide attempt? Doesn't he know canals are no more than three feet deep? That they were built for flat-bottomed barges?

Bar-goers, watching us drag him out. They must take this for some student jape . . . They must think Hector is an ordinary drunkard . . .

A very wet Hector, coughing on the towpath. Does anyone know first aid? Who wants to give him *mouth to mouth*?

But Hector's alive . . . Hector's breathing . . .

And now Marcie, talking to Hector. Hector's wet head in her lap. Hector's eyes closed. A pietà. And den mom, bent over him, talking very tenderly, very quietly. What's she saying to him? What's she whispering?

Something about badminton, no doubt. Something about their old partnership. About nearly lifting the trophy . . .

Marcie's tears, dripping into his. Is Hector going to rejoin her on court? Is Marcie thinking about the Manchester Postgraduate Badminton trophy?

# 10

## SATURDAY.

The Ees.

The sound of the Scandohorn. Unmistakable. The Dane's calling us. We're being Scando-summoned.

Through the tree-tunnel. Light through branches.

The land, sloping downwards.

The amphitheatre.

Weep, in their velvet dresses, busy with recording equipment. They're working on the film soundtrack, they explain. These are field recordings, to capture something of the Ees ambience. Of the *aural terroir*.

The Dane, incantatory on the Scandohorn. All rarefied. All austere. All restraint. No *fluid fury* here. No rising and falling runs. No arpeggiated flights. No screams and shrieks . . .

Now Vortek, with his hurdy-gurdy, singing out of tune, but with such emotion, playing songs of the Polish deepwood. Playing Polish forest glades. Polish toadstools. Playing secret Polish rivers, where unpolluted waters run. Playing the oldest woodland, that the chainsaws never reached.

My melodica. Playing the student hall in summer. Playing deserted corridors. Playing the song of everyone-away-but-you. Of everyone-with-their-families-but-you.

Playing summer silence. Playing the absence of noise, of chatter, of laughter. Playing empty post-trays. Playing unused basement washing machines. Playing steel shutters pulled over the bar.

Playing institutional carpet tiles. Institutional fire doors. Playing the wind in the trees on the grounds. Playing my student hall *view*, over the tennis courts.

Playing the perfect nothingness of the institution. Playing the Zen of the student hall. Playing the Uncontainable of postgraduate life. The limitlessness of the dissertation. Playing the Open of PhD infinitude . . .

## 11

### MICHAEL'S GARDEN.

Overcast. Simone and I, sitting side by side on the wrought iron bench.

Her bandaged wrist.

You wanted to talk to me, Simone says.

I wanted to know that you were okay, I say.

I'm okay, Johnny, Simone says. Thank you.

You're recovering? I ask. Healing?

I'm fine, Simone says.

Those bastards, I say. What . . . what did they do to you?

There was a tussle, Simone says. A misunderstanding. I'm fine.

Why do you go out to all those scary places? I ask. Why do you risk it? I mean, you're helping these people, and what for? . . . How dare they touch you! God, why must everything be so disgusting? Was it always like this? So vile? The horror's, like, *mounting* . . .

Even here . . . you can feel it, I say. Even sitting here in the sun . . . Michael should build the walls higher.

Michael's policy is to provide burglars with no cover, Simone says. Give them nowhere to hide. Let them look through the windows, if they want. They'll see there's nothing to steal.

Michael's not frightened . . . That figures . . . , I say. I'll bet if someone broke in, he'd light a candle and just sit down with them. And you'd be the same.

If you look evil in the face . . . , Simone says, if evil can see your face truly, then evil can't be evil anymore.

That's what happened with the guy on the bus, didn't it? I say. He felt ashamed. Evil felt ashamed . . .

There's something in us that expects the good, Simone says. Even the worst criminal feels that. That's the lifeline. That's what opens us to love and compassion.

So doing good disarms evil? I ask.

It *can*. But *sometimes* . . . , Simone smiles, holding up her bandaged wrist.

You need a friend, I say. You can't go through this alone.

You are my friend, Johnny, Simone says.

I . . . I don't want you to live a tragic life, I say.

What about my life seems tragic? Simone asks.

I don't understand who you are, I say. What you want . . . *Simone Weil*: Why did you even choose *that* name?

The saints used to model themselves on their predecessors, Simone says. You'd take the name of your favourite saint and try to live like them.

I don't know how you even *heard* of Simone Weil, I say. You were just a regular person, right? You weren't brought up with this. It seems crazy . . . I mean, how can you believe in anything—in God, in goodness and the rest? How can you be so *certain*?

Faith only makes things more *un*certain, Simone says. I don't think I've ever been less sure of anything.

But you know that God's real, I say.

Perhaps, Simone says.

You trust that there's faith . . . or that there can be, I say. You don't give in to doubt.

All I know is that I have to wait, watch and remain on guard, Simone says.

That's how you'll spend your whole life? I ask.

If necessary, Simone says.

Waiting for what? I ask.

I don't know, Simone says. I pray for direction. I try to do what I'm asked.

Can I ask you a question—another question, I mean? I say.

Simone, nodding.

When did you know? I ask. When did you know what you had to become?

A few years ago—it doesn't matter, Simone says.

You felt elected? I ask. A sense of vocation?

I felt called, but I didn't know how to respond—not at first, Simone says.

And you know now? I ask.

Our hearts can be changed, Johnny, Simone says.

I don't know what that means, I say.

There's more than absurdity and meaninglessness, Simone says.

Silence.

I think you're just a ghost—a ghost like me, I say. Like all of us—like every PhD student. But that you're pretending not to be a ghost.

We're not all ghosts, Simone says.

But you don't belong here, I say. Not in Manchester. Not even in Michael's house. I want . . . I want to protect you. You shouldn't be exposed to horror. You should be doing great things, I don't know what, but you should be doing them . . .

Moving closer to Simone.

Laying my hand over hers.

Simone, flinching. Pulling back her hand.

How long is it since you've been touched? I ask.

Simone, silent. Closing her eyes.

This is just a spiritual trial for you, isn't it? I say. It's another kind of evil. You probably think I've been sent by the devil. You probably want to say, *Get behind me, Satan.*

You're not Satanic, Simone smiles. You're confused, that's all. And you're an innocent.

Maybe I'm tempting you by my innocence, I say. Is that possible? That I've innocently laid an innocent trap . . .

Silence.

You don't want a romance because you're destined for higher things, I say.

I don't know what I'm *destined for*, Simone says.

Maybe God put me here, in front of you, did you ever think of that? I say. Maybe God's saying you don't have to decrease your way to holiness or whatever, like the real Simone Weil.

I've been reading about her, I say. She didn't like to be touched or kissed. She found all kinds of physical contact repugnant. She used to speak of her *disgustingness*. And I know what that means: to find everything disgusting. And corrupted. And ugly. That's the world, Simone. But you're not part of the world.

281

I try to be, Simone says.

You're not part of the world for *me*, I say. Because you are my hope. You're the living contradiction of the world. Of everything! . . . That you're alive at all. That you're *here* . . . How is it that you're here? How is it that you're alive at the same time as I am, and here, right here?

This isn't our world, I say. We didn't ask to be born into this world—into any world. We didn't ask to be lost here. We didn't ask to be marooned.

We've forgotten the simplest things, I say. My God, we don't even know the simplest things. We're so estranged from life. *Life*—we don't even know what that means. To live—just to live . . . It's impossible for us. It's forbidden—for *us*.

So we wander in the world's night, I say. Without knowing where to go. What to do . . . Just hoping for a twist in our despair. Just hoping for some turn in our despair. Some . . . peace. Some tranquillity.

Why must we desecrate ourselves? I ask. Why have we been made to desecrate ourselves? We live in the world of lies and are made liars. We live in the world of death and we are made dead.

And hatred is our truest feeling, I say. Hatred is our way of loving what is true, what is right. We hate because of what is good in us. We hate because of what is *true* in us. Our horror is the inverted image of the light. It's how we know the light.

No . . . no, Simone says. There's a death by love, Johnny. Where we consent to being nothing. And even love our own nothingness.

Decreation, right? I say.

Decreation, Simone says. The actual presence of the absent God.

Another name for death, I say. What you're saying is that death is the truth. Everything that exists is . . . crucifixion. I heard you say that yourself. Existence itself is a crucifixion of Jesus. Of us, too.

There's a period in which the soul is detached from the world but not yet attached to God, Simone says.

The purifying flame, right? I say. Atheism.

God needs atheism, Simone says.

There is no God! I say. There's death—that's all! I heard you say that.

But God is present in the void, too, Simone says. In terrible anguish. In the dark night. Which is where you are.

And you! You're there, too, I say. You're a void-seeker! A searcher after martyrdom!

We must not seek the void, Simone says.

But it comes, doesn't it: the void? I say.

It's part of our trial, Simone says. We must not seek it, but we mustn't avoid it either.

So here we are in the mancunian void! I say. On a lovely sunny day ... it's so beautiful today. Even I have to admit it's beautiful ...

Silence.

Simone, deliberately, slowly: We have to pass through affliction, forsakenness, to encounter God. A living death. We have to consent to death whilst we're still alive. But we serve life through death. We serve others in the world.

All the while wanting to die, I say.

We pass through death by love—the power of love, Simone says.

I want to believe in that, I say.

To be able to love others the way God loves them, Simone says. Supernaturally. There's a ... grace of compassion. Which is the descent of Christ on Earth.

To be crucified? I ask.

Yes, to be crucified, Simone says.

The world is the Cross of Christ ..., I say.

The world we have to love, Simone says.

I don't love it, I say. And I don't believe you do.

The void ... can be encountered as hell or as the entrance to heaven, Simone says. As the beginning of love, or damnation. As the opening to the absolute good, or to absolute godlessness. *Hell is a flame that burns the soul. Paradise also. It is the same flame.*

I wish the whole world would burn, I say. I wish we were somewhere outside the world—the two of us. Saving each other. Being *with* each other. Don't you want that? Why should it be impossible?

Silence.

Taking her hand.

Don't you feel that God is close to us? I ask. That God wants this? *Us?*

Simone, pulling her hand away.

You know I'd . . . become *Christian* for you, Simone, I say. I'd convert. I'd get down on my knees. I'd pray. And then I'd . . . I'd come with you onto the streets to see what you do. To keep you safe. To protect you. And I'd like to see you helping all these people . . . I'd keep quiet . . . I wouldn't distract you . . .

Simone, smiling.

Couldn't you put aside your . . . *vocation* for a day—just for a day? I ask. Couldn't this be a day of exception?

Silence.

I mean, Jesus was a fully human person, wasn't he? I say. He had fully human temptations . . . He knew what they were . . . He wanted to settle down with Mary Magdalene in that film, didn't he? Live a normal life . . . Well, this could be a day of normal life . . . An afternoon of ordinary life in the garden . . .

Silence.

Moving away from her. Standing.

I'm sorry, I say. I'm sorry for everything. I'm sorry for talking. Don't take me seriously. I'm talking too much, which I always do around you. I've said too many *stupid things* . . . All I ever say are *stupid things* . . .

Am I torturing myself, or is God torturing me? I ask. Is torture the way God shows himself to us? . . . I'm perverse. I'm disgusting. And I don't know how to be anything other than disgusting . . .

Simone, looking up at me. *Sick self-accusation is a Satanic counterfeit of the work of grace*, she says.

Am I sick? I ask. I know the answer: I'm sick. I'm sick and I'm making the world sick. I'm making *you* sick. I'm contaminating *you*.

Listen: you need to be loved, Simone says. You need to be forgiven. You need to fall in love with God, and know that God has fallen in love with you.

Yes, I say. *Yes.*

He will make of your heart a corner of heaven, Simone says.

I want that, I say.

We've been talking about you, Johnny—Michael, Ismail and I, Simone says.

Oh God, I say. I'm sorry, I'm sorry . . . I'm sorry you had to talk about me . . .

We don't think you should be living in your hall, Simone says. We'd like you to come and live in the house. To live with us. There's a room free.

You'd do that for me? I ask. Even after . . .

Come in from the cold, Simone says. Come to where you will be welcome. Where you can be with people who love you.

I . . . don't know what to say, I say.

You have to say *yes*, Simone says. That would make us all very happy.


## 12

### THE EES.

Thick mist over the pool, like smoke. Tendrils curling.

We've something special in mind for you, Business Studies Guy. We've decided you need a name—a proper name. A name that's worthy of you.

Business Studies Guy, looking expectant.

We've given it a lot of thought, Business Studies Guy. Something simple, to keep you humble. Something foolish. You've heard of the song *A Boy Named Sue*? Something like that, which won't let you get above yourself. A name you'll always have to *fight against* in some sense. A name you'll have to *ennoble*.

It was the same with Plato, Business Studies Guy. *Plato* was a nickname. It means *fat boy*, in Greek. But that's long forgotten.

You'll have to kneel, Business Studies Guy.

Valentine, producing his samurai sword.

Don't worry, we're not going to behead you—though Val took some persuading about *that*, Business Studies Guy. We're going to *knight* you, just like the Queen.

Business Studies Guy, kneeling. Bowing his head.

Valentine, tapping him on each shoulder with his sword. Arise, Bovril.

Bovril, looking confounded.

*Bovril*: that's the name we've found for you, Business Studies Guy. It's up to you to dignify it! Perhaps this whole epoch will become known as Bovrilian . . . Perhaps the name *Bovril* will take its place alongside the names of Aristotle and Kant . . . It'll mean one thing: *great philosopher*. And people will entirely forget that it's also the name of a beef-based beverage beloved of the working-class . . .

Bovril, weeping. Each of us embracing him in turn. He's carrying the humanities' fire, Bovril. He's bearing the humanities' hope. If he isn't the humanities' Word of God, then God never spoke . . .

# C H A P T E R          8

**1**

**METHOD CLASS.** Descent into the lecture room. Back to the Old
Inevitable . . .

Scrawled on the white board in thick, very thick lettering: *DIVINE
VIOLENCE.*

Wait a minute—that's not marker pen. It's something else.

Surely it's not . . . It has to be . . . It couldn't be . . . *Blood?! Human* blood?! Prof Bollocks's blood? Has there been a murder? Has
there been a human sacrifice?

And what the fuck is *that* on the podium?

Closer. Inspecting. A dead something, all bloody. A dead rabbit! A
brace of dead rabbits, on the podium and desk.

Blood on the keyboard. Blood on the monitor. And *DIVINE
VIOLENCE*, scrawled in blood . .

Who did this? Who snuck in early? Who snuck back out?

Head count. Everyone present except . . . Vortek . . . and Bovril.

Were you involved, too, Valentine? It's your sort of thing. Did you put them up to it?

Valentine, shaking his head.

Was it Weep? Through some kind of magic ritual? But Weep look as surprised as anyone.

So it was Vortek. Vortek and *Bovril*—our protégé. Vortek's protégé, now. Was this some drunken jape? Or was it planned and executed in advance, all deliberate? Were they cold-blooded or hot-blooded? Were they drunk or sober? Were they high on romance? Did they go all *Badlands*? Did they want to become *lovers on the lam*?

They must have brought rabbits from the Ees. Imagine that: transporting rabbits from the Ees. Were the rabbits already dead? Did they kill them here? Was there some weird magick-with-a-K rabbit-killing ritual?

Bovril did have a conspiratorial air . . . See what the humanities have done to him? See what *we've* done to him? He heard us complain countless times about method class. He had enough of our *method class lamentations*, and thought it was time to act.

But it was Vortek, surely, who put him up to this. Who *trained* him, probably. Imagining Bovril, under Vortek's eye, knife between his teeth, crawling through the undergrowth. Bovril, tracked by Vortek, busy with a one-man night raid on a gang of Northenden boys . . .

It must have started the day Bovril was shot. *Help me, Vortek*, Business Studies Guy must have said. *I don't want to be weak* . . . And it ended with this: supposed divine violence. Some weird leporine bloodletting . . .

But why rabbits? What's it all about? It's hardly May '68, is it? It's hardly the storming of the Winter Palace . . .

But it's still an act from nowhere for the uni. It's still, like, totally unexpected.

Discussion.

It's more confusing than anything else, we agree. Divine violence should be, like, a *real* catastrophe. This just looks like a prank . . .

But divine violence *has* to appear as a farce to the authorities. All genuine lumpen interventions look like pranks. It's the same with any move outside institutional logic ...

Because what can it understand of us, the institution? ... Our inability to bear things as they are ... Our *entire* hatred. Our *total* hatred. For the whole order of existence ...

Our theology of the dead God. Of the black sky. Of divine oblivion. Our sense that the conditions of the end are here. That the last of the seven seals has been opened. Our sense that the game is up—the human game. What does the institution know of that?

*Confuse the enemy*—that's the tactic. The only possible strategy.

Are the uni president and senior management confused? Probably. Are they afraid? Do they fear for themselves? For the university? Probably not. Do they believe they're under attack? Laughter. Have they moved to an underground war room? To a secret uni command centre? More laughter.

(A laughter unto death. Laughter unto laughter. That laughs at itself. At its own gratuitousness. This is laughter *at* laughter—the folly of laughter. At its excess, its hyperbole.

This is laughter at the endless *in vain* of laughter. Laughter unto apocalypse. Until the very end—but via the endless time until the end. And that laughs, too, because of the *length* of time. That laughs at itself, its imposture, for all the length of time ... )


## 2

MY STUDENT HALL.

I'm a jilted lover, and it's all your fault, I say. Why did you encourage me?

You can be so *passive*, Gita says. It's a relief.

I tried it on with you, didn't I? I say.

You were confused, Gita says. And drunk.

Let's get drunk now, I say.

Let's *not*, Gita says. I'm tired of drinking. Take me on a valedictory tour of the grounds. Show me Johnny-world. I want a taste of sweet Johnny melancholy.

Walking the grounds.

The high spiked fence around the perimeter.

Holding the horror back, I say.

Only just, Gita says. It's *scary* out here . . . There's a bad moon rising, Johnny.

It's always bad, I say.

Looking back at the hall. Imagining it without the student annex. Without the refectory out back. Just the old mansion.

They use it as a film set in the holidays, I say. They shoot exteriors here. Vintage cars, crunching up the gravel . . . Extras, standing around in frock coats.

See the way the old mansion pulls the whole setting together? I ask. The way it gathers the grounds around it? The lawn . . . The trees . . . This whole hall is an island. A patch of greensward in the midst of horror.

And do you see the way they laid this path—all winding? I ask. You turn a corner and suddenly everything opens up . . . They had a real sense of *drama* back then.

My favourite bench, by the flower beds, looking over the tennis courts.

There are views that *matter*: that's what I think, I say. That lift you out of everything. There are *landscapes* . . . You know what: I'll dream of this view in fifty years' time. It'll be the last thing I see before I die.

You're a real nature-boy, Gita says. Someone's going to love you for this kind of talk. Maybe not ol' nun-shoes, sure. But someone will rally to your cause. Someone's going to love you, and someone's going to love *me*. We're both *very* loveable.

But you're going to be okay, Johnny, Gita says. I'm glad you're moving to Michael's.

Do you think I'm clever enough? I ask. That I'll fit in?

I think they care about you, and that's the most important thing, Gita says.

I'll miss the *quality* of loneliness, I think, I say. The impersonality.

Stop it, Johnny, Gita says. Don't be ridiculous.

I like knowing where to be, I say. I like being certain of my duties.

You're going to be looked after, Gita says. You'll need it. Who knows—you might even finish your PhD.

Silence.

I was always waiting for the voices to start, but they never have, I say. I was always waiting to be possessed or whatever, but it hasn't happened . . . I always thought I'd become no one at all if I stayed here long enough. That I'd just fade into nothingness. Into the afternoon or whatever. And I liked that thought.

Silence.

I used to think I'd be the loneliest person in the world and that I wouldn't mind, I say. I used to think I'd just sit things out until the end of the world and that that would be okay.

And now? Gita asks.

I don't want to be alone anymore, I say.

Because of Simone? Gita asks.

I want to be with her, I say. I want to save her from all the horrors. And I want for her to save me from being alone forever. And I know it's impossible. Unless . . . Unless there's some miracle. Do you think miracles happen?


3

WEDNESDAY.

On the Ees.

Vortek's den, deserted.

His thinking place, his fortress of solitude, cleared out of books.

Vortek's prepping store, empty. No more tuna tins. No more sacks of lentils. No more bags of rice. His weights have vanished. His field hospital. His shrunken Northenden-boy heads . . .

Where have they gone? The Ees doesn't make sense without Vortek. Without Bovril. But perhaps Vortek and Bovril have only gone further into the Ees. Perhaps they've only gone *farther up and farther in*—perhaps they've reached a dimension of the Ees that lies beyond us.

The sense that the Ees is withdrawing from us, gathering up its treasures. The sense that the Ees is retreating into obscurity, that it's on the ebb . . .

The sense that we've never *reached* the Ees. That we haven't *got* there yet. That we're just wandering . . .

But that's what the Ees is: wandering. You can only ever be lost here, right? It can only be a matter of *not knowing your way about*.

Which is why our PhD lives haven't been wasted. Why our prevarication and procrastination and masturbation were leading us somewhere: *here*.

Won't we have to trust the Ees, when the time comes? Give ourselves over to the Ees? Farther up and farther in: Isn't that where we'll have to go, too? *The wind bloweth where it listeth.* But where will it blow us?

## 4

*(WE WON'T NEED PHILOSOPHY, THE DAY AFTER TOMORROW. All our questions will be answered, the day after tomorrow.*

*There'll never be a need to write up, to share your results, to write a conclusion, the day after tomorrow.*

*Completion will be part of a greater Incompletion, the day after tomorrow. Finishing will be but a fold of a greater* Unfinishing. *There'll be no last word, the day after tomorrow.*

*Your bibliography will be as long as your life, the day after tomorrow. As long as everything you've ever read. Everything you've seen. Bad spelling won't matter, the day after tomorrow. Bad grammar... You'll write by walking, write by wandering, write by drifting... You'll write by lying in the sun... You'll never have to open your laptop. And you'll complete only as you close your eyes to die, the day after tomorrow.*

*And God will be your examiner, just as God was your supervisor. God will run your viva on the Day of Judgement. You'll be questioned, and forgiven. And you'll pass, because it will have been your life's work to pass. And you'll sit alongside God's throne as doctors, as angels. As PhD immortals, shining souls in heaven... )*

## 5

**THURSDAY.**

Victoria campus.

The Manchester Postgraduate Badminton Tournament.

Marcie and Hector, up against Victoria PhD students—the cream of Victoria PhD students. Now they're up against a century of the hegemony of analytic philosophy, of functionalised philosophy. A hundred years of fetish-of-logic philosophy. Of technocratic philosophy...

Rounds, passing quickly.

Marcie, pinning down their opponents, smashing into forecourt. Hector, taking the speed off the 'cock. Hitting fast, flat midcourt moves down the sides.

They're crowding their opponents. Keeping them under pressure. Forcing lifts. Seizing win after win after win...

Quarter finals. Marcie and Hector, playing touch. Flicking the 'cock off the top of the net. Gliding over the court, skimming the court. It's all *Crouching Marcie, Hidden Hector* ..

Semi-finals. Marcie and Hector, using deceit. Marcie and Hector, forcing errors. Making unpredictable replies. Hairpin drops . . . 'Cock barely crawling over the net . . . High lobs . . .

Observations. Marcie plays more sadly now. With more wisdom, perhaps. There's a *humility* to her badminton. A sombre beauty. Marcie's regret strokes. Her strokes for Jen—for lost love. Marcie's strokes of sorrow. Of mourning . . .

Whereas Hector's game has become freer. Wilder. He's learnt something from his failed viva. A new recklessness—an *abandon*. A fuck-the-morrow attitude.

Hector's joy strokes. Hector's play-of-the-universe strokes. Hector's play of play of play . . .

And what do the Victoria student spectators see, sitting on the bleachers? Don't they understand that Marcie and Hector have declared war on the Victoria kind? On the middle-class humanities? Don't they understand that they're implicated, too? That Marcie and Hector are prophesying their end, too?

The finals. Marcie and Hector versus . . . *Kubus and Komissov*. Oh wow! The Logic Twins! Kubus is supposed to be the grandson of A.J. Ayer. The author of *Language, Truth and Logic*. Komissov is the product of some Iron Curtain breeding plan to create the *ultimate analytic philosopher* . . .

Marcie and Hector, disappearing into the changing rooms.

Marcie and Hector, emerging in fluorescents. With matching luminous sweatbands. Is that allowed?

Kubus and Komissov, black shorts. Black vests.

About to begin.

Thundering from above. Rain on the roof. A darkening of the sports hall skylight.

Marcie, closing her eyes. Is she seeing the battle ahead in her mind's eye? Is she visualising what will happen ten strokes ahead?

Hector, closing his eyes. Is he praying? Meditating? Gathering strength? Is he calling on the *gods of badminton*?

Marcie and Hector, opening their eyes again.

The signal to begin.

Silence, except for swishing rackets. Except the sound of air through catgut or whatever they make racket strings from . . .

Silence, except for the occasional squeak of court trainers . . .

Marcie and Hector, playing from surprise. Playing from the miracle. Perpetual novelty. Perpetual *Ursprung*.

How to describe what's happening? With what vocabulary? What badminton technical terms? Drive serves and crosscourt whips and dink shots and slow drops and attack-clears and power-smashes? . . . But that doesn't capture it.

Needed: another vocabulary. A vocabulary of light . . . Religious words . . . Theological ones . . . An *apophatics*, that only says what badminton is *not* . . .

How to describe it? How to describe our game? Non-tactics, larger than tactics. Non-strategy, vaster than strategy . . . A war of peace. A battle of gladness.

. . . A sport that depends upon *holding back*. Upon remaining with potential. A sport where it's not as much about how you play as about how you *don't* play. A sport where it's not all about optimisation. About *performance enhancement* . . .

A *floating* sport, played from detachment—from a peace within action. Where you're not attached to the *fruits* of action. You simply fulfil your *badminton dharma*, that's all.

A *divine* sport, that happens without you. *Decreative* sport, where you move in God, *with* God.

Improvisation. Where the rules are there to be played with. *Laughed* at. Acknowledged and exceeded—both at once. Where you deign to be contained, but are not contained.

Gesture: that's what it's about. The *beauty* of badminton—its *splendour*. The outspread fan of peacock's feathers.

It was all about what the 'cock does. How it flies, in great golden arcs. In 'cock rainbows … It was about trajectories of joy—of superabundance.

But—what's this?—Marcie's *forfeiting* shots (deliberately?). *Mis-hitting* (on purpose?). Marcie staggering (mock-staggering?).

But they're going to win, aren't they? They mean to win, don't they? They have to triumph this time—there's a question of *All Saints honour*. Is this some kind of stunt? Does she have something planned? Is it a Drunken Master thing, all over again?

Kubus and Kossimov, deft shot after shot. Kubus and Kossimov, drawing level.

Match point.

Kubus and Kossimov, looking confident.

Hector serving. The 'cock, sailing. Kubus, ready to power-smash it back. Ready to drive it down to the court. But—*what?*—the 'cock, *swerving* in midair. The 'cock, darting in midair, breaking all the laws of classical physics. The 'cock, unhittable in midair. The 'cock, landing at the end of the court.

Point to All Saints. Marcie and Hector win …

Marcie and Hector *WIN*!

*MARCIE AND HECTOR WIN!*

(Have they triumphed over farce? Have they cancelled farce? Have they out-farced farce? Are we ready to live directly now?)

## 6

### MICHAEL'S EIGHTIETH.

It's not a *party* party, Ismail explains. There isn't going to be, like, a DJ. Why would he even invite us? Valentine asks. What can we bring to the occasion? We're not the sort of people who should be invited to anything.

Michael asked for you to come, Ismail says. He wanted you here.

But what do we have, like, in common with Michael's friends? Marcie asks. Look, Michael on his own is nice, but everyone else . . .

Michael gathers up people, Ismail says. He's gathering us up, too. Think of it like Noah's ark. Anyway, everyone here's okay. They're not fakes. They're not *middle-class in the wrong way*.

This party will be *good* for us, right? I say. We'll learn how to associate with other people. Like, non-PhD people.

But we're so unsociable, Valentine says. We're so alienated. We're strangers in a strange land . . . When we open our mouths, we just scare people . . .

Maybe we shouldn't be brought into the throng all at once, Marcie says. Like when you can't bring up divers too quickly, or they get the bends . . .

Ismail, pointing out the guests.

That's Michael's old professor, who's about a hundred and two . . . That's Brian from Mad Lib. He's always leaving poems for Michael on his answerphone . . . There's royalty here: that guy's the heir to some vanished Byzantine kingdom. And that woman's the widow of the head of some ancient Christian order. She's got this six-foot crusader's sword in the boot of her Renault 5 with which to knight people.

And check out the choir singing roundelays. That's Arvo Pärt's son leading them. He's a student at Victoria. And monks—Michael knows lots of monks. And assorted Indian types from the temple where Michael gives talks. And undergraduates from Michael's Indian philosophy module. From his Plato module. (Undergraduates in your home?! A lawsuit waiting to happen.)

That guy's a mineralist—he doesn't eat animals or plants. And that's Michael's mechanic from the garage—he's kinda bicurious. He always comes round here with gifts—flowers and the like. That guy was Michael's roofer, who ended up moving into the attic flat . . . That guy was a street drinker for fifteen years . . .

Maybe Ismail's right: Maybe they're not fakes. Maybe they really are not *not* our people. Maybe we won't actually want to suicide-bomb them . . .

The garden. Hanging out.

I'm glad you're moving in, Johnny, Gita says. It's like you're being saved. Like Michael's house is saving you.

Along with all the other waifs and strays, I say.

You actually are a waif and stray, Gita says. You need looking after.

That's what my mum used to say: *you need looking after*, I say. And maybe I do . . .

Valentine and Marcie, joining us.

I actually *conversed*, Marcie says. I actually talked to, like, normal people.

They're not actually that normal, Gita says.

I'm not even drunk, Valentine says. I'm not even high. And I haven't talked about ritual suicide for the entire night, which counts as a tremendous exception . . .

Agreement. No signs of *condescension* here. No sense that this is anthropology for them. That this is some kind of *lower-class ethnography*. That this was like some kind of *working-class outreach* . . .

(Remembering that All Saints lecturer's party, when we were fledgling PhD students: All Saints lecturers praising the homemade baba ganoush and the homemade Lebanese bread. All Saints types, marvelling at cheese in a pot, to be served with a spoon.

All Saints types, talking about *going away this summer*. About getting their front garden done. About jackhammering the concrete. About paving slabs, shipped from Kerala . . .

All Saints academics, kind enough, well-meaning enough. There was a sweetness to them, a gentleness. They weren't serious careerists, like their Victoria equivalents. Not grant-gatherers. Not turbo-academics. Not *major players* in their subject areas.

Happy enough to have found their level, working at one of our shittier universities. Doing their bit for diversity. Getting the likes of us onto the PhD programme—the outsiders, the excluded. The mongrel kind, the working-class kind. And inviting us to their party. Getting us to exhibit ourselves, at their party. Putting us essentially *on show*, at their party.

Which is why, in gratitude, we busied ourselves doing our *thank-you work* for our scholarships. Our *gratitude rounds* for three years off the dole, off suicide watch, off anti-depressants . . . for three years' postponement of our *deaths of despair* . . . )

I like the monks, Valentine says. I've never spoken to a monk before. We were talking Antichrist for half the night. Luciferians and the hijacking of the church. We were talking about the *beast system* . . . They're onto things. They're, like, conspiratorial monks. I think I might become a monk, one day. I might grow a beard—or a moustache at least.

Even Simone's fitting in. Talking to Michael's professor and his son. Actually, it's pretty clear the son kinda *likes* Simone . . .

And there's Michael, talking to everyone. Buoying us up. Giving life to the place. Showing us all the immensity of living.

And because of him, we're not just anyone. Because of him, we're not anonymous, not randomers. We're guests—*Michael's* guests. Maybe all the candle stuff isn't bullshit . . .

We haven't fallen out of life after all. We haven't been left to fall and fall . . .

We've been brought close to the flame. We're warming our hands. We know now what makes the world liveable. What prevents it from becoming Hell.

And what about all the others out there—the homeless, the mad? Shouldn't they have been invited, too? Shouldn't they be here, feasting with us? Maybe this party will reach them somehow. Maybe they'll see the beacon of Michael's house, lights blazing . . .

# 7

**SATURDAY.**

Festival.

Our film (*Simone Weil*: we agreed on the title). Watching it in a room full of others is like seeing it for the first time.

First epigraph, from Emily Dickinson: *I dwell in Possibility— / A fairer House than Prose—*

Second epigraph, from Nietzsche: *Are we not continually falling? And backwards, sideways, forwards, in all directions?*

Third epigraph, from Jonas Mekas: *You don't have to go anywhere . . . your work will come, it will come by itself. Just have trust and knowing and be open and ready.*

Footage we've seen before. An Ees ice-cream van. We all eating choc-ices. An early Weep party. Before Weep were really Weep. When they hadn't yet become each other. Curry nights out in Rusholme, spending our scholarship money.

Sure, we've seen all this. We know the aesthetic. A mad collage—a mad mash-up. A jumble, like some weird lucky dip. Like some rummage sale. There's a logic here, if only we could follow it (an *il*logic. An *un*method).

Film made up solely of beginnings. That's all beginning—all threshold. And never even a starting-to-happen. Never even a going-to-happen . . .

Intertitles, almost random. From Thomas à Kempis: *Do not turn your face from me. Do not delay your visitation.* From Gilles Deleuze: *We need an ethic of faith, which makes fools laugh.* From Psalm 22: *Be not far from me, for trouble is near . . .*

Now old footage, from the archives, Tarkovsky's *Mirror*–style. The last untouched warehouses. Uncleared bombsites. Soot-blackened buildings, tramps in demob suits. Street urchins, playing in the rubble, making V-signs at the camera.

Now pop footage. Mark E. Smith, dancing, and smiling at the idea of himself dancing, from the *Eat Y'self Fitter* video. Morrissey, with his gladioli, with his Evans blouse and outsize hearing-aid, on *Top of the Pops*. Barney from New Order in dubious white shorts in the *Age of Consent* video. The ardent young Joy Division, playing *Transmission* on Tony Wilson's TV show . . .

And now *Simone footage*. A silent interview, with her just standing, saying nothing. Her half smile. A Warhol-style screen test, with Simone, amused by us—amused at being filmed. And even laughing at us, a little. Laughing at Ismail, with his earnestness. Laughing at art, and the pretensions of art . . .

Simone, doing ordinary things. Tidying up. Wandering in and out of shot. Simone, sudden sun behind her. Sunflare, behind her. A halo of light . . .

And the soundtrack. Found sounds. Mutterings. Sound-scraps. Elements fading in and out. Elements, intermittent . . . As though the signal had been lost. And found again. And lost again . . .

Scandohorn stylings. My children's-home melodica. Blurts of Val's noise experiments.

And now Simone's voice, moving in and moving out of clarity . . . Now Simone's voice, with a tranquillity beneath it. There's something at *rest* in Simone's voice. A kind of *peace* in Simone's voice . . .

Simone's voice, as a kind of stillness within tumult. Simone's voice: a silencing within noise. That draws a holy peace around it. That speaks and brings peace with it. That speaks from peace, out of peace . . .

This is how God speaks. These are his words. We hear the calm of his words. Of the divine Word. A voice, *for* God. That is *of* God. That rests in God . . .

*Nothing in the world is the centre of the world. Nothing here below has the right to say I.*

*Accept that reality is death. Accept that death is a mercy.*
*Death by love—that's how we enter what's outside of us.*
*That's how we become other than ourselves.*

And footage of enormous days on the Ees. Get-lost-in-the-them days. Empty-archway days . . .

Only the Ees has room for us: that's what's shown. Only the Ees is broad enough for us. Only the Ees will leave us in peace. Will give peace back to us.

Only the Ees can make everything possible again, even if nothing actually happens. Only the Ees can suspend the fatality of the world, even if it can't actually *change* it.

As though the film were just part of the Ees—of its unfolding. As though we'd brought the Ees here, to the screening room, and we're simply letting it flower . . .

And now valedictory stuff. The last images. Last glimpses of the world.

Tarkovsky dog, facing the camera. Breaking the fourth wall . . . Looking directly at the viewer, before turning and padding away.

Last image of Simone Weil, haloed by light in her room. Last image of an Ees experience, an Ees view . . . Last magic hour . . . All of us in silhouette. All of us, at sunset. Like the last people in the world.

Applause. Wild applause!

They like it, those bastards! It wasn't made for them! It's precisely an attack on them! It was meant as an all-out assault on them and their kind! How could they like it?! How *dare* they like it!

Resolution: Let's leave before the prize-giving. Let's leave before the glad-handing. Let's let the dead bury the fucking dead.

But no, we're here, with all the other saps. We're here, we're waiting . . .

Drama—opening the envelope. *And the WINNER of the MANCHESTER SHORT FILM FESTIVAL iiiis . . .*

They're doing the suspense thing. Like it's *MasterChef* or something. We're supposed to be excited . . .

The head judge, reading: The All Saints Disaster Studies Collective. Fuck—it's us. We've *won* . . . How could that be?

*The Disaster Collective* . . . Don't they understand to whom they're giving the award? Do they *see*?

The head judge: *All great films find a new genre or destroy one, both at once. And tonight's winner really does do both at once.*

The head judge, talking about disjunctive montage . . . Disassemblage . . . Micro-scenes, in rapid montage . . . About our film of moments: of one exhilarated microscene after another . . .

That bastard—he's trying to *plaque* us. Block your ears! Don't listen! The film wasn't made for those fuckers! It's a war on them—on their kind—even as it's peace to us. It's a declaration of hatred for their world, even as it's a declaration of love for ours. It's a bomb thrown right at them, and they *like* it?!

Don't they see that the Collective can't make films, not really? That this isn't a matter of *expanding the stylistic repertoire of the art-house film*. That we have no interest in starting some new movement (*lumpencore*, the equivalent of mumblecore, but with less depression, more larking about . . . ).

That we have no investment in inspiring others. In seeing crappy imitations of *Simone Weil*, aping our anti-techniques. In seeing knock-offs of our lumpen thing. Of the freedom-circulating-between-us thing. What could be worse than someone imitating our *game of laughter*? Our *ethos of laughing despair*?

Don't they see we wanted simply to dissolve film—all film? To expose the lie of film for what it was—the lie of *art*? Don't they see that this film was made about a time when there will be film no longer? When there won't *be* art?

Don't they see that the Collective has given them a vision of the world *after* the apocalypse—after the end of *their* world? That we want only to show ourselves in our *eschatological* role? As the lumpen-to-come, as *inheritors of the ruins*?

Don't they see that the Collective's made an anti-film? A non-film? Don't they see that this is essentially the *last* film—that there can be no others? That we've left film behind—all film and all festivals of film?

Don't they see that *Simone Weil* points beyond film, beyond art—to *post artistic life*, when film and life are reconciled? When film has been destituted in the name of life? When creation is identical with decreation?

No—no awards. We're not going up to collect our award. We're already walking in the *opposite direction*—away from the podium. Away from the head judge, and all the judges. We're already walking in the *opposite direction* to the Manchester Short Film Festival and all film festivals and all films and all art and all everything . . .

# C H A P T E R     9

**TIME, PASSING.**

Weeks at Michael's house. We live deep in time, deep in life. And it's like we've found some secret valley of time. Some secret flowering. Some opening of time in time.

Time, passing.

Ceremonies of the day, that ground the day. That let the day revolve. Out to Al's café in the morning, just as the offies open, just as the alkies step out. And then walking our great round of Chorlton, waiting for the macchiatos to hit. Our Chorlton orbit—our daily circuit, that keeps the world in its place.

Back home, in the early afternoon. Then up to our rooms. Simone in her room, Ismail in his, I in mine (but I barely work. I stare into air. Leaf through books . . . ).

Then outside in the late afternoon, to sit in the walled garden. To take tea in the walled garden, whilst Michael naps stretched out on his sofa . . .

Time, passing.

In the fridge: aloo gobi; piles of great round oatcakes; slabs of Lancashire cheese; thick ham, each slice resting on its own sheet of waxed paper. In pans on the oven top: chicken in sauce, pork in pilau rice, salmon cooked in milk.

We do not eat alone. We do not live alone. We're not deserted. We have a place to which to return. A place to arrive. Where we're greeted—*welcomed*. Where we tell of our days to one another.

Time, passing.

All the things of our world—particular things, real things, caught up in our living. *This* cutlery. *This* candlestick. *These* Chinese print plates. *This* calendar. *This* coffeepot. *These* knives, *these* forks. *This* cupboard. *These* soup bowls. *These* dried flowers. Humble things . . . Not-particularly-special things . . . But that are here, around us. That have washed up at our feet. That we clean, put away, bring out again.

Time, passing.

And new places set at the table—for unexpected guests. For all-comers. This is a place where people gather. Like a watering hole. People visit. Drop by.

Intense debate here, a guest asleep on the couch there. A player of computer games here, earnest church discussions there. Guests who say nothing, but who want to be at the edge of conversation, just to listen. To draw on the intellectual energy, on non-stupidity, on non-triviality . . .

And all invited to sit around the common table. All invited to join us around the candle for our collective meal. All to enjoy the good things of life, and together. In celebration. In thankfulness. All to know that there is no futility. That nothing's wasted. That our days on Earth are not a shadow. That the world isn't evil after all . . .

Time, passing.

Michael and his coeditors, busy with their encyclopaedia. Working on a collection of Orthodox mystical writings. Michael, translating works of Indian philosophy for his website.

Smoking breaks in the coach house, by the headless saint. Crap football in the long grass. Sitting on the mattresses in the basement, looking through piles and piles of Michael's books. (A bunch of Loeb editions, green and red: Plutarch's *Table Talk*, Athenaeus's *Deipnosophists*, in seven volumes, Boethius's *Theological Tractates*. Selected Sacred Books of the East (the *Dharmaśāstra*, the *Grihya Sutras*, the *Vedic Hymns*). *The Book of Chuang Tzu*. The *Zohar*, in two thick volumes. Seventies Illich books, all piled up. A bunch of Ellul's. Kropotkin's *Mutual Aid*, Mumford's *Technics and Civilisation* . . . )

Time, passing.

This is somewhere the Man can't destroy (isn't it?). This is somewhere hidden from the coming technate (we hope). An idyll—a pocket of time (hide us in this pocket of time). We're safe. We can play for a while (please, God, let us play here for a while).

The *vulnerability* of the house. Will it endure? Will the garden walls stand? Will the front door hold? Will maniacs smash the windows? Climb through?

And the friends of the house—will they survive? Will they be stabbed in the street when the supply chains snap, when hyperinflation hits? Will they be sky-zapped as domestic terrorists? Heart-attacked or cancered as enemies of the state? Suicided as *fifth columnists*? Sent to reeducation camps for *extra processing*?

Time, passing.

Lengthening days. Blue skies, sometimes. Sun on our faces, when it isn't actually raining. Summer on its way.

Larger life—that's what we know now. *Warmer* life.

We'll spend the last days at Michael's house, learning how to live. We'll live deep in life at Michael's house . . .

# CHAPTER 10

1

GITA, CLOSING UP THE SHOP. Rolling down the shutters.

Your last day, I say. Are you really going to submit tomorrow?

Russell approves, Gita says. He said it was *solid stuff*. *Solid*—it's hardly what you dream of it, is it?

You did it, I say. You finished.

I'll *do* it, Gita says. I only have to dot the Is and cross the Ts.

So what are we going to do to celebrate? I ask.

I'm supposed to be working tonight, Gita says. I'm supposed to be compos mentis . . . Anyway, how's your work going, dare I ask?

Like Zeno's arrow, I say. The closer I get to the end, the farther it recedes.

Which is how you like it, Gita says. Infinite philosophical eros, right? Where it's not about results.

Sure, I say. Where what you desire is desire itself, and there's no need to finish. Waiting, Simone might call it.

Waiting for what? Gita says.

Just waiting, I say.

Through the Ees woods.

Rain, very soft, that seems to drift horizontally through the air.

Gita, complaining: One last trip to the Ees, you said . . . Part of the ritual of finishing your dissertation, you said . . .

I think you have unfinished business, I say. In fact—that's what the Ees is: unfinished business.

Why does it rain here more than anywhere? Gita asks.

The Ees makes its own weather, I say.

And it's so *foggy*, Gita says.

Because the Ees doesn't want us to leave, I say. The Ees wants to keep us here forever . . .

Descent.

Are you sure this is the way out? Gita asks.

It's where the Ees is leading us, I say.

Have you noticed that nothing's, like, growing properly? Gita asks. The trees are all twisted. There must be something wrong in the soil. Like it's been cursed or something . . . And the *smell* of it. Like something vast was just left to rot. Like it's all *decaying* . . .

The black earth, bubbling. The earth, seeming to become liquid. To run.

Stunted trees. Weird trees.

It's so *warm* down here, I say. It has its own microclimate.

It's so damp, Gita says. The air's full of spores. We're, like, breathing them in. We're walking through a spore-cloud. There are spores, like, coating the inside of our lungs . . .

How heavy, the air. How heavily the branches hang.

And life—flourishing. Can this be called *flourishing*? Can this be called *life*?

It's like some giant tumour, we agree. It's like gangrene. Like some nano-level disaster. Some corruption of life, turning it all into black goo.

I swear you can watch it grow, if you can call it growing, Gita says. It's like anti-gardening. Anti-farming . . .

Swamp woods. Marsh woods. Stagnant water. Agreement: there's something monstrous abroad . . . *Burgeoning* . . . Some excessiveness of life—no, excessiveness *as* life. Sprawling, untamed, unformed. Multiplying in the darkness.

There's some weird Ees biology, some aberrant Ees chemistry. A perverted Ees *physics*. The laws of nature have gone strange here. No—the laws were never laws.

This is the Ees's chaos. Ees's queerness. Its miscegenation. Its lumpenness.

This is the Ees's potential. The way it could be anything. And be more than anything.

This is the Ees's lawlessness. Its unmanageability. This is the originary anarchy. From which everything rulebound emerged.

Where are we going? Gita asks.

*Through*, not back, I say. I don't think we can go back.

The valley, bottoming out.

A clearing. A field of shrooms, growing in the filth.

They're so fleshy, Gita says. But it's *wrong* fleshy. Like they've been irradiated or something.

The sound of some mass humming. Droning. Like Tibetan monks. Like Tuvan throat singing. Like a tanpura drone. Like echoes in an underground temple.

Where's that coming from? Gita asks.

The shrooms, I think, I say.

Things are getting weirder, Gita says.

At the centre of the clearing.

A giant shroom, ten feet across.

The god-shroom, I gasp. It must be . . .

The what? Gita asks.

What the Wizard was always after, I say. It's probably hundreds of years old. It must have been growing here for centuries, right at the bottom of the trench.

It's alive, I think, Gita says. It's, like, *vibrating*.

It's *thinking*, I say. It looks like a giant brain . . . What does the god-shroom think about?

Uh . . . how disgusting it is, Gita says. God.

How come we were allowed to find this? I ask. Why is the Ees giving us the god-shroom now?

Because it's decided to poison us? Gita says.

I can feel it *throbbing*, I say.

Gross, Gita says.

I can hear something, I say. I think . . . I think it's telepathic.

Talk to it, Gita says. Talk to the shroom. Say, *Hi, shroom!* Say, *Wassup, shroomio!*

Closing my eyes.

Are you actually the god-shroom? I ask.

No reply.

Is Gita going to finish? I ask.

*NOTHING CAN FINISH*, comes the voice. *JUST AS NOTHING CAN BEGIN.*

Did you hear that? I say. The shroom says you're not going to finish.

I bloody am, Gita says. Tell the shroom to fuck off.

Will we ever find the Room? I ask.

*THE ROOM WILL FIND YOU*, comes the voice.

We're going to find the Room, I tell Gita.

Whoop-de-do, Gita says. Ask it whether you'll ever win the heart of ol' nun-shoes.

I'm not asking that, I say.

Yoo-hoo, shroomio—will Johnny ever win the heart of nun-shoes? Gita asks.

No reply.

The shroom's stumm, Gita says.

Will Gita ever find a lover? I ask.

No reply.

The shroom's still stumm, Gita says.

What's the capital of Turkmenistan? Gita asks.

No reply.

What use *is* this shroom? Gita asks.

Will we defeat the Man? I ask.

*THE ENEMY IS ALREADY DEFEATED*, comes the voice.

We've won against the Man or the Antichrist or whatever, I say.

Phew, I can breathe again, Gita says. What a relief!

You ask it some questions, I say.

I'm not even going to *touch* it, Gita says.

This is as close as we're going to get to talking to the Ees, I say.

I don't want to talk to the Ees, Gita says.

*EAT ME*, comes the voice.

The shroom wants us to eat it, I say.

The shroom can fuck off, Gita says.

Breaking off bits of the shroom. Stuffing them into my pockets.


# 2

## WALKING BACK.

A text. Simone stabbed earlier today. In hospital.

Rushing to Michael's house.

The living room.

Bowls of saag aloo.

We're having a kind of wake, Marcie says. Michael's at some church thing. It's some Orthodox feast day.

Discussion. Who stabbed her? Some street thug? Some mugger? Some random mancunian maniac?

God, how does a stabbing even *work*? Did it pierce her vital organs? Puncture her aorta? Will she need to be sewn up or whatever? Will she live?

The stabbing was inevitable, we suppose . . . It had to happen . . . This is Manchester after all . . . She was out on the mancunian streets, wasn't she?

There are human jackals out there, and she was out among the human jackals . . .

Her goodness: that's why they stabbed her, I say. Because they could not endure it: her goodness. Because it made them feel shameful, and they were ashamed of their shame.

Come on—she was pretty much *trying* to be martyred, Gita says. You can't go to the worst possible places in Manchester and expect nothing to happen. What did she think she'd find there?

People in need of help, I say.

She was playing at being a saint, Gita says. And this is what happens to would-be saints—

They saw her, Ismail says. They looked into her face. They saw what the madman saw on the bus. They saw her and they couldn't bear what they saw: their own tenderness—their own vulnerability. They couldn't stand what she awakened in them.

I've said it all along: Simone has a death wish, Valentine says. She wasn't attached to life. And now she's got what she wanted: martyrdom.

Imagine her falling, I say. Imagine her, knees buckling. Imagine her, clutching her side . . .

Don't be so *melodramatic*, Gita says.

Do you think she's conscious? I ask. Awake?

She'll be lying there on a drip, with all the other mancunian stab victims, Marcie says.

What's she thinking of, lying there? I ask.

*God*, I should imagine, Gita says. She's probably thanking him for being stabbed.

Suddenly: lights off in the house. Darkness. Alarms ringing in the street.

Gita, flicking the light switch off and on. A power cut...

Maybe it's something worse than a power cut, Valentine says. The internet's down.

My phone's not working, Ismail says.

God—I was due to submit my dissertation tomorrow, Gita says.

Marcie standing. Pacing the room. The Man's set his plan in motion, she says. It's happening right now. The grid's gone down. The lights are out.

Probably just some brownout, Gita says.

The Man's white-tabled this, Marcie says. He's done the war games. The drills. He knows what he's up to. This is what it was leading up to: the Man's Armageddon. The Man's apocalyptic battle. They're readying the smart grid: the new global governance system. They're going to switch civilisation off and then back on again.

The whole street's dark, Valentine says. The sky, too. The clouds aren't orange from the streetlights.

Fuck... Marcie's right...

Everything's lined up, we know that. Every major logistical element. It'll be one thing, then another—blam, blam, blam. Coordinated attacks. Energy weapons. Stuff to grab the attention. To panic the population. To unleash paranoia. Wild fear. Driving out all common sense, all compassion, all love...

Pumping us up with hatred of concocted enemies. Psy-opsing us into mass panic. Cutting off our energy. Our food supplies. Our internet access. So that we cry out for help. And the Man aka Antichrist will come in to *save us*...

Fuck the Man! Fuck the power-grab! Fuck human conditioning! Fuck the rat maze! Fuck psychological warfare!

Where's Simone, to drive back the demons? Where's Michael, to light a candle?

We'll have to figure things out for ourselves.

What are we supposed to do? Gita asks.

I don't know, I say. Something.

Pondering.

Suggestions. Prepping?

Too late for that.

Looting?

Too early.

Hoarding?

There's plenty of saag aloo . . .

Holing up at Michael's with a shotgun?

We don't have a shotgun.

Preemptive suicides?

But there's life in us yet!

Ismail, in a trance: The world is a den of thieves, and night is falling. Evil has broken its chains and runs through the world like a mad dog. The poison affects us all. No one escapes.

Ismail (is he quoting?): Evil increases automatically. Inertia, laziness, cowardice, death are self-multiplying. Not everyone does evil, but everyone stands accused. No one is good, even if the word or act that links us may be good.

Ismail: Our whole lives: nothing but futile wandering and pursuits, a great deal of talk without meaning. Our whole lives, waiting in vain. What's happened so far was just the expectation of life, nothing more . . .

Ismail: Our whole lives, hoping for things that lie within this world, and not the *end* of this world. Our whole lives, lived within the senseless horror of this world—the Man's world. When what we should have been hoping for is the end of this world—the Man's world.

Which is what I've been saying all along, Marcie says.

Ismail (decisively): We have to act *as if* we could beat the Man. *As if* we could destroy the Beast-system. *As if* we were responsible for the future of the world . . .

Think of Alexander in *The Sacrifice*, when he pleads with God to save the world, Ismail says. *I've been waiting for this all my life*: that's what he says, isn't it? He realises his whole life has been meaningless. That his entire life had been building to this moment . . . And he acts *as if—as if* he could save the world.

And he really does save the world, doesn't he? Ismail says. The world's saved and Alexander's carried off mad in an ambulance . . .

Unless it was all taking place in his head: *that's* possible, Valentine says.

So we've got to do something crazy to save the world? Marcie says.

This is it—what we've been waiting for, Ismail says. No more farce. No more laughing at ourselves. No more taking ourselves unseriously . . . We have to kneel—*plead*. We should be ready to give everything up. To use up our lives. Go mad, if necessary.

I'm in, Valentine says.

We have to act *as if* the absence of belief could become belief itself, Ismail says. *As if* the absence of seriousness could become seriousness itself. *As if* we believed in belief—in miracles. *As if* we could be helped. *As if* there were a power greater than us—*better. Truer*. More *beautiful*.

(This is Ismail's revenge. We're Ismail's Collective, all serious and intent. Where it's not about farce. Where it's not just laughter at the world and laughter at laughter. This is the *As If* Collective, where we can be as serious as arthouse protagonists. As Andrei Rublev in *Andrei Rublev*. As Stalker in *Stalker*. As Gorchakov in *Nostalghia*. As Alexander in *The Sacrifice*.)

You've grown, Ismail, Marcie says. You're positively prophetic—

—*Apocalyptic!* Valentine says.

Cometh the hour, cometh the madman, Marcie says.

A madman I want to follow, Valentine says.

See, we knew all along what you might become, Marcie says. Who you might be. We saw it in you.

Are you taking the piss? Gita says.

We're absolutely sincere, Marcie says.

We are! We are! Valentine says.

It's the last night of the world—the old world, Marcie says. The last night of the great evil, of the Antichrist. The final surge. And we're here to see the night through. To come out the other side.

*Transcendence*: that's what we want, Valentine says. A transcendent blow . . . That'll strike our heads from our shoulders.

So what now? I ask.

We go to the Room, Ismail says.

What Room? I say. We've never even *found* the Room.

Eschaton recording studio—that's Room enough, Ismail says. It's *as if*, right?


3

OUTSIDE.

No screams, no shouts. Burglar alarms ringing, but no one out on the street . . .

People don't know what's hit them yet. They don't grasp the implications. The looting and burning hasn't started . . . The mass mancunian panic . . . But it'll come.

Walking, as if we had a sense of absolute mission. *As if* the night were behind us, propelling us. *As if* Manchester were looking to us. *As if* we were hope, and it's only hope.

And we're not scared. For once in our lives, we *dare* someone to attack us. We actually *want* someone to jump us . . . Let them try . . . We're afraid of nothing on Earth. We could walk through the roughest parts of Manchester and still feel no fear.

We're on a mission. No one could harm us, even if they harmed us. No one could kill us, even if they killed us. No one could destroy us, even if they destroyed us . . .

# 4
## THE EES.

Flickering in the skies.

Is it some radiation thing? Some energy-weapon thing? Some solar-storm thing? Some geomagnetic-disturbance thing? Some extreme-space-weather thing?

Is it an *alien* thing? Tonight might be the night of *full disclosure.* The UFOs might show their real purpose at last. We'll know what the greys and the reptiles were up to all along. The hybrid alien/human breeding project. The whole secret space programme . . .

Extraterrestrials . . . Maybe *ultra*terrestrials, who come from another dimension. What for? Why are they here? What have aliens got to do with the Man? Are they for him—against him? Are they doing their own thing? What do they even *want*?

It's ambiguous, we agree. It's unclear . . .

Is this the night when the Ees will reveal itself as what it is? Will we be shown what the Ees was *for* all along? Is this the night when we'll understand its messianic role? Will the Ees finally get to *wake up*?

Darkness, stirring around us . . . Leaves rustling . . . Ghost tulpas, maybe, waiting for Judgement Day . . . Or the dead of Manchester in the darkness, ready for resurrection . . . Or the mancunian lumpen, keeping to the shadows, ever watchful . . .

Through the shroom fields, glowshrooms lighting our way. Offering us a light-path . . .

Through the valley of the lost postgraduates. Through the field of drumlins.

Through the *Ees fairy fort*. Through the valley of the *portal dolmen* and the *psychometric stones*.

The Room—we're coming to the Room. The Room can't refuse us . . .

## 5

**THE RECORDING STUDIO, NOW ROOFLESS.** Now *blasted*. It's like something took off from here . . . There are scorch marks on the walls . . .

It's the Beast from the Ees, it has to be, I say. In its inaugural flight. It's official: the world's ending tonight.

Is this it: the Room?

It must be.

Downstairs.

The basement. Wet brick.

A crack in the wall.

A passageway.

Following.

Must be part of an underground drainage system . . .

Maybe it was part of an '80s bunker—a really big one, that was going to form Northwest Command if they dropped the big one.

An opening.

Climbing over piles of rubble.

Water, in long puddles.

It's like a secret lair, Valentine says. Like the Batcave or something.

There's something, like, *swarming* over here, Ismail says. Insects . . . Scuttling over one another . . .

I think they were spontaneously generated from the horror, Gita says.

And there are plant . . . *things*, Ismail says.

Anti-plants, more like, Marcie says. Opening their petals in darkness . . .

There's a whole *bush*, Ismail says.

The tree of death, Marcie says. An anti-tree.

It isn't very Room-y—even you guys have to admit that, Gita says.

Maybe it's the Room we deserve, Valentine says.

We don't deserve much, apparently, Gita says.

The Room's what we make of it, right? Ismail says.

I think it's actually *raining* in here, Gita says. How's that possible?

Too bad there aren't *Room instructions*, I say.

Weep always say you have to charge up things with psychic energy, Marcie says. Like, switch things on at a primal level.

How do we do that? I ask.

Marcie, musing. I have an idea, she says.

Forget it, den mom—no wank magic, Valentine says.

A better plan, I say, unwrapping my package. I've been saving this up . . . Behold: the god-shroom.

Is that it? Marcie says. Are you sure?

It's actually alive, Valentine says. It has veins . . .

It's, like, pulsating . . . , Marcie says.

It's *glowing* . . . , Ismail says.

Do you think it was any coincidence that you found the god-shroom on the very last night of the world? Valentine asks. This is the Ees in a shroom. Totally fateful . . .

The god-shroom unlocks the Room, that's what I think, Ismail says. The Room can be anywhere on the Ees, pretty much. Mystery solved.

All of us, chewing on the shroom.

Now what?

I think we just have to make our wish . . . , Ismail says. Like, pray.

We have to make an offering, Valentine says. Give something up.

We could start with your *alleged homosexuality*, Gita. Marcie asks. Not much of a sacrifice, is it?

I'll sacrifice wanting to be sacrificed, Valentine says.

We can all do that—easy, I say.

321

Yes, but I actually *want* to be sacrificed, Valentine says. I'd like nothing better . . .

I thought the Room was supposed to know what we want, I say. Like, better than we know ourselves.

Discussion. What *do* we want? For Simone to be safe—to rise from the dead or whatever? For the Man's blackout not to work? For the Antichrist to be defeated? To believe in something? In God? In the world? To actually *finish* our dissertations—or to never have to finish them?

For Ismail to become a real arthouse director? For me to disappear the moon from the sky? For Marcie to receive Ultimate Destruction Girl back doublefold, one Jen for each knee? For Valentine to be sacrificed by Bovril and found a new religion?

All these things! Of course! And more! Because what we Desire, capital D, lies deeper than that. We're surrounded by lack, loss, powerlessness, evil. We live in the void. We taste the void. Which is why we want what is absent. Which is why we love emptily, without sense or reason. But we do Love, capital L—and that's what the Room must know.

What we Want, capital W: for this night to have been what we waited for. For this night to have made our lives meaningful, finally. Not to have lived for nothing. Not just to have fallen.

What we Want: for our entire lives to have been building to this moment. To act *as if*—*as if* we could save the world; *as if* God were real; *as if* we could defeat the Antichrist. (*As if* there even were an Antichrist. *As if* there was a Christ.)

What we Want: to fully suffer the depth of our stupidity. To be truly pained by lives that have only turned in tiny circles. To have been penitents after all. To have been prayerful, despite everything.

A longing for longing. A faith in faith. Is that what the Room knows in our hearts? Is that what it discerns?

Something's happening, Gita says. Something's hitting.

A rumbling. A drone. Almost too low to hear . . .

A roaring, as of the centre of the Earth. As of an earthquake without end, but buried, buried. As of the movement of magma in magma, deep beneath our feet. As of tectonic plates grinding, subducting.

Something vast is happening.

A destruction? A creation?

The apocalypse?

Could be.

But whose apocalypse is it: the Man's or God's?

Let's go up and have a look.


## 6

### ABOVE GROUND.

Wow—it's, like, magic hour, Ismail says. The threshold of dawn . . .

It's kinda . . . foggy . . . , I say.

It tastes *sweet*, Valentine says.

Somehow I don't think we're in Manchester anymore, Marcie says.

Is this real, or is this a trip? Marcie asks.

The eternal postgrad question, Valentine says.

Tarkovsky dog, appearing from the mist. There she is again—so classy. So much *better* than us.

T-dog, bidding us to follow.

Through the woods.

So where actually are we? Gita asks.

Our wish worked, Ismail says.

For what—to be in weird postgrad heaven? Gita says. I don't remember wanting *that*.

This is an in-between place, Ismail says. It's like in *Tree of Life* when Jack O'Brien is being led through these landscapes, deserts and the like, by his guardian angel. Through this, like, *dream landscape*.

How come it all looks so much like the Ees? I ask.

I think it shows itself as what we're familiar with: favourite land-scapes or whatever, Ismail says. That's why it's quite recognisable at first—the grass is grass, the trees are trees. This place sort of reads our mind, showing us what we're familiar with, just to put us at ease. Like an airbag when you crash, or a protective coma.

Discussion. Are we hallucinating? It's like some kind of Limbo. Somewhere between our old lives and the next one . . . between successive rebirths of a soul . . .

Are we still PhD students? Will we have to finish?

Maybe we're *dead* in some way. Maybe they'll give us honorary PhDs, which would be handy. There'd be a speech about us at graduation. Professor Bollocks would tell everyone what wonderful students we were.

But what if he's up here, too? What if the old world's no more? What if God got tired of it all and destroyed everything? What if the world's actually *ended*?

The pressure's off . . . No more studies . . . No uni . . . No deadlines . . . It's the Sunday of life . . . It's like the '80s all over again, but permanently. This is '80s life on the dole, forever.

Less gravity up here, we notice. The ground's spongier and springier. It's like being on the moon . . .

And look at the moon itself: it's *green*! Luna's alive . . . and there are trees growing all the way up, growing through space. You could climb to the emerald moon . . .

So what is this place? we wonder. Why are we here? To learn something? To come to terms with our pasts? With suffering? Is there something we have to consent to—to *affirm*?

Remembering when the mother consents to her son's death in *Tree of Life* . . . Angels holding her. Close-ups of hands bathed in light, touching, praying and giving thanks. And her face, beatific—radiant with light. *I give him to You*, she says. *I give You my son . . .*

So we should say, *We give Simone to you. We give you our friend*?

Too bad we couldn't bring Simone here, to the Ees. Too bad she's lying there in some hospital bed.

It'd be like Dreyer's *Ordet*, when what's-her-name is resurrected . . . Or *Star Trek III: The Search for Spock*, when Spock's, like, come to life again.

But what about saving the world? I ask. Is that what we're trying to do?

That will come, I think, Ismail says. For now we just have to trust. Follow.

T-dog, paddling ahead of us.

I can hear *Ceremony*, Gita says. Someone's playing *Ceremony*.

I'll bet they're always playing *Ceremony* up here, I say.

I can hear *beats*, Marcie says. Maybe there's dancing. Maybe it's some nightclub . . .

A *dawn*club, you mean, Valentine says. A *day*club . . .

I'll bet there's, like, a heavenly Haçienda, Marcie says. Like God's own nightclub. Like the Haçienda, but turned inside out . . . The Haçienda without walls. Open to the elements. To whoever comes . . .

Should we go? I ask. Do proles wanna dance?

Proles are too tired to dance, Valentine says.

Walking on.

A couple, walking hand in hand through the trees.

I recognise him . . . that's *Ian Curtis*, right? Valentine says. And who's with him?

His girlfriend—Annik, Marcie says. The one for whom he was going to leave his wife. The classy Belgian . . .

What are they doing here? I ask.

Everyone's here, somewhere, Ismail says.

We mustn't disturb them, we agree. Let them be. Let them have a happy night before Ian hangs himself. But maybe he doesn't hang himself in heaven . . .

And isn't that the young Morrissey, walking with Linder in the forgotten graveyard, musing upon life and death and the *fourth gender*? And there's Mark E. Smith, walking with Una Baines in Heaton Park, talking Can and Lou Reed and feminism and the patients at Prestwich mental hospital. And there's Nico, an Amazon in biker boots, playing pool with a spindly John Cooper Clarke. And there's Tony Wilson, Mr Madchester in a baggy linen suit, having the *best conversation in the world* with the rest of the Factory Four. A grove for everyone . . .

Groves and groves in an endless wood. Probably a grove for Victoria PhD students, a grove for Business Studies PhD students . . . A grove for Professor Bollocks and pals . . .

And we, making our way through the groves. Looking for what? Working on our karma, maybe—but how?

Perhaps we have to find our way to the equivalent of the beach in *The Tree of Life*. To the eternity scene, where everyone's gathered on the sand to forgive and be forgiven.

Perhaps we have to find the place where God is. Where He acts in our place. Where we're finally decreated into the light . . .

But we're not there yet. We're not far enough for that . . .

A grove, full of softly glowing shrooms. Moss. T-dog, sitting down, curling up.

Sitting on the moss.

We could just lie down here and sleep . . . Maybe we should . . . maybe things will become clearer after a night's rest . . .

But where will we wake up? we wonder. Back on Earth again? Back before the blackout—before Simone was stabbed? Back in Michael's house, and passing time in the house? Is this place forever or is it just a trip?

Yawns. The stretching of arms. Does it matter? Can't it wait till tomorrow?

Valentine, lying down on the moss. Closing his eyes. Sleeping.

What's happening in the world? Marcie says. Has the Antichrist won? Has God? Why does none of it seem important? I thought it would always be important—that it was the most important thing in the world. But I don't suppose we're actually *in* the world anymore . . .

Marcie, closing her eyes. Falling asleep.

Ismail, Gita and I, sitting on the mossy ground.

I'm going to miss the world, Gita says. All my cool outfits. All the stuff in my room . . .

They're all up here somewhere, I'll bet, Ismail says. Nothing worthwhile is lost.

So it's like a giant vintage shop? Gita asks.

It's like God's version of our film, Ismail says. God's own home movie. (Quoting:) *You are now looking at the Narnia within Narnia, the real Narnia. And in that inner Narnia no good thing is destroyed.*

And what about worthwhile *people*? Gita asks. Where are they? Where are my parents? Where are my brothers?

They'll be up here, too, Ismail says. We'll run into them tomorrow, or the day after that . . .

How do you know? Gita asks.

Everyone will be saved when the time comes, according to Michael, Ismail says. Everyone will be forgiven and redeemed and united with God. Salvation for everyone: I always liked that idea. Where it's not a matter of faith or deeds, or belief or piety . . .

So this is actually heaven, Gita says. And we're all dead . . .

*I* don't agree, I say. Everyone saved!? What about, like, abusers? What about evil people?

Perhaps they'll need to be forgiven, too, Ismail says. Abusers were usually abused themselves, weren't they?

They should be punished for what they've done, I say. They should be in Hell.

They should be allowed to forgive and to be forgiven, Ismail says. They should be allowed to feel God's grace.

What about the homeless—are they here, too? I ask.

They're here, I'm sure of it—they have a home now, Ismail says.

Do the addicted become unaddicted up here? I ask. Do the mad become unmad?

I don't know—I think so, Ismail says.

And what about the screamers? I ask.

There's no need for screams anymore, Ismail says.

What about the horrors and terrors? I ask. All the suffering?

All gone, Ismail says. Vanished. Forgotten.

Forgotten? I say. *I* won't forget, I say. No one should forget.

*The term is over and the holidays have begun*, Ismail quotes. *The dream is ended: This is the morning. This is the end of all stories and we really will live happily ever after.*

Ismail, lying back on the moss. Ismail, eyelids flickering, closing... Ismail, asleep...

I don't want to live happily ever after, I say. Not yet...

Poor Johnny—you'll be all on your own, Gita says, closing her eyes.

Don't you sleep, too, I say. Don't leave me all alone.

But I'm tired—*so* tired—and the moss is *so* soft, Gita says, closing her eyes.


# 7

THROUGH THE GROVES, MICHAEL BESIDE ME.

Michael pointing upwards. Look!

I look. The whole of Manchester, filling the sky. The whole city, all spread around us. All the bus routes. All the train lines. The whole plain, right out to Wigan and beyond. To Alderley Edge. And all of it luminous—*shining*. Brighter than in life.

The New Manchester, Michael says. The earthly paradise.

I don't know what that means, I say.

The creation has been fulfilled, Michael says. Manchester has been taken into the hands of God.

All of Manchester? I ask.

Everything worthwhile that ever was in Manchester, Michael says. All good works—artistic, technological, scientific . . . All good deeds—all charity. All mancunians, who will now receive the fullness of what they hoped for.

And what if they hoped for bad things? I ask. Disgusting things?

No one truly hopes for bad things, Michael says.

That's where you're wrong, I say. That's where heaven's wrong . . . Look, we're not all innocents at heart. What about serial killers? Ian Brady? And Myra Hindley? What about Cyril Smith? I don't believe in the New Manchester, turning above us in the sky. I don't believe in a Manchester without brute force and pain . . .

You're determined to see only suffering and evil . . . , Michael says.

Because the world is overrun by suffering and evil, I say.

Not anymore, Michael says. Suffering, misery and death have been assumed into God and overcome. The Creation has been regained. The victory over disorder and chaos is complete.

I can still hear the screams, I say.

You hear echoes of screams, Michael says.

I hear the screams everyone's forgotten, I say. That are still like a knife through the heart of the world. That should wake God up from his death.

Those are old screams, Michael says. There's no reason to scream anymore.

There's been too much pain. I say. Manchester was built on pain.

There'll be a great feast, Michael says.

There'd *have* to be a feast, I say.

There'll be tables and tables, covered in white tablecloths. With candles. Glasses for wine. Great plates. Food will be brought! Michael says. Food for all!

And everyone will sit down together—every mancunian who's ever lived, Michael says. All of us. Good and bad. Saints and sinners. Rich and poor. Everyone's who's ever suffered—who's screamed in the night. Only no one will suffer anymore.

No one? I ask. The madman on the bus?

He'll be there—and no longer mad, Michael says.

The alleyway crack addict? I ask.

Among us, and no longer addicted, Michael says.

And the man I saw being beaten? I ask.

Breaking bread with his assaulters, Michael says. Drinking wine.

And the man I saw striking at his face with his fist? I ask.

Quiet as a lamb, Michael says. At peace, among friends.

And who will serve us? I ask. Who will prepare the meal?

Angels, I should think, Michael says.

And what will we eat? I ask.

Manna, perhaps, Michael says. I wonder what manna tastes like? Or maybe chunks of the Leviathan, the monster of chaos.

And after that? I ask.

I think there'll be a messianic nap, Michael says. A messianic siesta. We'll all just lie in the meadows. And it will rain. There'll be heavy drops of sweet rain, refreshing the Earth, scenting it.

And then what? I ask.

Then, in time, we'll each be brought into the light, Michael says. God will make us anew. He'll renew our hearts. We'll be welcomed home. We'll find the place where we should be, and to which we really belong. All separation will be destroyed—all contradiction—and God will be all in all.

It sounds wonderful, I say. It sounds fabbo. No more pain and suffering... Who wouldn't love that? Who doesn't love a happy ending?

But it won't make up for everything that happened. It won't compensate for all the horrors and terrors . . .

The sky, empty again. Dark.

Simone, beside us.

You don't believe in the New Creation or the messianic feast or all the other consolations, do you, Simone? You don't think the world's ended. You know the *evil of the city*. You know the meaning of glass and steel and cement and asphalt. You know the city's rooted in blood. That its great buildings stand in blood. You know Manchester's foundations are sunk right into Hell.

Jesus wept for Jerusalem, remember that, Simone says.

Because he thought it could be saved? I ask.

Because he longed for its peace, and knew peace would not come, Simone says.

And do you weep over Manchester? I ask. Over all that it's been? Because there'll be no peace, will there? The city is cursed—just as every city is cursed. The city cries out . . .

Its cries are prayers, Simone says.

Do you believe that? I ask.

Despair is hope—a version of hope, Simone says. Manchester wants to be changed.

It cries out because it's gone mad, I say. Because the city has driven its inhabitants mad. Because it's in endless debasement. In ceaseless fucking nihilism. Because it's ruled by despairing powers that don't even know their despair.

Manchester has never been abandoned, Simone says.

But who helps Manchester? I ask. Who answers its prayers?

Some of us try to, Simone says.

But look what happened to you! I say. Look what they did to you! I'll bet you're dead in real life. I'll bet you're lying dead in hospital. *The light shined in the darkness and the darkness did not receive it*: Isn't that right?

Where the darkness is present, so, too, is the light, Simone says.

Of course, I say. *Dialectics* . . . Conjuring something from nothing. Pulling God out of the devil's hat . . .

There's a harmony that resounds in tension—in the divergence of terms, Simone says.

Manchester screams, and God is silent: Where's the harmony there? I ask. Manchester cries out, and God does nothing . . .

Opposites can be brought together in their separation, Simone says. It's heartbreaking—*terrible*—but it's also beautiful.

You can find beauty in pain? I ask. In Job on his ash pile? In Jesus on the Cross?

The cry of the Son rises to meet the silence of the Father, Simone says. That's the most beautiful harmony of all.

Did you cry when you fell? I ask. Did you scream out against the *counter-creation* when they stabbed you on the streets? Against Babylon? Against the city of mortal sorrow?

Silence.

And did you know transcendent joy? I ask. Joy from beyond the world, that *passeth understanding*?

I knew that joy, Simone says. I know it now.

Do you consent to necessity, to the infernal machine? I ask.

I consent, Simone says.

And you hear God's silence? I ask.

I hear it, Simone says.

And you know God's absence?

I know it, Simone says.

Even in your pain? I ask.

I know my pain is a way God shows his love, Simone says.

You're mad, Simone, I say.

Yes—I'm mad, Simone says. Gladly mad. Because I know—truly know—God's madness.

A doorframe, standing in the grass before us.

I know what this is, I say. I'm supposed to step through. Supposed to receive a vision—see myself as I was: as an innocent, a child, before all the bad things happened. I'm supposed to be led to the *beach of reconciliation* or whatever. Kneel in the sand.

I'll see you, Simone, and you, Michael: I'll see Gita and my friends, I say. I'll see my mum—as she was when she was young and beautiful, before . . . all the trouble. And then she'll embrace me and I'll embrace her, and I'll say, *Thank you, God, thanks for it all.* I'll say, *I give you my mum, I give you my suffering, I give you my loneliness, I give you the sweetness of my solitude. It was all worthwhile.*

But do you know what? I'm not going to step through, I say. I'm never going to step through. This is just another illusion.

Georges-with-an-S, rubbing up against the doorframe.

You're being called home, Johnny, Michael says. You're going to be found at last, healed, forgiven by the one who made us.

Why should I be forgiven? I ask. What do I need to be forgiven for? What did I ever do wrong?

You long for a place to be, where you really belong, Michael says. And there is such a place. You're right at the edge of the kingdom of heaven. It's real. And there will be a point where you must fall to your knees and ask to be saved.

You don't have to say anything, Simone, I say. I know I'm supposed to accept order even as it places me in chains. Accept beauty, even as I drown in ugliness. Accept goodness, even as I'm submerged in *ATROCITY.* Accept harmony, even as I hear only screaming. Well, I don't accept!

Forgive God, Johnny, Simone says. Forgive him and receive his forgiveness.

I don't need forgiveness, I say. And I don't forgive *him.* God should pray for us, don't you see? God should be on his knees, praying to us . . .

**8**

WALKING AWAY.

Into the Ees.

Through the meadows.

A rough track, along the reservoir.

Vortek and Bovril, walking beside me. Bovril, transitioned, with flowers in her hair. She's girl-Bovril now. She's Bovrilla. She's smiling. Laughing . . .

Their cottage, Vortek and Bovrilla. Smoke, from the chimney.

Their long garden. Flagstones on the curving path. Robins, flying in and out of the hedge.

An Oxford bench, set for breakfast. A jug of milk. Granola. Ees berries. A vase of Ees wildflowers. A teapot and teacups.

Sitting down to eat.

The hill, opposite. A field, running into woodland.

This view, I say. I'm going to remember this view . . .

Bovrilla, feeding robins from her palms. Telling us the names she's given to the robins. Anaximander. Aristophanes. Adi Sankara . . .

Vortek, pointing out the tree house where Weep and the Dane live. There's Originary Ron's hermit's cave. There's Rainer Maria Dillwood and Animadab Jones's teepees. There's Plastic Bertrand's bivouac. There's the hobbit-hole where The Torn Curtain's shacked up with Spiral Stairs . . .

Disaster Studies PhD students, no longer living abstractly. No longer theorising. No longer out on peculiar limbs. No longer burrowing alone into the night. No longer writing their *notes from underground*. No longer living in mouldy bedsits.

Disaster Studies PhD students, in mass secession. Gone Ees-native. Raising their own flag. Founding a new Ees Christiana.

Disaster Studies PhD students, blinking in the sun. With sun-

bleached hair. With pollen in their beards. Drinking homemade
mead from Ees bee honey . . .

Disaster Studies PhD students, studying only the Unfinishable.
Only the Infinite, opening beyond this world and every world . . .

The Wizard, arriving with a basket of shrooms.

The Wizard, passing me a shroom.

Alone on the Ees.

Kneeling on the earth. Kneeling in the Ees mud, under the
Ees sky.

Help me, I pray. You know what I want, better than I know.
You know who I love, better than I know.

Let me renounce all things, except for her, I pray. Let me disappear from everything, except for her. Let me be less than myself,
except for her. Let me stay out of use forever, except for her.

Hide us where we will not be found, I pray. Where we will not
be disturbed. Hollow out a place for us, where no one goes. Keep us
from the Man and the minions of the Man.

Don't let us starve, in the coming famines, I pray. Don't let us be
killed, in the coming riots. Don't let us lose our minds, in the coming madness. Don't let us be bombed, in the coming wars.

Don't let them mutate us, I pray. Don't let them irradiate us. Free
us from demons that live on our terror and panic. Keep us from the
reign of sociopaths. Of psychopaths.

Give us the real skies, I pray. Give us real earth. Real air.
Real rain.

Give us real words, I pray. Don't let us lie . . . Don't make us have
to lie. Give us our own thoughts, not the Man's thoughts. Not the
thoughts of evil.

Don't let us hate ourselves, I pray. Don't let us destroy ourselves.
Save us from deaths of drinking, deaths of despair.

Give us what was good, I pray. Gather what was good, what was worth preserving. Let the best things be born again. Let them return ...

And let me remember what was good, what was worth preserving, I say. Moments of joy. Skylarking. Let me write of them and remember. Let me tell the story of Simone Weil's rebirth in Manchester. And let it also be my story, about my hope. Let her be *my Weil* ...

**∞**

**1**

**A HOUSE.** A kitchen.

Sitting at the table, across from her.

I had a dream, she says. I dreamt I was a student. In a great city. I dreamt I was reading . . . studying . . .

Manchester, I say. You—or a version of you—were at All Saints Uni.

I dreamt I was living in this upstairs room, she says. Looking out over rooftops. Over trees.

Michael's . . . , I say.

I dreamt I had friends . . . You were one of them, I think, she says.

You had friends, I say. I was your friend.

Where am I now? she asks. Where is this?

The Ees, I say. The heart of the Ees.

The . . . *Ees*, she says.

Where whatever you wish for comes true, I say.

I don't remember wishing for anything, she says.

Maybe all this is *my* wish, I say. This house . . . You—a version of you. A *tulpa* of you.

Maybe it's *my* wish, she says. Have you considered that?

You used to despise the idea of wishing, I say. Saints don't wish: that's what you thought. They just empty themselves and follow the will of God.

A saint . . . , she says. I don't know what a saint is . . .

What *do* you remember? I ask. How you came to Manchester? Your studies?

Shaking her head.

Your charity work? I say. Out on the streets with the homeless . . .

Shaking her head again.

Simone Weil, the philosopher: Do you know who that is? I ask. The one you named yourself after?

No . . . , she says. Those aren't my memories. I don't remember much.

I like you like this, I say. I like it, you not knowing anything . . . I think you're a tulpa. Simone's tulpa.

What does that mean? she asks.

A version of All Saints PhD students born on the Ees, I say. Like us, but not the same as us. The Ees's dream of who we are, maybe. And in your case: someone who won't have to suffer. Who won't have to be a martyr.

I don't remember suffering, she says. And I don't remember being . . . *martyred*.

And in my case . . . , I say. Someone who doesn't have to suffer suffering. The suffering of others. I think the Ees wants another life for me, too . . . Am I a tulpa? Am I the Ees's version of me? Am I a man who dreamt he was a butterfly, or a butterfly dreaming he's a man?

Maybe all this is the *Ees's* wish, I say. To place us among the simplest things. To let us live in the simplest way. Where living isn't some desecration. Where we don't have to lie. Where we're not lost. Not abandoned. Where we're not just *dead*...

It's springtime on the Ees, I say. Our time. Our new beginning. We're being shown what's beautiful. And uncorrupt. And un-... mangled. And *loving*.

Taking her hand.

I think that we knew a lot of things, and it's now time to forget it all, I say. I think it's time to unlearn our old lives. To begin again, afresh. From zero...

I've already forgotten it all, she says.

Then I'll have to catch up with you, I say.

Sitting beside her.

*The beauty of the universe: no other trace of the divine mercy is to be found in creation*, I quote. Your beauty. Because I find you beautiful.

What does that mean: *divine mercy*? she asks.

The chance we are given to receive the grace of God, I say. But I don't know if we need it anymore. God's been forgotten, here on the Ees. God's forgotten himself...

No more *contradictions*, I say. No more *crucifixion*. No more *Simone Weil*. Everything's here. Everything we need.


## 2

THIS IS OUR HOUSE. At the centre of the Ees. That gathers the Ees around itself. Over which the Ees sun arcs. Around which the Mersey bends.

This is our house, made of Ees stone. With foot-thick walls. That winds drive themselves against. That storms squall around.

This is our house. Where our precious things are. My children's-home quilt. Simone's iron teapot, for mint tea. Her pepper mill, made

from an old stair spindle. A few handpicked books. (Not philosophy—
*poetry*; not theology—books for children.) Our LPs (music you can
dance to. Because proles wanna dance . . . ).

This is our house. With painted chests in the bedrooms. With
framed fairy prints on the wall (Little Red Riding Hood in the
woods; the owl and the pussycat, rowing across the waters). With
centuries-old witch-marks cut into the beams.

This is our house. Where we speak of earthly things. Of real
things. Where we've retired the words *eschatology* and *Gnosticism*.
Where the word *apocalypse* never passes our lips.

This is our house. Where we only read lightly, almost *accidentally*.
Where our gaze may or may not fall upon the pages of a book. Where
we only write casually. A few words jotted down without forethought.
For no particular reason.

This is our house. Where evil can be kept at bay—by doing ordinary things. By chopping carrots, by setting the table. Where we can
banish the horrors and terrors by emptying the washing machine. By
hanging out our clothes.

This is our house. Where violence does not come. (Except when
Georges, king of cats, brought in a hatchling blackbird, fallen from
its nest. Except when Georges-with-an-S brought in a tiny, bewildered mouse.)

This is our house. Where tomato plants sprawl along the sun-
soaked wall of the ruined oast. Where lavender grows . . . Sweetpeas
and ornamental quince . . . Where the pixie hats of California pop-
pies push back to show the flower.

This is our house. Where jackdaws chuckle. Where goldfinches
sing busily. Where the woodpecker drills at the dogwood tree.
Where foxes bark in the high woods at dusk. Where badger cubs
play in the set on the ridge. Where owl screeches echo in the hollow
of the field.

This is our house. Where the stars come out one by one in the evening. Where bats fly, jagged, drunken. Where a phosphorescent barn owl hunts at twilight.

This is our house. Where Tarkovsky-dog lies at our feet. Where Georges-with-an-S curls round our ankles. Where we'll sit out the collapse. Where we'll await the Reveal. Await the Awakening. And the moment when, in time, we'll go out to reclaim the world.

# ABOUT THE AUTHOR

**LARS IYER** is a Professor in Creative Writing at Newcastle University, where he was formerly a longtime lecturer in philosophy. He is the author of the novels in the Spurious Trilogy—*Spurious*, *Dogma*, and *Exodus*—and more recently, the widely acclaimed *Wittgenstein Jr* and *Nietzsche and the Burbs*.